SOUTH
TO
GASCONY

SOUTH TO GASCONY

BY

MICHAEL BROWN

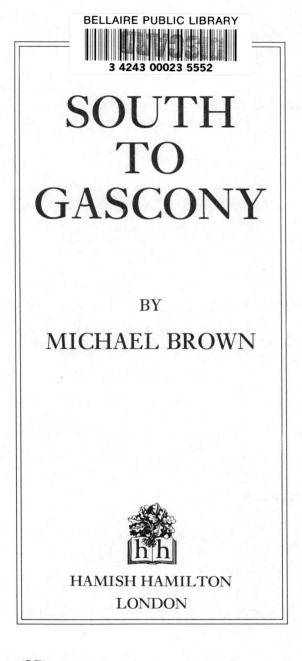

HAMISH HAMILTON
LONDON

HAMISH HAMILTON LTD

Published by the Penguin Group
27 Wrights Lane, London W8 5TZ, England
Viking Penguin Inc, 40 West 23rd Street, New York, New York 10010, U.S.A.
Penguin Books Australia Ltd, Ringwood, Victoria, Australia
Penguin Books Canada Ltd, 2801 John Street, Markham, Ontario, Canada L3R 1B4
Penguin Books (N.Z.) Ltd, 182–190 Wairau Road, Auckand 10, New Zealand

Penguin Books Ltd, Registered Offices: Harmondsworth, Middlesex, England

First published in Great Britain 1989 by Hamish Hamilton Ltd

Copyright © 1989 by Michael Brown

Maps © 1989 The Kirkham Studio

1 3 5 7 9 10 8 6 4 2

British Library Cataloguing in Publication Data

Brown, Michael
South to Gascony.
1. France. Gascony. Description & travel
I. Title
914.4'7704838

ISBN 0–241–12694–0

Printed in Great Britain by Butler and Tanner Ltd
Frome and London

CONTENTS

FOR SYBIL

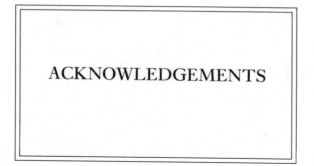

ACKNOWLEDGEMENTS

S o many people have helped me while I was researching and writing this book that it would be impossible to name them all, but I must single out my editor and publisher, Christopher Sinclair-Stevenson, who has given me great support throughout, and Clare Alexander who was very encouraging at the start. Special thanks are also due to my Gascon friend Guy Dubuc who accompanied me on many trips and made many valuable introductions.

I am most grateful to Monsieur Georges Courtes of the Comité Départemental Tourisme et des Loisirs du Gers, and to Monsieur Goyet of the French Tourist Office, London, both of whom have given the book their official blessing. I would also like to thank Monsieur Terrade, Monsieur Laulom and Monsieur Dudon who gave me much interesting information on the exciting new discoveries at Labrit.

Finally, I owe an enormous debt to my wife, Sybil, who accompanied me on my journeys to every part of Gascony and acted as interpreter whenever, as often happened, my shaky French proved inadequate.

ILLUSTRATION ACKNOWLEDGEMENTS

Colour Illustrations

The colour illustrations are reproduced by kind permission of the following: Zodiaque, La Pierre-qui-vire (Yonne) 1, 5, 7 and 8; Mike Busselle's Photo Library 2, top and bottom; Papigny 4; Scope – Jean-Luc Barde 3; Scope – Jean Daniel Sudres 6; Sybil Brown 9 and 10; Mayotte Magnus 11.

Black and White Illustrations

The black and white illustrations are reproduced by the kind permission of the following: Zodiaque, La Pierre-qui-Vire (Yonne) 1, 8, 9, 10, 11, 12; Comité Départemental du Tourisme et des Loisirs du Gers, 2, 3, 4, 5, 6, 7, all taken by Robert Nimitz; Mayotte Magnus 13.

LIST OF
ILLUSTRATIONS

MAPS

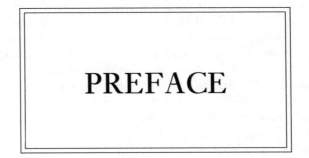

PREFACE

WE DISCOVERED Gascony by accident. In 1971 my wife Sybil and I bought an old stone farmhouse near Pujols in the Lot-et-Garonne. One evening we were talking to our French estate agent, Monsieur Colling, and asked him which part of the surrounding country he liked best. His reply surprised us: 'Le Gers'. As soon as Monsieur Colling had gone we rushed to look at the map and discovered that the Gers is a *département* immediately south of Lot-et-Garonne that takes its name from the local river.

For the next year or so we were too busy with the house to do much exploring but at last, one fine June morning, we set off south to Lectoure. We were immediately captivated by what we found: the rolling hilly country, meandering streams and old towns delighted us, but it was some time before we realized that this was Gascony. Once the connection was made we were eager to see more. As it happened, we were starting research for our book *Food and Wine of South-west France* so that, at the same time as we were seeking out little-known wines like Pacherenc du Vic-Bilh, we were extending our knowledge of Gascony.

It soon became clear that there was no easily accessible guide to Gascony. Not even the excellent Michelin Green Guides cover the region fully and the information they do give is contained in two titles, *Pyrénées* and *Côte de l'Atlantique*, both published in French only. The best guide is the *Guide Bleu, Pyrénées-Gascogne* but this has been out of print for some years, has a French text and is set in such a minuscule size that it is very difficult to read. It seemed to me that there was room for a new guide, in English, that would not only detail the main sites but supply background information on Gascon life and history that would set the duchy in context.

In describing the region I have stuck to the old names such as Armagnac and Bigorre. The departmental names such as the Gers date only from the time of the First Republic and, although they are administratively firmly entrenched, they have quite failed to eradicate the old titles from the consciousness of the local inhabitants. In fact, since we first started to explore the area we have noticed that the Gascons themselves have become increasingly aware of their ancient heritage and are proudly reverting to the original medieval names to establish their separate identities.

The book starts at Agen, partly because it is near our house, but chiefly because it is the gateway to Gascony. You can, of course, go by way of Bordeaux but this brings you first to the Landes, which until the end of the nineteenth century was a wilderness and lacks the historical sites found in profusion in the Gers and further south. Much better, then, to cross the Garonne and make straight for Lectoure.

Most of the book is based on personal research. Sybil and I have been to every part of Gascony and wherever possible we have visited the sites described and made our own judgements: only occasionally have we been frustrated by finding a church locked or been refused entry to a privately owned château. The major exception is the Pyrénées where we have not always been able to follow the backpackers to the highest slopes.

Our research has taken us to many interesting places that we would never otherwise have seen and we have met many charming and delightful people. In the process we have often found that the information in other guidebooks was out of date or just plain wrong. We hope this guide will prove to be reliable and will serve to introduce the reader to a little-known but fascinating region of France.

INTRODUCTION

A MONUMENTAL staircase sweeps up from the river to the cathedral square high above. Halfway up, at the top of the first flight of steps, stands the sculpted figure of a man. His right hand, holding gauntlets, rests lightly on his hip; his left caresses the handle of a sword, slung from a broad belt buckled diagonally across his chest; his elegant calf-length boots have huge buckles on their insteps; a full-length cloak is draped loosely round his shoulders; his hair is long but his moustache is neatly clipped; a broad-brimmed hat sits at a jaunty angle on the back of his head.

The statue commemorates one of the most famous of all Gascons, D'Artagnan, the swashbuckling hero immortalized by Alexandre Dumas in *The Three Musketeers*, and it is to be found in Auch, the ancient capital of Gascony on the river Gers, seventy-eight kilometres west of Toulouse.

Gascons are traditionally courageous, quick-witted, hot-tempered but warm-hearted; bad men to have as adversaries but the staunchest of friends. The leader of the three musketeers embodies all these qualities in the highest degree; what is more, although most of the exploits related in *The Three Musketeers* are pure invention, D'Artagnan was in fact based on a real-life hero, Charles de Batz, who was born not far from Auch in the Château of Castelmore. Small wonder then that when the worthy citizens of Auch were looking for an ideal representative of Gascony to adorn their staircase it was D'Artagnan they chose.

But where is Gascony to be found? Certainly not on a map of

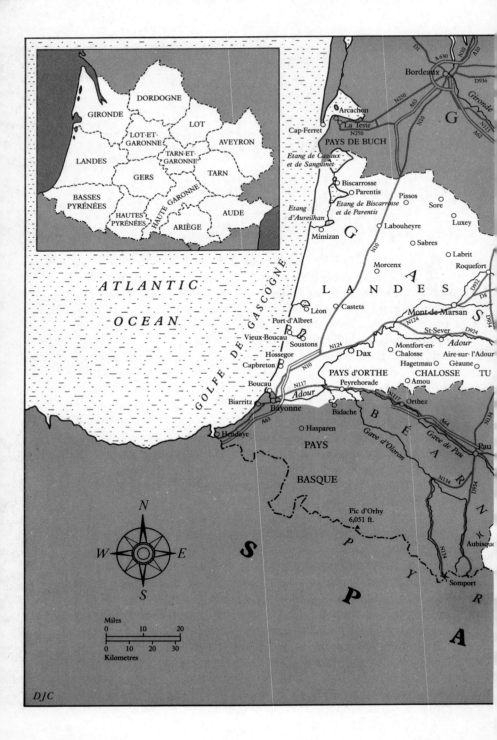

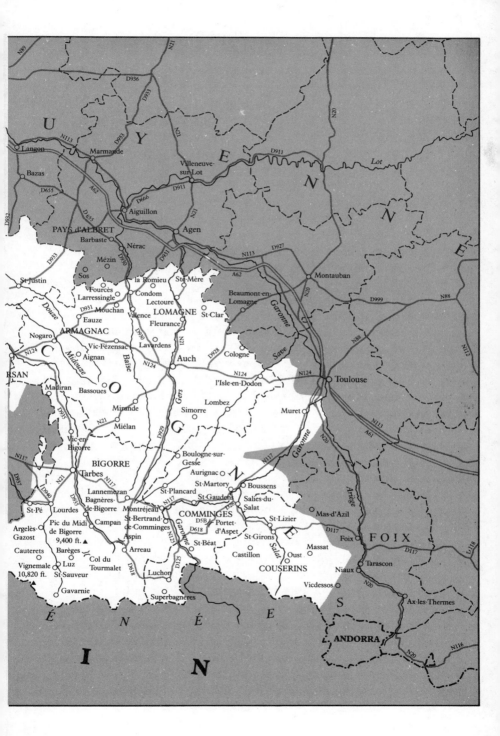

modern France, for it was abolished at the time of the French Revolution. Before then Gascony was a duchy in south-west France. The exact boundaries are difficult to define but at its greatest extent, just before the outbreak of the Revolution, it covered an area stretching from the left bank of the Garonne westwards to the Atlantic and from the Pyrénées northwards almost as far as Bordeaux. This was an enormous territory including the whole of the modern départements of the Gers and the Landes and much of the Ariège, Hautes-Pyrénées, Haute-Garonne and Lot-et-Garonne.

It may seem odd to write about an ancient duchy that ceased to exist nearly two hundred years ago, but legislation can never completely eradicate a sense of local identity: the people of Somerset resolutely refuse to acknowledge that they are part of Avon, even though the legislation that expunged their county was passed as long ago as 1974, and what true Yorkshireman would ever admit to living in Humberside? So, once you have crossed the Garonne and started to drive south from Agen, you soon find yourself among people who still proudly think of themselves as Gascons and who jealously preserve their traditions and cultural heritage.

Gascony is a beautiful land. Much of it is green and hilly and the landscape is very open. Unlike the Dordogne, to the north, where the roads corkscrew laboriously up and down over one hill after another within a framework of concealing trees, the roads of Gascony follow the crests of a chain of hills with magnificent views on either side over a pastoral landscape dotted with fine old farmsteads and hilltop villages, some dating back to the thirteenth century. The valley bottoms often have small, brown sluggish streams running through them or little lakes or ponds, frequently surrounded by flocks of fat, contented-looking ducks.

This makes for an exhilarating journey if you are driving north or south; on the other hand, a journey from east to west is rather like a roller-coaster ride: you swoop joyously down the western slope, climb laboriously up the eastern one to the top, only to fly dizzily down the next, and the pattern is seemingly endlessly repeated. The reason for this peculiarity of the landscape lies further south in the Pyrénées. The birth of this massive mountain chain was accompanied by the production of great quantities of debris that poured down the flanks of the new mountains and was deposited in a series of undulating ridges making the foothills we see today. The most remarkable example of this process is the plateau of Lannemezan, just east of Tarbes.

Most of Lannemezan consists of barren moorland called *touya* and the few farms found there tend to concentrate on raising veal calves and piglets for the local markets, but recently a large area to the north and west of Pau has been reclaimed and successfully planted with maize. From this plateau rise numerous small streams that fan out northwards, flowing through a series of narrow, asymmetrical valleys with steep western slopes and long gradual eastern ones, hence the roller-coaster effect. The unusual profile of these valleys is due to the west-facing slopes having layers of impermeable rock closer to the surface than the eastern ones, so that in the thaw that followed the last ice age the eastern slopes were eroded much more rapidly than the western ones. The asymmetry is more noticeable close to Lannemezan than further north where the streams have become rivers and the valleys wider.

Traditionally the Gascony farmers have always cultivated the gentle eastern slopes, planting vines, cereals and tobacco higher up and raising ducks and geese. These pampered birds are lovingly reared by farmers' wives for they are a potential source of one of France's most prized delicacies: *foie gras*.

Between Agen and the plateau of Lannemezan lies the Gers, which roughly corresponds with the ancient county of Armagnac. The Gers is the least populated *département* of France (175,366 persons at the last census) and the most rural with over sixty per cent of the working population engaged on the land. Apart from Auch there are no towns of any size and even the farms are few and far between: the land will not support large numbers and there is a long tradition of younger sons or *cadets* leaving home to seek their fortunes. Many of them chose soldiering as a career and some, like D'Artagnan and Blaise de Monluc (see page 57), were so successful that they became national heroes. There were, however, many other down-at-heel Gascony captains whose only assets were their swords and their reckless courage. Edmund Rostand painted a vivid picture of these swaggering, happy-go-lucky adventurers in his witty, romantic play *Cyrano de Bergerac*.

CYRANO: They are the Gascony cadets,
Captain Castel Jaloux's their chief.
Braggers of brags, layers of bets,
They are the Gascony cadets.
Barons who scorn mere baronets,
Their lines are long and tempers brief –
They are the Gascony cadets –

For those left behind life was far from easy. The soil of this part of Gascony consists of heavy clay that is extremely difficult to work. Nowadays tractors have taken most of the back-breaking drudgery out of the work but as recently as ten years ago it was still possible to see two massive white oxen yoked together stolidly dragging the ploughshare through the lumpy yellow soil. In summer the earth dries and bakes hard but as soon as the winter rains start it turns to glutinous mud, hence the saying that a true Gascon can always be recognized by the yellow clay sticking to his boots.

In the centre and the east of the Gers most farmers concentrate on raising single crops: cereals, especially maize, are most common but in 1983 many producers took advantage of favourable EEC subsidies and planted sunflowers. The scene in July when the *tournesols* were in bloom was quite extraordinary; mile after mile of heavy-headed deep yellow flowers nodding gently on their six-foot stalks made a dazzling sight in the intense *midi* sun.

Further west cereals give way to the vine, for here, deep in the heart of Gascony, they make what is arguably the finest brandy in the world, at least it is better not to argue about it if you are in Armagnac; Gascon pride brooks no comparison with Armagnac's famous rival made north of Bordeaux in the Charente.

The western limits of Armagnac merge slowly into a very different kind of landscape: the hills are left behind to be replaced by a seemingly endless vista of maritime pines intersected by long, dead-straight roads along which one can sometimes drive for an hour without seeing another car. This is the Landes, the greatest forest of France, which covers most of the coastal region, from the estuary of the Gironde in the north as far south as Bayonne. Yet less than a hundred and fifty years ago there were almost no trees, only an empty barren heathland fringed by coastal dunes, inhabited by a few poverty-stricken shepherds and their flocks. The advance of the dunes eastwards at a rate of more than seven metres a year convinced the government that something must be done. So began the planting of the dunes which within fifty years radically altered the whole ecology of the area. The reclamation of this wasteland will be described in more detail in the chapter on the Landes.

Although so much of Gascony consists of poor farming land, this very fact makes it attractive to tourists who find there a largely unspoiled countryside with occasional farmhouses that blend beautifully with the landscape and old villages of great charm and considerable historical interest. What is more, Gascony enjoys a pleasant climate with mild winters and hot, dry summers.

In winter temperatures rarely fall below four degrees centigrade; on the coast it is usually a degree or so higher. Frosts are rare, only forty days or less in the year, and snow is almost unknown, except in the foothills of the Pyrénées, but the winters are wet and this, as well as the rivers and streams that flow northwards from the Pyrénées, accounts for the lush greenness of the region.

The rainy season continues until the end of May; then, after a short but spectacular early spring (about twenty days in advance of the south of England), a long hot summer begins with a period of drought in July, August and September. The average temperature over this period is twenty degrees centigrade although in 1982 and again in 1983 we languished in a torrid heat of forty degrees and more. Hot spells like these are more often than not broken by a furious electric storm with a day, sometimes two, of almost continuous thunder, accompanied by lightning so bright that at night the landscape shows up in the flashes with the clarity of a silvered negative. After this unsettled period, which usually comes in late August, the good weather returns. Autumn is a good time to visit Gascony: the days are fine but not too hot for touring and the countryside, suffused in a warm honey-coloured light, looks particularly beautiful.

The story of Gascony starts with the invasion of south-west France by Caesar's lieutenant Crassus in 56 BC. The Romans called the region they had conquered Aquitania and the people they found living south and west of the Garonne the Novempopulani, or nine tribes. The Novempopulani were not Gauls but descendants of Celtic tribes, who had crossed the mountains from Spain in the fifth century BC and settled down north of the Pyrénées, as Strabo (c63 BC–cAD 21), the Greek geographer, makes clear: 'In short the Aquitanians differ from the Gallic race both in physique and language; rather they resemble the Iberians. Their country is bounded by the Garonne; they inhabit a country situated between the river and the Pyrénées. The peoples of Aquitaine consist of more than twenty small, obscure tribes, most of them living close to the sea.'

The nine most important tribes that made up the Novempopulani were the Ausci, whose capital was Eliberris (Auch); the Lactorates (Lactora = Lectoure); the Elusates (Elusa = Eauze); the Aturenses (Atura = Aire-sur-l'Adour); the Tarbelli (Aquae Tarbellicae = Dax); the Bigerriones (Tarba = Tarbes); the Convenes, whose capital Lugdunum Convenarum (Saint-Bertrand-de-Comminges) was created by Pompey the Great; the Consorani, with another capital created by the Romans, Lugdunum Consoranorum (Saint-Lizier) and the Boiates who inhabited the area south of Arcachon that in the Middle Ages was called the Pays de Buch. Later the Romans recognized three more tribes on the borders of the Novempopulani: the Vasates in the north, with Bazas as their capital, and the Benearnenses and Iluronenses in the mountains south of modern Pau.

Proof of the Novempopulani's sense of their separate identity is provided by an inscription carved on a memorial tablet found at Hasparen in the Pays-Basque, which is thought to date from the third century AD: FLAMEN. ITEM. DUMVIR. QUAESTOR PAGIQ. MAGISTER VERUS. AD AUGUSTUM. LEGATO. MUNERE. FUNCTUS PRO NOVEM. OPTINUIT POPULIS. SEIUNGERE GALLOS URBE REDUX. GENIO. PAGI. HANC. DEDICAT ARAM. Roughly translated, this says that Verus, a local worthy, went on a mission to the Emperor

Augustus to ask that the Novempopulani should be separated from the Gauls. On his return, he dedicated this memorial of his trip to the local god.

Apart from a small tribe called the Sotiates, who fought a fierce battle with the Romans near Sos, the Novempopulani put up little resistance to Crassus. They appear to have adjusted quickly to benign Roman rule and Latin became their adopted tongue. It was the Novempopulani who formed the indigenous population of what was eventually to become Gascony and the borders of the territory that they occupied when the Romans arrived conformed very closely to those of the medieval duchy.

The Pyrénées to the south, the Atlantic Ocean to the west and the river Garonne to the east all form natural frontiers but it is not clear why the first northern frontier of the Novempopulani, and later of Gascony, should have been where it was. The answer, I think, is that north of Arcachon lay an area of swamps that was virtually uninhabitable until it was drained by the Dutch in the seventeenth century. Further east the Novempopulani would have come up against a Gallic tribe called the Nitiobriges, whose stronghold was on the heights above the modern city of Agen, from which they commanded the fertile valley of the Garonne between Agen and Marmande. The Garonne itself curves westwards at this point and would have been a further barrier to progress northwards.

The Romans ruled Aquitania for over four hundred years during which time cities like Burdigala (Bordeaux) and Elusa (Eauze) grew rich and powerful. Among other good things the Romans brought the vine to south-west France and it was at this period that the first vineyards were planted close to Burdigala in the areas now called Graves and Saint-Emilion.

This era of peace and prosperity was rudely interrupted by the arrival in AD 275 of the first Barbarian invaders who stormed into Aquitania from the north and terrorized the province for the next eight years. Before this onslaught the villas and cities of Aquitania were apparently undefended and, at the approach of the Barbarians, the wealthier citizens seem to have panicked and, stopping only to bury their valuables, to have taken to their heels. Abandoned treasure hoards dating from this period have been found at Lectoure and a number of other sites. For the next seven hundred years the south-west suffered from successive waves of invaders: Vandals, Visigoths, Franks, Arabs, Vascons and Normans all fought over and despoiled this lovely land, but only the Franks and Vascons left a lasting legacy.

The greatest contribution was made by the Franks who in 507 AD drove out the Visigoths and made Aquitaine part of the Frankish Empire. It was the Franks who introduced the system of dividing their kingdom into counties and grouping a number of counties under the control of a duke and it was during their rule that the first Duke of Aquitaine was created.

The domination of the Franks was challenged at the end of the sixth century by the Vascons, an Iberian tribe or tribes who had never been conquered by the Romans and spoke their own language rather than Latin. They crossed the Pyrénées from Spain and quickly over-ran the whole of Aquitaine south and west of the Garonne. In AD 602 we find for the first time the land of the Novempopulani called Wasconia in a contemporary chronicle. It is only a short step from Wasconia to Gasconha and so to Gascogne, which is the French name for what we call Gascony. But apart from bestowing their name on the Gascon state the Vascons left no other memorials and seem to have settled down alongside the Novempopulani and adopted their ways.

Meanwhile, despite this takeover by the Vascons, or Gascons, Aquitaine remained technically part of the Frankish Empire and from time to time the stronger rulers like Charlemagne descended on the province to remind the Gascons of the fact. Nevertheless, the Franks were usually so busy defending their extensive empire against attacks by their powerful neighbours the Burgundians, the Saxons and the Ostrogoths of Italy, or suppressing internal rebellions, that they had no time to worry about their remote territories in the south-west. This led to a long-drawn-out, but ultimately unsuccessful, rebellion by the Gascon nobles. Somehow, the Franks managed to retain a tenuous hold on Aquitaine until AD 844, when the first Norse longships appeared at the mouths of the rivers Garonne and Adour.

There now began more than a hundred years of pillage and destruction that was even worse than the ravages of the Vandals. Year after year the Norse raiders reappeared, penetrating further and further upriver into the very heart of Gascony. Agen, Bazas, Lectoure, Condom, Eauze, Dax and many more towns besides were completely destroyed and the constant raids caused widespread fear and despair. During this period the authority of the state disintegrated and the remaining vestiges of Frankish rule crumbled. Power now passed into the hands of local lords who turned their manor houses into strongholds, refuges to which peasants and villagers could retreat in times of danger. This was the origin of the feudal castle.

So, by AD 987, when Hugh Capet unseated the last of the Franks, the new king found himself ruling a small territory, stretching only from Dreux, north of Paris, to Orléans on the Loire, entirely surrounded by overmighty subjects, all of whom wielded more real power than he did: one of these subjects was the Duke of Gascony.

Exactly when Gascony became a duchy is not known; it must have been some time in the tenth century but because of the depredations of the Norsemen there are very few documents surviving from that period and the origins of the first dukes are obscure. What is clear is that by the time Hugh Capet became King of France, Gascony was recognized as a separate entity and Duke Guillaume-Sanche ruled the whole region south and west of the Garonne.

The first Capetian kings were not strong enough to assert their authority over the Gascon dukes and the latter tended to look to Spain to help them maintain their independence, but in 1032 Duke Guillaume-Sanche died without an heir and the duchy passed to his sister's son, Eudes, who was also Count of Poitiers and Duke of Aquitaine. As a result Gascony lost its independent duke and was now merely the southern half of the Duchy of Aquitaine although its separate identity was still recognized.

The acquisition of Gascony made the dukes of Aquitaine extremely powerful. In theory they were vassals of the kings of France but as they ruled a territory much larger than that of the

Capetians, covering the whole of western France south of the Loire, they behaved in fact like independent princes. Their court at Poitiers was one of the richest and most sophisticated of the age. Here the bizarre rituals of the code of courtly love were preached, if not practised, while the troubadours, whose lyrics gave expression to that code's romantic view of women, were not only encouraged by the Duke and nobility, but were often the friends and even lovers of their patrons. Indeed, Duke Guilhem VI was himself a famous troubadour as was a later duke, Richard Coeur de Lion.

In Gascony, however, the rule of the dukes was for the most part nominal. The disintegration of society brought about by the Norse raids had led to the division of the region into a number of semi-independent fiefs, each ruled by a powerful local family. Chief among them were the Counts of Armagnac, whose lands lay right in the middle of Gascony with Aignan as their capital. To the south was Astarac, ruled by a viscount and centred on the town of Mirande. Further south again, in the foothills of the Pyrénées, was the territory of the Counts of Foix, the Armagnacs' bitter rivals. To the north of Auch was the Lomagne with Lectoure as its chief town. The Lomagne was also controlled by the Armagnacs. There were many more *petit-pays* which it would be tedious to mention here, but one that cannot be omitted is the Pays d'Albret which lay west of the Lomagne in the sandy wilderness of the Landes. A more unlikely power base than Albret would be difficult to imagine but it was from this obscure and barren region of Gascony that there emerged the family that produced one of France's greatest kings, the ruler who united France after the ravages of the wars of religion, Henri IV.

In 1137 Guilhem VII, Duke of Aquitaine, died while on a pilgrimage to Santiago de Compostella and the duchy passed to his only daughter Eleanor. In the same year Eleanor married the future Louis VII of France in Bordeaux cathedral. Eleanor's dowry was the Duchy of Aquitaine, a gain of territory that added enormously to the power and prestige of the French throne. This piece of practical statesmanship was confounded by the incompatibility of the marriage partners. Eleanor behaved less than discreetly, was divorced by the furious king and promptly married Henry Plantagenet, the heir to the English crown, thus sowing the seeds of the long and bitter struggle known as the Hundred Years' War.

The existence of such a huge territory on their borders, owing allegiance to a foreign power, was something that no French king could tolerate. The situation was complicated by the fact that in theory the King of France was suzerain over the Duke of Aquitaine who owed him homage. However, the duke was also the King of England and as such the French king's equal in rank; what is more he ruled a much larger realm in France than the French king himself, consisting not only of Aquitaine but Anjou, Maine, Touraine and Normandy as well.

War soon broke out and ended in 1259 with the loss by England of all her fiefs except Gascony and the adjacent territories of Agenais, Quercy, Périgord and Limousin. There was then a period of peace until 1337 when the Hundred Years' War began. It has been said that the Hundred Years' War was neither a war nor did it last a hundred years: it consisted mainly of a series of skirmishes and sieges with only one or two set-piece battles, such as Poitiers and Agincourt, most of which were won by the English. Little by little, however, the French whittled away the English territories until only Gascony remained. Eventually that too was lost when 'Old Talbot', the Earl of Shrewsbury, was defeated and killed at the battle of Castillon (1453) and Bordeaux fell.

Most Gascons fought on the side of the English in the Hundred Years' War and they soon became renowned as doughty fighters. The most famous of the Gascon captains were the Captals de Buch, a family of rather obscure nobles whose base was a *petit-pays* called Captalat de Buch near Arcachon. They loyally supported their English overlords and were richly rewarded as a result.

Indeed, the loyalty of the Gascons was far from disinterested. However ruinous the war may have been for France as a whole, many Gascons did very well out of it. The English kings developed a taste for Gascon wine and so did their subjects. In 1308 Edward II ordered a thousand barrels (roughly 1,152,000 bottles) to celebrate his marriage to Isabelle of France.

Bordeaux became a thriving port again and by the middle of the fourteenth century was exporting over three million gallons of wine a year to England – this at a time when our population numbered only four million!

Under the protection of the English kings, Bordeaux flourished, reaching its apogee after the English victory at Poitiers in 1356 when the Black Prince ruled Aquitaine and made the city his capital. The Black Prince may have been a great soldier but he was no administrator and his court soon became a by-word for luxury and extravagance, something that did not please all Gascons who paid heavily for his pleasures.

Further south, the port of Bayonne also prospered and her fleet fought alongside the English against the French. Elsewhere in Gascony, however, the picture was rather different. Inland towns like Condom and Auch had no option but to send their goods a long way downriver to Bordeaux or Bayonne for export. But because of its position on the estuary of the Gironde and its privileged position as the capital of Aquitaine, Bordeaux enjoyed a monopoly of the wine trade with England, a situation that the shrewd Bordelais exploited quite unscrupulously to promote their own wines at the expense of those that came from higher up the rivers Garonne, Dordogne and Lot. This may be one reason why Armagnac, which is far from the sea, was less enthusiastic about the English connection than other parts of Gascony.

The end of the Hundred Years' War was followed by a period of relative peace and prosperity during which trade increased and towns flourished. A sign that life was indeed returning to normal is the large number of *gentilhommières*, small manor-houses, that were built at this time with mullion and transom windows replacing arrow slits and ground-floor entrances instead of temporary wooden stairs to the first floor.

But it was not to last. In 1562 the first of the Wars of Religion between the Catholics and the Huguenots broke out and Gascony became a battle-ground in a bitter civil war that lasted, off and on, for over thirty years. During this period many churches and other religious buildings were either destroyed or suffered terrible damage at the hands of the Protestant Huguenots.

The Huguenot leader was the Gascon Henri of Navarre and his

accession to the throne as Henri IV, in 1594, brought the war to an end. It also brought an influx of Gascon nobility to the French court where Henry's former companions in arms were well rewarded for their loyalty. Many of these nobles later returned to Gascony where they used their new wealth to enlarge their châteaux or build new ones. The ordinary Gascon soldiers also flocked to Paris to enroll in the French Guards, the élite regiment sworn to defend the person of the King, and the flamboyant Gascon captains soon became a familiar sight in the capital.

The assassination of Henry IV, in 1610, brought a waning of Gascon influence at court and a renewal of persecution of the Huguenots, culminating in the Revocation of the Edict of Nantes in 1685, which forced hundreds of thousands of Huguenot Protestants to flee France.

Because of its history of unrest and disaffection, Gascony was never looked on kindly by the French kings and after the Revocation of the Edict of Nantes it seems to have been forgotten completely. A long period of neglect ensued during which there were no serious upheavals until the French Revolution and even this had less impact than elsewhere in France, although some châteaux and churches were pillaged and destroyed.

As a result of this isolation Gascony became a backwater: the south-west has always suffered from poor communications, both internally and with the rest of France. Right up to the middle of the nineteenth century roads were so few and so bad that the rivers were the only reliable means of transport. As late as 1832 when Georges Haussmann, later to become Baron Haussmann, was travelling in the south-west corner of Lot-et-Garonne there were no roads and his guide had to use a compass to find his way. Not only were roads lacking, but there were few bridges either. Not a single bridge was to be found on the Garonne all the way from Toulouse to Agen, a distance of three hundred kilometres. With such a poor communications network, Gascony inevitably turned in on itself and operated a closed economy, the main exception being brandy which did not suffer from the long voyage downriver. Apart from the havoc created by marauding armies, there were few outside influences and the pace of change was very slow.

Not until the end of the nineteenth century did new roads and the coming of the railway open up new horizons. Meanwhile, cut off from the outside world Gascons developed a strong sense of their separate identity. Like the British they are proud of their history and jealously guard their rich cultural heritage. Not that they are sunk in a nostalgic torpor: the farmers use the very latest tractors, and modern technology is as much in demand here as anywhere else, but Gascons seem able to absorb the best of the new without destroying their past. It is our good fortune that they feel this way: thanks to them we can visit villages and towns that have survived intact since the Middle Ages, set in a landscape that you feel must have looked to the original inhabitants very much as it does today.

So now let us delay no longer but cross the Garonne and start to explore the beautiful and historic land that lies south of Agen.

CHAPTER 1

SOUTH
FROM
AGEN

1 The Lomagne

AGEN IS a frontier town: it straddles the wide Garonne at the point where the river is forced westwards by the first ridge of limestone hills that stretch northwards to the Dordogne and all the way east to the Massif Central. When the Romans came here in 56 BC there was no riverside settlement but the heights to the north were commanded by the Nitiobriges, a Celtic tribe whose rule extended about twenty miles south of the Garonne; from there to the Pyrénées was the territory of the Novempopulani which in the early Middle Ages became the Duchy of Gascony.

It is always a relief to quit Agen, cross the Garonne and head south for Gascony. Not that Agen is completely lacking in interest: it has one of the best markets in the region, a good local museum containing a famous Greek sculpture, found locally, the Vénus de Mas, and a cathedral with a twelfth-century apse; yet the town lacks charm, has no obvious centre and, most damning of all, always seems full of traffic.

The best route out of Agen is the Passage d'Agen (RN21) which after crossing the Garonne, here a broad, slow-flowing rather boring river, follows its left bank for a short way. After only five miles a turning to the right (D268) leads to Moirax, a Cluniac priory founded in 1049. It is a small church but the proportions are beautiful; the east end, with its half-round apse and smaller radial chapels on either side, is particularly satisfying. The west

3

front is of little interest but once inside you have a feeling of great peace and harmony. The oldest part, built at about the time William the Conqueror was invading England, is the nave; this has six bays surmounted by a pointed tunnel vault. The tall arcade has round piers, with shafts attached from which spring both the arches of the arcade itself and the stone cross-ribs that reinforce the vault and, at this level, define the limits of each bay. The capitals of the shafts are crisply carved, sometimes with simplified acanthus leaves, sometimes with figures. One capital shows Adam and Eve and the serpent and St Michael slaying the dragon. The easternmost piers are octagonal with acanthus-leaf capitals again but here carved with much finer detail. These piers belong to the late eleventh century as does the transept, although the vaulting here is Gothic. The north transept has a splendid capital showing what looks like a pack of dogs but is apparently a pride of lions.

Beyond the crossing is the twelfth-century choir. There are only two bays but, unlike the nave, it has a clerestory, above which is a dome on squinches. Finally we come to the lovely semi-circular apse, lit by five plain windows set within blank arcades with beautifully carved capitals and crowned by a semi-dome, a simple but very satisfying resolution not just of the east end but of the whole interior.

Sybil and I are both addicted to Romanesque architecture and it is one of the joys of Gascony that you can find good examples of the style everywhere. We love its simplicity of form, its satisfying sense of mass, something that modern sculptors like Henry Moore have taught us to appreciate, and its clear lines, uncluttered by the kind of decorative fripperies that mar many late-Gothic buildings. Not that Romanesque is unadorned, its bizarre sculpture, which often includes the most fantastic monsters and chimaeras, is one of its delights but for the most part these carvings are sparingly applied and do not interfere with our appreciation of the churches' lines.

In the eleventh century there was an explosion of church-building all over France. By then the Dark Ages were coming to an end and life was more secure but, perhaps even more important, the year 1000 had passed without the world coming to an end as

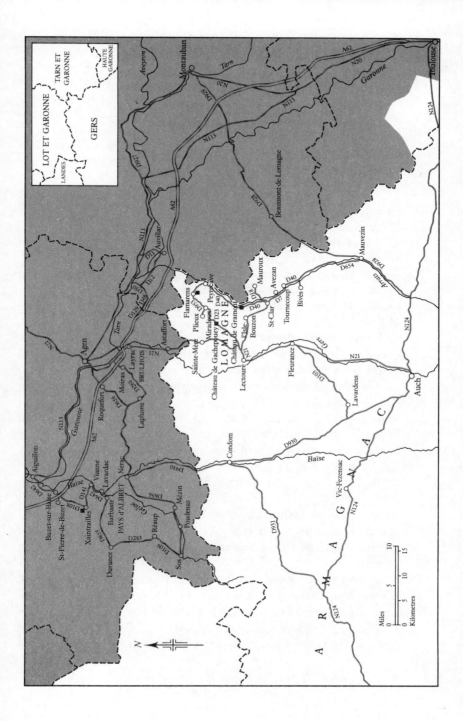

many Christians had confidently expected. The contemporary chronicler, Radulphus Glaber, has given us a vivid account of what it was like at this period: 'So on the threshold of the aforesaid thousandth year, some two or three years after it, it befell throughout the world, but especially in Italy and Gaul, that the fabrics of churches were rebuilt ... so it was as though the world has shaken herself and cast off her old age and were clothing herself everywhere in a white garment of churches.'

So in the eleventh and twelfth centuries new churches were built all over Gascony, but because of the distance from Paris and the Ile de France, and perhaps because of the antipathy of the peoples of the south to those of the north, the Gothic style was slow in arriving in the south-west (the Romanesque style spread from Italy and the south) and there are very few Gothic churches of any kind and nothing to compare with masterpieces like Chartres and Notre-Dame. As a result Gascony is a happy hunting ground for lovers of Romanesque.

A little further down the RN21, at Layrac, is another Cluniac church consecrated in 1096. After parking, go first to the east end where there is a fine prospect of open country stretching down to the Garonne. This is also the best view of the church, whose chevet has the same harmonious proportions as Moirax, although here, unfortunately, the effect is marred by an overpowering modern dome. The wall surface of the apse is divided into three bays by flat buttresses rising to roof level and each bay contains a window framed by a blind arch. At roof level there are carved corbel heads.

At the west end the doorway has archivolts ornamented with billet moulding and rosettes. To the right is a capital carved with lions and birds. Inside is a seven-bay aisleless nave with a pointed barrel vault. The windows on the north side are blocked up and the attached half-round columns dividing the bays are hideously painted.

Beyond the crossing with its shallow dome is a fine large apse whose semi-dome has paintings by Franceschini. Below the windows the wall surface is divided into nine bays by blank arcades supported on shafts with stiff leaf capitals. The entrance to the apse has tall columns on each side with beautifully carved capitals:

6

on the left lions and on the right lions and birds.

After Layrac the road follows the valley of the Gers, a tributary of the Garonne, which it crosses at Astaffort. On this stretch in summer you will see wayside stalls selling local fruit: peaches, nectarines, delicious orange-fleshed Charentais melons and the local delicacy, prunes, which here are not a subject for schoolboy mirth but are sold like luxury chocolates, beautifully packaged and stuffed with all kinds of succulent fillings. There is a large stall at the Caves de Bruilhois where you can also buy a very drinkable local red wine. They sell Armagnac here, too, but it is better to wait as you will find better quality brands and more choice further south.

Beyond Astaffort the road begins to wind and climb steeply up to a height of 700 feet and here, from the top of the ridge, you will see for the first time, stretching far away on either side, the rolling green countryside of Gascony. Close by, right on the northern frontier of Gascony, appear the massive square towers of the fortress of Sainte-Mère first on one side of the road and then on the other as the RN 21 twists and doubles back on itself.

Sainte-Mère is worth a closer look. Built in a commanding position on a hill to the west of the main road, it is one of the best examples of a type of castle peculiar to Gascony called the Gascon *château-fort*. Unlike conventional castles they do not have curtain walls or a keep but consist of a massive rectangular block, in which lived the lord and his retainers, defended by two or more square towers built at the corners. The north-facing façade of Sainte-Mère is very imposing: the two towers are both on this side of the castle, their northern sides built flush with the main block; the eastern tower is much higher (88 feet) than that on the west. Originally there were only three narrow arrow slits on this side, a clear indication of the defensive nature of the building. Even with the later addition of a window and what looks like an entrance opening, the severity of this sheer wall is very impressive.

The castle has four floors. Access was at second-floor level, on the south side, by a wooden stairway that could be dismantled in times of danger. Here were the lord's apartments, lit by twin-lancet windows and containing a fireplace. The ground floor held the castle's stores but exactly what the arrangements were in the other two floors is not clear; probably the first floor was occupied by the retainers and the top floor contained the bedrooms.

There is some argument amongst scholars about the exact purpose of the castle. It was built round about 1274 by Gérard de Monlezun, Bishop of Lectoure, and Philippe Lauzan, who first identified the 'château-fort Gascon', believed that it was a frontier fort built to defend the territory of the Count of Armagnac against invasion by the English, who occupied the Agenais to the north. Other scholars point out that technically the Counts of Armagnac were vassals of the English kings at this period and so had nothing to fear from the English but this, I think, betrays a lack of knowledge of the Armagnacs who were devious in the extreme and chiefly concerned to increase their already considerable power at the expense of both the English and French kings. Certainly when you look at that cliff-like north wall of Sainte-Mère, you cannot help feeling that this was the direction from which an attack was expected; what is more, the almost complete lack of any decoration and the massive size of the *château-fort* of Sainte-Mère is a grim reminder of the insecurity of life in fourteenth-century Gascony. Apart from the *château-fort*, Sainte-Mère has the remains of the medieval village that surrounded it, including a stone entry arch and a small twelfth-century church.

Twelve miles further south is the ancient hill town of Lectoure. It has a fine position on a steep promontory that juts out westwards like the prow of a ship, giving extensive views to the south and west; indeed they say that on a clear day you can see the Pyrénées, more than seventy miles away. Coming from the north, however, the ascent is more gradual. One of the first things you will see on the outskirts of the town is a signboard with a dashing picture of a musketeer advertising a local restaurant, so now you know you are really in Gascony. It certainly makes a change from the ubiquitous pigs promoting the local *charcuterie* shops, although I must confess a sneaking affection for these perky porkers, cheerfully brandishing a string of sausages or a pot of *rillettes*, like a Christian saint embracing the symbol of martyrdom.

Lectoure is a very old city; it was founded by one of the Celtic–

Iberian tribes that settled the region in the fifth century BC. They were one of the Novempopulani, and were given the name of Lactorates. Nothing is known about the pre-Roman town but there are fascinating relics of the Roman occupation in the town museum next to the cathedral. When the Gothic choir of the cathedral was being rebuilt in the sixteenth century the builders discovered a large number of *taurobolia*. These are stones recording the baptism of initiates into the cult of Cybele, an oriental religion that rivalled Christianity in popularity for a while. New members of the cult stood in a pit while above them a bull was slaughtered, showering them with its blood. The bull's blood washed away the candidate's sins and in celebration a stone was set up with a carved inscription commemorating the event.

The first thing you see, after passing the musketeer signboard and the men playing *boules* in a tree-shaded park, is the massive bell tower of the cathedral of Saints Gervais and Protais looming over the narrow main street and looking more like a castle keep than part of a church; indeed the tower does have a round stairway turret on its eastern side. The tower has five stages. The first two have enormous corner buttresses and narrow windows which reinforce the first impression that this is a defensive construction; on the other hand each of the top three stages is slightly recessed and the top two have twin windows attractively decorated with late Gothic carving and ornamented corner niches: the whole is crowned by a graceful balustrade. Apart from the east face, with its menacing turret, the tower looks at once both powerful and elegant. The rest of the church is a disappointment: it has one of those typically gloomy Gothic interiors so common in France and there are no monuments of any interest.

Although in the Gothic style, the church of Saints Gervais and Proteus was largely rebuilt in the sixteenth and seventeenth centuries following serious damage inflicted during the siege and sacking of Lectoure in 1473, the most terrible event in the town's history. At this period Lectoure was the capital of the Lomagne, one of the many feudal sub-divisions of Gascony that resulted from the weakness of the Gascon dukes during the tenth and eleventh centuries. In 1325 the Viscounty of the Lomagne passed by marriage to Jean I, Count of Armagnac and Lectoure became an Armagnac stronghold.

During the fourteenth and fifteenth centuries the Armagnacs were one of the most powerful families, not just in Gascony but in the whole of France. Their story will be told in more detail in the next chapter but by 1473 their fortunes were in decline. Jean IV, who was Count from 1418 to 1450, ruled his territories like an independent prince and continually flouted royal authority. Eventually he went too far when he intrigued with the King of England: a royal army was despatched to Gascony, Jean was defeated, taken prisoner and ended his days in disgrace.

The Count's son, the Viscount of Lomagne (the title given to the eldest sons of the Counts of Armagnac), started well. He fought bravely on the side of the French king against the English, taking part in the successful campaign in Normandy in 1449, when Rouen was captured. In 1450 he became Count Jean V and the same year fought in the final campaign of the Hundred Years' War in Gascony, which ended in the fall of Bordeaux and the defeat of the English forces at the Battle of Castillon in 1453.

The expulsion of the English from Gascony seems to have left the bellicose Count of Armagnac at a loose end. His behaviour became increasingly erratic: one of his more extraordinary interventions was in the succession to the archbishopric of Auch, the capital of Gascony. Jean V was determined to have his own nominee, Jean de Lescun, elected instead of Philippe de Lévis, who was favoured by both the Pope and the French king. To get his own way Jean V marched to Auch and held the canons of the cathedral virtual prisoner while he tried to force them to accept his candidate. An emissary sent to serve a writ on the Count to prevent him interfering with the election was chased away and his writ thrown into the river Gers, and when some followers of Philippe de Lévis tried to take possession of property belonging to the archbishop at Vic Fézensac, the furious Count had them thrown into a dungeon in his castle at Lavardens and instructed their gaoler not to give them any food until they had shouted '*Vive Armagnac*' three times.

Eventually the Count was forced with ill-grace to give way but these bizarre events were soon overshadowed by his incestuous affair with his sister Isabelle. When his father died in 1450 the thirty-year-old Count was left living alone with his youngest sister, a beautiful girl of thirteen. Jean had three children by Isabelle but what really scandalized his contemporaries was that he went through a spurious marriage ceremony with her.

This was too much. Jean V was excommunicated by Pope Nicholas V and the French King, Charles VII, took advantage of the disgrace to topple him. In May 1455 an army of 24,000 men was despatched against the Count. The King's forces proceeded to Auch where Philippe de Lévis was installed as archbishop, then to the castle of Lavardens, which was quickly captured, and finally to Lectoure which held out for a while but eventually was forced to surrender. Jean V, however, was not there to see it; he had already fled to Spain.

After a four-year trial the Count was found guilty by the Parlement of Paris of *lèse-majesté*, incest, rebellion and disobeying the King and his justice, and he was sentenced to perpetual banishment and confiscation of all his lands. But once again Jean, who had returned to France to defend himself, seeing the way the wind was blowing, had already fled.

In 1461 Charles VII died and his son, Louis XI, pardoned the Count and restored his lands to him. He was soon to regret his generosity.

In 1464 Jean V joined an alliance of great nobles who were determined to limit the growing power of the French monarchy, although they united under the pretext of defending the people against royal abuses, so that the civil war that followed became known as the 'war of the public weal'. The part played by Jean V in the conflict was hardly glorious. He contrived not to commit his forces in any major battle; instead they remained on the sidelines, ravaging the countryside and doing the public weal no good at all.

The war ended in a stalemate with the King forced to make concessions and the nobles, including Jean V, reaffirming their loyalty to the crown, but from then on Louis was looking for an opportunity to destroy the troublesome Count of Armagnac.

Jean V did nothing to allay the King's suspicions. He increasingly behaved like an independent prince, ruling his territories without reference to the authority of the crown and maintaining his own army, which continued to lay waste the royal realms in the south-west.

But in 1468 Louis found the pretext he needed. In that year the English King, Edward IV, sent a secret emissary called John Boon to Jean V to find out if the Count would support an English invasion of Gascony. Boon's account of his meeting with the Count has survived and fascinating it is. He was, it appears, acting as a double agent for afterwards he gave a full account of the negotiations to Louis, who rewarded him with a handsome pension. According to Boon, Jean agreed to come to the English King's aid with an army of 15,000 men and to pay homage to him as his sovereign lord. Whether or nor this was a true record of what took place is unclear but it was enough for Louis: he accused the Count of treachery and launched an attack on his territories.

Once again Lectoure was besieged by a royal army and once again Jean V escaped across the Pyrénées to Spain. The royal troops captured Lectoure and remained in control there until August 1471 when the Count of Armagnac returned secretly to Gascony and took the town by subterfuge.

Louis XI was furious. A new army was despatched and in 1472 the siege of Lectoure was resumed, but this time Jean V was there to conduct the defence of the town. Given the primitive nature of fifteenth-century artillery the town was virtually impregnable. To the west the steepness of the escarpment made attack impossible while the more vulnerable eastern slope had been reinforced by a double curtain wall and a massive tower known as 'le grand boulevard. After a preliminary artillery barrage which achieved little the royal army settled down to a long siege.

A year later Lectoure had not fallen and the royal army was still camped outside: it was stalemate. Negotiations began to bring the siege to an honourable end and eventually Jean V agreed, in return for a royal pardon, to surrender the town. On 6 March, 1473, the gates of Lectoure were opened to the royal troops. What happened next is not clear; all that it known is that there was a fracas in the streets in the course of which Count Jean V was stabbed to death, after which the King's men went on the rampage, burning and looting the town.

On the royal side it was afterwards claimed that there was treachery by the Count's men and that the royal troops were merely defending themselves. The adherents of the Armagnac cause claimed that the royalists never intended to honour the truce. Whatever the truth, it was the beginning of the end for the house of Armagnac. The King took possession of the Count's lands and with the death of Jean's brother Charles in 1495 the territories of the Counts of Armagnac finally passed to the French crown.

After the cathedral there is nothing else to see in Lectoure except the so-called Fontaine Diane which lies on the north side of the town, but the original opening is now covered by a grille from which rises an unsavoury smell.

The Lomagne lies to the east of Lectoure. It is one of the least-known regions of Gascony and one of the most sparsely populated but well worth exploring for all that. A turning just north of Lectoure, the D7 marked to Saint-Clar, leads straight into a pleasant, gently undulating landscape. This is good farming country and there are enormous fields devoted largely to single crops: maize, sunflowers or rape. Farms are few and far between, but soon the first hill village, l'Isle-Bouzon, appears attractively set on a hilltop to the left of the road. There is not much to see there, a few old houses being restored, a crumbling watchtower that is all that remains of the ancient fortifications, and an extraordinary *pigeonnier*. There are many of these pigeon-towers on farms all over the south-west. The pigeons that covered the roof were originally kept not as a supplementary food supply but for the sake of their droppings. In areas where there were few cattle the guano was a valuable source of nitrates. So strong was the fertilizer that it could not be spread on the ground until the rain was starting to fall, otherwise the stalks and surface roots would have been burned by the concentrated nitrates. Until the Revolution, the pigeon-tower and its guano belonged exclusively to the local lord who thus controlled the sale of this commodity. Today the pigeon droppings are no longer used but there is still a certain cachet in possessing a pigeon-tower, although now it is just as likely to contain a smart tiled bathroom as pigeons. The towers can take many forms, some of them very attractive. The simplest ones are straightforward stone towers, square or round, capped by pointed tiled roofs with openings for the pigeons to fly in and out. Further south, where stone is scarce, the *pigeonniers* are often half-timbered and stand on mushroom-headed stone stilts. There is a very pretty one like this at Mauroux off the D13, north-east of Saint-Clar. The *pigeonnier* at l'Isle de Bouzon is very bizarre indeed; built of stone, it is conical in shape and looks like the shell from some enormous First World War long-range gun, except that the pointed top is crowned by a saucy little tiled roof which gives it a rather comic appearance, like a heavyweight boxer wearing a school cap.

Down the road is Saint-Clar, one of our favourite Gascon towns. Saint-Clar is the Gascon form of St Clair, who was the first bishop of Albi and a martyr. The original town grew up around a Benedictine church founded in the tenth century and a few of the old streets are still to be found round the medieval church on the west side of the town. Most of the church is twelfth-century but the lowest part of the bell tower is tenth-century, whilst the recessed top stage is fourteenth-century.

Saint-Clar is unusual in combining two different kinds of medieval town, the organic town and the *bastide*.[1]

Organic towns, as the name suggests, were unplanned. They usually grew up round a castle or church which offered the townsmen protection in return for their services. A town based on a castle was called a *château neuf*, in Gascon a *castelnau* or *castelneu*. Both words are quite commonly found in place names in Gascony and almost certainly show that the town originated in this way in the late eleventh or twelfth centuries; examples are Castelnau-Tursan, Castelnau-d'Anglès and Castelnau-sur-l'Auvignon. Other words which are clues to these early towns are *castet*, meaning castle (Castet-Arrouey), *mothe* or *mont* referring to the artificial mounds on which these early castles were often built (Montpezat), *pouy* or *puy*, a high place on which a castle might be built

---

1 The word *bastide* derives from a langue d'oc word *bastida*, meaning to build.

(Puylausic, Monsempuy), *roque*, a rocky outcrop cliff or escarpment (Pouy-Roquelaire), and *fort* (Roquefort), although these last three are to be found in the names of bastides as well.

The *castelnaux* sometimes grew up spontaneously round the castle in times of danger, but often the lord of the castle deliberately set out to attract townsfolk who would help to dispose of the surplus produce of his land and provide the skilled tradesmen like carpenters and blacksmiths that he and his retainers often needed.

The towns that had churches at their centre were always voluntary creations which came about because the churches offered sanctuary to anyone who took refuge within their boundaries. The limits were marked by crosses and once you touched the cross you were safe. For this reason these towns were called *sauvetés* and this word also crops up in place names like Sauvetat-de-Savères, although more rarely than *castelnau*. These towns were undefended, a fact which sometimes tempted wicked local barons to sack them.

Bastides, on the other other, were planned from the start and can easily be recognized by their distinctive grid pattern of streets and their central squares surrounded by arcades, usually with heavy stone pointed arches. There is often a covered market in the square with a tiled roof supported by wooden posts or stone piers. The town church is nearly always to be found at one corner of the main square.

A large number of *bastides* were built in Gascony in the late twelfth and thirteenth centuries. Many of them were royal towns, founded by the kings of France or of England in partnership (*pareage*) with a local lord or prelate; others were created by great nobles like the Counts of Armagnac. The aim seems on the one hand to have been to establish local communities who would owe their allegiance to the founder and thus maintain his presence in the region; this was, of course, particularly important in disputed territories like Gascony. On the other hand, these new towns also encouraged trade which resulted in greater prosperity and increased revenue in the form of taxes for their founders.

Usually the foundation of a new *bastide* was marked by a ceremony in which a pole flying a pennant bearing the coat of arms of the founder was erected at the centre of what was to become the main square. A cord was then used to mark out the grid of streets and the prospective townsmen were summoned to hear the announcement of the liberties granted to the town and to receive the official charter.

The building of a new *bastide* was sometimes the cause of great local friction and once it actually precipitated armed conflict between France and England, the so-called War of Saint-Sardos, a minor episode in the Hundred Years' War. Saint-Sardos was a Benedictine priory north-west of Agen. In 1323 the abbot entered into an agreement to build a *bastide* at Saint-Sardos even though at that time the Agenais belonged to the English King Edward II. The pole was duly set up the evening before the ceremony but next morning the horrified monks found instead of the pennant the King's representative hanging from the pole and some of the priory buildings set on fire.

The crime had been perpetrated by the men of Monpezat, a nearby English *bastide*. One thing led to another and soon the two countries were at war. The fighting only lasted two years but by the end the English had lost effective control of the Agenais.

In 1289 the Bishop of Lectoure signed an agreement with the English King Edward I, who at that time was the Lomagne's overlord, to create a *bastide* at Saint-Clar and the new town was founded alongside the old. Apart from having this mixture of ancient and modern, Saint-Clar is unusual in possessing more than one arcaded square. The place de la Mairie, at the centre of the town, has arcades on all four sides and a small covered market in the centre abutting on the north side a larger building, with a curious clock tower, that houses the *mairie* itself. In the north-east corner of the square is a shop specializing in Gascon gastronomic products: it stocks a wide range of local wines and Armagnacs and tins of such delicacies as *foie gras de canard* and *confit d'oie*.

The rue de Château-Vieux and the rue Gambetta both lead out of the square into the place de l'Eglise, which separates the bastide from the old town where you will find the twelfth-century church. This is not to be confused with the church in the place de l'Eglise itself which is a nineteenth-century construction of no interest.

South of the place de l'Eglise is the place de la République which used to be called *la plaçotto*; here there is a long stretch of arcades on the east side and two shorter lengths to the north and south.

Besides the charm of the town itself, Saint-Clar has two more claims to fame: it is one of the biggest garlic markets in the Lomagne and it was the birthplace in 1594 of Jean Géraud Dastros, a Gascon poet who was amongst the first to realize the importance of preserving the Gascon language:

> Crey-me, Gascoun, n'ajos bergouigno
> De nosto lengouo de Gascouigno
> Ni de l'augi ni d'en parla
> Coumo a Laytouro e a Sent-Cla.[1]

Just south of Saint-Clar, dominating the valley of the Arrats, is the grim stone fortress of Avezan. It was built in 1237 by Raymond Sans de Manos and remained largely unaltered until it came into the hands of the Larocan family in the seventeenth century who punched windows in the austere façade and transformed the interior with a grand staircase and huge chimneypieces.

Not far from Avezan is the hilltop village of Tournecoup. Its exact origins are unknown but it was granted a charter of customs in the fourteenth century. It has a fifteenth-century Gothic church with a powerful stone bell tower, octagonal at the top on a square base; inside there are seventeenth-century frescoes in the apse. At the west end of the church is a short street ending in a stone arch framing a beautiful landscape. If you go through the arch you will find yourself walking on top of a stretch of the original town wall and looking over the fertile valley of the Arrats. You cannot help feeling that nothing has changed here for hundreds of years. You would be wrong: during the Revolution three churches and a château were destroyed in Tournecoup.

We once saw on a corner of the steep road that winds up to the village a notice advertising garlic for sale. Pulling into the farmyard we found the farmer's wife sitting at the door of a vast barn making up tresses; behind her the inside of the barn was festooned with

1 Believe me, Gascon, there is no need to blush for our Gascon language as it is heard or spoken at Lectoure or Saint-Clar.

strings and strings of the finest garlic imaginable. Soon the boot of our car was reeking with its heady odour.

This part of France is top of the league when it comes to the production of garlic: the modern *département* of Tarn-et-Garonne produces 6,000 tonnes annually, amounting to eighteen per cent of the national total. Early in June or July the market stalls offer bunches of new garlic looking more like overgrown spring onions than the garlic we are accustomed to seeing. These can be chopped and added, discreetly, to salads or used in stews or soups. Later, in September and October, the more familiar strings and bunches appear on sale. There are three main kinds: pink, violet and white. The pink is generally smaller and is highly prized for its flavour. In the Lomagne it is the white variety that is mostly grown but you will find the pink and violet as well. If you do buy a string, hang it in a cool airy place and you will find it stays juicy and sweet the whole winter.

The garlic capital of the Lomagne is Beaumont-de-Lomagne where every September a garlic fair is held. It takes place in the magnificent wooden market hall that covers an area of three thousand square metres. It is a splendid example of the medieval carpenter's skills, the wooden piers and complicated structure of roof beams being remarkably well preserved, no doubt due to the annual fumigation (the aroma inside the hall can be overwhelming).

Another town famous for its garlic fair is Mauvezin, south of Beaumont. Amongst the festivities, held every August, is a competition to create sculpture from garlic heads, which was won one year by a wishing well, and the crowning of a Garlic Queen who leads a procession accompanied by her ladies-in-waiting.

Cooking with garlic is a feature of Gascony gastronomy. It is said to have been rubbed on the lips of the infant Henri IV when he was baptized and certainly no concessions are made to those squeamish noses that can detect the smell at fifty paces. Strangely enough very few people actually smell at all offensive; we noticed this with a local farmer we came to know well and his family. Garlic soup, rabbit or chicken cooked with copious amounts of chopped garlic, a boiled egg with a garlic clove sliced into it – yet no one ever smelled of it. Perhaps we didn't notice the garlic because we were eating it ourselves but the more likely explanation seems to be that the more you eat the less you smell. Whatever your personal feelings on the subject, if you are in Gascony you will have to come to terms with garlic sooner or later. And remember, recent medical research has shown that garlic is good for you: it is diuretic, reduces the amount of fats produced by the body and lowers blood cholesterol, so it is definitely not to be sniffed at.

Mauvezin lies to the south of the Lomagne whilst Beaumont is on the easternmost fringe of Gascony where the hills grow smaller and the valleys wider as you approach the great flat plain that stretches endlessly north of Toulouse. Indeed, Beaumont looks towards Languedoc rather than Gascony and possesses, besides its market hall, a fine church built in the Toulouse style which is commonly found in Languedoc and derives from the thirteenth-century nave of the cathedral of Saint-Etienne in Toulouse, although the most famous example is the magnificent rose-red cathedral of Albi.

These churches are usually built of narrow red bricks identical to those used by the Romans, stone being scarce in these parts. They have high wide naves without side aisles but with internal buttresses enclosing a series of side chapels. From the outside all you can see is a sheer brick wall articulated by tall slim buttresses that often end above the roof line in what look like little turrets, giving the church a decidedly military air, which the narrow windows do little to dispel.

A feature of these churches is their very attractive brick bell towers. They are built in tiers, each succeeding stage being slightly smaller than the one below, and capped by ornamental balustrades. At each level and on every face of the octagon there is a pair of pointed window arches, contained within a larger blank arch which because of its shape is called a mitre. Above the window is a white stone lozenge punched into the red brick and adding to the graceful appearance of these elegant towers.

Beaumont is a good example of the genre. Apart from an ornamented porch, the west front is very severe with massive side buttresses, ending in turrets, and a line of machicolation at roof level. The base of the bell tower is a heavily buttressed watch-tower with a battlemented sentry-walk at the level where the ornamented stages begin. The church was built between the thir-teenth and fifteenth centuries.

For much of the Middle Ages the frontier between Gascony and Languedoc followed the course of the river Arrats which winds its way northwards to join the Garonne near Auvillar. On either side of the river were castles and fortified manor houses built not so much to hold a defensive line as to provide protection in times of trouble. Avezan has already been men-tioned and there is a charming small château at Bivès, south-west of Tournecoup, which was largely rebuilt in the Renaissance period; but the most interesting of them is the Château de Gramont.

Gramont is a delightful example of the kind of château that Sybil and I like best of all: that is to say a medieval building that has been given an early Renaissance facelift, before French architects had learned the grammar of classical architecture so thoroughly that they were able to design correct and, to my mind, rather dull châteaux whose worth one can appreciate intellectually but which are much less enjoyable than the earlier transitional ones whose owners were joyfully experimenting for the first time in an exciting new style.

The story of Gramont begins in 1215 when Simon de Montfort, the ruthless butcher of the Albigensian heretics of Languedoc, granted it to one of his faithful followers, Eudes de Montaut. As you approach the château you will see on the left a simple stone tower, the so-called tower of Simon de Montfort. This is the earliest part of the château and probably dates from the thirteenth century. It was once much higher but the top was taken off, for no good reason, in the last century. Halfway up the tower there is a projection added at the end of the fourteenth century so that the defenders could use firearms to protect the entrance below. The four-storey building to the right of the tower also dates from the thirteenth century, although the windows, watch-tower and tiled roof were all added in the nineteenth century. The rusticated entrance is seventeenth-century but originally there were a drawbridge and portcullis here and the grooves for the latter can still be seen.

The way in is now at the base of Simon de Montfort's tower and leads to a barrel-vaulted stone hall and thence to a terrace and the Renaissance wing. This is built of an attractive blue-grey stone. The unevenness of the stonework still suggests a medieval building but the windows and doors give quite a different impression. The main entrance to the wing has twin doors surmounted by an entablature with a broad frieze, showing *putti* holding the family coat of arms, above which is a triangular pediment. The entablature is supported by curious truncated pilasters. The style is early French Renaissance, round about 1540, but compared with what was being done in Italy at this period the details are far from correct. The same thing applies to the windows which are un-evenly distributed along the façade and are all different, although they all have Renaissance trimmings. Above, at roof level, is a classical cornice but the effect is rather spoiled by some cheeky gargoyles, although Sybil and I relish just this kind of bizarre juxtaposition.

On the opposite side of the house, there was some attempt to arrange the windows in a rhythmic pattern, although not one that would have been approved of in Italy. Looking from left to right, there are four pairs of windows. The first two, one above the other, are wide mullion and transom windows, then there are two narrow ones with transoms only; this arrangement is then repeated in the remaining two pairs of windows. To the far right, however, there is another odd window that does not fit the pattern. All the windows are set within classical frames of columns or pilasters and entablatures, but here again they are not classically correct. But the carving is skilful and the detail delightful. We particularly like the charming children's heads at the base of the pilasters of the lower narrow window on the right.

Inside, the château has been sensitively restored by the present owners, Monsieur and Madame Dichamp. There is a splendid *grande salle*, with a fine Renaissance chimneypiece, a kitchen and bakery and near the entrance the old stables have been beautifully converted into an exhibition gallery.

Gramont is splendidly placed on its own hilltop and there are fine views from its terrace over the valley of the Arrats.

Continuing north along the valley bottom you come to Peyre-cave, where a left-hand turning leads to the château of Flamarens. Originally a *château-fort*, the present building was built in 1471 by Jean de Grossoles and consists of a rectangular main block flanked by two huge round towers adorned with machicolation. A disastrous fire in 1944 destroyed the interior which according to a local saying must have been very fine indeed: 'lo castet de Flama-rens, bet dehoro, bet deguens' (in English 'the castle of Flamarens, beautiful within and without'). There is talk of restoration work being undertaken at Flamarens though it would cost a fortune to restore the château to its former glory.

Flamarens lies at the extreme north-east of Gascony so the time has come to turn westwards taking the D953 to Miradoux. At the next road junction a sign points to the Ferme de la Hitte. This is meant to be a typical Gascon farm but from the outside it looks more like those found in nearby Languedoc, long low buildings with enormous tiled roofs reaching down almost to ground level. At the Ferme de la Hitte there is a central round-headed arch with the living quarters on the right and a cattle byre on the left. This again is unusual in Gascony where the living quarters are normally kept quite separate from the barns and accommodation for the animals. Inside, however, you will find a typical Gascon interior.

The main room contains a stone sink with a groove lip at one end for the water to drain away, a heavy table and some simple chairs but it is dominated by an enormous fireplace, in which hangs a large black pot that Macbeth's witches would have gloated over. The top of the fireplace has a pretty scalloped pelmet designed to help prevent the fire smoking, there are fire-dogs, a fire-back, tongs and bellows.

The fireplace was always the centre of the Gascony farmhouse and was built on such a large scale so that old people could sit comfortably in the chimney corner away from draughts, keeping an eye on the fire and stirring the pot. Even when wood-burning stoves were introduced, the open fire was still used for cooking much of the time. Ovens were a luxury in the country districts until butane and propane gases revolutionized both the cooking and the kitchen utensils. But old customs and traditions die hard and as late as 1972, when we were looking for a house in the area, we saw jam being made on an open fire in one of the farmhouses we visited. The farmer's wife tended both jam and fire, stirring the one and feeding the other with twigs and small pieces of wood. We asked her why she cooked her jam on the fire when she had a large gas cooker in the corner of the kitchen. She shrugged and then laughed: that was how her mother had always done it, she explained, and besides jam needed very little heat and she could control it with two or three twigs at a time. We tasted a spoonful before we left; it was melon jam, smooth and sweet with all the ripeness of autumn days.

Lacking an oven, and with strictly limited fuel supplies, the farmer's wife learned to provide a variety of appetizing food cooked with a minimum of fuel.[1] The basic utensil was the cauldron, a large cooking pot with a handle and three small legs: it could be hung from the *crémaillère* (the series of hooks over the open fire) or set securely on the hot fire itself, or even stood in the hearth near the fire to keep warm and continue cooking slowly. Inside the cauldron such composite dishes as *garbure* (ham and mixed vegetables), the *pot-au-feu* and the *poule-au-pot* (chicken and mixed vegetables) would be cooked. Puddings could be boiled in cloths in the water and, like the suet dumpling, these could be sweet or savoury. Many desserts and sweetmeats were made by boiling cereals with water until they formed a thick mass which was spread on a board and allowed to cool and thicken; the slab of porridge was then cut into shapes and fried in lard or goose fat and sprinkled with sugar or cheese. One such accommodating mixture is *cruchade*, made with semolina and flavoured with orange-flower water, sugar and honey if it is served as a tea-time snack, or sprinkled with grated cheese if eaten with apéritifs.

Cakes, tarts and sweet puddings that we would automatically cook in the oven were made either in a covered frying pan or a heavy copper or iron dish with a close-fitting lid on which glowing

---

1 Before the Revolution the landlord often had a feudal right prohibiting his tenants collecting fuel on his land.

embers were piled, so that when the vessel was put on the fire there was *feu dessous, feu dessus*. Many desserts were made simply in the open frying pan, including *flaugnarde* (prunes in batter) which was fried slowly on one side, turned carefully and fried again.

Next door is the bedroom where Sybil and I were amazed to find a high-sided wooden bed. We own an old French farmhouse north of Agen which contains a bed just like the one here, as well as an open fireplace and many other features identical to the ones to be found at the Ferme de la Hitte, so it seems we are living in a museum.

The bed is covered with a heavy eiderdown which served as an unexpected addition to the Gascony cook's *batterie de cuisine*. At times like the *vendange*, when all hands, including grannies and great-aunts, were in the vineyard, the eiderdown came into its own. The thick feather-filled duvet, relegated to the top of the *armoire* (wardrobe) during the hot summer months, was brought down and wrapped round the tureens and *faitouts* to keep meals hot and to allow the *ragôuts* and other stews to continue their long slow cooking, leaving the women free to take their scissors and start snipping off bunches of grapes. Besides keeping the food hot, the eiderdown also maintained the yeast paste, so essential to bread-making, at a constant temperature and served as a cocoon for the bread dough, which was put into a warm bed and covered with the eiderdown so that the yeast would work and the dough rise.

Every household kneaded its own dough which was either baked in an oven belonging to a neighbouring family or taken in a handcart, wrapped in its eiderdown, to the communal oven which might be several miles away in the next village. There are still old people who remember how families and neighbours co-operated in making the bread: one minding the yeast paste and feeding it between one baking and the next; another providing the wood to heat the rough communal oven; a third releasing her children from work for the day to keep the oven supplied with wood or to assist the baker, if the village could afford the services of a professional to bake for them. Each loaf was marked with the family's cross or sign, or could be distinguished by its shape. Some loaves weighed eighteen pounds or more and were almost the size of a cartwheel, one or two of them sustaining a family for two weeks until the next baking.

Old farmhouses like the Ferme de la Hitte are one of the joys of Gascony. They blend beautifully with the landscape, sometimes seeming to grow naturally out of the hillsides. Building methods vary according to the local materials available but, except in the Pyrénées, there is a recognizable Gascon style. The feature that nearly all these old farmhouses have in common and that establishes their regional character is the use of the Roman roof-tile, which gives their roofs a beautiful warm terra-cotta colouring and a most attractive undulating rhythm.

The tiles are long, have a shallow U-curve and are narrower at the top than at the bottom. They are arranged in rows stretching vertically down the side of the roof. The topmost tile is cemented at its narrower end to the roof ridge; the next fits under the broader end of the first and so on down, the last tile being sealed off again with cement. The next row, however, has the titles laid the other way up, in other words the curve, seen from above, is concave rather than convex and the two rows, looked at together, make a shallow S. The sides of this concave row are overlapped by the tiles in the rows to right and left, so that there are a series of channels all along the roof to carry away the rainwater. There is no guttering or drainpipes on these old farms, so the ends of the bottom-most tiles project slightly to carry the drips clear of the wall. When the sun is in the right direction they cast a delightful shadow on the side of the building below. The eaves are also decorated with *génoise*, a row of curved tiles set end-on directly into the wall which are also intended to act instead of a gutter. The grander the house the more rows of *génoise* there are, although three is the limit.

These roof-tiles tend to slip down and to crack easily but replacements can easily be bought. Unfortunately, for some reason the new tiles are lighter in colour than the old, so you can always tell when a roof has been heavily repaired because it results in a speckled effect, which it must be said is not unattractive. The tiles are supported by light battens on a timber frame.

25

It is worth trying to get a look into the roof space of one of these old farmhouses. There you will find some excellent examples of the carpenter's art, including massive oak beams, trusses and crown posts, all shaped by the adze and held together with wooden pegs and not a nail in sight. These attics are used to store cereals or tobacco and because of the tiles they are dry but sweet and airy.

The farmhouses of the Lomagne are usually built of stone. For the most part they are one-storey buildings with an attic and sometimes a cellar. Quite often they have a *pigeonnier* which is part of the house itself. Usually it is at one end of the building but sometimes it is in the middle. Exceptionally there are two, one at either end, giving the farm at first glance the appearance of a fortified manor house.

Two miles south of the Ferme de la Hitte is Miradoux, the oldest bastide in the Lomagne, founded in 1283. Despite its age, the town has little to offer the visitor except some stupendous views of the surrounding countryside. Nearby, however, on the road to Castet-Arrouy are the spectacular ruins of the Château de Gachepouey. All that survives of the original late sixteenth-, early seventeenth-century building is one ruined wing and a tall rectangular tower standing out against the skyline like an admonishing finger; even so it is an impressive sight.

From Gachepouey, continue south on the D23 to Castet-Arrouy and then take the D218 to Plieux, a hill-top village dominated at its western end by a Gascon *château-fort*. The castle of Plieux consists of a massive rectangular main building with a tower at the south-east and north-west corners. Like Sainte-Mère the castle has a blind ground floor, used for storage, above which are two more floors that contained the living quarters and in which later fifteenth-century windows were inserted. The heavy machicolation that projects from the top of the walls, together with the spiral staircase in the upper half of the north-west tower, show that Plieux was built later than Sainte-Mère, probably in the second half of the fourteenth century.

Avezan, Flamarens, Gramont, Plieux, Gachepouey, Sainte-Mère: the remarkable number of these powerful fortresses, standing aloof on their high hills, often within sight of one another, has led some scholars to suggest that they were originally built as part of a defensive scheme to protect the north-eastern border of Gascony. Today this is thought unlikely: rather they reflect the uncertainties of an age when warfare was endemic, the rule of law only fitfully enforced and strongholds like these the only source of security.

2 Nérac and the Pays d'Albret

Gascony's favourite son is not, as might be supposed, D'Artagnan, who after all was largely the creation of Alexandre Dumas, but Henri de Navarre, better known as Henri IV, the first of the Bourbons and France's most popular king. Henri's affectionate nickname was the '*Vert Galant*', a reference to his sexual vigour, which continued undiminished until his assassination at the age of fifty-six, but in Gascony he was familiarly known as *le noustre Henri*, our own Henri. You will find bars and restaurants with this name all over the south-west: a proof of the warmth with which he is still remembered.

Henri was born at Pau in 1553 and at his baptism his grandfather Henri d'Albret is said to have rubbed his lips with garlic and moistened them with the local Jurançon wine to make him a true Gascon. The Albrets were one of the great Gascon families that, like the Armagnacs, played an important part in the politics of the south-west during the Middle Ages. Their origins are obscure: the first we know of was Amanieu I, who in 1050 had his stronghold at Labrit (the name is a corruption of Albret) about seventy miles south-west of Agen, right in the heart of the sandy wilderness, as it was then, of the Landes. From these unlikely beginnings the Albrets built up a position of power in north-west Gascony, chiefly by a shrewd policy of political marriages, although their allegiance to the French crown in the Hundred Years' War (Charles d'Albret led the fatal charge against the English at Agincourt and was amongst the ten thousand French nobles who perished on that bloody battlefield) did not go unrewarded.

In the last quarter of the fifteenth century the house of Albret made a great leap forward. Alain le Grand d'Albret was small, fat, coarse and lame but he was also very astute. His great coup was to marry his son, Jean, in 1484, to Cathérine de Foix-Béarn, an alliance that doubled the Albrets' territories, for the house of Foix-Béarn united two of the largest and most powerful Pyrenean states that lay on the south-east and south-west borders of Gascony. The marriage also made Alain's great-great grandson, Henri, the King of Navarre, although this was a title with more prestige than real power.

The old Kingdom of Navarre dated back to the ninth century AD and straddled the Pyrénées, although the greater part of the territory lay on the Spanish side with Pamplona as its capital. In 1481 Navarre became part of the Foix-Béarn inheritance as the result of another fortunate marriage and thus in 1484 passed to Jean d'Albret. Unfortunately the Spanish portion of Navarre was conquered in 1512 by the dynamic King Ferdinand of Aragon, leaving only a small enclave on the French side of the Pyrénées in what is now called the Pays-Basque. Nevertheless, the King of Navarre was a respected title and carried some weight at the French court.

Henri de Navarre's mother was Jeanne d'Albret, a formidable woman who had embraced the Protestant faith with a fierce ardour. She made the Pays d'Albret a Protestant stronghold and at her instigation Henri was made leader of the Huguenots when he was only fifteen years old. Because of his royal blood Henri escaped death in the Massacre of St Bartholomew's Eve, although he was in Paris at the time, and over the next seventeen years he became a hardened campaigner. The Wars of Religion only came to an end when Henri III, the last Valois king, died childless leaving Henri of Navarre as his legitimate heir. With his famous remark 'Paris is worth a mass' Henri became a Catholic convert and was duly crowned King of France.

With the help of his able finance minister Sully, Henri ruled wisely and well for twenty years until his assassination in 1610. His courage on the battlefield and political ability were qualities that earned him respect but he also had a common touch that made him loved. It was Henri who made the famous comment when he became king that he wished every household in France to have a chicken in the pot (a typical Gascon dish, by the way) and he always moved freely amongst his subjects without the least suggestion of condescension. A testimony to Henri's popularity is the large number of stories about him. The one I like best tells how Henri made an unexpected call on his mistress Gabrielle d'Estrées who, as it happened, was not alone. Her new lover barely had time to leap for safety under the bed before Henri entered the room. The King sat down and asked the petrified Gabrielle to have a sumptuous dinner sent up. When it arrived, he took a whole partridge for himself, handed another to Gabrielle and tossed a third under the bed saying, 'Can't let the poor devil starve!'

Before he became King of France, Henri de Navarre held court at Nérac, the capital of the Pays d'Albret, the family having moved to more congenial surroundings. To visit Nérac and the Pays d'Albret you cross the Garonne by the Pont de Pierre, Agen, and take the D656 marked to Nérac. When you reach Roquefort (not the place where the cheese is made: that is in the Aveyron a long way to the east) be sure to fork right onto the D7 which follows a ridge route with marvellous views north and south over the Brulhois. This was one of the many *petit-pays*, or small medieval fiefs, that came into existence in the tenth century in Gascony when central rule broke down. The Vicomté de Brulhois survived until 1304 when it was absorbed into the County of Armagnac. Its chief towns are Laplume and Layrac. Look out *en route* for a fine farm close to the road on the right with a beautiful *pigeonnier*. Soon the road begins to switchback in typical Gascony fashion at the same time dropping gradually until it reaches the valley of the Baïse, one of the numerous small rivers that rise on the plateau of Lannemezan and flow northwards to join the Garonne.

Nérac lies astride the Baïse and just across the main bridge stands the château of Nérac, or at least one wing of it, the other three having been destroyed in the French Revolution. What remains is a charming example of early French Renaissance architecture, especially the first-floor loggia with its depressed arches and twisted fluted columns surmounted by curious carved capitals.

Note in particular the lively carving of the siren, Melusine, on the fifth capital from the left.

The entrance to the château, at the left-hand side of the gallery, leads into a series of rather dull first-floor rooms, but a descent to the ground floor reveals some fine vaulted apartments. The Salle des Archives, in particular, has a beautiful ceiling, covered with a complicated web of ribs. This room contains a collection of Gallo-Roman artefacts and some Merovingian jewellery. The vault of the last room on this floor has bosses with intertwined double 'a's carved on them, indicating that this wing was built by Alain le Grand, the great-great-grandfather of Henri de Navarre, who died in 1522.

With its red-tiled roof and modest proportions the impression the château of Nérac gives is of a somewhat domestic and provincial palace and it is difficult to believe that here in the sixteenth century resided one of the most brilliant courts in Europe.

This reputation was largely due to Henri's grandmother, Marguerite d'Angoulême, the much-loved sister of François I of France, who married Henri d'Albret in 1527 and brought to his court a love of the arts that transformed the life of this provincial kingdom.

Marguerite delighted in the company of artists and men of ideas and under her tolerant rule Nérac became a safe haven for any writer or thinker whose views had aroused the wrath of Church or State; but her special love was poetry and many poets, among them Clément Marot and the classical scholar Jean de Sponde, benefited from her generous patronage.

Marguerite was herself a gifted poet, best-known for her collection of verses called *Les Marguerites de la Marguerite des Princesses* but she is more famous in France as the author of the *Heptaméron*, a series of linked tales that clearly derives from Boccaccio's *Decameron*, although in this case the story-tellers are trapped by a flood high in the Pyrénées and their narratives are not so relentlessly sexual in content as Boccaccio's.

Nérac is believed to be the setting for Shakespeare's *Love's Labour's Lost* which, according to the stage directions, takes place at the court of Navarre. Amongst the lords in attendance on the

King of Navarre are Berowne and Dumaine, who had real-life counterparts in the Duc de Biron and the Duc de Longueville, both of whom were companions in arms of Henri de Navarre and were with him at Nérac.

But there is another, perhaps more tenuous connection: the plot of *Love's Labour's Lost* turns on the visit to Navarre of a French princess and her ladies and the merry war that ensues between them and the king and his followers, who have taken an oath to forswear the company of women and devote themselves to study. In 1578 two queens made a famous visit to Nérac: Catherine de'Medici, the Queen Mother who had virtually ruled France for thirty years after the death of her husband Henri II, and her daughter Marguerite de Valois who was Henri de Navarre's estranged wife. On the face of it Catherine had come to effect a reconciliation between Henri and Marguerite after a three-year separation; in reality she was there to negotiate a settlement between the reigning King Henri III of France and his legal successor the Protestant King of Navarre.

With the two queens came the 'flying squadron', a bevy of young aristocratic beauties whose charms Catherine exploited quite shamelessly to further her political ends. As Sully wrote, 'La reine qui connoissoit les dispositions de Henri à la galanterie, avoit compte sur elles pour le séduire.' Catherine certainly seems to have been successful. 'Love,' continues Sully, 'became the most serious business of the courtiers. The mixture of the two courts, neither of which was to be outdone in affairs of gallantry, created the effect that was to be expected: all gave themselves up to festivities and fêtes of gallantry. I too became a courtier and played the lover like the rest.'

Not surprisingly, Marguerite enjoyed her stay at Nérac. Discussing her marriage in her memoirs she wrote: 'My happiness only lasted for the four or five years that I was in Gascony with my husband the King. Most of the time was spent at Nérac where our court was so beautiful and so pleasant that we never missed the French court . . . we used to meet to stroll in a beautiful garden with long alleys of laurels or cypresses; or we would roam in the charming park where I had made avenues, three thousand yards long on the banks of the river.'

This park, the Promenade de la Garenne, with its long tree-shaded walks, still exists just opposite the château and very pleasant it is, on a hot, somnolent afternoon, after a good lunch at the Hôtel du Château, to amble gently along the cool alleys, idly glancing at the slow-moving stream and imagining the elegantly dressed lords of Henri's court making their assignations with the fair maids of the flying squadron.

A little way along the Promenade de la Garenne, on the left-hand side, you will see a grotto containing an amusingly kitsch sculpture commemorating Fleurette, the gardener's daughter who, according to local legend, was Henri de Navarre's first youthful conquest and who is supposed to have drowned herself in the Baïse after the *Vert Galant* abandoned her. Alongside is this sad inscription:

> A peine ils s'étaient vus qu'ils s'aimèrent d'amour.
> Elle comptait seize ans; lui trois de plus. Ravie,
> Fleurette à cet amour donna toute sa vie,
> Henri, prince d'Albret, ne lui donna qu'un jour.[1]

Next to Fleurette's grotto is the Fontaine des Marguerites erected in 1903 to commemorate Marguerite d'Angoulême.

On the opposite bank is the so-called bath-house of Henri de Navarre, a delightful hexagonal stone building, not much bigger than a *pigeonnier*, whose slate-tiled roof has a graceful ogee curve. In fact, the bath-house was probably used by Henri to entertain his lady friends.

Further along the Promenade is the Théâtre de Nature, where we once watched the local school children giving displays of dancing and gymnastics, including some five-year-olds dressed up as chickens who flapped their arms and staggered uncertainly through a routine to the music of 'The Four Seasons.'

[1] As soon as they saw each other they fell in love.
She was sixteen; he only three years older.
Seduced, Fleurette gave her life for love,
Henri, Prince of Albret gave a single day.

Nearby is the Fontaine du Dauphin, erected in 1602 to commemorate the birth of Henri's son François, on 27 September, 1601.

If you walk right to the end of the Promenade de la Garenne (about half an hour) you will find, on a bend of the river by a weir, the sad ruins of the water-mill of Nazareth, the setting of Marcel Prévost's novel *Le Moulin de Nazareth* (1894). Prévost, a famous novelist and playwright, was born in Paris in 1862 but spent much of his childhood at Tonneins on the Garonne, north-west of Agen. He died at Château de la Roche, near Vianne, in 1941.

Opposite the entrance to the Promenade is Petit Nérac, the old quarter of Nérac. You get a good view from the new bridge, especially of the beautiful old stone bridge, now no longer used. There used to be a busy port here handling cargoes to and from Bordeaux, for until the nineteenth century this was an important trade route, especially for the transport of Armagnac from further south. The port fell into decline when it was by-passed by a new canal. Petit Nérac has some attractive old buildings including l'Hôtel des Présidents, a beautiful seventeenth-century house, and in the rue de la Conférence a Renaissance building with a charming gallery.

South-east of Nérac, on the D656, is Mezin, a fortified hill town which was the scene of much fighting during the Hundred Years' War and which changed hands more than once. It still has extensive remains of the original walls and, as Mezin has never expanded outside them, a walk through its narrow streets is like returning to the Middle Ages. At the top of the hill, in the centre of the town, as befits its position in medieval society, is the church, a grey solid-looking edifice with a severe, screen west-front, flanked by two round towers. A Gothic porch has been inserted into this front without diminishing its grim aspect. At the opposite end of the church the chevet and transepts are twelfth-century but the harmony of the ensemble is spoiled by a later square crossing tower that replaced the original octagonal one. The walls of the apse and side chapels are articulated by pilasters, surmounted by half-round columns and there are sculpted corbel heads at roof level. Inside, the Gothic nave has aisles that are the same height as the nave,

33

giving a great deal of light but imposing stresses on the solid round piers that they can scarcely bear, so that looking down the length of the nave you can see quite clearly that they are leaning out of true. Cross-bracing prevents complete collapse.

Behind the church, at the entrance to the rue Saint-Jean, is a pillar with a capital carved with three heads, which was used for public executions. On the north side is the arcaded place A. Fall-ières and at the west the rue Saint-Cauzemis, leading southwards to the rue des Capots. Here, in the Middle Ages, dwelt the *capots* or *cagots*, lepers and other social outcasts who were forced to live in a ghetto. The rue des Capots leads down to one of the original gateways, the narrow Porte des Anglais.

From Mezin the D656 leads through the pretty valley of the Gélise to Poudenas. This is a good example of the asymmetrical valleys commonly found in Gascony, although usually further south, that have a very steep west flank and a gently sloping eastern slope. Poudenas is tiny but boasts an excellent restaurant with a Michelin rosette. Marie-Claude Gracia, who owns La Belle Gasconne along with her husband, is very proud that she was once called upon to cook for President Giscard D'Estaing. Her *foie gras d'oie* and *de canard* is the best we have tasted anywhere in the south-west. Opposite the restaurant is a water-mill, which is being converted into a hotel, and an old stone bridge across the Gélise: it makes a delightful picture.

On top of the steep hill, directly above the village, is the château of Poudenas. Unfortunately it is only open for a short time in July but outside there is a park that can be visited as any time: it contains some fine stone farmhouses and a modest thirteenth-century church. There is a good view over the village and eastwards across the Pays d'Albret.

Further down the valley is Sos, a small hill-top town that is believed to be the site of the *oppidum* of the Sotiates, the only people of the Novempopulani to put up any serious resistance to the Roman army lead by Crassus in 56 BC. After a preliminary skirmish the Sotiates retired to the *oppidum* but after a siege of some days were forced to surrender.

Crassus treated the Sotiates generously: their leader, Adietuanus, was allowed to continue as king and was even granted the great privilege of minting his own money. Sos was in fact destroyed not by the Romans but by the Saracens in the eighth century and again by the Normans a century later. However, a new town was built in the Middle Ages, although little remains to be seen today but a single arcade and some half-timbered houses.

Sos lies on a stretch of Roman road that follows a prehistoric ridge route called the Ténarèze. There is a Gascon saying that you can travel all the way from Bordeaux to the Pyrénées along the Ténarèze without crossing a bridge or taking a boat. The route starts on the left bank of the Garonne near Aiguillon and after Sos follows the crests of the hills right through the heart of Gascony via Eauze and Miélan to end in the Pyrénées near Bagnère-de-Bigorre. The Ténarèze was followed in part at least by the medieval pilgrims making their way to the great Spanish shrine of Santiago de Compostella.

If you take the D109 to Reaup and then the D283 to Durance you will see a distinct change in the landscape. The limestone hills that dominate the landscape further east have finally petered out to be replaced by a flat sandy terrain dotted with the first scrubby stands of pine, although the deep forests lie still further to the west.

Durance is a thirteenth-century *bastide* that was once enclosed by walls. Only two square towers and the fortified main gate survive. Durance also contains the vestiges of the so-called château of Henri de Navarre, where the *Vert Galant* often stayed when he was on a hunting trip.

About six miles east of Durance on the D655 is Barbaste. Just to the right of the main crossing of the Baïse is another much older stone bridge and at the end of it, on the right bank, a massive stone tower with a turret at each corner. It looks like a castle keep; in fact it is a fourteenth-century fortified mill. No more eloquent testimony to the insecurity of the period of the Hundred Years' War can be imagined. The mill is called the Moulin de Henri IV because Henri is supposed to have stayed here, no doubt with the hapless Fleurette.

On the opposite side of the river to Barbaste is Lavardac, a former *bastide* that was completely destroyed by the Catholic forces of the Duc de Mayenne during the Wars of Religion. From Lavardac the D642 leads to Vianne, an English *bastide* granted a charter by Edward I in 1284. Unlike Lavardac, Vianne is almost perfectly preserved. Except for a short stretch along the riverbank, the original walls, with their defensive towers, are intact, while inside is the standard grid pattern of streets with the central square. The church was there before the building of the *bastide* and the whole of the choir and part of the nave are Romanesque. Like the fortified mill at Barbaste, Vianne is a salutary reminder that there was nothing romantic about the Middle Ages: it was a period of instability and fear.

A minor road, the D141, leads to the tiny hill village of Xaintrailles. Here there is a château that belonged to a famous Gascon soldier, Poton de Xaintrailles, who was an ardent supporter of Joan of Arc and fought bravely at her side at the siege of Orléans. Poton also took part in the final French campaign that drove the English out of France in 1453. The château dates from the twelfth century but was largely rebuilt in the eighteenth century although a square keep and some curtain walls survive from the earlier building. It is only open by special request. There is a grand view of the Landes from Xaintrailles.

North of Xaintrailles are the vineyards of Buzet, which produce an excellent local wine made from the same grape varieties as Bordeaux clarets, Cabernet Sauvignon, Cabernet Franc and Merlot. Buzet is just as good as, if not better than, the wine produced by some of the minor properties of Bordeaux. There is a large, efficient Cave Coopérative where you can buy wine by the bottle or straight from the vats into any container you care to take along. You can buy a plastic container (*cubitainer*) holding twenty-five litres, which has a tap on it and can be re-used. The Coopérative sells a range of wines from a *vin de table* to Cuvée Napoléon, which is made from the best grapes grown in the best vineyards in Buzet. They also sell a very good rosé, which is easier to drink when the weather is hot.

Buzet-sur-Baïse was the site of an ancient Benedictine abbey, of which there is now no trace, while a single round tower is all that remains of a thirteen-century castle destroyed by the English. The old medieval town was built on an escarpment overlooking the Benedictine abbey but here again there is little to see except for a Gothic church with an impressive bell tower and inside a vast nave and a three-bay choir lit by flamboyant windows.

At nearby Saint-Pierre-de-Buzet is an earlier church with some strange features. The west end is very stark and looks as though it was once a fortified bell tower. However, either it was never finished or the top was destroyed or fell down, because now it is capped by an uncomfortable pointed gable that projects above the roof line and has three arches, one containing bells.

Gable-ended churches with open arches in which bells are hung are quite common in Gascony but unlike Saint-Pierre-de-Buzet they were not afterthoughts but intended as part of the original design of these churches whose communities could not afford the expense of a proper bell tower. They can have anything from one to five round-headed arches for the bells and some of the more elaborate ones can be very attractive. The bells were sometimes given names like 'the Trinity' where there are three and 'the Evangelists' if there are four and so on.

The entrance to Saint-Pierre is on the south side. Inside, to the right of the door, is a simple aisleless nave ending in a narrow apse lit by three windows with below them five blank arches supported on small columns with carved capitals. The entrance to the apse has a tall column on either side, again surmounted by finely carved capitals; but to the left of the entrance is something very odd, an enormous, thick, round pier dividing the bay into two, from the top of which spring three diaphragm arches, presumably a device to give more support to the original west tower.

From Buzet the D642 leads to Aiguillon on the Garonne and the north-western frontier of Gascony. Here the RN113 leads eastwards to Agen or west to Bordeaux.

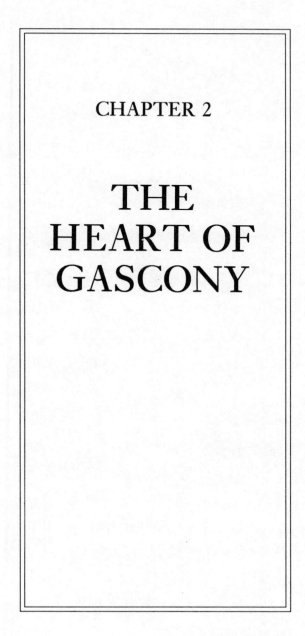

CHAPTER 2

THE
HEART OF
GASCONY

T HE HEART of Gascony is Armagnac. This ancient county, which roughly corresponds to the modern *département* of the Gers, stretched south from Lectoure to the foothills of the Pyrénées, eastwards nearly to the left bank of the Garonne and was bounded to the west by the sandy wastes of the Landes. It first came into existence in the tenth century, following the invasions of the Norsemen which undermined the authority of the Duke of Gascony and allowed the first counts of Armagnac to carve out a territory for themselves. Technically the counts were vassals of the Duke but in practice they were independent. They quickly consolidated their position and rapidly extended their boundaries. By the fourteenth century they had become a force to be reckoned with in France and they played a major political role during the Hundred Years' War. At this period Armagnac was a disputed territory right on the frontier between English Gascony and the domains of the French King, a fact testified to by the many castles, *bastides* and fortified churches to be found here.

In the seventeenth century Armagnac was chiefly remarkable as a recruiting ground for the French army. It became a tradition that the younger sons of noble families should leave home to seek their fortunes. They really had no choice since most of the nobility of Armagnac lived in genteel poverty and could not support an extra son who contributed nothing to the household. That is why Charles de Batz, better known as D'Artagnan, left his home near

Lupiac and went to Paris to join the King's musketeers.

The economic pressures that forced de Batz to leave home still apply today. The Gers is the least populated *départemente* in France: only 32 per cent of the population lives in towns and 51 per cent of the working population is engaged in agriculture, figures that underline the rural character of the land. There are no large towns to speak of: Auch, the ancient capital of Gascony and *chef-lieu* of the Gers, is the biggest with a population of 25,543, whilst Condom and Eauze, both well-known centres of the Armagnac brandy industry, have 7,836 and 4,338 inhabitants, respectively.

But, just because the region is so sparsely populated, the countryside of Armagnac is delightful to drive through. The rolling wooded hills are relaxing to the eyes and the roads often follow the valley routes alongside one of the many small rivers that wind half-hidden by trees and bushes through the landscape. There are few towns or villages to interrupt a leisurely journey and the farms are often obscured by trees or a fold in the land. It is easy enough to turn off the road and find an empty meadow by a stream where, mosquitoes permitting, you can enjoy an uninterrupted picnic. We once spent a languorous hot afternoon in the shade of a ruined mill on the banks of the Gers. The slow-moving brown river flowed over a weir at this point, creating a convenient back-eddy where we could put our bottle of Côtes de Buzet to cool; the birds were silent in the intense heat but enormous brightly coloured dragonflies flitted back and forth over the water as we ate our delicious Charentais melons from nearby Lectoure and sipped our wine.

There are many such idyllic spots to be found in Armagnac, for the countryside is threaded by numerous rivers and streams which rise on the plateau of Lannemezan to the south and spread fanwise as they flow northwards.

Much of Armagnac has heavy clay soil that is very difficult to work. In the past sturdy oxen were used to drag the plough. When we first went to Armagnac fifteen years ago we did see yoked oxen in use in the more remote areas but now they have all been replaced by tractors, and the beautiful wooden yokes are now only to be found adorning the walls of restaurants. In the west of Armagnac

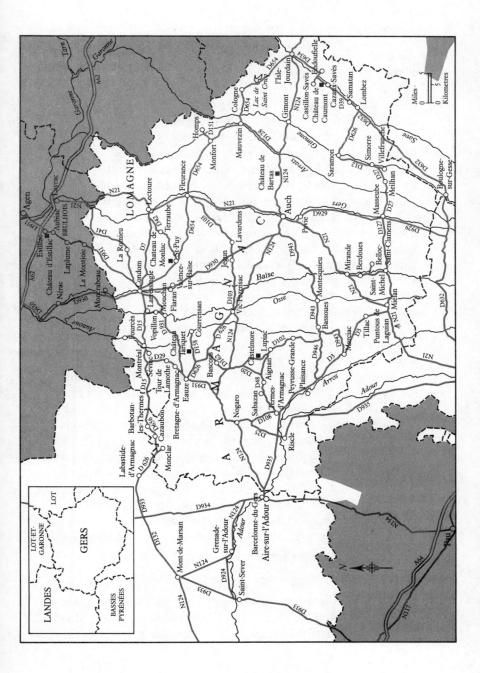

the soil is lighter and sandier and here, in the neighbourhood of Eauze, the best Armagnac brandy is made.

The quickest way to reach Auch, the capital of Gascony, is to follow the RN21 down the valley of the Gers. Seven miles south of Lectoure is Fleurance, a *bastide* founded in 1272. It was the capital of a tiny medieval fief, the County of Gaure, which, despite being entirely surrounded by Armagnac territories, managed to remain independent until the fifteenth century; and then it was the Count of Albret, not Armagnac, who became its new overlord. The County of Gaure was united with the French crown in 1505.

Fleurance is named after the Italian city of Florence. There are a number of thirteenth-century *bastides* in Gascony that bear the names of famous European cities: Barcelonne-de-Gers (Barcelona), Cologne, Grenade (Granada), Boulogne-sur-Gesse (Bologna), Pavie (Pavia) and many more. Their founders seem to have deliberately given these new towns the names of well-known and successful foreign cities to attract people to settle in them – a case of glory by association, in fact, and an early example of the public-relations man's art.

Fleurance has preserved the original grid plan of streets and the central square surrounded by buildings built over arcades; in the middle of the square is a handsome seventeenth-century market hall. Just off the square is the church of Saint-Laurent, a Gothic building dating from the fourteenth and fifteenth centuries but much restored after Fleurance was sacked by Protestant troops in 1562. The church is of no great interest but it contains three magnificent stained-glass windows by a famous Gascon artist, Arnold de Moles, who was born at Saint-Sever in the Landes.

Little is known about Arnold de Moles but he was one of the greatest exponents of the art of stained glass of his age, the early sixteenth century. His masterpiece is the series of eighteen windows that he made for the cathedral at Auch which he signed and dated 1513.

These windows are very different from the ones found in the great Gothic cathedrals of the north. For a start they were not made in the same way: instead of being composed of individual pieces of coloured glass, laboriously assembled, the images were painted on white glass which was afterwards hardened in the oven. This means that the windows do not have the rich depth of colour found at Chartres or Bourges; on the other hand these painted windows transmit more light than the earlier ones which makes them more luminous. This effect is accentuated by Arnold de Moles' frequent use of a warm golden yellow and his habit of leaving areas of white glass unpainted. De Moles' palette contained a wide range of intense colours, including red, blue, green, violet and amethyst, all of which help to give his windows a rich translucent glow.

De Moles was a Renaissance artist and his work shows strong influences from both Italian and Flemish painting. He often used typical Renaissance architectural settings, for example. His figures are beautifully drawn, with strong characterization, and are particularly interesting to historians because the clothes that his Old Testament worthies wear are obviously based on contemporary models.

The windows at Fleurance show in the centre the Trinity and the Virgin Mary; to the right the Tree of Jesse and to the left St Lawrence, Mary Magdalene and St Augustine.

A dull stretch of fifteen miles to the south of Fleurance brings you to Auch, the capital of Gascony, but long before you arrive you see high up on a hill to the right the massive outline of the cathedral and, close to the east end, the tall fourteenth-century Tour d'Armagnac.

The name Auch derives from the Ausci, one of the Celtic-Iberian tribes that had settled the south-west long before the Romans arrived and who had built their capital, Elimberris, on top of the hill. The Roman legions of Crassus stormed and took the *oppidum* during his campaign of 56 BC and the Ausci were forced to submit to the rule of Rome. The Roman city took the name of Augusta Auscorum and it was re-sited at the foot of the hill on the banks of the Gers. Christianity arrived in the fourth century, brought by St Taurin, and Auch became a bishopric and later an archbishopric. The power of the archbishops of Auch was enormous and extended throughout Gascony and, with the dismemberment of the duchy in the eleventh century into a number of independent and competing fiefs, they became a major force in the region.

At this period Auch came under the influence of the Armagnacs but was never the capital of Armagnac and power was shared uncomfortably between the counts and the archbishops.

In 1455 Auch was occupied by royal troops sent by Charles VII to bring Jean V, the troublesome last Count of Armagnac, to heel; the city also suffered during the Religious Wars of the sixteenth century, but, under the Bourbon kings, the city flourished: Auch became the capital of the newly-created Province de Gascogne at a time when Gascony covered more territory than at any time since the Dark Ages with its northern border extending as far as Agen.

It was in the eighteenth century that Auch reached its apogee under the enlightened rule of Antoine Megret d'Etigny, the Intendant of Auch. D'Etigny was a most remarkable man in that, at a time when nearly all public officials were corrupt and inefficient, he was neither. He was born in Paris in 1719 into a family of royal civil servants that came from Picardy. He was made Intendant of Auch in 1751, a post that meant he was responsible not just for Auch but the whole of Gascony and the Pays-Basque. D'Etigny immediately set about reforming the local finances, judiciary and police, policies which quickly brought him into conflict with the local nobility and other vested interests; but he managed to overcome these difficulties and change Auch from a medieval town into an eighteenth-century capital with elegant classical buildings like the Hôtel de l'Intendance which today is the Hôtel de la Poste.

Outside Auch, d'Etigny's greatest contribution was the development of a road system where one had hardly existed before: in particular the main east–west route from Toulouse to Bayonne and the north–south road from Agen to Tarbes and thence south into Spain. This improvement in communications encouraged both internal and external trade in Gascony and helped to bring about a much-needed economic revival in this backward region.

D'Etigny also encouraged local agriculture and did his best to persuade the conservative Gascon peasants to change their inefficient methods; he also made frequent appeals to the King to give them aid in times of drought or when their crops had been destroyed by floods or hail.

D'Etigny died at Auch in 1767 and fifteen years later the grateful town raised a statue to him at the beginning of the grand promenade that he himself created and that bears his name.

The road from Agen crosses the river Gers and climbs steeply up the hill to the place de la Libération. In the south-west corner of the square stands the Hôtel de Ville, built in 1777, and leading off it on the west side the allée d'Etigny and the Intendant's statue. On the opposite side the place de la Libération opens into the place de la République, on the north side of which is the beautiful Maison Fédel, half-timbered with brick in-filling and dating from the fifteenth century, which now houses the local tourist information offices.

Overshadowing everything else in the square is the magnificent Cathedral of Sainte-Marie. The classical west front has a three-storey elevation based on the Roman triumphal arch. The ground floor has three arched openings with paired columns that clearly reflect its Roman inspiration: the second and third stages continue as towers with the double columns repeated, although at the top they change to pilasters and this level is recessed, both modifications designed to prevent the towers looking top-heavy. The first two storeys were designed by Jean de Beaujeu between 1560 and 1567 but the top stage was not added until 1665. The whole west front is a good example of French classical architecture of the period but I have to admit it leaves me unmoved.

Behind this impressive façade is a totally different building, Gothic, built of brick and typical of the Midi. The Cathedral of Sainte-Marie was begun in 1489 but it was not completed until the seventeenth century and it shows how backward Gascony was at this time that, apart from the classical façade, it should have been designed in a style that dates back to the thirteenth century.

At first sight the interior, with its immensely tall arcades and narrow nave, gives an impression of great height. This, however, is misleading because the width of the building is 37 metres compared with a vault height of 26 metres. The illusion is created by the massive internal buttresses which create a series of deep

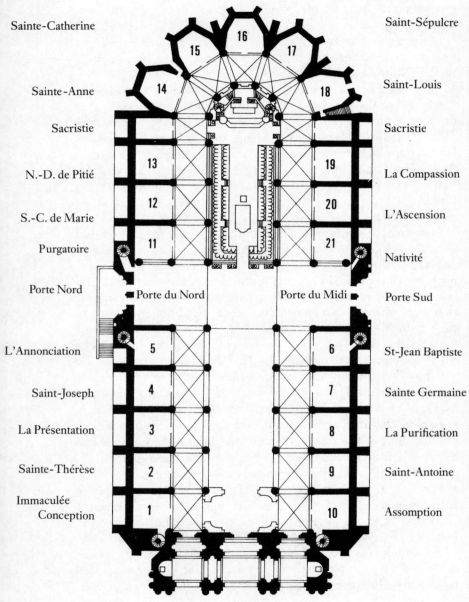

Saint-Sacrement

Sainte-Catherine

Saint-Sépulcre

16

15   17

Sainte-Anne   Saint-Louis

14   18

Sacristie   Sacristie

N.-D. de Pitié   La Compassion

13   19

S.-C. de Marie   L'Ascension

12   20

Purgatoire   Nativité

11   21

Porte Nord   Porte du Nord   Porte du Midi   Porte Sud

L'Annonciation   St-Jean Baptiste

5   6

Saint-Joseph   Sainte Germaine

4   7

La Présentation   La Purification

3   8

Sainte-Thérèse   Saint-Antoine

2   9

Immaculée
Conception   Assomption

1   10

Porte Ouest et Tours

PLAN OF THE CATHEDRAL
OF SAINTE-MARIE D'AUCH

chapels to left and right, leaving only room for a narrow nave flanked on each side by a single aisle.

But hardly anyone comes to the Cathedral of Sainte-Marie to admire its architecture: instead they make straight for the east end to look at the magnificent series of stained-glass windows by Arnold de Moles and the richly-carved choir stalls.

There are eighteen Arnold de Moles windows altogether and they start in the Chapelle du Purgatoire, which is the first chapel east of the crossing on the north side (number 11 on the plan).

11 Chapelle du Purgatoire
Window number 1. Theme: The Creation and Original Sin
Top, within the bars of the tracery: Abel, the first martyr; Enos invokes the name of the Lord and Enoch cries to God. In a band below God creates harmony out of Chaos and makes the first man and woman.
Middle: The main scene shows Adam and Eve either side of the tree of knowledge. Note that the serpent has the bust and head of a young woman and the Renaissance decoration behind the figures.
Below: The expulsion from Paradise, Eve amongst her children, and Cain murders Abel.

12 Chapelle du Saint-Coeur-de-Marie
Window number 2. Theme: After the Fall
Top: God the Creator amongst his Angels.
Middle: Noah, Jacob, St Peter and the Erythraean sibyl holding the stem of the Tree of Jesse. The sibyl is famous for the beauty of her profile.
Below these four figures is the coat of arms of the Cardinal-Archibishop Clermont de Lodève (1507–38).
Foot: Four scenes showing the Drunkenness of Noah, the Blessing of Jacob, Christ walking on the water, and the Annunciation.

13 Chapelle de Notre-Dame de Pitié
Window number 3. Theme: The Birth of the Jewish People
Top: Samuel and Elias.
Middle: Four splendid Bible figures standing in Renaissance niches. From left to right: Abraham, Melchizedek, the apostle Paul and the Samian sibyl.
Foot: The Sacrifice of Isaac, the Conversion of Saul, the Nativity.

49

14 Chapelle de Sainte-Anne
Windows 4, 5 and 6. Theme: God the Father and the Desert

LEFT-HAND WINDOW (4)
Top: The Persian sibyl questions the high priest Eli. Below them the Virgin Mary.
Middle: The patriarch Isaac and the prophets Samuel and Hosea standing against a splendid Renaissance architectural background with cupids.
Foot: Medallions bearing portraits of the architect of the west front of the cathedral, Jean de Beaujeu, and his wife Anne.

MIDDLE WINDOW (5)
Standing figures: Jacob, Jonah and the evangelist Mark.
Foot: Jonah and the Whale.
On either side of the Renaissance arch which frames the scene of Jonah and the Whale are two symmetrical medallions showing the last Count of Armagnac, Jean V.

RIGHT-HAND WINDOW (6)
Top: The amorial bearings of the Armagnacs. Immediately below an angel displaying a pennant bearing words celebrating the glory of the Virgin Mary.
Middle: Moses carrying the tablets engraved with the laws; the Libyan sibyl holding a torch symbolizing the ancient promises which formed the basis of the laws; Enoch prays to be raised to heaven.
Foot: Moses and the burning bush; the sibyl shows the Emperor Augustus a vision of the future King of the World, the infant Jesus in his mother's arms; Enoch is raised to heaven by two angels.

15 Chapelle de Sainte-Cathérine
Windows 7, 8 and 9. Theme: The Promised Land
LEFT-HAND WINDOW (7)
Top: The preferment of Joseph.
Middle: Joseph, the apostle Andrew and the prophet Joel.
Foot: Joseph sold by his brothers.
MIDDLE WINDOW (8)
Top: Angels making music.
Middle: Joshua, wearing armour; the European sibyl armed with a sword prophesying the Massacre of the Innocents; the prophet Amos.
Foot: The Flight into Egypt.

RIGHT-HAND WINDOW (9)

Top: Mary Magdalene; just below her Saints Barbara and Lucy on the left and Saints Catherine and Agatha on the right.

Middle: The patriarch Caleb, St Bartholomew the apostle, and the prophet Obadiah. Below these three standing figures is a strip depicting the story of Susanna.

Foot: The Martyrdom of St Bartholomew by flaying.

16 Chapelle du Saint-Sacrement

Windows 10, 11 and 12. Theme: The Crucifixion

LEFT-HAND WINDOW (10)

Top: The coat of arms of Cardinal Clermont de Lodève

Standing figures: The prophet Isaiah, the apostle Philip and the prophet Micah.

MIDDLE WINDOW (11)

Top: A fleur-de-lys, symbolizing Christ, against a blue background speckled with stars with the sun on the left and the moon on the right. The rest of the window is a beautiful depiction of the Crucifixion with Mary on the left and John on the right. At the base of the cross is Mary Magdalene.

Foot: Jerusalem the Blessed.

RIGHT-HAND WINDOW (12)

The window shows St James the Greater dressed as a pilgrim; on the right King David and on his left Azariah.

17 Chapelle du Saint-Sépulcre

This chapel has no stained glass but there is a moving piece of sculpture, the Entombment, which is generally attributed to Arnold de Moles. It shows Christ in his winding sheet which is held at one end by Joseph of Aramathea and Nicodemus while Mary and other mourning women look on with St John. On the far right is Mary Magdalene. The man standing apart on the left may be a self-portrait of Arnold de Moles. This works shows a strong Flemish influence.

18 Chapelle de Saint-Louis

Windows 13, 14 and 15. Theme: The Exile

LEFT-HAND WINDOW (13)

The window shows Jeremiah, the Agrippine sibyl holding a whip, symbol of Christ's flagellation, and Nahum. Below is shown the Flagellation.

MIDDLE WINDOW (14)
The prophet Daniel, the Cimmerian sibyl and the apostle Matthew.
Below: Daniel in the Lion's Den.
RIGHT-HAND WINDOW (15)
The three prophets Zephaniah, Elijah and Uriah. *Below*, Elijah is taken
to heaven in a chariot of fire.

19 Chapelle de la Compassion
Window number 16. Theme: The Return from Exile.
Standing figures: The apostles Matthias, Ezra, the prophet who tran-
scribed the books of Moses which had been burned by the people of
Ur and the Chaldees; Habakkuk, who brought sustenance to Daniel
in the lion's den and the Tiburtine sibyl, the latter another beautiful
portrait. This window contains a number of medallions commemorating the founders and protectors of the cathedral. At the top
is the coat of arms of the Cardinal of Lescun (1463–83). Lower down
is an arch containing angels bearing a banner. On either side of the
arch is a portrait of King Louis XII of France.

20 Chapelle de L'Ascension
Window number 17.
Top: In the centre the coat of arms of Auch; on the right those of the
Cardinal of Savoy; on the left the arms of the Cardinal of Trémouïlle
(1490–1507). Just below the coats of arms a double fleur-de-lys representing the two branches of the French crown, the Valois and Orléans,
with on the right a medallion showing the future François I and on
his left his fiancée Claude de France, daughter of Louis XII.
Middle: The prophet Elisha, the apostle Jude displaying the saw that
was the instrument of his martyrdom, and the Delphic sibyl holding
in her right hand the crown of thorns, heralding the passion of Christ;
the prophet Haggai.
Foot: Elijah cures Naaman, the martyrdom of the apostle James the
younger; Christ crowned with thorns; the coat of arms of the Cardinal-
Archbishop Clermont de Lodève.

21 Chapelle de la Nativité et de Notre-Dame-d'Auch
Window number 18. Theme: The Resurrection
The theme of this window is the Resurrection. Mary Magdalene and
St Thomas are shown meeting and recognizing the risen Christ against
a beautiful green background decorated with pearls. Below this scene
are the words LO XXV IHUN CENS XIII FON ACABADES LAS
PRESENS BERINES EN AUNOUR DE DIEV DE NOTR. which

translated means "these windows were completed on 25 June, 1513, in honour of God and Notre-Dame".

Below is a scene depicting Christ revealing himself to the disciples at Emmaus by the symbolic act of breaking bread. On the right is the name of the designer of these windows, Arnold de Moles.

From this chapel it is but a short step to the Cathedral's other great glory, the carved stalls of the choir. There are over a hundred beautifully sculpted figures and scenes within a three-sided architectural setting made entirely of wood. Although the choir stalls were carved at the beginning of the sixteenth century the first impression is that this is the work of a Gothic master: the screens at the east end and on the north and south sides have niches with pointed arches and Gothic tracery while all round the top run delicate pointed finials. But the carved figures within the niches often show the influence of Renaissance Italy: Mary Magdalene (23), for instance, is clearly modelled on a Roman matron, while here and there you will find *putti*, those plump cherubs so beloved of Italian fifteenth-century artists. Elsewhere there is sculpture in the Flemish or Burgundian style, such as the small scene of Christ before Pontius Pilate. But some of these carvings hark back to a much earlier tradition; these are the small, grotesque figures found on some of the desks in front of the seats or on the seats themselves, such as the bent figure of a man blowing a horn. There are too many carvings to describe in detail but the main ones in the niches are identified in the plan on page 54.

Below the apse at the east end is a crypt containing a remarkable sarcophagus which holds the remains of St Léothade (619–718) who was Bishop of Auch for twenty-seven years. The tomb is made of white marble from the Pyrénées and is carved with classical motifs: the front and sides are divided into panels by crude pilasters and the spaces in between are decorated with vine scrolls and acanthus leaves. The sarcophagus pre-dates St Léothade and is thought to have been carved in the seventh century: it is a fascinating example of how the art of Rome survived into the Dark Ages, although in much debased forms.

On the way out, stop at Chapel 9, the Chapel of St Antoine. Here there is a monument to Auch's great benefactor Antoine

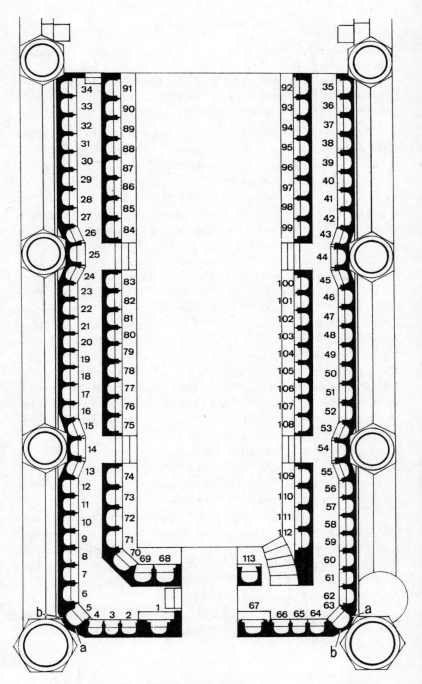

The choir stalls of the Cathedral of Sainte-Marie d'Auch

Key to the figure sculpture of the choir stalls in the Cathedral at Auch.

Above the door of the choir: St Jerome, the Virgin and Child, St Augustine. On the backs of the stalls, starting from the right of the high altar:

1	Adam	37	Saul
2	Charity	38	David prepares for battle
3	The Seer	39	Goliath
4	The Libyan Sibyl	40	David with his sling
5a	Moses	41	David's friend Jonathan
5b	The Samian sibyl	42	David with his trophy
6	The Prophet Amos	43	Judith makes her choice
7	The Persian Sibyl	44	Holofernes as a soldier
8	The Prophet Habakkuk	45	Judith sets off on her
9	The Phrygian Sibyl ·		mission
10	The Prophet Malachae	46	Holofernes in his robes
11	The Cumaean Sibyl	47	Judith decapitates
12	John the Baptist		Holofernes
13	Religion	48	Tobias and his faithful dog
14	John, the first disciple	49	Prudence
15	Hope	50	The Prophet Ezekiel
16	Mark (the Evangelist)	51	The mourner
17	Charity	52	The Prophet Jeremiah
18	Matthew (the Evangelist)	53	The European Sibyl
19	Justice	54	The Centurion at Calvary
20	Luke (the Evangelist)	55	The Hellespontic Sibyl
21	Patience	56	The Prophet Jonah
22	John (the Evangelist)	57	The Delphic Sibyl
23	Mary Magdalene	58	The Prophet Daniel
24	The disciple Peter	59	The Tiburtine Sibyl
25	Martha	60	The Prophet Haggai
26	Noah	61	The Cumaean Sibyl
27	Faith	62	The Prophet Isaiah
28	Joshua	63a	The Agrippine Sibyl
29	Jael	63b	Caleb, Joshua's Second in
30	Sisera fleeing		Command
31	Faith	64	The Erythraean Sibyl
32	Jephthah	65	The Prophet Zacharias
33	Abraham	66	Triumph
34	Melchizedek	67	The Apostles Peter and
35	King David		Paul
36	Bathsheba		

Megret d'Etigny. The Latin inscription at the base translates as follows:

> D. D. Megret d'Etigny, Intendant of the Province, scrupulous observer of the divine will. He displayed a rare solicitude for his parents, a very faithful love for his wife and a truly paternal affection for his children. His great generosity was extended to everyone; he was beloved of God and men. Afflicted by a cruel illness his virtue enabled him to overcome his distress. Holding fast the Cross of Christ he fell asleep the ninth day of September 1767, aged 48. His faithful sorrowing wife Françoise-Thomas de Pange, raised this tomb to her much loved husband in the year 1772.

The last thing you will see as you leave the Cathedral is the magnificent organ that fills most of the west end. It was built by a famous constructor of organs, Jean de Joyeuse (c.1635–98), and installed between 1688 and 1694. It is embellished with some fine carving, including a panel showing King David playing a dulcimer.

Leaving the Cathedral, turn right and walk along the north side, where you will have a clear view of the Gothic nave and the vast buttresses. At the east end is the Archbishop's palace, a noble eighteenth-century building articulated by Corinthian pilasters. On the opposite side of the cathedral is the tree-shaded place de Salinis which terminates to the east in a terrace giving an extensive view over the lower town and the Gascon countryside beyond. A magnificent monumental staircase of 232 steps descends in stages to the river Gers. On a landing near the top is a statue of D'Artagnan.

On this side of the cathedral, the east end is flanked by a twelfth-century hall which has one of the earliest Gothic vaults in the whole of Gascony. Alongside it rises the fourteenth-century Tour d'Armagnac. In fact, it has nothing to do with the Armagnacs but belonged like the hall to the old town prison.

Straggling down the hillside, south of the place de Salinis, are the houses of the old quarter that date back to the Middle Ages. The steep narrow streets that link the city above with the river below are known as *pousterles*, a name that derives from the low Latin *posterula*, meaning gate. In many of them the incline is so severe that there are long flights of stone steps. An exploration of this part of Auch is not to be lightly undertaken. But take courage:

a morning's strenuous sight-seeing will whet your appetite for the excellent cuisine of one of Gascony's most famous chefs, André Daguin, who specializes in regional dishes. You will find him at the Hôtel de France, place de la Libération.

There is a cross-country route to Auch which is much more attractive than the busy N21 and has less traffic. You cross the Pont de Pierre in Agen and take the left-hand turn to Condom D931. After passing the airport and the entrance to the Autoroute de Deux Mers, the road begins to curve and climb, and plane trees border the route. Almost immediately you will see on the right a sign pointing to the Château d'Estillac, the home of one of Gascony's most famous sons, Blaise de Monluc, Marshal of France who lived from c.1502 to 1577. Monluc is the supreme example of the Gascon *cadets* who left home to seek fame and fortune on the battlefield. He was born at Saint-Puy, between Condom and Fleurance, into a noble but impoverished family. He was the eldest of six boys and four girls and such was the state of the family's finances that Blaise left home at the age of nine to serve the Duke of Lorraine as his page. Under the Duke's tutelage he learned the military arts and at the age of twenty went to fight in François I's Italian campaign against the troops of the Emperor Charles V. At first Monluc was not particularly successful: when he was taken prisoner at the Battle of Pavia his family was so poor that it was unable to find his ransom, and eventually he was released without one. Nevertheless his skill and bravery soon brought him to prominence and he became famous in 1555 for his doughty defence of Siena against the imperial troops, which although it ended in the city's surrender was still regarded as a magnificent achievement against overwhelming odds.

In 1560 Monluc returned to Gascony and took up residence at Estillac. This was just at the outbreak of the first of the Wars of Religion between the Huguenots and the Catholics, and Monluc was quickly appointed Governor of Guyenne with instructions to suppress the uprising. A staunch Catholic, Monluc treated the Huguenots with the utmost ferocity, earning him the title 'the King's butcher'. Monluc, himself, boasted in his memoirs: 'One might see, wherever I had passed, the trees on the highway wearing my livery. One man hanged terrified more than a hundred that were killed.' Elsewhere he describes how after the taking of Montségur 'the slaughter continued till ten of the clock or after, because they were fain to ferret them out of the houses and there were not above fifteen or twenty taken prisoner, whom we presently hung up ... There was no talking of ransoms unless for the hangmen.' But not too much should be made of this savagery: it was a cruel age when both sides were guilty of the most appalling acts of brutality and Monluc was a simple soldier with a firm unquestioning faith, and a deep patriotism that left no room for doubt when dealing with the King's and God's enemies.

Monluc's military career came to a bloody end at the siege of Rabastens, in the south of Gascony, in 1570, where he received a terrible wound in the face, so bad that ever after he was forced to wear a mask in public. He retreated to Estillac where he spent his last years writing his *Commentaires*, an account of his military career which Henri IV called the Soldier's Bible and which was the King's favourite reading. Monluc was created Marshal of France in 1574 and died in 1577.

Estillac is an interesting example of the transitional military architecture of the sixteenth century that preceded the prodigious fortifications built by Louis XIV's great engineer, Vauban.

The château stands in a commanding position on a narrow ridge with extensive views on all sides except the south. Originally it was a thirteenth-century Gascon *château-fort* with one large rectangular building flanked by a single tower. By the beginning of the fifteenth century the defences were out of date and round towers, designed to resist gunfire, were added on the east and west sides. At the same time a spiral staircase was introduced and some other internal modifications made.

Monluc retired to Estillac in 1560 and soon set about enlarging the old building and improving its defences. Because of the narrowness of the site he could only extend the château by adding two long wings projecting south, resulting in a narrow trapezoid plan like an inverted V, with a south front nearly twice the width of the north. Each wing terminated in a massive bastion, jutting out like the prow of a ship, designed according to the very latest military principles to give a good field of fire and to withstand artillery. A curtain wall containing the entrance stretched between them. The eastern bastion was destroyed at the time of the French Revolution but the western one survives, as does another smaller bastion half-way along the west wall.

In the courtyard is the pulpit from which Monluc was accustomed to harangue his troops and in the oldest part of the building is the vaulted kitchen with its great open fire-place beside which Monluc is said to have sat while he wrote the *Commentaires*.

Just south of Estillac is the village of Aubiac and another splendid Romanesque church. The first sight of the village comes as a surprise. You climb to the top of a hill, snatching glimpses of the Gascon countryside through the plane trees bordering the route as you go, and there, perched on a ridge directly opposite is Aubiac. Seen from this viewpoint, Aubiac looks like a fortified village but this is an optical illusion created by the church, which is fortified, merging with the windowless wall of a large nearby house.

The church of Sainte-Marie stands in a narrow square to the left of the road. The west front, which looks more like a castle keep than part of a church, has a massive stone tower crowned by a low-pitched tiled roof. The north-west corner of the tower is flanked by a round turret containing a spiral staircase which apparently doesn't go anywhere. This suggests that the roof was a later addition and that originally the top of the tower was used as a look-out post. The entrance is very simple, only relieved by dogtooth ornament on the outer moulding of the arch above the door. Inside is a simple aisleless, three-bay nave, the first bay being the ground floor of the tower. The most interesting part of the interior is the choir which has three semi-circular apses in a trefoil arrangement surmounted by a tower, a most unusual design. The tower is lit by paired windows on three sides, each pair separated by a massive rectangular cross-rib supporting a shallow vault decorated with corner paintings of the four evangelists.

Outside, the east end is particularly interesting with its three linked apses, undecorated except for flat simple buttresses, dominated by the powerful tower. The east end is the earliest part of the church, in fact there are fragments in the extrerior walls of the east and north chapels that pre-date the twelfth century. Just west of the north apse is another round turret, containing a spiral staircase, which presumably also served as a watch-tower. No wonder that Aubiac, when first seen from a distance, looks more like a castle than a church.

The road continues south to Laplume, a *castelnau* dating back at least to the tenth century, which was capital of a tiny medieval fief, the Viscounty of Brulhois, stretching westwards from the left bank of the Garonne to the Pays d'Albret and from Layrac, south of Agen, to just north of Condom. The Viscounty remained independent until 1304 when it fell into the hands of the Armagnacs. In 1452 it was sold to Poton de Xaintrailles, the companion in arms of Joan of Arc, for 2,000 *écus*.

The ancient town centre of Laplume is undergoing extensive and much-needed restoration. The sixteenth-century church is flanked to the north by an enormous porch surmounted by an octagonal bell tower.

Eight miles further down the road is La Montjoie, a *bastide* founded in 1299 by Philippe le Bel. The route follows the valley bottom for much of the way and if you turn off down one of the narrow side roads you will find lush meadows which are ideal places for picnics.

Just north of Condom a turning to the left (D41) leads to La Romieu, a village originally founded in the eleventh century on a prehistoric site, although the arcaded square and grid plan of streets clearly indicate a *bastide* dating from the fourteenth century. There are one or two old houses, the remains of the earlier walls and the old gateway to see, but the real reason for a visit to La Romieu is to admire the considerable ruins of the collegiate church founded in 1318 by Arnaud d'Aux who was born in La Romieu in 1210. As a young man Arnaud went to study at the University of Bologna where he made friends with his cousin Bertrand de Goth, the future Pope Clement V, the first of the French popes who ruled the Catholic world from Avignon rather than Rome. Their friendship endured and when Bertrand was elected Pope he appointed Arnaud his chamberlain and made him a cardinal.

The Gothic church has a simple, aisle-less, four-bay nave, supported by tall, narrow external buttresses, and a pentagonal east end with chapels radiating from the ambulatory. There is a tower at either end, the one at the east being particularly fine. Octagonal in plan, it has a four-stage elevation with paired arches in the uppermost one and quatrefoil openings punched into the stone right round the top, giving a decorative finishing touch to this otherwise massive structure. The ground floor of the tower has a vaulted chamber decorated with paintings of angels in the compartments between the ribs. Above are the manuscript room and the chapter. The roof is reached by a steep staircase of one hundred and sixty steps where you will be rewarded by a magnificent view.

On the north side of the church are the remains of a beautiful fourteenth-century cloister. The arcades have twin openings into the central court divided by elegant central shafts, surmounted by cinquefoil roundels, unfortunately not all of them complete because the cloister was partly destroyed by Protestant troops in the sixteenth century and also suffered damage in the French Revolution.

South of the church is the Cardinal's Tower, all that remains of Arnaud d'Aux's episcopal palace.

The approach to Condom is down a long hill giving an excellent view of the Cathedral of Saint-Pierre. The town's unfortunate name has nothing at all to do with prophylactics; the contraceptive sheath was invented by a Monsieur Condom who was not even a native of the place. How the town did get its name is not clear. According to local legend it grew up around a monastery founded by Honorette, wife of Garcia Sanche le Courbe, Duke of Gascony. Condom was part of Eleanor of Aquitaine's dowry to Henry Plantagenet, so from 1152 until 1419 it was under English rule. In 1317 Pope John XXII made Condom a bishopric which it remained until the Revolution. Its most famous bishop was Bossuet who lived in the reign of Louis XVI and was such a successful orator and writer that he never came near his Gascon diocese.

Condom boasts that it is the capital of Armagnac (a claim disputed by at least two other Gascon towns); it is certainly the main commercial centre for armagnac brandy, a pre-eminence due not only to the proximity of the armagnac vineyards but to the situation on the banks of the River Baïse which, up to the nineteenth century, was the only reliable route for transporting goods northwards to the port of Bordeaux.

The centre of the town is the place Saint-Pierre and here on market days (Wednesday) you will find an animated scene as local businessmen rub shoulders with weatherbeaten farmers from the surrounding countryside and dispute the merits of rival armagnacs. Towering above them is the great Gothic cathedral, built between 1506 and 1531 by Bishop Jean Marre (1496–1521) on the site of a ninth-century chapel.

The west end of Saint-Pierre is dominated by an impressive stone tower, supported at the front by four solid-looking attached buttresses and to the north and south by flying buttresses. On the south side is a beautiful flamboyant porch with twenty-four sculptures in the voussoirs. At the base of an empty niche on the central column is the coat of arms of Bishop Marre.

Inside the cathedral is an aisle-less nave lit on the south side by modern stained glass and crowned by an admirable ribbed vault with a complex pattern made up of those subsidiary ribs called liernes and tiercerons. The glass in the choir is nineteenth-century as is the altar screen. On the left side of the choir, above the entrance to the sacristy, is an inscription commemorating the consecration of the cathedral.

On the north side of the cathedral is a sixteenth-century cloister embellished with flamboyant tracery but much damaged in the Revolution. The cloister is flanked to the east by the ancient chapel of Ste Catherine, formerly the chapter house; it, too, has a fine vaulted roof with central bosses decorated with polychrome armorial bearings. On the north side is the Bishop's Palace which now serves as the vestibule to the Palais de Justice. The chapel is Gothic but from the garden behind you can see a Renaissance doorway surmounted by a window ornamented with sculpted medallions.

On the first floor there used to be the Museum of Armagnac but there are plans to move it and you should check with the tourist office. The museum is largely dedicated to the display of artefacts connected with the armagnac industry. There are tools for making barrels, eighteenth-century bottles, ancient stills and a gigantic grape press that looks as though it is made from two trees.

Today, Condom is a sleepy provincial town but before the Revolution it was wealthy and important. This more prosperous era is reflected in a number of elegant stone mansions dating from the seventeenth and eighteenth centuries. Just north of the cathedral in the Rue Jules Ferry is the Hôtel Bloy-Richon which has a beautiful cast-iron staircase and the Hôtel de Polignac with a fine entrance court closed by cast-iron gates and a stone balcony that runs the whole length of the façade. To the south are two stately homes dating from the eighteenth century, the Hoîel du Cugnac and the Hôtel de Riberot at numbers 36 and 38 rue Jean Jaurès, respectively.

Condom boasts one of the best restaurants in Gascony, La Table des Cordeliers, where you can eat splendid food in what was once a fourteenth-century monastery. The town is also a good centre for exploring the heart of Gascony, for there is a great deal to see in the area. A number of roads converge here: the D931 from Agen continues south-westwards to Aire-sur-l'Adour, while the D930, which follows the valley of the Baïse southwards from Nérac to Condom, goes on south-eastwards to Auch. To the east, two minor roads wind through typical Gascon countryside to Lectoure and Fleurance. The approach to Lectoure, on the D7, is particularly good with striking views from some way off of the town standing out on its escarpment.

Another country road on the west side of Condom, the D15, takes you in less than half an hour to one of Gascony's most remarkable sites, Larressingle, a completely fortified village dating from the thirteenth century. Larressingle is known locally, with typical Gascon exaggeration, as the 'Carcassonne of the Gers': at first sight it looks like a small castle but the encircling defensive wall is in fact made up of the backs of a ring of houses, huddled together like a covered wagon-train drawn up in a circle at night against an attack by redskins.

At intervals along the wall are small crenellated watch-towers while the entrance is defended by a much larger machicolated tower which was originally preceded by a drawbridge across a now dry moat. Inside is one narrow circular street with some charming small houses. Towering over them are the ruins of the thirteenth-century *château-fort* which, up to the sixteenth century, was the residence of the Bishops of Condom.

Behind the château is the thirteenth-century church. It was begun from the east end with an apse, vaulted with a semi-dome. This is preceded by a barrel-vaulted rectangular choir. The projected nave was never built, the *château-fort* taking its place, and the entrance to the choir was blocked off by a screen wall topped by a bell gable. Later a refuge chamber was built above the choir that was reached by a spiral staircase. Above the chamber a lean-to was constructed against the back of the screen-wall which gave access to the bells. Finally, because it was impossible to extend the church westwards, the apse was breached and a rectangular choir added to the east end. The entrance to the original choir and to the apse both have Romanesque columns with sculpted capitals.

In the eleventh century there was a small earlier church and one or two secular buildings on this site and that was all. It is not until 1279 that we find a reference to a *castrum* here, indicating that by then it was fortified, in a document in which King Philippe III of France acknowledges that the Agenais, which included Larressingle, was part of English Gascony. A later document refers to the extension and fortification of the *château-fort* by the then Bishop of Condom, Arnaud-Oden de Lomagne (1287–1306).

Otherwise nothing more is heard of Larressingle until 1589 when the town councillors of Condom appointed two guards to protect the village against troops of the Catholic League who were in rebellion against King Henri IV. The Leaguers, under their leader Antoine-Arnaud de Pardeillan, Seigneur de Montespan, captured Larressingle quite easily and held it for seven years, terrorizing the surrounding countryside until Montespan surrendered in 1598 to be made Senechal of the Agenais and Gascony.

Fifteen kilometres west of Larressingle is Montréal, a *bastide* founded in 1289 on the site of a Celtic *oppidum*. The main square still has a few arcaded houses and there are some half-timbered dwellings in the side streets. Much of the original defensive wall survives as well as the original gateway, but the chief interest lies in the fortified church: this was built in a commanding position right on the edge of the escarpment so that its southern wall is aligned with the town ramparts and like them is pierced with narrow arrow slits.

The strength of Montréal's fortifications reflects its position right on the frontier of English Gascony and French Armagnac. During the Hundred Years' War Montréal was firmly attached to the English cause and evidence of this loyalty is to be found in two remarkable letters written by the English King Edward II to the town council. Under English rule Montréal prospered, only to suffer during the Wars of Religion when the Huguenot leader Montgoméry sacked the town, badly damaging the church in the process.

Montgoméry's name crops up frequently in this part of Gascony, always in the context of destruction and iconoclasm. He is the Protestant counterpart of Blaise de Monluc and every bit as savage and, like Monluc, he was a brillant commander.

Gabriel de Lorges, Sieur de Montgoméry, was born in 1530 into a family belonging to the minor nobility of Normandy. Like Monluc, he left home at an early age to join the King's bodyguard, the Scottish Guards, at the court of Henri II of France.

In 1559 the King held a tournament to celebrate the marriage of his daughter Elizabeth to Philip of Spain. Montgoméry entered the lists against Henri and after two inconclusive tilts his lance struck the King's helmet so hard that it broke in two and the lower half penetrated Henri's vizor. A splinter entered the King's eye and he died a few days later. Montgoméry, fearing reprisals, fled to England.

In 1562, when the first of the Wars of Religion broke out in France, Montgoméry returned from exile to help the Protestant cause and quickly proved himself an able leader.

In 1568 a Catholic force, under the command of Antoine de Lomagne, Seigneur de Terride (the castle of Terride still stands just outside the extreme north-east border of Gascony), attacked the Protestant Viscounty of Béarn in the Pyréneés just south of

Gascony, and Montgoméry was sent to the rescue. He quickly liberated Béarn, defeating and capturing Terride at Orthez, and then embarked on a campaign of terror as a reprisal for the atrocities committed by Terride's troops. Marching north into Gascony, he captured Tarbes and put it to the sword, then moved on into Armagnac, sacking and burning Nogaro and Samatan but sparing Marciac from whose burghers he extracted a huge ransom. Numerous Catholic churches were also attacked and wholly or partly destroyed. Melancholy evidence of this frenzy of destruction can be seen in many ruined or rebuilt churches all over southern Armagnac.

In 1570 the Peace of Saint-Germain proclaimed an amnesty for Huguenots but on August 24, 1572 the Massacre of St Bartholomew took place. Montgoméry, who was in Paris at the time, was one of the few Huguenots leaders to escape, fleeing south from Paris on a fast horse. Once again he took refuge in England and a year later took part in the abortive attempt by an English fleet to raise the siege of the Protestant stronghold La Rochelle.

In 1574 Montgoméry landed in Normandy and took the towns of Carentan and Argentan. This success was short-lived: he was captured at Domfront, taken to Paris and beheaded on June 26.

Montréal has a small museum, the centrepiece of which is a fine fourth-century mosaic from the Gallo-Roman villa excavated at nearby Seviac. This is one of the most important archaeological sites in Gascony and excavations have been in progress there since 1959, although the first mosaic was found as long ago as 1868.

The villa covers an area of over five acres and includes a large courtyard surrounded on three sides by rectangular rooms and on the east by a large vestibule beyond which is a series of chambers with more sophisticated ground plans, many of them having apses. There is also the remains of the heating system for the hot baths. But what most people go to see are the mosaic pavements. For the most part these have geometrical patterns of the kind commonly found all over the Roman world but there are also some very attractive designs with patterns made up of fruit and leaves. The base colour of the mosaics is a creamy white with the designs picked out in terracotta, olive green and dark blue.

Just north of Montréal is one of Gascony's most delightful *bastides*, Fourcés. It lies to the left of the D29 in a loop of the river Auzoue, which formed part of the original defences. To enter Fourcés you cross a short bridge at the inner end of which is a small château built at the end of the fifteenth century. At that time life was returning to normal after the alarms of the Hundred Years' War so, although it still has corner towers, they look as though they are there for the sake of their appearance rather than for defence while the arrow slits have been replaced by mullion and transom windows. Indeed, with its warm, honey-coloured stone walls, low-pitched Roman tile roof and the river Auzoue flowing gently past, the château makes a charming picture.

The inside of Fourcés comes as a surprise: instead of the usual rectangular plan there is a circular *place* planted with plane trees, surrounded by the usual houses over arcades but here built in a ring. Such circular *bastides* are very rare. Originally Fourcés had a defensive wall but of this little remains. However, the rue de l'Horloge leads down to one surviving arched entrance, sur-mounted by a tall tower to which has been added an off-centre clock and a jaunty little belfry capped by a pointed tiled roof. If you go through the arch you will see the backs of the houses (not by any means their best aspect), some remains of the ramparts and, beyond, the river Auzoue marked by a line of poplars.

Fourcés takes its name from Guillaume de Fourcés, the younger son of the Count of Fézensac, one of the great Gascon nobles of the early Middle Ages whose territories were later to be subsumed into those of the Count of Armagnac. The Fourcés owed their allegiance to the English crown and in 1315 Bertrand de Fourcés actually accompanied the English King Edward III on his ill-starred campaign against Robert the Bruce of Scotland. The bastide was founded at the end of the thirteenth century and was granted a charter by Edward I of England in 1289.

In the parallel valley of the Baïse, to the east, there are a number of handsome farms with *pigeonniers* standing in very desirable positions on the steep western slopes. Ten kilometres north of Condom in the same valley is Moncrabeau, a hill-top hamlet where once a year a curious Gascon ceremony takes place when the

Académie des Menteurs enthrones the winner of a contest to find who can tell the tallest story. The stone throne where the *menteur* is crowned can be seen on the north outside wall of the church.

On the road south from Condom to Fleurance is Saint-Puy where Monluc was born. Very little of the original Château de Monluc is left: there is a terrace above the remains of the ramparts from which there are extensive views south; an arched entrance to the courtyard, covered with Virginia creeper glowing crimson in the autumn and, inside the house, the original flagstones into which is set a large stone trough where, in the days of Monluc, the grapes were trodden to make wine for the household.

Wine is still made at Monluc but today it is for sale. Both white and rosé are produced by the *méthode champenoise*. The rosé is caled *tuilé* because of its beautiful colour, reminiscent of Roman terracotta tiles. Another drink, with a distinct kick to it, made at Monluc is *pousse rapière* or rapier thrust. It consists of a measure of orange liqueur topped up with sparkling wine and garnished with orange peel. The name is supposed to derive from the fanciful idea that the effect of the apéritif is like the thrust of a rapier in a duel – this is after all the land of D'Artagnan. *Pousse rapière* is now being marketed by the Château de Monluc in special packs containing one bottle of armagnac mixed with orange liqueur and a bottle of sparkling white wine.

There are conducted tours of the beautiful stone cellars and tastings in the tourist season.

From Saint-Puy a road leads through typical undulating country north-east to Lectoure. On the way you pass through the hill village of Terraube where there is a beautiful sixteenth- and seventeenth-century château built by the Galard family and still occupied by their descendants. Unfortunately it is rarely open.

The name Terraube is interesting: it derives from the Latin *terra alba*, meaning white earth, and indeed from here on northwards you are in limestone country and the soil has a distinctly chalky look. South of Condom you find a heavy yellow clay that is glutinous in winter and turns to dust in the summer. The clay is very hard to work so smallholdings are not really viable and farms are few and far between compared with further north.

2 Fourcès: *above* the fifteenth-century chateau and gothic bridge; *below* looking from the market place down the rue de l'Horloge.

PREVIOUS PAGE: 1 The red roofs of this hill-top village of Aubiac cluster round the massive fortified church of Sainte-Marie.

3 The romanesque church of Saint-Just-de-Valcabrère with, in the background, the cathedral of Saint Bertrand-de-Comminges.

4 Looming above the roof of the covered market the abbey of Simorre looks more like a castle than a church.

5 The twelfth-century church of Saint-Savin, in the village of the same name, occupies a beautiful site in the Lavedan, just south of Lourdes.

OPPOSITE PAGE: 6 The cirque de Troumouse, an impressive natural amphitheatre high in the Pyrénées.

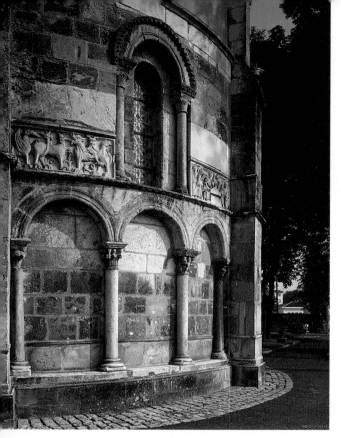

Because stone is scarce in these parts only the rich could afford it so, although there are stone churches and châteaux, most of the old farm buildings are built of mud brick or half-timbered. The mud-brick walls are sometimes reinforced with odd stones, occasional bricks and here and there a wooden post or beam; the half-timbered houses, on the other hand, started with a wooden frame and the interstices are filled with a mixture called *torchis* made of yellow clay and straw. You find many of these half-timbered buildings in the towns and here they usually have a cladding of Roman bricks. Sometimes the arrangement of beams and posts in the frames is quite complicated and produces elaborate patterns made up of verticals and diagonals. Many such buildings have been recently restored with a modern cement used instead of *torchis*. Although not strictly authentic the result is perfectly acceptable and certainly much better than letting the houses rot – as was the case when we first started to explore Gascony.

On the south-west outskirts of Condom, where the D931 to Eauze and the D15 to Barbotan diverge, is the church of Saint-Jacques. Of little interest in itself, this modest building reminds us that Condom was a stop on the medieval pilgrims' route to Santiago de Compostella. There are a number of these *chemins de Saint-Jacques*, as they are called in France, for the shrine of Saint James the Great at Compostella was so famous that it attracted more pilgrims than any other, except for Jerusalem and Rome. One of the most important of these *chemins* started in Paris and proceeded south via Tours, Poitiers and Bordeaux; another extremely long pilgrimage began in Trier, in Germany, and followed the Rhône southwards to Arles. Eventually, all the routes converged in the western Pyréneés, where the pilgrims gathered their strength before tackling the difficult journey over the mountains into Spain.

The *chemin de Saint-Jacques* that passed through Condom originated in Saint-Puy, in the Massif Central, and entered Gascony in the extreme north-east, near Flamarens, continuing via Lectoure, La Romieu, Condom, Montréal, Eauze, Aire-sur-l'Adour and finally on to Saint-Jean-Pied-de-Port, at the foot of the Roncesvalles pass into Spain.

There are many reminders of the *chemin de Saint-Jacques* to be found all over Gascony and the *coquille*, or cockle-shell badge, which was worn by pilgrims on the route to Compostella and after which the dish of scallops is named, is frequently found carved at the entrances of churches and ancient hostels along the route.

Due south of Condom is the Cistercian abbey of Flaran which houses a small exhibition devoted to Gascon *chemins de Saint-Jacques*. Flaran was founded in 1151 on the west bank of the Baïse. The monks dammed the river and dug a canal that turned the site into an island. The waters of the canal served to carry away the discharges from the kitchens and latrines and to turn the wheel of a water-mill. The abbey soon acquired land on both sides of the river and by the early years of the thirteenth century had grown rich and powerful. This prosperity aroused the envy of the local lord, Centulle d'Astarac, who ravaged the abbey lands. Centulle was excommunicated for this sacrilege but made amends by leaving Flaran a fortune in his will when he died in 1230.

By 1247 Flaran was confident enough to found a *bastide*, Valence, on the opposite side of the river, but this was the abbey's apogee: during the Hundred Years' War it was under constant threat from one side or the other and was in fact sacked by the English who controlled Valence and the surrounding territory from 1315 to 1324.

Flaran recovered after the end of the war only to suffer in 1569 at the hands of Montgoméry who demolished three sides of the cloister and set fire to the church, destroying the abbey's archives in the process; only four monks survived this attack. The church was repaired during the subsequent two centuries but even so at the time of the Revolution only three monks remained. The abbey was sold off by the revolutionaries to a private buyer who used it to store brandy; now it belongs to the *département* of the Gers who are busy restoring it.

The west front of Flaran has the austerity typical of Cistercian architecture: the arch over the entrance is sparsely decorated with geometrical ornament, above which are two simple round-headed windows surmounted by a wheel window embellished with plate tracery. Inside is a short nave of only three bays, very bare except for some modestly carved capitals, and covered by a pointed tunnel vault. The stone is blackened by fumes from the barrels of Armagnac once stored there. The left-hand aisle shows some early rib vaulting. Beyond the crossing and transepts is a shallow choir terminated by an apse and to left and right four apsidal chapels in a line, there being no ambulatory.

A door in the last bay of the left-hand aisle leads to the cloister. The tympanum above the door has a shallowly carved chrisme (Christ's monogram) on either side of which is a simple medallion with Greek crosses.

Although only one side of the original cloister survived Montgoméry's onslaught (the one with pointed arches and paired columns), it still has a certain charm created by the gallery above being half-timbered. On the east side of the cloister is the most beautiful part of Flaran, the chapter house. You enter through a round-headed arch springing from short compound piers with attached columns standing on a low wall. The arch is unadorned but the capitals of the columns have finely carved leaf ornaments. To the left and right of the entrance arch are two more round-headed arches, of the same dimensions as the one in the centre, whose lower third is blocked off by the continuation of the low wall, so that they are more like windows. Inside, the chapter house is divided into nine bays covered by rib vaults springing from four slim columns of different-coloured marble, two white, one red and one black. These capitals are also ornamented with leaf carving. The spatial effect created by the four graceful columns and the interweaving of the vaulting ribs is both complex and satisfying. A similar visual impression, but on a smaller scale, is found in the sacristy, a square chamber in the corner of the chapter-house building with one central column supporting four vaults.

The exterior of Flaran is not particularly interesting: even the east end, having no ambulatory, lacks the harmony usually found in Romanesque churches.

Valence-sur-Baïse, the *bastide* founded by the monks of Flaran, is situated on a small hill just east of the D930 from Condom to Auch. Of the original ramparts only a fortified gate, the Port d'Espagne, remains. There are some old houses in the place de l'Hôtel-de-Ville. The fourteenth-century church is much restored. North of Valence, just off the D232, are the ruins of a once-fine Gascon castle, the Château de Tauzia.

The road from Condom to Eauze runs through pleasantly undulating country increasingly given over to the cultivation of the vine. Five miles down the road from Condom is a turning to Vopillon, where you will find the remains of the twelfth-century chapel of the Dames de Fontevrault. All that is left is the east end, the rest having been destroyed by Montgoméry. A new entrance was made by inserting a porch in what had been the transept: the present door is classical in style and dates from 1774. Inside the church a blocked-up arch on the west shows where the nave began; now there are only two bays and an apse. The architecture is very basic with primitive capitals and simple billet moulding the only sculptural decoration. Inside the door to the sacristy, however, are a series of panels with Gothic arches above containing thirteenth-century frescoes depicting the life of Christ. They are in a very poor state but one can see that originally they must have been of a very high quality.

Near the church is a medieval tower that was converted into a handsome classical house. You can still see some of the original arrow slits but an imposing classical entrance with french windows opening onto a gallery above was inserted in the eighteenth century on the north side of the tower. Here in the seventeenth century lived a prior of Flaran who drowned himself because he had overspent the abbey's funds and feared the wrath of the Archbishop of Auch.

A footpath leads northwards from Vopillon to the Pont d'Artigues, a famous stone bridge with five unequal arches, that for hundreds of years was used by pilgrims on the *chemin de Saint-Jacques* to cross the river Osse. Although the bridge is now right off the beaten track it can be reached on the D278.

A little further down the main road to Eauze is Mouchan, where there is an interesting Romanesque church, Saint-Pierre. The church is best viewed from the south-east: from here you see the apsed east end with closely abutting it a tall square tower joined onto the south-west corner of which is a round staircase turret. Beyond this unusual complex of structures, largely hidden from view, is the entrance to the church in the transept end and the nave.

The apse at the east end is divided into five by four stone buttresses reaching up to what looks like the original roof line where there are carved corbels. The stonework above looks different, as if the roof was raised later, perhaps to accommodate the vaulting of the choir. In between the buttresses are round-headed windows, ornamented with billet and hood mouldings, and recessed shafts on each side with well-carved capitals.

From research it appears that the tower is earlier than the church: it probably dates from the end of the eleventh century and was presumably a watch-tower. Originally the arches at the bottom were open and access was by the blocked door at first-floor level via a wooden staircase. Once again the stonework at the top looks different and later.

Inside Saint-Pierre is a two-bay nave of no interest. The east end, however, is altogether more exciting: it consists of a wide tunnel-vaulted transept and a deep choir, also tunnel-vaulted, ending in a semi-domed apse. The choir is flanked on the north side by a large chapel which in modern times was walled off from the transept and turned into a sacristy. The north transept and sacristy are the earliest part of the church and there is a decorative link in a strip of billet moulding that runs along the walls of both and round the heads of the sacristy windows. On the south side the building of an apsidal chapel was inhibited by the tower. The quadripartite vault of the crossing with its massive stone ribs is one the earliest in Gascony.

But the chief glory of the east end is the sculpture, especially the carving of the capitals of the blank arcading of the choir. Many of the subjects found here are common in Romanesque sculpture but some are unique: note in particular the fourth capital on the right which has on one face a bell-ringer, sitting inside an arch representing the church with the bell-tower above, and on another Vice represented as a woman in a barrel encircled by a serpent. The third capital has splendid eagles on the corners. More eagles and some engaging lion heads appear on the capitals of the shafts at the entrance to the sacristy.

Not far down the road is Eauze. Now a modest market town, in Gallo-Roman times it was the capital of the Elusates, one of the Celtic–Iberian tribes conquered by Caesar's legions. Under Roman rule Elusa, as Eauze was then called, became the capital of the Novempopulani and such was its prestige and power that it was granted the right to mint its own coinage. Archaeological excavations have brought to light inscriptions showing that in early Roman times the Elusates worshipped at the shrines of Mithras and Cybele but in the fourth century the Novempopulani were converted to Christianity and Elusa, as the chief city of the region, became the see of a metropolitan bishop with eleven suffragan bishops under his rule. One of the first Bishops of Elusa, Mamertius, participated in the Council of Arles in AD 314.

Elusa's prosperity made the city an obvious target for attack and it was sacked in turn by the Vandals in the fifth century and the Saracens in the seventh. The city survived the first two disasters but in the ninth century it was devastated by Viking pirates and never recovered. The modern town of Eauze was rebuilt on a new site slightly to the west of the old. You can visit what remains of Elusa but there is very little to see. Nevertheless it was here in October 1985 that one of the most important archaeological finds ever made in France was unearthed. In the course of digging the foundations for a new building, on a site just north of the road to Vic-Fézensac, a workman uncovered a man-made hole 20 inches in diameter and 11 inches deep. In it were 28,000 Roman and Gallo-Roman coins comprising the complete range of currency issued between the reigns of Commodus (AD 177–192) and Grallienus (AD 253–268) and covering the reigns of thirty emperors. There is also a coin issued by Posthumus, a rebel soldier who proclaimed himself Emperor of Gaul and governed from AD 260 to 273. The hoard was probably hidden by a rich Gallo-Roman noble during the period of civil war that followed Posthumus's seizure of power.

With the coins were many exquisite items of jewellery, including gold rings, emerald and pearl earrings, cameo brooches, some delicate emerald and pearl necklaces, gold bracelets and, perhaps most remarkable of all, a dagger with an ivory handle superbly carved to represent the god Bacchus.

This treasure trove, which may well prove to be the richest ever found in France, is now in Paris being carefully examined and catalogued. Eauze is hoping that the Ministry of Culture will fund a local museum, although if this happens it will almost certainly contain copies rather than the originals.

There is not a great deal of interest in the modern town: what there is will be found in the place de la Cathédrale where there is a particularly fine half-timbered house dating from the fifteenth century and, built out over an arcade, the so-called Maison de Jeanne d'Albret, although there is no evidence that it belonged to her or that she even stayed there. The brick cathedral of Saint-Luperc was built at the end of the fifteenth century in the typically austere Gothic style of the Midi. Inside is a wide aisleless nave with side chapels between the buttresses. The bosses of the rib vaults are ornamented with the arms of France, Eauze, Jean Marre who founded the cathedral and the Duke of Alençon. Perhaps the nicest feature of the cathedral is that all the plaster has recently been stripped off the wall of the nave revealing a very attractive surface of red brick and occasional white stones.

Eauze disputes with Condom the title of capital of Armagnac, the brandy rather than the county, for it is in this area that the best armagnac is made.

The region where armagnac is distilled, and which is legally entitled to the *appellation*, covers three-quarters of the modern département of the Gers, the extreme south-west of the Agenais (Lot-et-Garonne) and a small part of the Landes, near Villeneuve-de-Marsan. Within these boundaries Armagnac is further subdivided into Haut-Armagnac, a large area embracing the whole of the eastern half and a good portion of the south of the region; Ténarèze, a smaller stretch in the north and centre; and to the west Bas-Armagnac, with Eauze, the 'capital' of Armagnac as its main town. (Auch is the departmental capital of the Gers.)

Although armagnac rivals cognac in excellence, it is much less well-known. This is in part due to the fact that the Charente,

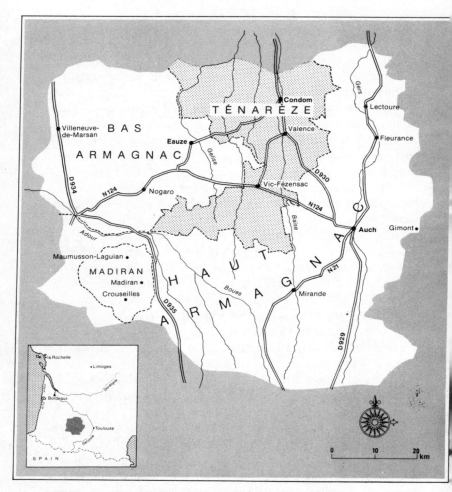

THE THREE ARMAGNAC BRANDY *APPELLATION CONTRÔLÉE* REGIONS

where cognac is made, is much nearer to Bordeaux and has therefore always had an outlet for its product, while armagnac had a
much longer journey, either down the Adour to Bayonne or along
the Garonne to Bordeaux, through what was often hostile country.
The building of the railways and later better roads at the end of
the nineteenth century eased the communication problem, but
because the Gascons were cut off from the outside world for so
long they were also less energetic in exploiting their brandy than
the producers of cognac. It is only very recently that serious efforts
have been made to reach export markets, so that names such as
Janneau, Clés des Ducs and Marquis de Caussade are becoming
better known.

Armagnac is made in an alembic, a kind of double boiler in
which the wine is distilled only once, unlike cognac which passes
through the still twice. The strength of armagnac is also lower. At
the end of the distillation the spirit leaves the alembic with a
minimum of 52 degrees of pure alcohol compared with cognac
which starts with a minimum strength of 70 degrees. During its
years in the barrel it will lose by evaporation between one and one
and a half per cent per year. By law armagnac must be sold with
an alcoholic content of between 40 degrees and 48 degrees. But in
practice bottles above 42 degrees are rarely found.

The Gascons learned the art of distillation from the Arabs whose
influence was strong in this part of France until the Moors were
expelled from Spain in the fifteenth century. The word *alembic*
comes from the Arabic *el embic*. In the archives of the Musée de
l'Armagnac at Condom there is a document dated 1411 which
mentions an *ayga ardenterius*, in other words a distiller of *eau-de-
vie*, but it appears that this spirit was used for medicinal purposes
only. So far as we know it was not until the seventeenth century
that armagnac was distilled to be drunk. Until then, Armagnac
was still a wine-growing region although, during the troubled
period of the Hundred Years' War and subsequently the Wars of
Religion, the growers found great difficulty in exporting their
product because of the problem of reaching a port.

In the seventeenth century, however, the Gascons were encouraged by Dutch merchants to distil their wine. The advantage of

this to the Dutch was that the volume of the *eau-de-vie* was much less than that of the wine and so their transport costs over a long distance were much reduced. When the spirit reached Holland it was mixed with wine purchased from more accessible parts of France such as Périgord. The idea was to help preserve the wine as well as to fortify it. This fortified wine was shipped in the following year to ports in Germany and the Baltic.

It was the Dutch seamen who first started drinking the spirit.

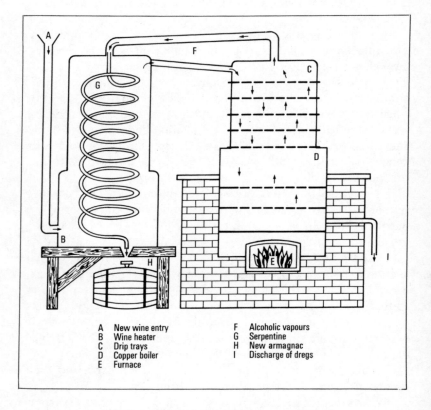

A	New wine entry	F	Alcoholic vapours
B	Wine heater	G	Serpentine
C	Drip trays	H	New armagnac
D	Copper boiler	I	Discharge of dregs
E	Furnace		

THE ALAMBIC ARMAGNACAIS

78

They were given a barrel of *eau-de-vie* on each voyage as part of their contract and seem to have acquired a taste for it that led to more and more of the imported spirit, rather than French wine, finding its way into the Dutch taverns. The sailors called the spirit *Brandewijn*, which is Dutch for *vin brûle*, or 'burnt wine'. 'Brandewijn' was anglicized into 'brandy'.

The original alembic used in Armagnac was the *double chauffe* which meant that the liquid was distilled at least twice to purify it. In 1801, however, a chemist from Montpellier, Edouard Adam, invented a single-distillation method which was further refined by a Gascon peasant named Verdier, and this *alambic armagnacais* is still in use today.

To understand how the *alambic armagnacais* works one needs to know the basic principle of the ordinary pot still. This is simple enough: the wine, contained in a large kettle or pot, is heated so that it starts to vaporize. The first highly volatile elements, known as 'headings', escape into a copper coil called the *serpentine*, which is immersed in water. As the vapour passes through the *serpentine* it condenses and by the time it has reached the end it has changed into spirit. The 'headings' are full of impurities that contribute nothing to the final spirit, so they are drawn off into a barrel. Meanwhile the process is continuing and as the heat increases the alcohol in the wine is also vaporized and is collected in a second barrel. The liquid alcohol contained in this second barrel is called the *brouillis*. A residue of wine is left behind in the pot and this goes into the third barrel under the name of 'tailings'. The *brouillis* is returned to the pot and is distilled a second time, in exactly the same way, and this time the second barrel contains the *eau-de-vie* that, after a period of maturing in the barrel, is sold as brandy. The headings and tailings are added to the next pot of wine to be distilled.

In the case of the *alambic armagnacais*, the wine does not go straight into the pot but into a copper cauldron called the *chauffe-vin*, inside which is the *serpentine*. From the *chauffe-vin* the wine flows into a second receptacle which is divided into two parts: at the top is the *colonne à plateaux* and beneath it the *chaudière-en-cuivre*, which is heated by the furnace immediately below. The

colonne à plateaux, as its name suggests, contains a series of per-
forated trays and the wine drips slowly down from tray to tray
becoming hotter and hotter as it gets nearer the furnace until the
water, alcohol and other volatile elements all evaporate. The vapour
now rises, finding its way back through the trays and becoming
impregnated as it does so with the subtle aromas of the incoming
wine in the process of vaporizing as it drips downwards. These
aromas are preserved throughout the rest of the distillation and
account for much of armagnac's individual character. The alcoholic
vapour (for most of the water content disappears) continues on its
way into and through the *serpentine*. In the case of the *alambic
armagnacais*, it will be remembered, this is immersed not in water
but in the wine itself, which enters at the base of the *chauffe-vin*.
Thus, as the vapour descends, the *serpentine* is slowly condensed
by the cooler wine outside, so that by the time the bottom is
reached it is *eau-de-vie* and is drawn into a barrel. Conversely, the
rising wine is warmed by the *serpentine* and by the time it reaches
the top of the *chauffe-vin* it has already attained a temperature of
80°C. Inside the *colonne à plateaux* the temperature averages 100°C
but at the base of the *chaudière* it rises to between 105°C and
110°C. Here the last traces of alcohol evaporate, leaving the liquid
residue full of impurities called the *vinesse*, which is regularly
drained off.

Once started, the distillation process is continuous until the
whole of the new vintage has been converted into *eau-de-vie*.
Although the method is basically straightforward, a great deal of
skill is needed to produce the best results. For example, it is
claimed that even the kind of wood used to heat the alembic plays
an important part: oak and alder are considered the best.

Armagnac is distilled from white wine made from a variety of
grapes and here again the choice of grapes will significantly affect
the final quality. In the past the grape most widely used in Armagnac was the Picquepoult, a local word meaning *pique-lèvres*, referring to the high acidity of the wine made from it, but today this
has been largely supplanted by Saint-Emilion, Colombard and
Bacco 22A. The last is a hybrid made by crossing Folle Blanche
with the American grape, Noah. It can only be grown in the sandy

soil of Bas-Armagnac. Other authorized grape varieties are Folle Blanche, Jurançon, Meslier Saint-François, Plant de Graisse and Mozac.

All these grapes are low in sugar but rich in the subtle perfumes that distinguish brandy made in Armagnac from all others, although the wine made from them is thin, acidic and low in alcohol. By law the wine must not be racked or filtered and distillation starts as soon as the fermentation is over. The grape harvest is late in Armagnac so the distillation period begins in late November or early December and lasts until the end of April. The process goes on day and night and the roaring flames of the furnace seen against the blackness of the night make a dramatic sight. Most of the small producers in Armagnac have no alembic of their own but rely on an itinerant still, which in days of yore used to be transported slowly from farm to farm behind two sturdy blond oxen. Nowadays the alembic comes by lorry, which is quicker but much less picturesque. The larger concerns have their own stills and some of them are adopting the cognac method of double distillation, but this is frowned on by the purists.

After distillation the spirit is kept in new barrels for a minimum of a year. The barrels must be made of local oak, most of which comes from the forest of Monlezun. This is unfortunately becoming rarer and consequently very expensive, but no substitute will do. Limousin oak has been tried instead but the resulting brandy is not armagnac. The local oak is dark and sappy and by some mysterious alchemy this helps to give armagnac its peculiar character as well as its beautiful colour. It follows that the cooper has an important role in Armagnac. Indeed the larger establishments employ their own. The cooper (*tonnelier*) chooses the trees and supervises their felling; he then sees that the logs are cut into manageable lengths from which the staves can be made. Because the oak is so full of sap the cooper cuts out the staves by hand with an adze. The staves are then left to dry out at the rate of a centimetre a year. The cooper himself matures slowly, serving an apprenticeship that lasts ten years before he is considered fully fledged. His chief art lies in making the finished barrel watertight but not airtight, for the contact of the air with the spirit contributes to the maturing process.

Armagnac must remain at least one year in the barrel before it can be sold, in which case it carries three stars on the label. If the label bears the letters 'VSOP'[1] it means that the brandy has been in cask for a minimum of four years, whilst the words '*Hors d'Age*' indicate a minimum period before bottling of at least five years, although it could be much longer than that. Armagnac can mature in the cask for anything up to thirty years before it starts to decline, in rare cases even longer, and indeed it is possible to find bottles whose labels claim this length of age. Brandy does not mature in the bottle, of course. In passing, it should be pointed out that the flask-shaped bottle in which armagnac is sold has no particular significance; the old bottles that can be seen in the Musée de l'Armagnac are all the same shape as a claret bottle.

It would be wrong to suppose that when you buy a bottle of armagnac the brandy it contains comes from a single barrel of a particular year. It may do, but in practice nearly all armagnac is blended. In the case of the smaller producers the blend is made by mixing different years to produce a quality that is individual to the house but does not vary too much from year to year. A good example is Château du Tariquet, a small *domaine* near Eauze. The château has an attractive façade flanked by small round towers. Close to the house there are oak trees and flowerbeds but otherwise the château is surrounded by vines, Saint-Emilion and Bacco 22A predominating. The *chai*, of which the proprietor Monsieur Pierre Grassa is rightly proud, dates back to the seventeenth century, the period when armagnac was first distilled to be drunk. Inside, the *chai* has a beautiful timbered roof made from the same local oak as the barrels it contains.

At Château du Tariquet, as we have said, the armagnac is the result of the careful blending in cask of spirit from different years, the exact combination being the secret of the *maître de chai*, in this case Monsieur Grassa himself. Monsieur Grassa believes fervently

---

1 VSOP is short for Very Special Old Pale. This classification is also used for cognac.

in upholding the traditional methods of making armagnac and the finesse of his brandy is the best of tributes to the care and skill that goes into its production.

In some of the larger firms, however, the grapes may come from a number of different growers, so the wine from which the distillate is made is already a blend. After the distillation the years are blended as at Château du Tariquet, but in some cases spirit from one area may be mixed with that from another, Haut-Armagnac with Ténarèze, for example. Such a blend could not carry the appellation of either Haut-Armagnac or Ténarèze, but would be sold under the simple label, '*Armagnac Appellation Contrôlée*'. The bigger companies often market several different qualities of armagnac, from the simple *appellation* up to a very expensive twenty- or thirty-year-old '*Hors d'Age*'. If you wish to buy a very fine armagnac the words to look for on the label are 'Bas-Armagnac', the best area, and '*Hors d'Age*', but remember that all this means is that the brandy has been in the barrel a minimum of five years and in these days when all good businessmen are anxious to turn their money over as quickly as possible it probably will not have been longer. If you would like a really old bottle you will have to look out for one that actually states the number of years in cask.

Should you be fortunate enough to enjoy a tasting before buying your armagnac – and there is no shortage of opportunities for a *dégustation* – you should look first of all at the colour. A young armagnac should be a pale amber, whilst an older one will be a deeper, richer shade. Unfortunately some young armagnacs have sugar and other elements added to them so that they take on a darker hue which, for some obscure reason, is how most people think a good armagnac should look. This artificial colouring makes the brandy look slightly more opaque than it should do if it has gone through the proper ageing process. A good armagnac will also have a strongly perfumed aroma and a high viscosity. The latter can be tested by swirling the spirit in the glass, this will leave a film on the inside of the glass from which long tears will slowly drip down like rain on a window pane. To the palate armagnac should be smooth and dry with an aftertaste that gives a comfortable warm glow. A poor armagnac will be fiery and will make your eyes blink.

Armagnac should always be warmed by cupping the hands round the glass before tasting. This will help to release the fine aromas. The locals, however, claim not to need a glass to assess the quality of an armagnac, they merely pour a little into the palms of their hands, rub them together and sniff!

Armagnac is an *eau-de-vie de vin*; in other words, like cognac, it is distilled from wine, which largely accounts for the superior quality and comparative rarity of these brandies. Most *eau-de-vie* is distilled from *marc*, the residue of the grapes that is left behind after the wine has fermented and been transferred to another container. *Eau-de-vie* can also be made from the mash of fermented fruit, hence *eau-de-vie de prune*, a plum brandy popular all over the south-west, but especially associated with the Agenais.

Many farmers in France have the hereditary right to distil twenty litres of *eau-de-vie*, duty free, for their own use each year. At one time it was possible to transfer the privilege to a new owner when the farm was sold but the French government, worried by alcoholism in France, has clamped down and stopped the practice. This has reduced the number of people entitled to distil their own *eau-de-vie* from four million in 1956 to under two million today. Even so, every farming family seems to have its supply of *eau-de-vie* and it is common when you are invited in to be given a small dish containing two large prunes swimming in a dark alcoholic liquid or a similar dish of cherries. This is not a true brandy for the fruit has been bottled in the *eau-de-vie*. To begin with the spirit is quite clear but after a year or so it takes on the colour of the fruit while the plums or cherries swell as they absorb the alcohol. The result is delicious and extremely potent.

A less powerful drink is Floc de Gascogne (Bouquet de Gascogne), a Gascon version of Pineau de Charente. It is made from grape juice drawn off before fermentation and mixed in a proportion of 3:1 with armagnac. Floc de Gascogne has an alcoholic content of 17 degrees. Served chilled it is delicious.

South-east of Eauze are the vineyards of Côtes de Gascogne, a small area producing a light, dry-white *vin de pays* from the Ugni

Blanc grapes, and a modest red. Monsieur Grassa markets an
excellent example of the white under the labels Château du
Tariquet and Domaine de Plantérieu.

A little way north of Eauze is the Tower of Lamothe. You take
the D29 to Montréal and the tower is on the left about two miles
north of Bretagne d'Armagnac. It was built in the thirteenth
century as a watch-tower and is very well preserved. Nearby are
the curiously named lakes of Zou-fou-dou where you can fish and
swim.

Another even bigger lake with excellent facilities for all kinds of
leisure activities, including windsurfing and sailing, is situated
about 10 miles north-west of Eauze at Barbotan-les-Thermes. Half
a mile further west the D626 crosses into the modern *département*
of the Landes, although in the Middle Ages this territory was still
part of the County of Armagnac, as the many towns with the
termination 'Armagnac' testify. By now the landscape has changed
radically: the hills have been left behind to be replaced by a flat
sandy plain dotted with trees. Here and there the first stands of
pine trees are forerunners of the great forest of the Landes that
lies to the west.

Soon afterwards a sign on the right-hand side of the road points
to Notre-Dame-des-Cyclistes, a small Romanesque chapel which
is now a shrine to the favourite French sport of cycling. Sport is
often described as a modern religion and here at Notre-Dame-des-
Cyclistes the truth of this observation is only too evident. The
west end of the chapel has been converted into a shop flogging
sweatshirts, postcards, badges and every other kind of tawdry
memento associated with the sport; but this is nothing to the shock,
even for a non-Christian, of finding the nave festooned with what
look like Christmas decorations and the altar covered with yellow
jerseys once worn by such cycling saints as Eddie Merckx and
Raymond Poulidor.

The N626 continues west to Labastide-d'Armagnac. Founded
in 1284 by Edward I of England, the Count of Armagnac, the
town seems to have escaped unscathed during the Hundred Years'
War but in the sixteenth century it sided with the Protestants and

was sacked by Catholic troops led by Monluc. Even so, Labastide-d'Armagnac is one of Gascony's most beautiful *bastides*.

The centre is the Place Royale, a spacious square surrounded by well-restored half-timbered houses built over arcades. The unusual size of the square, emphasized by the absence for once of a market hall, the unpaved floor surface of hard-packed sandy soil and the predominantly creamy yellow plaster of the houses all combine to give the Place Royale an airy elegance rare in such towns.

Local legend says that the square served as the inspiration for Henri IV's place Royale in Paris (now the place des Vosges), which served in turn as a model for the Georgian squares of England, but this sounds like a typical piece of Gascon exaggeration. In the north-east corner of the square is a fifteenth-century church with a huge west tower. Inside there is a fifteenth-century *pietà* and a sixteenth-century primitive Virgin Mary carved in wood.

Wandering round the town with our Gascon friend Guy Dubuc we were very struck by the number of lovingly restored houses not only in the Place Royale but in the side streets as well. One house was having a new roof of Roman tiles and the workmen were laughing, chattering in Gascon, according to Guy.

East of Eauze the D626 leads to Vic-Fézensac. After two miles a left-hand fork onto the D158 takes you to Château du Tariquet, if it is brandy you are after, and then on to Courrensan, a well-preserved fifteenth-century château still in private hands. South of the D626 the brick church of Bascous has a splendid battlemented bell-gable. Inside is a stoup made from a hollowed-out marble capital reputed to date from the seventh century.

Vic-Fézensac was originally the capital of the County of Fézensac which in the tenth century was twice the size of the County of Armagnac but which nevertheless succumbed to its predatory neighbour in the thirteenth century. Practically nothing of its former glory remains: the eleventh-century church was ravaged in the sixteenth century by the Huguenots and very badly restored while the castle of the Counts of Fézensac lies in ruins. The prefix Vic, by the way, often found in southern Gascony derives from the Latin *vicus*, meaning a village.

From Vic-Fézensac a cross-country road (D103) takes you to the pretty hill-top town of Jegun. The name is Celtic in origin, *ju* meaning tree and *guen* wine, so the cultivation of the vine clearly goes back a very long way in this part of the world.

The medieval town originally grew up round the collegiate church but in 1180 it was fortified by the Count of Armagnac, Bernard IV. Stretches of the original walls and gateways still survive. Inside are some charming medieval houses and a Renaissance one supposed to have been slept in by the *Vert Galant*. At the top of the hill, surrounded by trees, is the lovely old church. The east end is fifteenth-century but the four-bay nave is Romanesque. Jegun has an excellent small restaurant, Le Bastio, where you can eat well and inexpensively.

Continuing eastwards you cross the D930 from Condom to Auch and follow a winding road to Lavardens. Long before arriving at this hill village the great rectangular block of the Château de Lavardens can be seen jutting out on its rocky promontory, looking more like a prison than a private mansion. Closer to, the château looms gloomily over the approach road, completely dominating its surroundings.

The origins of the village go back to the Merovingian era but nothing is known of its history until the twelfth century when the church and original *château-fort* were built. During most of the Middle Ages it belonged to the Counts of Armagnac, but after their fall from grace it passed to the Seigneur de Roquelaure.

The village church has a gigantic west tower which is the only surviving part of the original castle. The rest was demolished on the orders of Henri IV at the end of the sixteenth century.

The château we see today was begun in 1620 under the orders of the Seigneur de Roquelaure. The new building was always intended to be bigger than the old and was extended westwards where the ground drops away by projecting it out over two corner arches which act as cantilevers, a brilliant solution for the times.

The main apartments are on the first floor: here there is a tunnel-vaulted hall stretching the length of the building, off which, on the north side, lead two vaulted rooms with mullion and double-transom windows. Until very recently Lavardens was in a dreadful state of repair and it will be many years before restoration work is completed and all the rooms open to the public. Nevertheless the château is well worth a visit not only for its forbidding but magnificent exterior, but also, in the apartments that can be visited, for the remarkable tiled floors arranged in a series of ingenious geometric motifs, each one different from the last. They are believed to derive from the Mozarabic art of southern Spain and are unique in France.

If Armagnac is the heart of Gascony, the country south of Eauze is the heart of Armagnac for it was here that the fortunes of the race were founded. Towards the end of the tenth century the Viking raids had reduced Gascony to such a state of anarchy that it broke up into numerous petty states whose noble overlords, while nominally still subject to the authority of the Duke, reigned supreme in their own domains.

This process of disintegration was hastened by the reigning Duke, Garcie-Sanche, who divided the Duchy between his three sons: the western and largest part he left to Sanche-Garcie, who kept the title Duke of Gascony; the middle of the region, in the vicinity of Auch, fell to Guillaume and formed the County of Fézensac; and the third portion, to the south-east, became the County of Astarac and went to Arnaud. In his turn, Guillaume subdivided the County of Fézensac, giving the south-western portion to his second son Bernard, who thus became the first Count of Armagnac.

The size of Bernard's territory was tiny, stretching only from Cazaubon south-eastwards to Riscle on the river Adour, with Nogaro, Riscle and Aignan as its chief towns: the ambitions of the Armagnacs, however, were large. Following the death in 1039 of Eudes, Duke of Aquitaine, who had inherited the title of Duke of Gascony, Bernard Tumapaler, the third Count of Armagnac, stepped in and took the Duchy by force. This success was short-lived. In 1062 Bernard was defeated by Eudes' legitimate heir Guy Geoffroi in a decisive battle near Grenade-sur-l'Adour and surrendered his rights to his conqueror: henceforth Gascony was subsumed into Aquitaine.

Undeterred by this disaster, the Armagnacs pursued their

ambitions and over the next four centuries they acquired, by one means or another, more and more territory, until they became one of the most powerful families not just in Gascony, but in the whole of France. By the middle of the fourteenth century, when Gascony was under English rule, Armagnac already occupied a key position sandwiched between English Gascony to the west and the French territories to the east. Count Jean I was nominally subject to the English king, Edward III, but when war broke out between the French and the English in 1355 the Count sided with France, so fervently that the Black Prince led a *chevauchée*, or raid, from Bordeaux into Armagnac where he captured many towns and castles and laid waste the countryside, while the Count looked helplessly on at a distance.

When the war was over, for a time at least, Jean refused to submit to the Black Prince, who had been made Duke of Aquitaine, and complained to the French King of the Prince's treatment of his Gascon subjects, thus precipitating the outbreak of renewed hostilities.

During this same period Jean was engaged in a fierce struggle with his powerful neighbour the Count of Foix which ended in his defeat and capture at the Battle of Launac in 1362. Jean was only released after paying an enormous ransom of three hundred thousand florins. He died in 1373.

The most famous of the Armagnacs was Bernard VII who through the marriage of his daughter Bonne in 1410 to Charles, the son of the Duke of Orléans, became the brother-in-law of the French King Charles VI. At that time the King suffered from intermittent bouts of madness and because of this weakness two opposing factions struggled for control of the country, one headed by his brother, the Duke of Orléans, the other by his cousin Jean the Fearless, Duke of Burgundy. When the Duke of Orléans was murdered by followers of Jean the Fearless, Bernard became leader of the Orléanist faction. For a time the Armagnacs, as the Orléanists were now called, were in the ascendancy and Bernard one of the most powerful men in France.

The intense rivalry between the Burgundians and the Armagnacs brought untold suffering to France and prevented a successful defence against the English invasion led by Henry V, who in 1415 inflicted a heavy defeat on the French forces at Agincourt. In fact to achieve their ends the Burgundians actually allied themselves to the English so that for a while the Armagnacs became seen as the national party. The English victory inevitably spelled disaster for the Armagnacs and in 1418 the Burgundians attacked Paris, entered it by treachery and Bernard and all his followers were massacred.

The death of Bernard was the beginning of a gradual but inevitable decline in the Armagnacs' fortunes. True, his son Jean IV was able to increase the family's territories by gaining possession of Comminges, long disputed between the Armagnacs and the Counts of Foix, but he unwisely fell into dispute with the King and rose in arms against him. After an initial success he was defeated and imprisoned in 1444. He was soon released but died in 1450.

The decline was accelerated by his son Jean V, whose scandalous story has already been told, and although Jean's brother and nephew survived him, the power of the Armagnacs had been broken. Eventually the county passed by inheritance to Henri of Navarre and so, when he became king in 1589, it was united to the French crown.

The early capital of Armagnac was Aignan, something that is difficult to believe when you see it today. The arcaded square is much restored and all that remains of the original fortifications is a buttress at the east end of the church which was once the respond for an arch that stretched across the street to a house on the opposite side and formed part of the main gate.

The church is Romanesque but not very interesting except for the entrance on the south side which has an arch with billet moulding and attached shafts with carved capitals. The fortified bell-tower on the north side is impressive but ruined by a grotesque cupola. Inside are two naves of unequal size, the one on the north being the larger, and a choir with a blind arcade whose columns have carved capitals. The first one on the right shows St Jerome and his lion and the next Christ and the disciples.

An altogether more exciting church is to be found at Sabazan, a mile or so to the west. Saint-Jean-Baptiste is a Romanesque building with, for this region, an unusually high-pitched roof covered with flat brown tiles. The church has a single aisleless nave ending in a semi-circular apse that, seen from the outside, makes the east end look attractively streamlined.

But the most interesting part of Saint-Jean-Baptiste is the stone west tower which has a unique half-timbered bell-chamber built out on corbels at the top, looking not unlike those temporary constructions called 'hourds' used in time of siege to protect the upper parts of castle towers from Greek fire and other missiles. Above the bell-chamber rises a steep four-sided red-tiled roof. You can climb up inside the tower to the bell-chamber where you will be rewarded by the sight of the magnificent wooden frame supporting the roof: a splendid example of Gascon carpentry.

Aignan and Sabazan are almost due south of Bascous and can be reached by continuing on the D162, crossing the N124 and turning right onto the D20. About three miles north of Aignan on the D20 a turning to the left, marked to Lupiac, takes you on to a ridge route that is part of the Ténarèze and which also marks the watershed between the valley of the Garonne to the east and the valley of the Adour to the west. From the ridge there are wide views of typical Gascon countryside, dotted with trees and criss-crossed with hedges. Down in the valleys are quiet meadows while here and there the hillsides are splashed in summer with the gold of sunflowers. At intervals along the route are attractive stone windmills, many of them, alas, in ruins though at least one has recently been restored.

About two miles further on you will see on the left-hand side a modest fifteenth-century château: this is Castelmore where D'Artagnan is supposed to have been born.

Dumas's gallant musketeer is based on the real-life hero Charles de Batz-Castelmore but most of the swashbuckling adventures recounted in *The Three Musketeers* and subsequent novels are pure invention, since little or nothing is known of Charles de Batz's early years. He was the son of Bernard de Batz-Castelmore and Françoise de Montesquieu d'Artagnan in Bigorre but the exact date and place of his birth are uncertain, no birth certificate having survived. However, since his parents lived there at the time, Castelmore seems the most likely place and the year was probably 1611.

A typical Gascon *cadet*, Charles de Batz must have left home round about 1631 to seek his fortune in Paris but there is no record of what he did there until 1646 when he appears under his mother's name of D'Artagnan in the service of Cardinal Mazarin, Louis XIV's great minister. All the stories in *The Three Musketeers* of D'Artagnan's arrival in Paris and recruitment into Tréville's company of Guards are based on a book called *Mémoires de monsieur d'Artagnan, capitaine-lieutenant de la première compagnie des mousquetaires du roi, contenant quantité de choses particulières et secrètes qui sont passées sous le règne de Louis le Grand*, written by Gatien Courtil de Sandras, which was published in Cologne in three massive volumes in 1700–1 and which purported to be the true story of D'Artagnan's secret missions on behalf of Mazarin and Louis XIV. The memoirs, although almost a total fabrication, enjoyed a great success in their day and then were forgotten until they were reissued in an abridged form in the middle of the nineteenth century and caught Dumas's eye.

D'Artagnan's actual career, though successful, was less extravagant that that of his fictional namesake. In 1657 he became a lieutenant in the King's first company of musketeers and in 1660 was sufficiently well thought of to be chosen to accompany Louis XIV to Saint-Jean-de-Luz near the border with Spain to meet his future wife and Queen, the Infanta Maria Theresa. After this the King made him responsible for guarding the disgraced finance minister Fouquet, for three years. Having acquitted this task to his master's satisfaction, D'Artagnan was promoted to Lieutenant of the King's Musketeers and was further rewarded in 1668 by being made Governor of Lille, which had recently been captured from the Spaniards.

In 1672 the war against Spain was renewed and Louis' forces invaded the Low Countries and besieged Maastricht. Here, during a particularly dangerous attack on the Spanish defences, D'Artagnan was struck in the throat by a musket ball and died instantly; but, thanks to Courtil de Sandras and Dumas, his legend lives on.

The Château de Castelmore is in private hands and cannot normally be visited but the exterior can be seen easily enough from the road. The design is typical of small manor houses of the period with the two-storey main building being flanked by four corner towers. The two round towers on the west are original, the larger square ones on the east having replaced the earlier ones when this façade was extended, probably at the beginning of the seventeenth century.

Five miles south of Lupiac, at Peyrusse-Grande, is a most remarkable church, Saint-Mamet, dating from the beginning of the eleventh century. The earliest part is the east end, which, seen from inside, has a choir and side-chapels all ending in semi-circular apses. Outside, however, the east end is rectangular with no sign of the apses. The lower two-thirds of each of the three walls is articulated by two tall, narrow blank arcades with simple round stone arches and flat wide pilasters: the effect is very severe, looking more like an example of Roman secular architecture than a church. This impression is somewhat alleviated, on the east wall especially, by the mixture of red and yellow stones and their diamond arrangement in the wall space inside the arches.

There are some blocked-up windows in the east end which have very simple stone surrounds decorated with low-relief carving of complicated interlaced motifs. Inside, the capitals of the choir have similar carvings more reminiscent of the Byzantine sculpture of Ravenna than the deep-cut figurative sculpture of Romanesque France. The rest of the church has been much altered and restored and is of little interest.

South of Peyrusse-Grande the D102 meets the D946. Here a left-hand turn leads quickly to one of the most famous monuments of the region, the *donjon* of Bassoues.

The *bastide* of Bassoues was founded in the thirteenth century by the Archbishop of Auch on the site of a Benedictine convent dedicated to Saint Fris, the hero of a famous eighth-century victory over the Saracens. Bassoues is built on an east–west ridge and has one long main street lined with half-timbered houses and running straight through the middle of the covered market with its splendid timbered roof. But the whole village is dominated by the colossal brooding mass of the *donjon*. This magnificent tower and the château it belongs to were built by Archbishop Arnaud Aubert, nephew of Pope Innocent VI, in 1371. A wing of the château running north from the tower still exists but, like everything else in the vicinity, it is completely overshadowed by its huge neighbour.

The tower is beautifully built of dressed stone from a local quarry. It is a four-storey building surmounted by an octagon and although its ground plan is square the elevation is given considerable elegance by the angled corner buttresses, only marred on the north side by the inevitable external staircase turret.

The ground-floor chamber has no windows and was used as a store room. Access was originally by an external wooden staircase to an entrance at first-floor level. Here there is a rib-vaulted room with a central boss bearing the Archbishop's coat of arms. The ribs spring from corner shafts whose capitals have beautifully carved oak leaves. There is a large opening where there was once a fireplace in the south wall and nearby a stone washbasin. In the west wall is a large window with a window-seat and there is a smaller one on the opposite side of the room. There are latrines in the north-east and south-east buttresses. It really must have been a very comfortable room.

A spiral staircase leads to the next chamber which like the one below is rib-vaulted, although here the central boss has a representation of the Archbishop himself. Here there is a surviving fifteenth-century fireplace with a coat of arms on either side and a window with window seats.

The room above has no floor, only joists, and here the roof is not vaulted but the corners are built out to support the octagon which completes the tower. The spiral staircase leads outside onto the roof platform in the middle of which is the octagon itself with its tiled roof. The four angle buttresses terminate in watch-turrets and, in between, the walls are machicolated. From the top here, on a clear day, you have a good view of the snow-clad peaks of the Pyrénées.

If the *donjon* is closed the key may be obtained from the next-door house. The rest of the château is not open but anyway has little architectural merit.

Not far east of Bassoues is the pretty hill town of Montesquieu, the cradle of the great family of the same name. Its most illustrious member was Louis XVIII's famous minister the Abbé Montesquieu, who was created a duke. The village has a well-preserved medieval gateway from which there is an agreeable view of the valley of the Osse.

Just west of Bassoues the D943 turns south to Marciac. This *bastide* town was founded in 1298 by the Lord of Montlezun, Count of Pardiac, and the Abbot of the Abbey of La Case-Dieu. The charter was given to the town by the king's seneschal Guichard de Marciac, hence the name. The idea behind the founding of the bastide was to clear a vast, marshy forest, an unhealthy place that was the haunt of outlaws.

Marciac has an extremely large arcaded square and, for a town of this size, a huge Gothic church. The west tower is gigantic with enormous buttresses and a decorated nineteenth-century spire that rises to a total height of two hundred and thirty feet.

Inside the church is a three-bay nave with side aisles covered by a lierne rib vault. The elevation of the bays of the nave is very unusual, each having a twin arcade and a clerestory lit by a rose window.

Despite the architecture being pure Gothic, the church contains some remarkable sculpture that is Romanesque in feeling. The first main pier on the right of the nave has three attached shafts facing the south aisle which are decorated with leaves and animals, and a hooded figure with some pigs. On the opposite side of the nave are some grotesque heads. There is more sculpture in the choir including Daniel in the Lions' Den and Samson prising open a lion's jaws.

In the south chapel an interesting capital depicts the legend of Saint Eloi. He is shown unmasking the devil, who has unwisely entered his forge in the guise of a woman, and seizing his nose in a pair of red-hot pincers. In a subsequent scene the saint is shown making a horse-shoe on the anvil and shoeing a horse watched by a majestic sitting figure thought to be the Merovingian King Clothar.

On the left-hand side of the rue Saint-Jean, which leads to the south door of the church, there is a good half-timbered house with carved corbels.

From Marciac the D3 follows the valley of the Arros north-westwards to Plaisance, a *bastide* founded in 1322 by Count Jean I of Armagnac and the Abbot of La-Case-Dieu which was captured and burned down by the Black Prince during his *chevauchée* of 1355.

Hostilities between the English and French had broken out in 1352 and the Count of Armagnac had played a prominent part in the successful French campaign. In 1355 Edward III sent his son the Black Prince to Bordeaux to help restore English fortunes. After consulting his advisors the Prince decided on the raid. As he wrote to the Bishop of Winchester: '... it was agreed by the advice and counsel of all the lords with us and the lords and barons of Gascony that we ought to march into Armagnac, because the Count of Armagnac was the leader of our adversary's troops and his lieutenant in the whole of Languedoc, and had done more damage to the liegemen of our most honoured lord and father the King than anyone else in the region.'

The English force left Bordeaux on October 5 and marched south-east, skirting the Landes, to Arouille, a tiny hamlet on the southern border of English Gascony, just north of Labastide d'Armagnac. Here the English force regrouped before marching south into Armagnac. They first captured the castle of Monclar, south of Cazaubon and then, by-passing Nogaro, advanced on Plaisance where they took prisoner the Lord of Montlezun and set fire to the town, presumably as an example to the Count of Armagnac. From here they proceeded to Bassoues which the Prince spared because it belonged to the Bishop of Auch.

After Bassoues '... they left the fine town of Montesquieu to the left and came to the noble town of Mirande, belonging to the Count of Comminges, full of men at arms; and the Prince stayed in the great Cistercian monastery at Berdoues; where no living thing was found. On Thursday, they halted; no damage was done to the monastery. On Friday, they left the noble, fine and rich country of Armagnac and entered the country called Astarac.'

The campaign continued eastwards towards Toulouse, which was held by the Count of Armagnac. The Prince's army was too weak to take such a strongly defended city and the Count imagined that the Black Prince would now turn back. Instead he amazed the French by crossing the rivers Garonne and Ariège, a feat thought impossible, and striking at Carcassonne which he captured without difficulty. The *chevauchée* continued as far as Narbonne which was also taken by the Anglo-Gascon force.

This was the furthest point of the raid and the Black Prince now retraced his steps and with Count Jean I still avoiding battle returned safely to Bordeaux in early December.

The people of Armagnac had therefore little reason to love the Black Prince, although his prowess in war was universally admired.

The following year the Black Prince inflicted a crushing defeat on the French in the Battle of Poitiers and was rewarded with the title of Duke of Aquitaine. His court at Bordeaux soon became a byword for sophistication and extravagance, arousing envy and anger amongst the Gascons who had to foot the bills.

In 1361 the Prince joined an abortive expedition to Spain to defend the King of Castile, Don Pedro the Cruel, against the attempt by his brother, Don Henri, Count of Trastamara, to depose him. Despite a famous victory at the battle of Najara the campaign was a failure and Don Henri became king. For the Black Prince the adventure was a disaster: the cost of the campaign was so great that he was forced to levy a special tax to pay for it. This was so unpopular that the Gascons rose in revolt while the Count of Armagnac, who following the battle of Poitiers had been forced to accept Edward III as his suzerain, refused to pay and appealed to the French King for support. A fresh outbreak of hostilities soon followed. Even worse, the Prince contracted a wasting disease in Spain from which he died nine years later.

There is not much to see at Plaisance, much better to make straight for Termes d'Armagnac further up the road. On the way Saint-Pierre-de-Tasque is worth a quick look. It dates from the eleventh century but suffered terribly at the hands of Montgoméry in the Wars of Religion. Above the west door is the mutilated remains of a tympanum depicting Christ in majesty giving the keys to Saint Peter and the law to Saint Paul. The lintel is supported by some curiously carved corbels including one of a monkey playing a harp.

At Termes d'Armagnac is a fifteenth-century château with a magnificent rectangular keep dating from the thirteenth century. *Termes* derives from the Latin *terminus* meaning end or limit and indeed the castle was built right on the southern border of Armagnac facing the county of Bigorre which in the thirteenth century was under English rule for a time before it came within the control of the Armagnacs' mortal enemy, the Count of Foix. No wonder the *donjon* is so impressive. Six storeys high it stands on the edge of a cliff overlooking the valley of the Adour. Those brave enough to tackle the 149 steps to the top will be rewarded by a spectacular view of the river below and the mountains beyond.

Thibaut de Termes (1405–67) fought alongside Joan of Arc at Orléans and was a principal witness at her trial.

A cross-country route (D108 and D25) brings you to the ancient town of Nogaro. It was founded in 1060 by Saint Austinde, the Archbishop of Auch, and soon overtook Aignan as the chief town of Armagnac until superseded by Lectoure. Saint Austinde was also the founder of the church of Saint Nicholas built on land acquired from Bernard Tumapaler, the second Count of Armagnac, who was present at the consecration of the church in 1060. The church was dreadfully damaged by Montgoméry's troops in 1569 and suffered some heavy-handed restoration in the nineteenth century; even so what remains of the eleventh-century building is worth seeing.

The west front is nineteenth-century as is the first bay of the nave. The remaining three and the east end all date from the eleventh century except for the second pier on the left which was destroyed by Montgoméry's men. The church has a nave and side aisles of the same width, although the central nave is higher and has a tunnel vault. The nineteenth-century decoration of the apse and side chapels is appalling but the entrance arch of the apse has fine capitals carved with acanthus leaves. Inside the apse are five niches within arcades with carved capitals. These have suffered dreadfully from the nineteenth-century restoration but must once have been beautiful: one depicts a lion being hunted on one face and a centaur on another; the rest show biblical scenes, Daniel in the Lion's Den, King David with musicians and the entry of Christ into Jerusalem.

There are some good capitals in the nave too. In the south aisle the last pier before the apse has a curious one on the east side with strange bearded dwarf-like figures on the corners and in between savage-looking birds of prey. On the opposite side are bizarre monsters with the bodies of lions and human heads. Elsewhere are capitals with lions or with acanthus leaves, rosettes and other ornamental decoration commonly found in Gascon sculpture of the period.

Outside, the north door has a tympanum with Christ in a mandorla surrounded by symbols of the evangelists. The lintel is supported by carved corbels, one of them depicting a mermaid holding her tail, a symbol of sexual licence.

The saddest part of the church is the remains of the cloister now hidden in the chapter house at the east end. Here there are four blocked arcades whose arches have a beautifully carved intertwined floral motif, surmounted by palm leaves. The richness of this decoration gives some idea of the importance of the church of Saint Nicholas and the wealth of this part of Gascony in the eleventh century.

By the fifteenth century the territories of the Count of Armagnac extended a long way north and east of the original heartland. South of the Lomagne was Fézensaguet which, like Armagnac, was originally part of Fézensac and was created a viscounty in the tenth century. The name Fézensaguet is the equivalent of *petit* Fézensac or little Fézensac. The viscounty remained independent until the beginning of the fifteenth century when it became absorbed by Armagnac.

Fézensaguet's main town, Mauvezin, can be reached by taking the D654 east from Fleurance. On the way is Monfort, a drab little bastide with a large stone church with a Toulouse-style bell-tower. A minor road, the D151 from Monfort, leads to Homps, a mere hamlet on a hill with many ruined houses, some of which are however, in the process of being restored. At the far end of Homps, on the hillside, is a strange stone cross. The top is round and carved on it is the figure of a man wearing a robe and with arms outstretched. It looks very primitive and is thought to be a Cathar cross.

Mauvezin was founded in the tenth century. From the beginning it was the capital of Fézensaguet, although it was not granted a charter until 1275. After the decline and fall of the house of Armagnac, control of Fézensaguet passed to the crown. At the beginning of the sixteenth century François I gave the viscounty to his sister Marguerite d'Angoulême, who married the Count of Albret, and so Fézensaguet came into the hands of one of the Armagnacs' greatest rivals.

Marguerite d'Angoulême's daughter, Jeanne d'Albret, was a militant Protestant and made Mauvezin a Huguenot stronghold, so much so it became known as Little Geneva. The original town probably occupied the site of a prehistoric *oppidum*. A vast square surrounded by ramparts and protected by the Viscount of Fézensaguet's castle was built on an escarpment overlooking the valley of the Arrats. This strongpoint made the town impregnable during the Wars of Religion but in the seventeenth century, when the Protestants were finally defeated and many expelled from France, Cardinal Richelieu ordered the defences of Mauvezin to be demolished. Now the square is merely a pleasant place in which to stroll, shaded from the sun by avenues of trees.

The centre of the town is now higher up the hill. Here there is an unusually large arcaded square in which stands an imposing fourteenth-century covered market hall with a fine timbered roof supported by round stone piers. Further down the hill is a nineteenth-century church with a splendid thirteenth-century, two-storey octagonal bell-tower.

Two miles east of Mauvezin, just north of the road to Cologne, is the Château de Bartas, the home of Guillaume Saluste de Bartas (1544–90), a Renaissance poet who was one of the stars of the court of Navarre at Nérac, but whose long-winded poems are now of interest only to academics.

The château is a typical modest Gascon *gentilhommière* dating from the end of the fifteenth century but modified by Saluste de Bartas after he inherited the house in 1567. It consists of a massive rectangular block with three corner towers, one of them octagonal, the other two round, all capped by pointed red-tiled roofs. The main building is three storeys high, although the ground floor was originally almost certainly blind, the windows having been inserted in the eighteenth century at the same time as the old mullion and transom windows were replaced in the first and second floors.

Cologne is a *bastide* founded in 1286 by the French King Philippe le Bel and Odon de Terride. It lies on the eastern border of Gascony where the land starts to flatten out and merge into the great plain that surrounds Toulouse. Stone is scarce here and brick is the common building material. Cologne has the usual arcaded central square but here some of the arches are of brick and there are a number of half-timbered houses with very attractive brick in-filling. There is a very jolly market hall with a half-timbered building growing out of the middle of it capped by a little wooden bell-turret with a witch's-hat tiled roof.

The D654 now turns south-east past the large lake of Saint-Cricq to l'Isle-Jourdain. This was the capital of another medieval county of the same name which was sold to Jean IV, Count of Armagnac, in 1421. Like Fézensaguet l'Isle-Jourdain subsequently passed to the Count of Albret. The town was originally called simply l'Isle because of its position on the river Save. Jourdain was added after Raymond de l'Isle went on the First Crusade (1096–99) and was baptized in the river Jordan. But l'Isle-Jourdain's most celebrated citizen was Raymond's brother Bertrand (1044–1124) who became Bishop of Comminges in the Pyrénées and after his death was made a saint.

Like Mauvezin, l'Isle-Jourdain was a Protestant stronghold and its castle and fortifications were destroyed in 1621 by order of the King. As a result there is not a great deal to see. The church is eighteenth-century, although there is a fifteenth-century bell-tower at the east end spoiled by modern crenellation. The town has two squares. The older one, called the *marcadieu*, has arcades on two sides; the larger one has the market hall and an elegant classical town hall.

Due west of l'Isle-Jourdain is Gimont, a *bastide* founded in 1266 on a narrow ridge just south of the main road to Auch. The town square is almost filled by a market hall so large that the high street goes right through the middle of it. Like many similar halls in Gascony it has a splendid timbered roof supported on stone piers arranged so that there are two aisles on the north side of the road and one on the south.

East of the square is a Gothic church dating from the fourteenth and fifteenth centuries built of brick in the Toulouse style, with a tower restored in the seventeenth century. Inside there is one wide nave with side chapels and a pentagonal choir. In the first chapel on the right is a remarkable Renaissance triptych. The middle painting is an extraordinary crucifixion scene from which the main protagonist, Christ, is missing. The viewpoint of the picture is also unusual: it is painted as if from the top of Calvary. In the foreground, amid a landscape of jagged rocks, are various figures, a turbanned soldier holding a sword, a woman with a child at her breast and on the left a figure in a plumed hat preceded by another soldier and a dog.

To left and right are the two thieves crucified with Christ. The one on the right is being transported to heaven by his guardian angel while St Michael fights a rearguard action against demons. Meanwhile, devils drag the unrepentant thief down to hell.

The inside of the flaps have low-relief sculptures depicting on the left the sorrowing Mary and on the right St John. When the flaps are closed they show on the outside painted pictures of Mary Magdalene on the left and Martha on the right. There was probably originally a cross standing in front of the triptych which would account for its absence from the painting inside. The triptych is thought to be Flemish and to date from round about 1530.

Gimont's other great attraction is the Comtesse du Barry factory at the far east end of the town. This excellent firm is famous for the high quality of its preserved foods. Amongst the gastronomic delicacies processed here are *foie gras, civet de lièvre, cassoulet, salmis de palombe* and *pâté de foie truffé*.

South of Gimont and l'Isle-Jourdain the rivers Arrats, Gimone and Save grow closer as you approach nearer their sources in the Plateau de Lannemezan, flowing through narrow valleys, divided from each other by low ranges of hills.

From l'Isle-Jourdain follow the D634 southwards down the valley of the Save. Just north of Endoufielle turn right towards Castillon-Savès and then left onto the D39 to Cazaux-Savès. A little way along on the right is the entrance to the magnificent Château de Caumont.

A steep bumpy track climbs a thickly wooded hillside to emerge into a clearing bounded on the far side by a wall with towers at each end and a central gateway. Beyond the gateway is a large open space the other side of which is the château.

Caumont was built round about 1530 and is a good example of the transition between medieval and Renaissance architecture. Its plan is one that was to become common in France over the next one hundred and fifty years: a main building with a wing on either side projecting forward and enclosing a large courtyard completed on the fourth side by a screen wall in which is the entrance. This Renaissance ground plan is offset by the massive corner towers which hark back to the Middle Ages, although their military appearance is softened by their pointed slate-covered roofs.

From the outside Caumont certainly looks like a castle with its high walls and spectacular position on a spur of the hill with steep drops on three sides. In the sixteenth century this impression would have been reinforced by the fact that the approach was protected by a deep ditch that could only be crossed by a draw-bridge. This has now been replaced by a proper bridge and most of the screen wall has disappeared except for two smaller towers with pepperpot roofs that project from the side wings.

Once inside the courtyard things look different. Ahead is the main building. It is built of alternate courses of brick and stone and has two storeys surmounted by a high-pitched slate roof of the kind you would expect to see in the Loire rather than in Gascony. The mullion and transom windows on the first floor look original as do the dormer windows above, but only the stone surrounds to the two long windows on the ground floor are authentic. The entrance is on the left side and has a round-headed arch set within columns and surmounted by a cornice – all reasonably classical. Above, however, is a decidedly unclassical pediment which looks Flemish if anything. The left wing has mullion and transom windows on both floors and at first-floor level there is a brick balcony built out on heavy corbels so that it looks more like machicolation than a place to promenade. I feel sure that this reference back to the military architecture of the past must have been quite deliberate on the part of the architect.

The other wing is seventeenth-century and has a five-arch arcade on the ground floor. The arches are of brick with heavy stone rustication. The windows are mullion and transom again, which seems deliberately archaic. Certainly, despite the difference in dates, the whole ensemble is very harmonious.

The inside is of no great interest except for the turned staircase which is very early. Before this period there were only circular tower staircases.

Caumont was built by Pierre de Nogaret la Valette whose grandson was the famous Duke of Epernon (1559–1642), the favourite of the French King Henri III. According to legend he once entertained Henri IV at the château.

After Caumont, continue on the D39 through Cazaux-Savès to Samatan, an important market town which was pillaged and burned by the Black Prince during his *chevauchée* in 1355.

Immediately south of Samatan is the ancient cathedral city of Lombez. Originally a Celtic–Iberian settlement, Lombez flourished in the Gallo-Roman era under the name of Lumbarium. The Roman town was destroyed first by the Barbarians and later in the eighth century by the Saracens and its fortunes did not revive until a Benedictine monastery was founded on the banks of the Save in the ninth century. Such was the success of the monks in settling and farming the site that the monastery was promoted to an abbey in the twelfth century and became a cathedral in 1317. Meanwhile a prosperous town grew up in the shadow of the church.

The fourteenth-century Gothic cathedral of Sainte-Marie is built of brick in the style of the church of the Jacobins at Toulouse. The west front is rather plain but on the left, slightly set back, is a very elegant example of a Toulouse bell-tower. Octagonal in plan, it has five storeys, each one slightly recessed and smaller than the one below, with paired mitred windows on each face.

The tower is not easy to see from the west and anyway this is not its best side; much better to walk down the north side of the church to the east end by the river where there is a good view. From here, too, you can see the magnificent polygonal apse with its narrow Gothic windows between tall brick buttresses surmounted by pointed finials. If you have time, take the path along the opposite bank of the river which can be reached from the town's main bridge. From this distance it is easier to appreciate the fine proportions of the tower which looks almost frivolous contrasted with the austere fortress-like nave.

Inside the cathedral are two naves of unequal size, the one on the north being the smaller, although this is obscured by the fact that the right-hand piers of the main nave merge into the internal buttresses on the south side. The rib-vaulted roof is supported by tall round brick piers, unadorned except for the narrow capitals high up at the level of the small clerestory windows, and even these have very restrained decoration. The east end has three tall lancet windows with sixteenth-century glass.

Near the entrance are two Romanesque capitals used as stoups, thought to come from the twelfth-century abbey, and in the first chapel on the left is a thirteenth-century lead font with contrasting bands of decoration on the outside, the style of the upper being Romanesque and the lower Gothic. Also on the left is a collection of the cathedral's treasures behind glass.

Lombez is right on the southern border of the territories of the Counts of Armagnac. Beyond is the County of Comminges, the first of the mountain fiefs, which will be covered in the next chapter. For the moment then let us take the D626 west across the hills to the parallel valley of the Gimone. At Saramon turn left down the D12 to Simorre, where you will find one of the most remarkable churches in the whole of Gascony.

The name Simorre derives from the Celtic–Iberian *cimgorra* (*cim* = remarkable and *gorra* = height), the name given to the original prehistoric settlement on a hill south-east of the present village.

This site was abandoned after a disastrous fire in 1140 and a new town was founded in the valley close to a Benedictine monastery which at that time was already over three hundred years old, the first mention of it being in a document dated 817. The medieval town prospered and was granted a charter in 1280.

By the end of the thirteenth century the old Romanesque church was no longer big enough to serve the increased population of Simorre and a new church was begun, which was consecrated in 1309. Built in brick in the Gothic style of Toulouse this extraordinary battlemented building, bristling with turrets and towers, looks more like a castle than a church and seems designed to keep the world at a distance rather than welcome the faithful in. The plan of the church is cruciform with a two-bay nave, a transept and a single-bay choir, but this is only apparent inside; outside, seen from any angle except the west, the building looks centrally planned. What appears to be a battlemented keep, but is in fact a squat octagonal crossing-tower, is flanked on the north, south and east sides by the rectangular projections of the transepts and choir, each of which has corner towers and battlemented walls. This impression of a centrally planned castle is accentuated by a low square bell-tower built in the angle between the north transept and the nave.

It has to be said that the fortress-like appearance of the church owes a great deal to Viollet-le-Duc who completely restored the church in 1848. Originally the nave, crossing-tower and bell-tower all had low-pitched, Roman-tiled roofs which the great restorer had lowered so that they were hidden behind his newly added battlements. But, even allowing for these romantic alterations, the church of Simorre must always have looked a formidable construction. Inside, the architecture is equally austere but there are some good stained-glass windows. The earliest of them, high up in the east wall of the choir, dates from the fourteenth century. The three below and the window in the southern transept are fifteenth-century; that in the north transept is nineteenth-century and the remaining three in the nave date from the sixteenth century and may have been made by Arnold de Moles.

Simorre is in Astarac, a county created in the tenth century by the Gascon duke, Garcie-Sanche. Astarac lies south of Auch and stretches westwards from Simorre to the eastern borders of ancient Armagnac in the vicinity of Montesquieu. The Counts of Astarac seem to have been less successful in acquiring territory than their ambitious neighbours but they did maintain their independence until the fifteenth century when the line died out. It is significant that in 1362 the Count of Astarac allied himself with Gaston Fébus, Count of Foix in his quarrel with Jean I and fought on his side in the decisive Battle of Launac when the Count of Armagnac was crushingly defeated and taken prisoner.

In 1355 the Black Prince, in the course of his *chevauchée*, crossed Astarac from west to east, burning down Samatan *en route*. This was going against the grain of the country for Astarac is famous for its narrow asymmetrical river valleys with their steep wooded western slopes and more gradual eastern ones. The soil here is poor and farms are few and far between. Much of the country is wild and remote, so much so that during the Second World War the Resistance used these hills as a base for their operations in the region.

It makes good sense, then, to explore Astarac by journeying down the river valleys from north to south. The capital, Mirande, is eleven miles south-west of Auch on the N21. This *bastide* was founded in 1281 by Bernard IV, Count of Astarac, and the Abbot of Berdoues on the banks of the river Baïse. There is little of interest in Mirande: the Place d'Astarac still has some of the original arcades and on its north side a street leads to the fifteenth-century church of Notre-Dame, a building chiefly remarkable for its massive and ugly west tower built over a porch and supported in front by flying buttresses that arch across the road.

South of Mirande the D939 leads to Berdoues-Ponsampère where the great abbey, whose monks helped to found Mirande, once stood. Now, sadly, almost nothing remains to be seen. A mile further on is a left-hand turning to Belloc-Saint-Clamens. Here, in a remote valley, is a small church dating from the eleventh century, which houses a rare Gallo-Roman sarcophagus. Belloc itself consists of a few scattered houses, the largest of which has the key to Saint-Clamens.

The church stands, surrounded by trees, a little apart from the rest of the hamlet in a green field under the shadow of the hill. It is a beautiful setting, a sacred grove where the gods of nature were worshipped for centuries before the first Christian missionaries arrived (sometime in the sixth or seventh century), and founded Saint-Clamens on the site of a pagan temple.

It is a simple aisleless church with a two-bell western gable. The oldest part is the polygonal east end. This has three round-headed windows with short stubby columns on either side. Curiously, these columns are not responds for the arches themselves but for two stone slabs that jut out at right angles between the capitals and the springing of the arch. The capitals are carved in low relief with palm leaves, vine scrolls and some purely geometrical motifs.

It seems that there was once a Roman villa in the valley and in the south porch you will find a tombstone carved with the Roman letters D M CANTIST ARVILLIAN which is short for D M CANTISTII ARVLLIANI, some letters having been combined: NT and TII in the second line and NI at the end of the third line. Even so the sculptor seems to have miscalculated and the last line, especially, is very cramped. The full inscription, with everything spelled out, would have read DIIS (DEUS) MANIBUS CAII ANTISTII ARULLIANI meaning To the God of departed souls (or as we would say R I P) CAIUS ANTISTIUS ARULIANUS.

The inside of the church is almost bare and your eyes are immediately attracted by the sarcophagus that serves as the base of the altar at the east end. It has two parts: the upper is a piece of yellowish sandstone with large three-quarter profile heads on each corner with long wavy hair out of which pokes a small wing. The heads are presumably representations of a god of some kind, perhaps Apollo but more likely, in view of the wing, Mercury, a very popular Celtic deity. In the centre is an empty panel flanked on either side by winged cupids pushing wheels on the end of sticks which look like a child's toy but are meant to symbolize life. The first cupid on the far left looking straight ahead stands for childhood; the next looking back over his shoulder represents adolescence. On the right of the panel the third cupid, maturity, looks towards old age whose wheel is broken symbolizing death.

The lower part of the sarcophagus is of darker stone. In the centre is a medallion with the portrait of an unknown Roman supported below by two small figures and on either side by two larger figures, all of them naked except for cloaks. To left and right are allegorical representations of the seasons. The first figure on the left, holding a bunch of flowers, stands for spring; next, with a sheaf of corn, is summer. On the far right, bearing a basket of fruit and an olive branch is autumn. The last figure, the only one wearing a tunic, who holds a bare branch, is winter. In between the legs of the figures are stooks of corn and various animals, to the left a ram and a dog and on the right a deer and a wild boar. The ends of the sarcophagus are also carved: on the left two jolly cupids are harvesting the grapes and on the right they are carrying them off in a basket suspended from a pole between them.

In the nave is a painted Crucifixion thought to date from the twelfth century and to have been repainted in the sixteenth.

After our visit to Saint-Clamens we drove up into the hills above the church and found an idyllic picnic site full of butterflies. We were completely alone except for a shepherd and his flock on a hillside so far away that they were little more than specks. But, even at that distance, the shepherd's dog saw us and barked continuously until we moved out of his sight.

From Belloc continue south on the D939 to Saint Michel. Turn right here to Miélan; soon after, a right turn (D3) takes you to Tillac. This is a very old fortified village with a main street bordered by half-timbered houses with jettied upper storeys supported on wooden posts. At either end is a square defensive tower with an entrance arch, the eastern one having been blocked up at some time. Unlike many of these medieval towns Tillac has not been discovered and restored: it looks a bit scruffy and poverty-stricken and is therefore perhaps closer to what it would really have looked like in the Middle Ages than most.

Five miles west of Miélan is a famous viewing spot, the Puntous de Laguian, where there is an unsurpassed view to the south of the highest peaks of the Pyrenean chain.

CHAPTER 3

THE MOUNTAIN FIEFS

AT FIRST SIGHT it may seem odd that a book on Gascony should include the Pyrénées. For most people the word Gascony conjures up the sunny hill country of D'Artagnan's homeland, Armagnac, with its dusty yellow soil; yet the central part of the mountain chain has always had strong links with the country to its north.

Branches of the same Celtic–Iberian tribes that colonized the lowlands of Gascony in prehistoric times also settled in the mountains. This is hardly surprising since they had to cross the Pyrénées in the first place and one of the main routes they used led northwards down the Vallée d'Aren towards Tarbes. When the Romans conquered Aquitaine in 56 BC they identified three mountain tribes: the Bigerriones, who had settled a large area stretching northwards from Gavarnie in the mountains as far north as the left bank of the Adour, near Rabastens; the Convenes, whose territory lay to the east of those of the Bigerriones and had Lugdunum Convenarum (Saint-Bertrand-de-Comminges) as their capital, and, further east again, the Consorani who occupied a smaller wedge of land, much of it in the mountains, south of Saint-Lizier. All three belonged to the larger group of tribes living south and west of the Garonne, the Novempopulani.

But quite apart from these ethnic and cultural links there were good geographical reasons for the mountain tribes and their descendants to belong to Gascony. The Pyrénées have a series of north–south valleys and passes which communicate easily with the lowlands. East–west journeys, on the contrary, are very difficult, even by car. The passes are high up, with steep, twisting roads, and during the winter many of them are cut off by snow. Modern snow-clearing equipment can keep some of the passes open for skiers but many defeat all attempts and are closed for six months of the year.

So, right up to the twentieth century, if the mountain people wanted to leave their high valleys their natural route was north-wards and, indeed, since prehistoric times the Pyrenean shepherds have moved their flocks in the spring to spend the short summer months high up in the lush green mountain pastures, bringing them down again in the autumn preparing to winter in the Gascon lowlands. This twice-yearly *transhumance* as the migration is called often involved long distances, some of the shepherds taking their flocks as far north as the Pays d'Albret. Cattle were also pastured in the high mountains and brought down at the end of the summer to be sold in the market towns of Saint-Gaudens, Tarbes and elsewhere. But, while the mountain peoples of the central Pyrénées maintained this regular communication with the Gascon lowlands, the impenetrable mountain crests cut them off from their immediate neighbours in the County of Foix to the east and Béarn on the west.

In the early Middle Ages the lands of the Bigerriones, Consorani and Convenes were translated by the Carolingians into three great fiefs ruled by powerful counts, Bigorre, Comminges and Couserans, which remained independent until the fifteenth century, when they were united with the Kingdom of France. They were finally wiped off the political map in the French Revolution when they were absorbed within the départements of Haute-Garonne and Hautes-Pyrénées; but nine hundred years of history cannot be suppressed so easily and in the central Pyrénées the old names survive to this day.

1 The Comminges

If I had to choose the part of Gascony that I like best I would plump without hesitation for the Comminges. It must have been some time in the early 1970s that we first drove south from Agen to visit the famous cathedral of Saint-Bertrand-de-Comminges. From our first sight of this noble church in its splendid mountain setting we fell in love with the Comminges and have been going back there regularly ever since.

Not only does the Comminges have magnificent mountain scenery with remote lakes and thundering cascades but there are calm green valleys with lush meadows which in early summer are full of wild flowers. The high valleys are sparsely populated but here and there are isolated hamlets with two or three houses grouped round a tiny stone church, some of which date from the eleventh and twelfth centuries. Many of these churches have fragments of antique funeral monuments, altars or crude sculpted heads of pagan gods incorporated in the walls as if their founders were taking no chances and hoped to placate the ancient deities by including them in the fabric of the building. A number of these churches also have rare Romanesque frescoes inside.

There are no large towns in the Comminges but in Luchon it has one of the most attractive of all the Pyrenean resorts which makes an excellent base from which to explore the mountains. Man has lived in the Comminges for a very long time indeed. In 1949 the jawbone of a Neanderthal man between 300,000 and 400,000 years old was found in a cave near Montmaurin; but more interesting are the archaeological discoveries made by Edouard Lartet in 1860 near the village of Aurignac. He found finely knapped flint tools and beautifully carved reindeer bones dating back 40,000 years. Lartet was inspired by these finds to make the first attempt to elaborate a prehistoric chronology, giving the name Aurignacian to the earliest Palaeolithic era (40,000 to 20,000 BC). These Palaeolithic men were troglodytes who lived by hunting and there are a number of caves in the central Pyrénées where traces of them have been found. The most exciting discoveries are the beautiful cave paintings of bison and other animals which are the

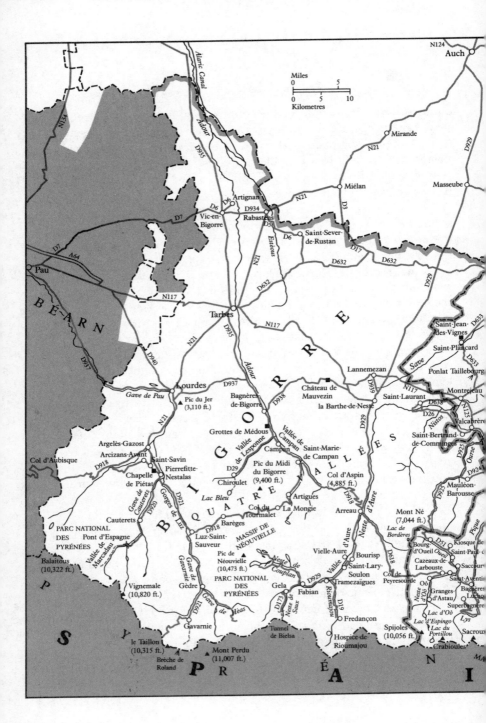

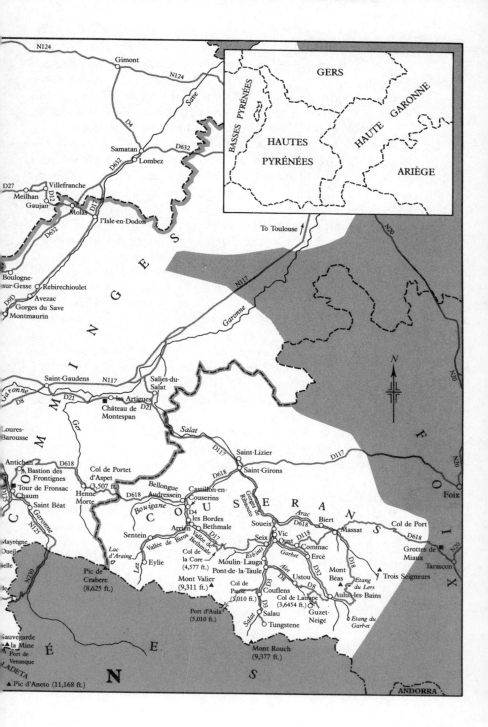

earliest known form of art. The best cave paintings in the region are to be found in the Grottes de Niaux, south of Tarascon in the Ariège. Strictly speaking this is outside the limits of Gascony but it would be perverse not to mention them when we are speaking of an era over 20,000 years before the Duchy was created.

Recorded history begins in the Comminges with the arrival of Pompey the Great. In 72 BC he spent the winter in the high valley of the Garonne on the way back from Spain after a successful campaign against the rebel Roman general Sertorius. The mountains to the south were inhabited by fierce mountain tribes who were constantly raiding the nearby Roman settlements of the Narbonnais, and Pompey decided to pacify the region by founding a city at the point where the Garonne leaves its mountain valley. The site he chose was at the foot of the Celtic–Iberian *oppidum* where the cathedral of Saint-Bertrand-de-Comminges now stands.

The citizens were made up of some of the veterans of his own legions, the remnants of Sertorius's defeated army and local tribesmen, and were known as *Convenae* or peoples brought together, hence the full name of Pompey's city Lugdunum Convenarum. The name *Convenae* was extended to describe the whole region north of the valley of the Garonne and gradually over nine hundred years changed to *Commenicus*, then *Commenge*, and finally Comminges.

Lugdunum flourished and by the end of the first century AD had 60,000 inhabitants. According to the Jewish historian Josephus, Herod and his wife Herodias (who asked for the head of John the Baptist) were exiled to Lugdunum Convenarum and it seems likely that they died there.

In AD 408 the Roman city in the plain was destroyed by the Vandals but the citadel on the hill survived until 587 when the rebel Gundovald was defeated by the Burgundian King Guntram. Gundovald was thrown to his death from a rock known to this day as the Matacan ('kill the dog') and the victorious Burgundians razed the citadel to the ground.

There is no record of the creation of the County of Comminges but it was almost certainly at the end of the tenth century. A Count of Comminges, Raymond, is mentioned in a church document of

979 but whether he was the first is unclear. Almost nothing is known about his successors until the early twelfth century when Bernard I became Count. Bernard's early years were spent crusading against the Arabs in Spain and he was clearly a belligerent character because on his return to the Comminges, some time after 1118, he began a long and ultimately unsuccessful dispute with his powerful neighbour, the Count of Bigorre, over possession of the Viscounty of Aure, a rich mountain valley south of Arreau. But Bernard's greatest achievement was his marriage to Dias, daughter of Godfrey the Seigneur of Samatan and Muret, which greatly enlarged his territories to the north and north-east of the county.

Two ineffectual Counts succeeded Bernard I and then in 1176 his grandson Bernard IV assumed the title. Bernard IV is the most famous of the Counts: his contemporaries regarded him as a 'very parfait gentle knight' and his deeds were celebrated by troubadours, but he was a shrewd politician as well. When the infamous Simon de Montfort, leader of the crusade against the Albigensian heresy, invaded the south of France, Bernard IV joined forces with Raymond of Toulouse to resist the aggressor. Yet, although he ended up on the losing side, indeed he participated in the crucial Battle of Muret (1213) when Simon de Montfort inflicted his most crushing defeat on the combined forces of the southern nobility, Bernard escaped largely unscathed and, in spite of the Comminges being occupied for a short time by the Crusaders, he managed to keep the county intact.

Bernard died in 1225. The subsequent history of the Comminges is dominated by dynastic quarrels and by the attempts of the county's powerful neighbours, the houses of Foix-Béarn and Armagnac, to gain control of it. During the same period the prestige of the Counts was eclipsed by the increasing power of the Bishops of Saint-Bertrand-de-Comminges. Eventually, after the death in 1336 of Bernard VIII, without heirs, the Comminges became a royal fief and was finally united with the French crown in 1454.

The direct route to the Comminges is down the D929 from Auch to La Barthe-de-Neste, just south of Lannemezan. Turn left onto the D938 which follows the river valley of the Neste and then at Saint-Laurent onto the D26 to Saint-Bertrand-de-Comminges.

The Gothic cathedral of Saint-Bertrand is one of the great sights of the Pyrénées. It stands on a small isolated hill, dominating the valley of the Garonne against a backdrop of thickly wooded mountains. The massive buttresses and west tower with its curious wooden bell-chamber can be clearly seen some way off as you approach across the plain. At the foot of the hill are the pathetic vestiges of the Roman city of Lugdunum Convenarum, but these are hardly worth a detour. Saint-Bertrand itself is still encircled by ancient ramparts and you have to pass the medieval Porte Majou before climbing up the steep, winding road to the cathedral square where you will find one or two old houses as well as a much-needed café.

Saint-Bertrand was founded by Bertrand de l'Isle who became Bishop of Comminges in 1073 and whose reforming zeal earned him his sainthood. Work on the cathedral began circa 1120 and continued until about 1140. Bertrand de l'Isle died in 1123 and was canonized at the beginning of the thirteenth century. Bertrand de Goth, who later became Pope Clement V, was Bishop of Comminges from 1295 to 1299 and during this time decided to enlarge and modernize the old building. Most of what you see today dates from this period: of the original Romanesque building only the west tower, the porch and part of the cloister survive.

The original entrance was by the west porch in the bell-tower. Above the door is a lintel with carvings of the twelve apostles. This is surmounted by a carved tympanum representing the Adoration of the Magi. The kings advance from the left bearing gifts while St Bertrand himself stands proudly on the right, his hand raised in benediction. Above this group angels with censers celebrate the nativity of Christ.

On the right of the entrance is a double capital showing a miser being swallowed by hell. A heavy purse hanging round his neck weighs him down and snakes and devils add to his torments.

Inside the tower is a large chamber with high pointed arches supporting an eight-ribbed vault. Once beyond the tower the rest of the church is Gothic and of little interest except for the carved wooden choir stalls. They were commissioned by Bishop Jean de

Mauléon and installed in 1535. The ensemble consists of a rood screen, the bishop's throne and sixty-six stalls. They are of course similar in style to the celebrated stalls at Auch but the carving is cruder and, to my taste, livelier. Although the composition and execution of the stalls belong for the most part to the Renaissance there are numerous small carvings that have the exuberance of medieval figure sculpture, witness the lascivious siren seducing a man and a schoolmaster flogging a pupil.

Easily the most attractive part of Saint-Bertrand, however, is the cloister. It is reached by the door to the right of the façade which nowadays is the usual entrance to the cathedral. The first sight of the cloister is unforgettable: on three sides is a gallery with round-headed Romanesque arches on the inside carried on twin columns with carved capitals. Immediately opposite the entrance is a column made up of four beautifully carved figures of the evangelists serving as caryatids; but what makes the cloister unique are the arches on the south side which are open to the exterior, revealing a beautiful view of the calm valley below with cows placidly grazing.

The fourth side of the cloister was rebuilt in the fifteenth century. It contains ancient tombs including one believed to belong to Bishop Hugues de Châtillon (d. 1352) whose marble monument can be seen in the chapel on the north side of the nave. In the east gallery is the famous epitaph of Canon Ardengost (d. 1134).

> Hic jacet in tumba rosa mundi, non rosa munda,
> Non redolet, sed olet quod redolere solet.

Roughly translated this means: 'In this tomb lies a rose of the world, not a fresh fragrant rose but one that smells of the grave.' This epitaph was used as a clue by Simon Raven in his bizarre novel *The Roses of Picardie*. M. R. James made Saint-Bertrand-de-Comminges the setting for one of his most chilling tales, *Canon Alberic's Scrapbook*.

Down at the foot of the hill the D26 continues to Saint-Just-de-Valcabrère which strikes me as architecturally more interesting than Saint-Bertrand. It stands surrounded by cypress trees in the open country just outside the village of Valcabrère. Before looking at the church itself, go to the east end where there is a wonderful view of Saint-Just in the foreground and beyond, in the middle distance, Saint-Bertrand on its hill, against a background of rugged mountains.

Saint-Just was built by St Bertrand at the end of the eleventh century on what was almost certainly a pagan burial site, since innumerable fragments of funeral monuments have been found there, some of which were incorporated in the fabric of the church. It is dedicated to Saints Just and Pasteur, two young brothers who were put to death in Spain during the reign of Diocletian.

The entrance, on the south side, has a round-headed arch with billet and heavy roll mouldings springing from carved capitals supported by column figures, two on each side. Those on the left represent Saints Just and Etienne; on the right are Saints Pasteur and Hélène. The capitals above their heads depict scenes from their lives or martyrdoms. St Etienne is shown being stoned to death but the significance of St Hélène's capital is unclear. Above the column figures is a carved tympanum with Christ in a mandorla flanked by the evangelists while angels fly overheard. Despite the difference in scale, the composition of the south entrance of Saint-Just is much more satisfying and harmonious than that of the west entrance to Saint-Bertrand.

The west end and side walls of the nave are very plain but the east end is complex and exciting: to understand it properly you need to look at the inside. The nave has four rectangular bays of unequal size covered by a barrel vault, with vaulted side aisles. The arcades of the nave have massive rectangular piers, with attached columns and twinned columns which are clearly much older and presumably come from the ruins of the Roman city. Fragments of antique architraves and friezes are also employed. Some of these, for example on the easternmost pier on the south side, mark the level of the supports for the original wooden roof, the nave having been raised when the vaults were constructed. On the west wall is an antique funeral plaque of Valeria Severa and of the priest Patroclus dated AD 347.

But the most interesting part of the interior is the east end, consisting of a barrel-vaulted choir terminating in a semi-circular apse with semi-dome. The entrance has twin columns which do not reach the springing of the vault and therefore have no function other than a decorative one. The interior of the apse has a wall arcade with simple carved capitals. The choir is flanked by vaulted apsidal chapels entered by horse-shoe arches supported by squat twin columns.

Back outside, the east end does not at first seem to reflect the interior plan: the apse can only be seen at roof level, below is a curious arrangement of shallow arches looking rather like radiating chapels turned inside out. In fact, the end of the church is rectangular with a buttress either side of the central window. The tops of these buttresses are linked by an arch and on each side again arches cover the space between the buttresses and the corner of the building, and the angles between these corners and the projecting side chapels. These five shallow arches produce delightful effects of light and shade which give the chevet of Saint-Just an unusual sculptural quality.

A more leisurely approach to the Comminges can be made by driving south from Auch on the D929 to Masseube and turning left onto the D27 to Villefranche and thence, via Gaujan and Molas, to l'Isle-en-Dodon. The route takes you through some wild hills which in the Second World War were a sanctuary for the Maquis. At Meilhan a vast monument commemorates Resistance heroes who were rounded up by the Germans and summarily shot. A more straightforward journey is from Auch to Gimont; down the D4 to Samatan and then five miles south of Lombez left on to the D9 and D17.

L'Isle-en-Dodon has another remarkable brick-built fortified church dating from the fourteenth century. The west end has a sixteenth-century octagonal tower built over a porch and capped by a witch's-hat roof. The Gothic nave, built in the Toulouse style, is undistinguished but in the chapel on the north side of the choir is a sixteenth-century stained-glass window showing St Sebastian being shot at by medieval bowmen: above his head is the sign of the Trinity and, below, Adam and Eve are shown in Paradise. Eve's anatomy is distinctly unconvincing.

But the best part of the church is the heavily fortified east end:

the polygonal apse, with its heavy angle-buttresses, extends high above the roof of the nave, so that at first sight it looks more like a castle keep than the chevet of a church, an impression reinforced by two rectangular crenellated turrets, which project from the corners, where the apse meets the nave.

There is little more to say about l'Isle-en-Dodon except that Wellington stayed there on the eve of Toulouse, the last battle of the Peninsular Campaign, after which Napoleon abdicated and was exiled to Elba.

From l'Isle-en-Dodon continue south down the valley of the Save to the hamlet of Rebirechioulet where a minor road (D9e) leads via Avezac to the Gorges de la Save. Here the river has cut its way through an isolated rocky outcrop that geologically is related to the Pyrénées. The gorge is narrow, only wide enough to contain the Save and a narrow road, and the cliffs are not high but this short stretch of about three miles is very pretty and an ideal place for a picnic. The Gorges are a favourite place for teaching novices the techniques of mountaineering.

Between 1912 and 1922 some important archaeological finds were made in the Gorges including the famous Vénus de Lespugue, a statuette carved from a piece of mammoth ivory that dates from the Aurignacian period. It has very exaggerated breasts and thighs and was probably a fertility symbol. It is now in the Musée de l'Homme in Paris but there is a copy in the small museum in the village of Montmaurin, a museum largely devoted to prehistory.

At the end of the Gorges is the chapel of Hillère which contains a beautiful wheel-shaped Roman mosaic. At the next junction turn left to the Gallo-Roman villa of Montmaurin. This archaeological site has the most extensive and best-preserved Roman remains in all Gascony, giving a remarkably clear picture of the life of a rich Roman landowner. The original building, dating from the first century AD, was a simple farmhouse surrounded by barns and other dependencies but in the fourth century this was replaced by a marble villa with every modern comfort: running water, under-floor central heating, hot baths and glass windows, decorated throughout with beautiful mosaics. The villa covered an area of forty-five acres and there were two hundred rooms, many of them faced with marble from the Pyrénées. This was no longer the house of a farmer but the country retreat of a rich Roman businessman or official, attracted, no doubt, by the beauty of the secluded valley.

The original entrance was approached via two long colonnaded, covered walks that projected in a semi-circle from the south side of the villa. Contained within the arms of the hemi-style, on the left, excavations have revealed the ground plan of a hexagonal Gallo-Roman temple.

Beyond the entrance wings was a large courtyard surrounded by a peristyle. Immediately to the left of the entrance is the wing which contained the hypocausts that provided the underfloor heating for the villa and here too was the *nymphaeum*, a pool surrounded by columns and bordered to the south by a small garden contained within an apse. Some of the columns of the *nymphaeum* have been re-erected and here, in particular, it is possible to imagine the luxurious life of these wealthy, pleasure-loving Roman colonists.

To the north of the main courtyard is another smaller one around which are arranged the private rooms. Outside were the vegetable gardens and the servants' quarters. The sheer size of Montmaurin, the number of rooms and the complexity of arrangements show that life in fourth-century Aquitaine had reached a high degree of sophistication, sadly soon to be eclipsed by successive waves of invaders.

From the village of Montmaurin take the D69c to join the D633 and drive south along the valley of the Save to Saint-Plancard. Just before you reach the village you will see on a low western hill the tiny chapel of Saint-Jean-des-Vignes, appropriately enough backed by a small vineyard. This little church has two features commonly found in the Comminges: it has an apse at both ends and the interior is decorated with frescoes.

The entrance to Saint-Jean-des-Vignes is on the south side alongside a projecting bell-gable. If the door is locked the key may be obtained from the *épicerie* in the same street as the *mairie*. The inside of the church is very plain with a flat wooden ceiling and plastered walls, only relieved at the east end by the frescoes, although these are very faded and not easy to make out.

The artist seems to have had dificulty fitting his composition round the three small windows in the apse, so the figure of Christ in Majesty is placed to the left of the central window. He is surrounded by the evangelists. On Christ's right hand, above the left window, a tall angel, holding a long sceptre, welcomes two of the blessed to paradise. Below them a battlemented wall represents the heavenly city of Jerusalem. The scene is balanced by one on the right-hand side showing a devil dragging the damned into the flames of hell.

Above the centre window are the Magi offering their gifts to the infant Jesus who sits on his mother's knee. The kings' jewel-studded crowns, their style of dress and staring eyes seem to suggest a Byzantine influence. Awkwardly placed between the centre and right-hand windows is the Crucifixion with Christ being pierced in the side by a soldier wearing twelfth-century dress. Above the Crucifixion the son of God is shown ascending into heaven accompanied by angels.

The best-preserved frescoes are to be found in the south side-chapel. To the right of the entrance to the chapel is a scene showing the serpent, coiled round the tree of knowledge, offering the forbidden fruit to a bald Eve. Only the top half of Eve survives but on the right of the tree the figure of Adam is almost complete. His face is expressively drawn and looks as though it may have been taken from life. Inside the chapel Christ in Majesty is depicted on the semi-circular vault. On the left-hand wall Christ speaks to two disciples who are separated by a column from another figure believed to be John the Baptist. On the opposite wall Herod demands the head of John the Baptist and the saint is shown decapitated. The Latin inscription reads: 'The infidel king ordered a detestable servant to decapitate John the Baptist.'

From Saint-Plancard the road switchbacks over a range of hills called the Côteaux de Gascogne. Just north of the bastide town of Montréjeau, at Ponlat-Taillebourg, there is a panoramic view south over the la Plaine de Rivière, the fertile river valley of the Garonne which, after emerging from the mountains, is deflected by the Côteaux de Gascogne from its course and turns a right angle to flow eastwards for fifteen miles before resuming a more northerly route at Cazères. La Plaine de Rivière is largely given over to agriculture, although there are a few factories, and viewed from Ponlat-Taillebourg the scene is of a peaceful prosperous-looking landscape dotted with farmhouses and chequered by fields and orchards with the thickly-wooded slopes of the advance guard of the mountains brooding in the background.

The main road into the mountains is the N125 which leads from Montrejeau to the popular resort of Bagnères-de-Luchon. To start with the road crosses la Plaine de Rivière, passing close to Saint-Bertrand-de-Comminges on the way (turn right at Labroquère), before entering the valley of the Garonne.

On either side are thickly-forested slopes belonging to a low range of arid mountains, preceding the high peaks, called the Petits Pyrénées. Largely uninhabited, the Petits Pyrénées are formed for the most part of limestone laid down in the second geological era over 200 million years ago when this part of Gascony was covered by the sea. Limestone is porous and water soaks through it until it meets an impermeable layer where it forms subterranean lakes and rivers which sometimes emerge from the bowels of the earth in spectacular cascades. The best examples are to be seen in the Arbas, a particularly inhospitable region which stretches eastwards from the right bank of the Garonne and possesses one of the deepest pot-holes in all France, sinisterly named la Henne Morte, the dead woman.

West of the Garonne is the Barousse, which like the Arbas is covered with forest but is less desolate. In fact, it has two tiny but delightful river valleys, the Ourse and the Nistos. The valley of the Ourse can be reached by turning off the N125 near Loures-Barousse, just south of Saint-Bertrand-de-Comminges. After Mauléon-Barousse the road passes the Gouffre de Saoule and the valley narrows so that the Ourse is invitingly near. This is an ideal place for picnics: access is easy across firm flower-freckled meadows and the river itself is bordered by trees so there is plenty of shade. Even in the summer the Ourse runs swiftly and the temperature is just right to cool a bottle of white wine. Add butterflies and birdsong and a more peaceful relaxing spot is hard to imagine.

The valley of the Nistos can be reached from the D938 by

turning south at Saint-Laurent-de-Neste. It presents less opportunities for picnicking than the Ourse until you get quite high up
at Haut Nistos (2,156 feet) but here there are good views down
across the forest.

Five miles further down the N125 a left turn (D618) leads to
Bastion des Frontignes where there is a good view south. Round
the next bend or so is Antichan where the Hôtel La Palombière
makes a good base for exploring the Comminges. The D618 climbs
up to the Col de Portet d'Aspet (3,507 feet), one of the easier east–
west passes in the Pyrénées, which links the Comminges with the
Couserans.

Back on the N125 the road soon divides, the left-hand fork
(N125) following the course of the Garonne to Saint-Béat, a small
dour town whose strategic position, where the Garonne flows
through a narrow pass, earned it the title 'the Key to France'. The
remains of the citadel that once defended the Comminges from
Spanish invaders can still be seen high above the town, but the
dignity of the only surviving tower is somewhat impaired by a
large clockface. Just outside Saint-Béat are marble quarries that
have been worked since Roman times. After Saint-Béat there is a
stiff climb of seven miles to the Spanish border.

The right-hand fork (D125) takes you up the valley of the Pique
to Luchon. It is an easy drive along a good road hemmed in by
sombre tree-covered slopes. After eleven miles the valley opens
out and there ahead is Bagnères-de-Luchon with directly behind
it the snow-clad peaks of Sacroux, Sauvegarde and la Mine.

Bagnères-de-Luchon, 'la Reine des Pyrénées ', occupies a splendid position in a narrow basin, little more than a mile across at its
widest, where the river One flows into the Pique. On every side
are high peaks, making Luchon an ideal base for excursions into
the mountains.

Luchon was famous for its healing waters in Gallo-Roman times.
A Latin inscription, preserved in the thermal baths, proclaims that
they are second only to those of Naples and they were also praised
by the Greek geographer Strabo. Archaeological excavations have
revealed traces of three enormous marble-faced baths with their
own central-heating system, as well as marble altars, inscribed

stones, statues and many other fragments testifying to the importance of the Roman resort. The baths were under the protection of a powerful local deity, Ilixo.

During the Dark Ages Luchon was sacked and pillaged several times and sank into obscurity. Its fortunes only revived in the eighteenth century when Anton Megret, Baron d'Etigny visited the town and decided to redevelop it. In 1762 he improved access to Luchon by building a good road from the resort to Montréjeau. He also created the elegant boulevard, planted with lime trees, that bears his name but, most important of all, he persuaded the Governor of Gascony and Guienne, the Maréchal de Richelieu, to visit Luchon. Richelieu was enchanted by the town and spread news of its attractions at the court of Versailles: the town's future was assured. Luchon reached its apogee during the Second Empire in the middle of the nineteenth century. It became especially popular with writers and Lamartine, Flaubert, Dumas and Maupassant all visited the resort; but perhaps its most enthusiastic admirer was Edmond Rostand, the author of *Cyrano de Bergerac*, who borrowed local place names, Antignac, Juzet and Crabioules, for his Gascon *cadets*. Nearer our own time François Mauriac describes a childhood visit to Luchon in his novel *The Knot of Vipers*.

The heart of Luchon is the allées d'Etigny, the long tree-shaded boulevard, lined with cafés, restaurants and shops, that runs roughly north–south through the town, ending at the thermal baths. All day long it is crowded with holiday-makers shopping, strolling or just idly sitting watching the world go by: it is an animated colourful scene. Halfway down the west side at number 18 is a large eighteenth-century house where Richelieu stayed during his visit. It now houses a permanent exhibition devoted to the traditions and culture of the Pyrénées. There are also some remains from the Gallo-Roman baths.

Except for a small casino there is little else in the way of entertainment at Luchon but, apart from the invalids who are there for the cure, most people have come to the town because it makes a convenient base for exploring the mountains.

The shortest and easiest excursion is to the Hospice de France.

You take the D125 south from Luchon along the valley of the Pique. After six miles the road climbs through a thick oak forest, hugging the shoulder of the mountain with a steep drop on the right. Far below, hidden in the trees, is the river Pique. After seven miles the road comes to an abrupt end and you must park your car as best you can and continue on foot. The ascent, though, is easy, along a well-marked path which toddlers and grannies can both manage. After about three-quarters of an hour you emerge from the trees into a beautiful natural amphitheatre overlooked by the Pic de Sauvegarde and the Pic de Sacroux. The lower slopes are covered with grass and intersected by fast-running streams. The Hospice, which was once a pilgrims' halt on the route to Compostella, now looks more like a run-down ranch, and indeed you can hire a horse there.

Backpackers may follow a mule track on up the mountain to the Porte de Venasque, a mountain pass into Spain. The climb lasts about five hours, there and back, and means a very early start. Another hour brings you to the summit of the Pic de Sauvegarde (8,983 feet) where you will be rewarded by a superb view to the south of the mountain range called the Maladetta.

If you prefer to transport your picnic by car you can return down the valley of the Pique to the Pont de Ravi and turn left up the valley of the Lys. After three miles this comes to a dead end at the Cascade d'Enfer, a spectacular waterfall.

Halfway along the north side of the valley of the Lys a steep road corkscrews up to the ski resort of Superbagnères. From here there are immense views of the mountains on every side; but make sure you go up in the morning before the clouds descend and blot everything out.

Another favourite excursion from Luchon is to Lake Oô. Take the D618 from the place Maréchal Joffre towards the Col de Peyresourde. An easy drive of three and a half miles brings you to Saint-Aventin and a fine Romanesque church.

Saint-Aventin is tucked into the hillside on the right, a little above the level of the road. Parking is difficult but there is just room on the steep ramp that leads up to the church. This can only be approached from the west but there is a turning place at the far end of the village. The building is remarkably large for the mountains, seventy feet long with a nave height of thirty feet and, unusually, it has two towers. Despite its size, Saint-Aventin has a distinctly rustic appearance, typical of the churches of the high Pyrénées which are almost invariably built of local undressed stone.

Saint-Aventin has a number of features that show it belongs to the first period of Romanesque: the plain style of building, the simple crossing tower with its twinned openings, the pilaster strips on the exterior wall of the nave and the arched corbel bands that run under the eaves are all derived from the Lombard architecture of northern Italy and point to a date of about 1100. The west tower is later, replacing an earlier bell-gable, but this too is in the Lombard style with characteristic window openings that increase in number at each stage. Here there are three openings, separated by slim columns at the first stage, and four on the next. The tower is capped by a tall pointed slate tower typical of the Pyrénées.

The entrance, on the south side, has a carved tympanum preceded by two archivolts supported on twinned columns with carved capitals. The tympanum shows Christ in Majesty surrounded by flying figures who support the frame of Christ's mandorla with one hand and bear symbols showing that they are the four evangelists in the other. This unusual composition is also found at Valcabrère. In his left hand Christ holds a book inscribed *Ego sum lux Mundi*. The inner capitals of the left show on the outer face Mary Magdalene anointing the feet of Jesus and on the inner the Massacre of the Innocents with a soldier wrenching a child from its mother. On the right are scenes from the martyrdom of St Aventin who, after being decapitated by Arab infidels, walked two hundred paces with his head in his hands. On the interior face, the saint is arrested by two armed men, one of whom is crippled. On the outer face an executioner brandishes a sword at the saint who is shown holding his decapitated head in his hands.

On a shallow buttress to the right of the porch is a fine marble sculpture of the Virgin Mary with the infant Jesus on her knee. They are covered by a canopy with the inscription *Res Miranda Nimis Mater Dei Erat Vi Nimis*, which roughly means 'Wonderful, the Mother of God was all-powerful'. Monstrous heads support the canopy on either side and more monsters writhe under Mary's feet, symbolizing her triumph over evil. The formalized carving of the folds of the robes, together with the hieratic pose and heavy features of both Virgin and Child, suggest that the sculpture belongs to the school of Saint-Sernin at Toulouse, or at least was influenced by work done there. Round the corner of the buttress is another robed figure, rather awkwardly compressed within the available space, presumably carved by the same hand as the Virgin. This is believed to be the prophet Isaiah foretelling the birth of the Saviour, hence the position of his right hand which points to Mary.

Further along the wall, to the right of the porch, is a curious carving showing another scene from the story of Saint-Aventin. After his martyrdom, the saint's corpse was lost for three centuries and only rediscovered by a divinely inspired bull which was led by an angel to the spot where St Aventin was buried. In the sculpture the bull stands astride the body of the saint with his head turned to listen to the directions given by the angel.

On the south-east corner of the church is a piece of a Gallo–Roman altar showing a twin deity. Such fragments are commonly found embedded in the walls of the mountain churches of the Comminges and make one wonder if their builders were not hedging their bets.

Inside the church is a strange baptismal font whose crude carving suggests that it was made locally. On the outside are doves drinking from a chalice, a fairly obvious symbol of baptism which is also found at Ravenna; there are also fish representing the faithful, but the meaning of the two human figures is far from clear: they may represent the newly baptized.

The narrow nave has six bays covered by groin vaults, as are the aisles. A fine wrought-iron grille divides the nave from the choir which, like the side chapels, ends in a semi-circular apse. Much of the interior is covered with faded frescoes which once again underline the fact that, despite its remoteness, the bones of St Aventin made this church a very important shrine in the early Middle Ages.

After Saint-Aventin the next stop is Cazeaux-de-Larboust where there is another twelfth-century church built of undressed stone with a Lombard tower topped by a slate spire. Inside is a series of remarkable fifteenth-century frescoes, alas much restored. On the wall opposite the entrance is an unusual Last Judgement showing the mother of Jesus intervening on behalf of mankind to prevent divine retribution. The frescoes are painted in a style similar to that found in late-fifteenth-century tapestries like the 'Lady and the Unicorn' in the Cluny Museum in Paris. There are several paintings devoted to the first chapter of Genesis; in one of them the Archangel Gabriel is shown expelling Adam and Eve from the Garden of Eden. The flowers in the garden are beautifully depicted but in a totally unrealistic manner so that they form a purely decorative backdrop to the scene. The Archangel is pretty rather than fierce and Adam and Eve look as though they have committed a *faux pas* rather than original sin. Even so, the paintings are very attractive and well worth a look. What makes them even more interesting are the Gascon captions below or alongside them: the Expulsion of Adam and Eve, for example, has a line reading 'Com langel jete adam e eba de paradis tareste'.

On leaving the church turn right up a narrow country road and then right again to the pretty hamlet of Bernet, where there is a charming, tiny double-ended church only forty foot long by sixteen wide.

Cazeaux-de-Larboust is where you turn south towards Lake Oô, but before doing so continue for a short way on the D618. The road runs along the north side of a huge morain, left behind by the melting glaciers of the Ice Age, on which are perched the villages of Cazeaux-de-Larboust and Garin. A mile further on is the pilgrims' chapel of Saint-Pé-de-la-Moraine. This rugged little church is remarkable for the extraordinary number of Gallo-Roman fragments incorporated in the walls.

Back at Cazeaux-de-Larboust you take the D76, leading to Lac d'Oô. About a mile further on is the small dull village of Oô, after which the road runs alongside the river Neste d'Oô through delightful meadows until it ends in a large car park at the Granges d'Astau. The journey must now be continued on foot across the dried-up bed of an ancient lake: the scenery is grim with ragged shrubs and twisted dwarf trees clinging to the rocks. After an hour and a half you arrive at Lac d'Oô. The scene is impressive but austere: the lake is surrounded by rocky slopes and the water is still and menacing, but on the far side of the lake is a magnificent cascade hurtling nine hundred feet down the rock face from Lake Espingo above. It takes another two hours' hard march to reach the upper lake, above which looms the high peak of Spijoles (10,056 feet). Experienced backpackers can spend the night at the refuge at Lac d'Espingo and continue the next day to the Lac de Portillon and on to the summit of the peak of Crabioules.

One of the most enjoyable excursions from Luchon is up the valley of the river Oueil. Take the D618 from the Place Maréchal Joffre and after five miles turn right onto the D51 marked to Saint-Paul-d'Oueil. After only half a mile a small turning to the left, easily missed, leads to the hamlets of Benque-Dessous and Benque-Dessus, each of which has a modest Romanesque church no more than forty feet long by twenty wide, with a bell-gable at the west end, an apse at the east and a nave without aisles. The more interesting of the two is Benque-Dessus, which you come to second. Built of rough brown local stone it stands a little apart from the rest of the hamlet in a small churchyard, planted with red roses, against a background of green mountain pastures.

But what makes this tiny church remarkable is that the interior is covered by frescoes which, judging by the costumes worn by the figures in the various scenes depicted, must have been painted at the very end of the fifteenth century or the beginning of the sixteenth. What is more, although they are no masterpieces, they are well executed. How a good artist was persuaded to decorate a tiny mountain church like this is a mystery. The frescoes were only discovered in 1965 under a layer of eighteenth-century whitewash, which accounts for their excellent state of preservation.

The most important paintings are in the apse and depict scenes from Christ's Passion. There are six scenes in all, reading left to right:

1 Christ and his disciples praying in the garden of Gethsemane.
2 The Judas kiss and Christ's arrest. Note the splendid devil in the left-hand bottom corner.

3 Christ before Pontius Pilate who wears the clothes of a fifteenth-century nobleman.
4 The flagellation.
5 Christ carrying the cross. Christ's head has unfortunately suffered damage.
6 The Crucifixion.

In the north chapel there are the remains of what was probably the Annunciation and on the north wall of the nave, near the apse, is St James in pilgrim's dress. Further west, opposite the south door, is the Archangel Michael. On the south wall of the nave is St Catherine, wearing a very smart fur-trimmed dress and holding the wheel that was the instrument of her martyrdom. To the right of the blocked-up window is St John the Baptist and to his right again, but higher up, is the Virgin Mary about to give birth to Jesus. She is lying in a four-poster bed and is attended by St Anne acting as midwife.

A mile or so further along the D52, at Saint-Paul-d'Oueil, is another typical small mountain church: Saint-Gordien. The most interesting feature here is the tympanum over the entrance. Crudely but vigorously carved, it shows Christ in a mandorla surrounded by the symbols of the evangelists. What is unusual is that the tympanum is framed by a plain, semi-circular arch with a keystone consisting of a fragment of Gallo-Roman sculpture with the ubiquitous twin busts carved on it. Inside the church is a baptismal font decorated with horseshoe arches and worn human heads.

A side road, the D51B, leads to Saccourvielle where the church of Saint-Barthélémy has a particularly fine Lombard tower with two openings on the first stage, three on the next and four on the top and last, all separated by slim elegant columns.

Half a mile beyond Saint-Paul-d'Oueil is the Kiosque de Mayrègne where there is a panoramic view of the mountains. In the foreground are the glaciers above Lac d'Oô. In the background, between the peaks of Sacroux and Sauvegarde, the Maladetta massif can be seen with, in the far distance, the Pic d'Aneto, the highest point of the Pyrénées (11,168 ft).

After the Kiosque de Mayrègne, the road continues through a delightful pastoral valley, with scattered hamlets clinging precariously to the green slopes on either side, to end at Bourg d'Oueil. Here there is a good rustic *auberge*, the Sapin Fleuri, and a small Romanesque church with a two-bell gable at the west end.

From Bourg d'Oueil a very rough, twisting, rock-strewn track climbs painfully up to the summit of Mont Né (7,044 ft). On all sides are the high peaks: to the west the Pic de Midi du Bigorre (9,400 ft) can easily be distinguished by its television transmitter, while on its left is the Pic de Néouvielle (10,473 ft). To the south, on the Spanish side of the border, are the highest mountains of the whole Pyrenean chain, the Pic d'Aneto (11,168 ft) and further west Mont Perdu (11,007 ft). Diminished by distance these great peaks seem to be on a level with Mont Né.

South-west of Mont Né is the beautiful but remote mountain lake of Bordères, which can, however, be reached on foot in half an hour. The walk is through very attractive scenery, made more beautiful by wild rhododendron, aquilegia and other alpine flowers. In every way an excursion to Mont Né makes a fitting climax to a tour of the Comminges.

2 The Couserans

The fortunes of the Comminges and Couserans have always been closely intertwined. Like the Comminges the Couserans owes its origin to Pompey the Great who assembled the local Celtic–Iberian tribes, together with his own veterans, to form the Consorani (peoples grouped together). Later, for the sake of euphony, the n became a u and so the name changed to Couserani, hence Couserans.

Pompey also founded a new capital on the site of a Celtic–Iberian *oppidum* and called it Lugdunum Consoranorum.

The Viscounty of Couserans was created at the end of the tenth century. After the death of Arnaud I, the powerful Count of Comminges, in 957, his territory was divided between his sons: Raymond, the eldest, inherited the Comminges while the new title of Viscount of Couserans went to his second son, Roger. From the beginning the Viscounty was dominated by its more powerful neighbours, the Counts of Comminges to the west and of Foix to the east. Over the centuries the original small territory was partitioned and dismembered until by the time of the French Revolution all that remained was a narrow strip of land on either side of the upper reaches of the river Salat.

The geography of Couserans is best understood by looking at its river system. Its backbone is the river Salat which rises in the high mountains near the Spanish border and flows north to Saint-Girons where it is deflected west for a short way by the Petits Pyrénées, a barren limestone belt that precedes the mountains proper, before continuing its northwards course to join the Garonne just below Boussens. On the way the Salat is joined by numerous tributaries, each of them flowing through its separate valley with its individual flavour: hence the Couserans has been called the country of the eighteen valleys.

The Couserans can be reached from the Comminges by taking the mountain route (D618). Driving north from Luchon, you turn off the N125 at Chaum and pass the Tour de Fronsac, the ruins of a castle that belonged to the Count of Comminges. The road winds up to the Bastion des Frontignes, where there are fine views south over the valley of the Garonne, and then enters the gloomy forest of Arbas. Eighteen miles further on you come to the entrance to the narrow valley of the Ger, whence a tortuous but beautiful mountain road leads back to Saint-Béat. On the other side of the road, but two and a half miles to the north, is the Gouffre de Henne Morte.

Another two and a half miles on the D618 brings you to the top of the pass, the Col de Portet d'Aspet (5,279 ft). From here there is a view to the south of Mont Valier (9,311 ft), the peak that dominates the whole of the Couserans. The road now leaves the dark forest and descends the sunny valley of the Bellongue into the Couserans. At the bottom of the valley, in a picturesque site where the rivers Lez and Bouigane meet, is the fourteenth-century pilgrim-age church of Notre-Dame-de-Tramezaygues at Audressein. The entrance is through a gateway with a pointed stone arch into what looks at first like a drive to a house. At the end is a rather curious hotchpotch of a building. The entrance is at the west end where two pointed arches, of unequal size, lead into a porch covered by a forward-sloping slate roof. Above the porch is a slate-roofed gallery built against the bell-gable. The latter has four arches and is capped by three turrets, the middle one being higher than those to left and right. The whole effect is made even more bizarre by a large clockface on the right-hand side of the upper gallery. Inside the porch are rather faded fifteenth-century frescoes and a crudely carved marble cross. The inside of the church is unremarkable except for two massive round piers and a primitive fifteenth-century *pietà*.

A pleasant drive of seven and a half miles through the valley of the Lez brings you to the capital of the Couserans, Saint-Girons. This small market town, at the junction of the rivers Salat, Lez and Baup, is the gateway to the mountains and makes a good centre for exploring the eighteen valleys.

An alternative route to Saint-Girons follows the valley of the Garonne from Montréjeau to Salies-du-Salat. Eight miles east of Montréjeau is Saint-Gaudens, the ancient capital of a *petit pays* called the Nebouzan which subsequently became part of the Comminges. Saint-Gaudens possesses a large Romanesque church with some good carved capitals but the church was partly destroyed by Montgoméry during the Wars of Religion and maladroitly restored in the nineteenth century. The crossing-tower, in particular, is a monstrosity, having no similarity at all to the original which was octagonal in the Toulouse style.

At Saint-Gaudens you can either continue on the main road north of the Garonne or cross the river and take a minor road (D21) through an agreeable pastoral landscape overlooked to the south by the thickly wooded heights of the Arbas. Near Les Artigues are the spectacular ruins of the Château de Montespan, perched on a crag above the road. The château belonged to the husband of Madame de Montespan, the mistress of Louis XIV, although it appears she never actually lived there.

Soon afterwards the D21 joins the main road to Saint-Girons (D117) just south of Salies-du-Salat. The next fourteen miles along a narrow traffic-congested road are trying in the extreme but at last patience is rewarded by the sight of Saint-Lizier, high up on a hill on the far bank of the Salat.

Saint-Lizier is the ancient Lugdunum Consoranorum. Tradition has it that Christianity was brought to the Couserans in the fourth century by a Spanish monk called Valier, after whom the mountain peak, whose brooding presence is ubiquitous in the Couserans, is named. However, the first definite record of the Church in the Couserans is dated 506 when Bishop Glycerius attended the Council of Agde, along with Suavis, Bishop of Comminges. Glycerius was subsequently canonized as St Lizier and Lugdunum Consoranorum changed its name in his honour.

During the early Middle Ages it was the Bishops of Saint-Lizier, whose diocese overlapped the territories of the Viscounty, who represented the most powerful political force in the Couserans. The authority of the Bishop was challenged in 1125 when the Viscounty came under the control of the bellicose Count of Comminges, Bernard I. The Count tried to enter the cathedral city of Saint-Lizier, only to find himself opposed by Bishop Pierre, who insisted on the Church's autonomy. Bernard was not a man to be thwarted: he took Saint-Lizier by force, sacked it and removed its citizens to Saint-Girons. Bishop Pierre remained a prisoner for seven years until a power-sharing accord was worked out and the Count took the Bishop under his 'protection'. That is why the arms of the Count of Comminges are to be found on some of the roof bosses in the cathedral. The town of Saint-Lizier never fully recovered from this disaster and the rise of Saint-Girons dates from this period.

The first sight of the cathedral is disappointing. The east end, usually the most visually satisfying part of a Romanesque church, is a mess. The best part is the polygonal apse of the choir. It is built of dressed stone, with some Roman fragments incorporated here and there, in particular a fine frieze on either side of the centre window. The latter looks almost Palladian with a round-headed arch supported by elegant fluted columns, presumably also Roman. However, the effect is marred by the awkward transition from a polygon to semi-circle at the top, where different stonework shows that the roof has been raised. On either side of the choir are small apsidal chapels built of undressed stone which look rather rustic compared to the main apse. Behind them the south transept is higher than the north, giving the building a lopsided look, while the crossing-tower, in the Toulouse style, has only two stages, making it look squat and ugly.

Inside you can see at once that the nave is out of alignment with the transepts and choir: in fact it is the oldest part of the church, built in the eleventh century, and the choir and transepts were added at the beginning of the twelfth century. At the same time the original wooden roof of the nave was replaced by Gothic ribbed vaults.

The most interesting part of the interior is the choir which is decorated with some remarkable, if faded, frescoes dating from the twelfth century. The semi-dome of the apse shows Christ in Majesty, surrounded by the four evangelists. Below, the walls on either side of the centre window are divided into eight panels, four at the top and four at the bottom. The top panels show the apostles: to the left of the window is St Peter and alongside him St Paul. Below, to the left, are the Magi before Herod and offering gifts to the Christ child. To the right are the Annunciation and the Visitation, the latter a moving composition in which the heads of the two women are united by a single halo, painted in sombre hues of dark blue, brown and ochre. In the apse of the north chapel is a fourteenth-century painting of the Virgin Mary suckling the infant Jesus.

But the most exciting part of the cathedral is the beautiful Romanesque cloister, dating from the end of the twelfth century, although the gallery was added in the sixteenth. It consists of thirty-two arches supported on alternate single and twinned marble columns with carved capitals. The corners and middles of the sides have square piers with attached columns, except on the west side where there is an entrance to the cathedral square with four grouped columns on either side. The quality of the carving of the capitals is variable: some are indifferently executed but others are exquisite. The most beautiful are to be found on the north side parallel to the south wall of the nave: they have intricate compositions of intertwined leaves and vines, often enclosing human figures or animals. But the charm of the cloister depends not so much on individual carvings as on the harmonious impression conveyed by the rhythmical repetition of the arches and the way the graceful marble columns and their delicate capitals contrast with the sturdy stone piers and the open gallery above.

From Saint-Lizier it is but a short step to Saint-Girons, after which you are soon in the mountains. To reach the high valley of the Salat take the D618 to Seix. Almost at once you plunge into the gloomy Gorges de Ribaouto, only just wide enough to contain the river itself and a narrow road on each bank. It is best to stick to the west side for on the east there is a short but frightening tunnel to negotiate.

After eight miles you reach the junction of the rivers Arac and Salat and the road divides. Turn right up the D3 to Soueix, a small holiday village. Soon afterwards the valley widens at the point where the river Garbet flows into the Salat forming a large triangle containing another larger holiday village, Oust, and some meadows suitable for camping. Oust lies on the left-hand fork but we continue on the D3 to the small town of Seix (pronounced Sèche) where there is yet another tributary, the mountain torrent of Esbints. Seix is an agreeable little town with a small fifteenth-century château with two round towers and a corner turret. There is also a seventeenth-century church with a bizarre bell-gable built on the end of the north transept. It is a popular base for exploring the mountains.

A bridge crosses the Salat at Seix and the D3 continues up the east bank of the river. The valley here is very narrow with passing places on the road. After about a mile you reach Moulin-Lauga where a track (GR10) leads from the left bank to the summit of Mont Valier: this is a stiff seven-hour climb for experienced backpackers. Another mile brings you to the junction of the Alet and the Salat at Pont de la Taule, where there is a good *auberge*, the Deux Rivières. Its rooms are minuscule but the food is excellent and there is a pleasant terrace overlooking the noisy torrent where you can take your aperitif and watch the wagtails flick backwards and forwards along the riverbed.

At Pont de la Taule a road to the left (D8) leads to the pretty valley of Ustou while the D3 continues for three miles, hemmed in by high slopes on either side, to Couflens, where the D703 to the right climbs up to the Col de Pause. Still on the D3 another couple of miles brings you to Salau, after which the road comes to a dead end at the tungsten mines half a mile further on.

Salau is a sad little village with dreary modern houses inhabited by the miners and their families. Once there was a fine Romanesque church here but in 1982 a terrible flood swept away the seven-hundred-year-old nave, leaving only the choir surmounted by a four-arch bell-gable: it is a pathetic sight. All around are the gigantic boulders that destroyed the nave, left behind when the waters subsided: an eloquent testimony to the scale of this natural disaster.

The antidote to Salau is a picnic at the Col de Pause. It is an exacting climb with seemingly endless tight bends on a very rough stone-strewn track but all the way there are beautiful views, first of the wooded valley of Angouls and then, after the hamlet of Faup, of the upper valley of the Salat, with the silver thread of the river winding through it. The track peters out just below the Col de Pause (5,010 ft), where there is a panorama including Mont Valier (9,377 ft) to the west and the twin peaks of Mont Rouch (9,377 ft) right on the frontier to the south. From here you can proceed on foot to the top of the pass and thence to Port d'Aula (5,010 ft) where you cross the border into Spain. It is best to make the trip to the Col de Pause in the morning as the clouds tend to build up from the south after midday and it can be very cold at that height, even in midsummer.

The valley of Ustou is surely the prettiest in the Couserans. I well remember walking along it one golden evening after an excellent meal at Les Deux Rivières. On the right was the Alet, little more than a swift-flowing stream really, with swallows darting over it, snatching at flies; on both banks a profusion of wild flowers and beyond them lush green pastures. A little way along the road a family was harvesting the hay, forking it onto a kind of sled drawn by two placid, pale brown cows; because of the steep slope of these mountain fields a wheeled cart would be useless.

Every so often, the farmer's wife tapped the muzzle of the nearest beast and the pair moved on a few paces and stopped again. The farmer stood on top of the pile of hay on the sled receiving loads from the rest of the family who collected it with old-fashioned pitchforks from bee-hive-shaped stooks dotted at intervals round the field. It was the kind of scene that must have been enacted in the Pyrénées for generations, although not so long ago there would probably have been bullocks pulling the sled instead of cows. Part of the special charm of the Couserans is that here, more than anywhere in the Gascon Pyrénées, the old way of life continues, even if, nowadays, the farmers have to be subsidized to persuade them to stay and farm this difficult, if beautiful, terrain.

Soon afterwards the valley broadens out and more farms and scattered hamlets come into view. Five miles further on at Ustou the road divides: the right-hand fork follows the river Alet upstream almost to its source, in a lake just above the Cirque de Cagateille, while the D6 starts to slimb steeply up to the Col de Latrape (3,645 ft).

The ascent to the col is punishing for this is one of the high passes that is only open in the summer and which, before the coming of the motor car, made communication between the valleys of Ustou and Garbet impossible, except for the mountain shepherds, even though they are only a few miles apart as the crow flies.

Less than four miles along the route to the Col de Latrape, a turning to the right leads to the ski station of Guzet Neige, where there are stunning views all round. The road up is excellent and kept open all winter. At the top of the pass itself, there is a welcome bar where you can enjoy a cold beer while the car engine takes a much-needed rest. The subsequent descent down a dizzy series of Z-bends brings you quickly to Aulus-les-Bains, a tiny spa town at the head of the valley of Garbet.

Few now go to Aulus to take the waters, although at the end of the nineteenth century it achieved some popularity because they were supposed to cure syphilis. Aulus has been saved from complete extinction by its proximity to the ski slopes of Guzet Neige but in the summer the few old-fashioned hotels are largely empty, so it makes a good inexpensive base for exploring the surrounding countryside.

The most spectacular of the local sights, the Cascade d'Arse, is very close to Aulus. You take the route to the Col de Latrape and on the left-hand side of the first bend is the beginning of a well-marked footpath to the waterfall. The track climbs steadily upwards, at first through a forest and later across some pretty glades, carpeted with wild flowers. All the time you are within sight or earshot of the torrent. The sound of the waterfall grows louder and louder the higher you go until, at last, you come out onto a rocky ledge and you can see the Cascade d'Arse itself hurtling three hundred and sixty feet down the cliff face and rebounding from the ledges below to disappear into a deep wooded gorge. It is a magnificent sight that the great nineteenth-century Irish traveller Henry Russell thought the most beautiful in the whole of the Pyrénées.

The walk up to the Cascade d'Arse is an easy one and takes only a couple of hours, there and back: another favourite promenade is to the Tuc de Caïzardé, lasting about three hours. The path starts just behind the church in Aulus and winds upwards through a wood to the summit where there are fine all-round views. A much longer all-day excursion takes you to the Lake of Garbet. The route begins three miles down the D8 south of Aulus and follows the upper course of the river Garbet through a wooded valley and eventually out onto the bare mountain-side. Unless you are very experienced it is probably advisable to take a guide to the lake. If the expedition seems too daunting, the stretch of valley near the road makes a good place for an idle picnic.

Downstream, between Aulus and Ercé, the valley widens into a fertile basin framed by steep wooded mountains. Ercé has a small Romanesque church whose west door is decorated with badly eroded geometrical sculpture. From Ercé a narrow country road leads to Cominac, a remote hamlet surrounded by beautiful pasture-land, with views over the valley of Garbet and south to the frontier.

Cominac looks pretty and tranquil enough but like most Pyrenean villages it has suffered badly from depopulation and its young people have left to seek a better life elsewhere. At the turn of the century things were even worse; life in the mountains was so hard that some of the men were driven to trap wild bears which they tamed and taught to 'dance'. The wretched animals were then led from town to town to entertain the locals. Some of these miserable troupes even found their way to England.

In the fields round Cominac you can see some of the small attractive barns which were once common in the mountains. They are built of local undressed stone skilfully fitted together without mortar. At either end is a stepped gable whose ledges support the roof ridge poles. The barns were originally thatched but this is rarely seen nowadays, most roofs having been re-covered with unsightly corrugated iron. The barns are built into the hillsides with an opening high up under the roof at the back into which hay can be be easily forked, to be retrieved, when needed, from the door lower down the hill at the front.

The harsh winters in the mountains dictate a very different kind of building to that found in the Gascon lowlands. North of a line between Montréjeau and Saint-Girons the houses look similar to those found in Armagnac and the Lomagne: the low-pitched Roman-tiled roof is still ubiquitous and the farms tend to be one-storey buildings with large attics used for storage. The materials used in the walls vary according to the nature of the terrain. In areas where stone is scarce you will still find mud-brick and half-timbered walls; elsewhere the round stones brought down by the ancient glaciers and left behind in the rivers when the ice melted are used. The stones are often arranged in horizontal courses alternating with brick, flint or some other material, producing some very pleasing effects: sometimes they are mixed with dressed stones in a chequerboard pattern.

In the foothills of the Pyrénées and the mountains themselves the old houses are all built of stone. They are usually narrow buildings, two or more storeys high, with slate roofs steeply pitched to shed the heavy rains and prevent the build-up of snow. The gable ends often project forward to give shade to wooden balconies built at attic level. There is considerable variation from one valley to another: sometimes the roof slates are arranged in a pleasing fish-scale pattern, elsewhere larger buildings have attic dormer windows with slate roofs known as *capucines* because they look like monks' hoods. In the high pastures you sometimes come across lonely shepherds' huts whose roofs and walls are built entirely of great slabs of local stone.

A narrow twisting road leads from Cominac, through remote mountain country to Massat. Back down in the valley of Garbet the D32 continues to Oust, where a comfortable hotel, the Poste, boasts a Michelin rosette. A mile further on at Vic there is an interesting Romanesque church with a semi-circular apse and side chapels. Inside is a remarkable sixteenth-century painted wooden roof. The surface is divided up into numerous square panels decorated with cherub-like heads and delicately painted flowers. The rich colouring and overall design suggest a Spanish influence. The roof has recently been beautifully restored by the Beaux Arts at Toulouse and is well worth seeing. Below Vic the road joins the D3 near Soueix. A mile further on and you are back to the junction of the rivers Salat and Arac where a right turn onto the D618 takes you to Massat.

The route follows the river Arac, at first along a narrow sombre valley and then, after five miles, into a gorge carved by the river through an outcrop of red rock. Near Biert the road skirts some huge, weirdly shaped boulders near the deep potholes called the Grottes de Ker.

It is difficult to believe that the small mountain village of Massat was once the civil capital of the Couserans. The only clue to its former glory is the rather grand sixteenth-century church which stands at the crossroads and is the hub of the village. Its west end has a screen front terminating in an elegant ogee-shaped gable, while to the right is a tall octagonal bell-tower capped by a slim spire. The eight sides of the final stage of the tower are curiously ornamented with stone cannons.

Massat is strategically situated at the foot of the pass that leads over the Col de Port into the County of Foix, the modern *département* of the Ariège, and no doubt the church's mock cannon are a reminder of the building's former defensive role. Two other minor roads strike south into the Couserans, the D17 which takes you back to Cominac and the D18 which leads to the Lake of Lers. Much of the journey is through rugged country covered with oak forests and dominated by the grim peaks of the Trois Seigneurs, which form a frontier between the Couserans and the County of Foix.

The Lake of Lers lies in a gloomy bowl at the foot of a barren rocky outcrop; it is a sinister place but in the spring and early summer the scene is transformed by the carpets of wild flowers that cover the lower slopes of Montbéas to the west. From the lake a zig-zag road descends to Aulus and the valley of Garbet. On the other side of the Couserans, south-west of Saint-Girons, is another valley network based on the river Lez. You take the D618 from Saint-Girons towards the Col de Porte d'Aspet and turn off onto the D4 at the junction of the rivers Bouigane and Lez, just before Audressein. Soon afterwards you arrive at Castillon-en-Couserans, a lively market town.

High up on a bluff, overlooking the town, is the twelfth-century pilgrimage church of Saint-Pierre, a fortified church built on the site of a former castle of the Counts of Comminges. A steep flight of worn stone steps climbs up to the church. The entrance, hidden by a lean-to roof, has a badly eroded Romanesque doorway with sculpted archivolts supported on marble columns with carved capitals. In a niche to the right of the door is the figure of St Peter with an inscription in Latin and Gascon.

At the junction of the nave and choir is a large five-bell gable with two large bells below, two smaller ones above and a tiny one at the top. The gable has impressive military-looking finials with pointed slate roofs. The roof of the polygonal east end has been raised but you can still see the battlements that once surmounted the parapet; below them are Lombard bands, resting on carved corbel heads, and pilaster strips.

Half a mile south of Castillon, at Bordes, is the pretty Romanesque church of Ourjout with a four-arch bell-gable and an apse with Lombard bands. A medieval stone bridge, the oldest in the Couserans, crosses the Lez at this point. At Bordes the road divides, the D4 continuing to follow the course of the Lez to its upper reaches while the left fork (D17) takes you up the valley of Bethmale and over the Col de la Core (4,577 ft) to the Haut Salat.

We travelled this route in reverse from Seix to Castillon and it was one of the most dramatic journeys we have made in the Pyrénées. The first part of the drive is through the charming valley of Esbints with beautiful views looking back over the Haut Salat. Higher up you enter a dark forest but eventually you come out above the tree line onto the bare mountainside following a rock-strewn road with frequent alarming notices warning against avalanches. The day we drove over the pass, the Col de la Core was wreathed in low cloud and there was no view from the top but, soon after we started our descent, the sun came out and the valley of Bethmale was bathed in a warm welcoming glow.

Bethmale is a fertile valley, famous for its cheeses, especially sheeps' cheese (*brébis*), which are made in the villages strung out along the route: Arrien, Aret, Ayet, Samortein and Bethmale itself. There is a cheese factory at Bethmale where you can stop for a tasting and to buy. There are good examples of local rural architecture in all the villages and in Ayet they hold an annual festival on August 15 when the villagers wear their traditional costumes including clogs whose toes curve inwards to a tapering point like the fashionable shoes seen in some fifteenth-century paintings.

The right-hand fork after Bordes leads to the pretty valley of Biros through which runs the river Lez. After five miles you come to Sentein where there is an interesting fortified church. It is a bizarre building: the west end has a tower with a square base and a two-arch opening on each face at the first stage. Above there is an awkward transition to a four-stage octagonal tower capped by a slate spire. The second storey of the octagonal section has dummy stone guns like those at Massat. The north side of the church is flanked by the remains of a curtain wall that once completely surrounded the building. It is reinforced by two very solid rectangular towers, linked to the church by massive buttresses and surmounted by jaunty witch's-hat slate spires. Presumably there were once towers on the other side of the church but even in its present reduced state the ensemble is impressive and, built as it is for the most part of undressed stone, looks more like a rugged frontier fort than a church.

Inside, the roof of the nave is decorated with fifteenth-century frescoes. Although now rather faded, they must once have been very fine and are painted in a sophisticated style similar to the tapestries in the Cluny Museum in Paris.

Above Sentein the Lez is little more than a mountain stream bordered by peaceful meadows and there are numerous places to picnic. The road finally peters out at the electricity station near Eylie. Serious backpackers can continue to the Lake of Araing and the Pic de Crabère (8,625 ft), the great peak that dominates the western valleys of the Couserans.

3 Bigorre

It is difficult to describe Bigorre without resorting to hyperbole: the highest mountains, the grandest *cirques*, the most turbulent torrents, the holiest shrine and, by far, the greatest number of tourists. Here, more than anywhere in the Pyrenean chain, the mountain wall seems an impenetrable barrier. Only twelve miles in depth, from the foothills to the frontier, the land rises quickly to a height of over 2,500 ft at mountain resorts like Saint-Lary and Cauterets, while the high peaks soar to over 10,000 (Vignemale 10,820 ft). This means that you can leave Lourdes or Bagnère-de-Bigorre in the lowlands and within an hour be high up in the mountains surrounded by superb scenery.

Bigorre derives from the Latin Bigerriones, the name given by the conquering Romans to the Celtic–Iberian peoples of the region. The mountain tribes of Bigorre have always been fiercely independent and, unlike the Convenes of Comminges and the Consorani of the Couserans, were never completely subdued by the legions but left to themselves in the vastness of the high valleys, while the capital of the Roman province, Tarbes, was sited some way to the north in the lowlands.

After the departure of the Romans at the end of the fifth century, Bigorre sank into almost total obscurity for five hundred years, only fitfully illuminated in the sixth century by evidence of the arrival of Christian missionaries in the region and the foundation of some primitive churches, one of which, Saint-Savin, survives to this day, although it was rebuilt in the twelfth century.

Early in the tenth century, Ramon I was created the first Count of Bigorre and made Tarbes his capital. The first Counts were fully occupied consolidating their position but in 1096 Bernard III succeeded to the title and set about codifying the legal system. Up until Bernard's time, Bigorre had no written laws; instead there were customs and privileges handed down by word of mouth and jealously guarded by the tribal elders. Bernard appointed a council of four of the most venerable of these greybeards to recall these ancient traditions and, for the first time, write them down. The culmination of these labours was the famous *fors de Bigorre*, which governed the relations between the people of the county and their rulers and is one of the earliest written constitutions known.

From the very beginning the fortunes of Bigorre were always closely intertwined with those of Armagnac to the north, Béarn to the west and Comminges and Foix to the east. Unlike France, the Salic law did not pertain in Bigorre and there were a number of Countesses of Bigorre who ruled in their own right. The most famous of these formidable ladies was Petronella who ruled for sixty years from 1191 to 1251. During this period she married five times, her third husband being Guy de Montfort, the son of the Englishman, Simon de Montfort, who led the crusade against the Albigensian heresy.

When Petronella died in 1251 she bequeathed to the County the most horrendous succession problem. It would be tedious in the extreme to detail the subsequent manoeuvres and machinations that dominated the politics of Bigorre for another fifty years. Suffice it to say that the Counts of Armagnac and Foix, the Viscount of Béarn and the Kings of France and England were all involved.

In 1300, after a direct appeal by the peoples of Bigorre to the French crown, Philippe le Bel sequestered the County and put it under direct rule until 1341 when it was granted to Count Roger Bernard II of Foix. In 1360, however, after the massive defeat of the French by the Black Prince at Poitiers, the County was ceded to the King of England as part of the terms of the Treaty of Brétigny. Soon afterwards the Black Prince himself, accompanied by the Princess of Wales, visited Bigorre to receive the homage of its nobility, and was given a magnificent reception at Tarbes.

But the English occupation was not popular and in 1406, infuriated by the heavy taxes imposed by the Black Prince after his ill-fated Spanish campaign, the people of Bigorre rose in revolt and expelled the enemy. The County now passed into the hands of the Counts of Foix and subsequently, after the unification of the houses of Foix and Albret, to Henri of Navarre and at last, when he became King in 1607, to France.

The northern frontier of Bigorre lies thirty miles south-west of Auch at Rabastens on the N21. Rabastens is a bastide founded in 1306 where the river Estéous joins the Alaric canal, which is supposed to have been constructed by the Visigothic King Alaric II at the beginning of the sixth century.

Five miles due west of Rabastens is Vic-en-Bigorre and just north of it, on the D6, Artagnan where you will find what is left of D'Artagnan's mother's home. The original building must have been modest indeed, judging by what is left, a small rectangular main building with a squat round tower. Sadly, although still occupied, the building is very dilapidated and the garden overgrown.

Another badly ruined building is the Abbey of Saint-Sever-de-Rustan, six miles south-east of Rabastens on the D6. Little remains of the original Romanesque building: on the south side is a portal with much-weathered sculpted capitals; inside are three Romanesque bays in the nave with an eighteenth-century roof and a crossing with a twelfth-century dome on pendentives, springing from columns with beautifully carved capitals. This is the most exciting part of the church and gives one some idea of how splendid the original building must have been. The choir is sixteenth-century.

Outside, to the west and north of the church, are extensive eighteenth-century outbuildings belonging to the abbey. They must have been magnificent for there are still traces of beautiful parquet floorings, finely wrought iron staircases and delicate plastered ceilings, but for the most part the scene is one of utter desolation with rooms engulfed by brambles and creepers and even some with large trees bursting through the floors. It would take millions of francs to restore the buildings to their former glory and it seems unlikely that the money will ever be found. Even more depressing is the fact that the fine fourteenth-century cloister, which has survived, was hijacked in 1889 by the town of Tarbes and re-erected in the Jardin Massey, since when the town councillors have steadfastly refused to part with it.

Tarbes is an industrial town, the largest in Gascony, with a population of 54,000. Founded by the Romans, it became the capital of the Counts of Bigorre in the tenth century and was occupied by the English from 1360 to 1406. In 1569, during the Wars of Religion, it was completely destroyed by Montgoméry's forces and the rebuilt town was subsequently badly damaged by opposing Catholic troops in 1592. In 1814 Wellington beat the French near Tarbes in one of the last battles of the campaign that drove Napoleon into exile for the first time.

Apart from the cloisters from Saint-Sever in the Jardin Massey, there is little to detain the traveller in Tarbes unless he loves horses, in which case he will want to see the famous Anglo-Arab steeds in the stables of Haras.

The twelve-and-a-half-mile journey from Tarbes to Lourdes is one of the best approaches to the Pyrénées in the whole chain, with magnificent views of the snow-capped mountain wall ahead. Lourdes is, of course, celebrated world-wide as the holy shrine to which hundreds of thousands of pilgrims flock every year to see the grotto where in 1858 the Virgin Mary appeared to fourteen-year-old Bernadette Soubirous, many of them hoping to be cured by the miraculous waters of some incurable disease. Such is the fame of Lourdes that in its centenary year, 1958, the town was host to over five million of the faithful.

Yet, at first sight, apart from the rather larger number than usual of nuns and priests, Lourdes looks much like any other prosperous, small provincial town with smart restaurants, comfortable cafés and enticing food shops. This is because the town is in two parts, divided by the Gave de Pau, a swiftly-flowing mountain river, and an isolated rock outcrop crowned by the medieval castle of the Counts of Bigorre.

East of the Gave de Pau, and higher up, is the old town where you will find hotels, shops, banks and offices; to the west, largely contained within a loop made by the river, is the 'religious city', all of it built since 1858 and consisting of basilicas, hospitals and shops selling religious bric-à-brac. Here, too, is the famous grotto.

Whatever your beliefs, the religious city is impressive. True, the approach via the Boulevard de la Grotte is extremely tawdry, with endless shops selling cheap religious souvenirs, but the view from the bridge that spans the Gave de Pau is very fine: on either side is the green river, curving from left to right, while ahead is a long straight avenue, bordered by trees, which ends in a hemicycle containing the lower church of the Rosaire, built between 1883 and 1901.

On either side of the church, projecting ramps, like arms extended in welcome, lead up to the basilica (1876–1908) built in the Byzantine style. There is a marvellous view from the top of the steps northwards over the Gave de Pau to the Convent of the Carmelites. Every evening a torch-lit service is held by the river in front of the convent and the pilgrims proceed along the bank of the river, over a bridge to Bernadette's grotto, which is at ground level on the north side of the basilica. The thousands of twinkling lights as the pilgrims move slowly to their goal is a moving sight.

The interior of the basilica certainly doesn't move one, except perhaps to laughter. It is dominated by a frightful Mabel Lucy Atwell mosaic of the Virgin Mary which fills the whole of the apse. The acoustics, however, are excellent. Sybil and I went to two concerts held in the basilica but, during a stirring rendition of the 'Dies Irae' chorus in Verdi's *Requiem*, we were alarmed to see bits dropping off the marble façade, so it looks as though the basilica is unlikely to last an eternity.

Walking back from the religious city one is uncomfortably aware of the menacing presence of the castle of the Counts of Bigorre dominating the river crossing from high up on its crag. During the Hundred Years' War, the castle was an English stronghold and

153

in 1363 the Black Prince paid it a visit during a tour of Bigorre. According to the contemporary chronicler Froissart '... while he was at Tarbes he had a great will to go see the castle of Lourdes three leagues distant, among the mountains. When he had fully examined that castle and country he was much pleased, as well with the strength of the place as its situation on the frontiers of several countries ...' In 1369 Lourdes was invested by French troops under the command of the Duke of Anjou. The town was quickly taken but the castle resisted all attempts to capture it for six weeks and at last the siege was called off. Eventually after a further siege lasting eighteen months the castle surrendered in 1403 and English rule in Bigorre was at an end.

Of the original castle only the keep survives: the rest was rebuilt in the nineteenth century and now houses a museum devoted to the history and traditions of the Pyrénées.

Lourdes is an ideal centre from which to explore Bigorre: it is full of hotels and because pilgrims come from all walks of life there are prices to suit every pocket. Lourdes is close to the mountains but in the immediate vicinity there is a great deal to see. Just south of the town is the Pic du Jer (3,110 ft) whose summit is easily reached by cable car. From the top are views in all directions: to the north is the plain with the dark mass of Tarbes sprawling across it; immediately below is Lourdes itself, the castle easily distinguished but the religious city somewhat hidden. To the south are the great peaks: on the left, clearly distinguished by its radio mast, is the Pic du Midi de Bigorre and further towards the right the two highest mountains on the French side, Vignemale (10,820 ft) and Balaïtous (10,322 ft). Nearby another smaller peak, Le Béout, is accessible by *téléférique*. A few miles west of Lourdes there is also a large lake where the townsfolk take their Sunday picnics and where there are facilities for windsurfing and other watersports.

Just south of Lourdes is the Lavedan, a network of seven valleys whose sturdy inhabitants are famous for their fiery independence. During the Middle Ages, the Lavedan was nominally under the control of a viscount, directly responsible to the Count of Bigorre;

in practice, however, the mountain peoples ruled themselves, each of the 'seven valleys' having its own customs and traditions, although a patriarchal system was common to them all. So jealously did the Lavedan guard its independence that, whenever a new Count of Bigorre succeeded to the title, it was the custom for him to go there, present himself to the elders and swear to uphold the rights and privileges of the 'seven valleys'. In their turn, the mountain peoples pledged their loyalty to their new overlord. Just as a precaution, however, hostages from the 'seven valleys' were taken beforehand and held in the castle of Lourdes to ensure the Count's safe return.

The gateway to the Lavedan is the mountain resort of Argelès-Gazost. The road divides here, the right-hand fork (D918) taking you out of Bigorre, over the Col d'Aubisque, to Béarn, while the left-hand road (D921) runs alongside the Gave de Pau, through a beautiful pastoral valley to Pierrefitte-Nestalas. Only a mile or so south of Argelès-Gazost a left-hand turning leads, via a narrow country road, to one of the most remarkable of the mountain churches, Saint-Savin.

The first sight of the church is unexpected: you round a tight bend and there is the massive apse of the chevet looming over the road like the bow of a great ship. You then arrive in a pretty square of which Saint-Savin forms the northern boundary.

Saint-Savin stands on the site of a Roman fort destroyed in the fifth century by Barbarian invaders. A monastery, Saint-Martin-de-Bencer, was founded here in the eighth century and changed its name to Saint-Savin in the eleventh century in honour of a Spanish saint who spent the last thirteen years of his life in the mountains above the village of Bencer, which like the monastery changed its name to that of the saint.

Seen from the square, the church has a simple grandeur, somewhat spoiled by the curious candle-snuffer slate spire over the squat crossing-tower. The high stone walls of the nave and crossing are devoid of windows, although there is a row of martial-looking embrasures just below the eaves where the roof level was raised in the fourteenth century. These features, together with the compact plan of the church, make Saint-Savin look more like a castle than a place of worship and indeed there is a sentry walk running right round the building at roof level.

The original entrance at the west end is now closed but there remains a large arch with nine recessed archivolts, supported by short half-round piers, alternating with attached shafts, which encloses a tympanum showing Christ in Majesty, surrounded by symbols of the evangelists. Unfortunately, the sculpture is so weathered and mutilated that little of its original beauty remains. To the left of the entrance, near ground level, is a small round-headed opening called the *fenêtre des cagots* where, so it is said, lepers and other unfortunates barred from the church were able to listen to the service.

The new entrance is via the south transept. Inside, you are immediately struck by the size and austerity of the interior: the bare stone walls are unlit and the only sources of light are the windows of the fourteenth-century tower and of the apse at the east end.

Although Saint-Savin is a cruciform church, the east end, with its crossing, wide transepts, apsed choir and side chapels, comprises a much larger spatial unit than the short three-bay nave, so that the usual dominant progression from west to east is lacking. Instead, you find yourself irresistibly drawn to the space below the crossing-tower just as you would in a centrally planned church. From here, it is the harmonious proportions of Saint-Savin and the sense of space that impress one most, rather than any individual detail.

The south transept contains a fifteenth-century font, supported by caryatids, called the *bénitier des cagots* because it was believed that it was once used exclusively by lepers and other pariahs; nearby is a remarkable organ case decorated with grisaille paintings of prophets and sibyls. It was built in 1557 but restored in the seventeenth and eighteenth centuries. In the nave there is a moving sculpture in wood of Christ on the cross, carved in Spain in the fifteenth century. The simple marble tomb of St Savin himself is to be found in the apse: it is eleventh-century.

Beyond the north transept is a chapter house containing some exceptionally fine treasures. In particular, there are two Romanesque statues of the Madonna and Child dating from the twelfth century. One, called the 'Black Virgin of the Crusades', is supposed to have been brought here by crusaders returning from the Holy Land: the Madonna sits in a hieratic pose with the infant Jesus on her knees, both are crowned and Jesus holds the Book of Life in his left hand. The sculpture has a golden patina. The other piece, the 'Virgin With Long Thumb', is similar in composition but here the infant Jesus is uncrowned and the left hand of the Madonna has a prominent raised thumb which once rested against a sceptre, now lost.

The architecture of the chapter house itself is interesting. In the centre of the room are two columns with Roman bases and archaic composite capitals, perhaps influenced by local Roman remains. The columns divide the chapter house into two and from them spring six primitive Gothic vaults with heavy, rather ugly ribs. On the west side of the room are two windows, each having a pair of arches supported on short twin columns, decorated with archaic carvings. The left-hand window has a column with a primitive head of the devil on the side of the capital facing into the room, the sides are decorated with cows, a deer and a complicated interlace motif. The right-hand window has a matching face of Christ, while the sides have carvings of flower heads, stars and birds. The meaning and origin of these strange carvings are a mystery.

A narrow country road leads from the south-west corner of the square of Saint-Savin to the hamlet of Arcizans-Avant and the so-called Château du Prince Noir, although there seems no reason to connect it with the Black Prince other than that he was in Bigorre in the 1360s and may have paid it a visit. Little remains of the original château except a small rectangular keep and two fifteenth-century doorways; the rest has been restored during the last ten years by the present owner. However, it is worth a detour for the view from the tower of the lovely valley of Argelès, with the mountains in the background. Another fine view of the valley can be had from the garden of the Chapelle de Piétat just off the D13, half a mile south of Saint-Savin.

The D13 rejoins the N21 at Pierrefitte-Nestalas, where the Gave de Cauterets makes a junction with the Gave de Gavarnie. Here a right-hand fork takes you to Cauterets and the Pont d'Espagne while the left-hand one (D921) leads to Luz-Saint-Sauveur and the Cirque de Gavarnie. Immediately after Pierrefitte-Nestalas, the D921 plunges into the Gorges de Luz but after five miles it emerges into another broad pastoral valley at the head of which is the charming mountain resort of Luz-Saint-Sauveur.

The town occupies a strategic position guarding one of the mountain passes into Spain, not an easy route for a would-be invader, it must be admitted, but one that was frequently used by marauding Spanish bands in the fourteenth century. It is also the starting point for the Route du Col du Tourmalet, leading via the mountain resort of Barèges over the highest pass in the Pyrénées (6,939 ft), which is normally only open from June to the end of October and leads to the valley of Campan.

In the Middle Ages Luz was the capital of the valley of Barèges, which although part of the Lavedan and nominally under the control of its viscount was in practice independent, with its own customs and traditions. The seventeen villages of the Barèges were divided into four Vics (from the Latin *vicus* = village) each with its own consul who served on a council presided over by the Consul of Luz which administered the affairs of the whole valley. The council had the right to administer justice, raise local taxes, and could even, as recognized by the French crown, negotiate treaties with the neighbouring Spanish valleys of Bielsa and Broto. Even now the 'Syndicat de Luz' looks after the rights of the valley peoples, although its role is hardly international.

Luz possesses one of the most remarkable fortified churches to be found anywhere in the Pyrénées. Saint-André was founded in the twelfth century by the Knights of Saint John to protect the pilgrim route to Compostella. To begin with the church was unfortified but in the fourteenth century an encircling wall was built at a time when Luz was under frequent attack from marauding Spanish bands. The wall is crenellated and pierced with loopholes, while the lower third is protected outside by a counterscarp. Originally the only way in was through the doorway in the barbican on the south side. This entrance was defended by loopholes in the walls on either side and by a machicolated parapet on the face of the tower above. The old door into the church, reached via the barbican, is now no longer used but on its left-hand side there is the tomb of a child contained within a simple arched opening, flanked by sculpted consoles and with carved capitals belonging to columns that have now disappeared. A Gascon inscription reads: 'Here lies Bene ... O ... bat daughter of Ramon de Barèges and Madame Na Hera. She died in the last week of April 1236. Gile de Sère made it.'

Once inside the wall you can see a sentry walk from which the defenders could fire at their attackers through the loopholes and at the east end a cemetery, now no longer used. The church itself is very simple with a three-bay nave and an apse at the east end. Just below roof level is another sentry walk with mitred shaped openings. On the south side is a campanile which also served as a watch-tower.

Nowadays access to the church is through a new doorway in the north-west corner of the wall which leads directly to the main entrance. This has a fine tympanum with Christ in a mandorla surrounded by signs of the evangelists. The two other archivolts of the arch are decorated with an intricate foliage motif and billet moulding. Above the tympanum is an inscription reading, 'The heavenly kingdom receives the just who quit the earth, provided that on their deathbeds they are close to Christ and the Virgin'. Below on the lintel is another inscription: 'The snake shrugs off his skin each year; he is very humble; avoid the worship of the flesh. If you wish to enter the temple do not pollute it ... fill yourself with the love of God.' On the base of the column to the left of the doorway is a quotation from Saint Paul: 'I cannot bend ... if anyone is right it is I.' On the base of the column on the right the inscription reads: 'I support those that are worthy; I reject the wicked' – a reference to judgement day.

Immediately south of Luz-Saint-Sauveur the road to Gavarnie (D921) crosses the Pont Napoléon, a single-arched bridge built in 1860 by order of Napoleon III. The view from the bridge of the mountain torrent surging through the narrow chasm far below is justly famous.

From here the road climbs steeply for five miles, hemmed in on either side by the narrow, forbidding gorge of Saint-Sauveur, until it reaches Gèdre, a mountain hamlet surrounded by steep pastures which, when we saw them, were covered with dwarf daffodils. After Gèdre a further five miles through wild rocky scenery brings you at last to Gavarnie.

The first impression is horrific: it comes as a considerable shock, after battling up the steep, stony route from Luz-Saint-Sauveur, to find a tourist village full of coaches, bars, restaurants and souvenir stalls. Luckily, however, as is always the case, you only have to walk a short way to leave the madding crowd behind. An easy, gradual climb, lasting only half an hour, brings you to a scrub-covered open space, through which the Gave de Gavarnie gently meanders. From here there is a magnificent view of what is generally considered the most majestic scene in the whole Pyrénées. You can, however, continue for another half-hour to the Hôtel du Cirque, from where there is an even better view. The faint-hearted can make the trip on horseback or by mule, which can be hired at the village. From the hotel a further journey on foot of about three-quarters of an hour, there and back, takes you to the foot of the Grande Cascade.

The Cirque de Gavarnie is a huge natural amphiteatre enclosed to the south by a curving mountain wall nearly five thousand feet high. The cliff-face is broken up by a series of horizontal, snow-capped ledges from which cascade innumerable waterfalls, one of them the source of the Gave de Pau. At its base the Cirque is nearly two and a half miles wide but the view at the summit stretches over a distance of nearly seven, taking in no less than eleven mountain peaks. Starting from the left (east) end there are the Grand and Petit Astazou (10,076 ft and 9,882 ft), the Pic du Marboré (10,656 ft), the three peaks of the Cascade (10,371 ft, 9,895 ft and 10,154 ft), the Epaule de Marboré (10,082 ft), the Tour and Casque de Marboré (9,872 ft and 9,862 ft), le Doigt de la Fausse-Brèche (9,666 ft) and le Taillon (10,315 ft). At the western end of the Cirque, between le Taillon and le Doigt, is a gap in the cliff-wall called the Brèche de Roland, which is supposed to have been made by a stroke of the Carolingian hero's sword.

Only a poet could do justice to this overwhelming sight, so let Victor Hugo have the last word: 'C'est une montagne et une muraille tout à la fois; c'est l'édifice le plus mystérieux du plus mystérieux des architectes; c'est le colosséum de la nature: c'est Gavarnie.'

Back at the village of Gavarnie (and probably by now not averse to downing a beer at one of the bars), you will see a twisting road that leads up the pretty valley of Espécières to the frontier at Port de Gavernie. At the start of it is a small fourteenth-century church, once belonging to the Hospitallers of Saint John of Jerusalem, where the pilgrims rested before resuming their arduous trek across the mountains.

Returning to Gèdre, on the D921, a turning to the right (going north) follows the Gave de Héas to its source in the Cirque de Troumouse. The first mile or so is through lush pastoral land but soon afterwards the landscape becomes grim with great stony outcrops and the Cirque itself is like a moon landscape: a savage, barren place compared with Gavarnie but impressive even so.

After Gavarnie, the most popular excursion from Lourdes is to Cauterets and the Pont d'Espagne. You take the N21 to Pierrefitte-Nestalas and branch right onto the D920. At once the road plunges into a narrow gorge through which tumbles the Gave de Cauterets. The route is much more tortuous and dramatic than the one to Gavarnie. Only at Cauterets itself does the valley widen sufficiently for habitation: this small town with a population of only one thousand is a popular ski-resort in the winter and in the summer makes an ideal base for excursions into the mountain on foot.

Above Cauterets the scenery grows even more rugged, although the steep slopes on either side are thickly wooded. All the time as you climb steeply upwards, the Gave flowing alongside gets louder and more boisterous. At every turn of the twisting road, so it seems, there is a new waterfall more spectacular than the last and the torrent ricochets from rock to rock sending up great sheets of spray which turn into rainbows as the sun glints through the water droplets. One of the most awe-inspiring of the falls is the Cascade de Lutour which crashes down in four separate, mighty jets.

Five more astonishing miles bring you to the Pont d'Espagne, a bridge crossing the Gave where two great waterfalls thunder into a narrow gully, full of seething white water. Nearby is a bar restaurant where you can pause to recover breath. From here a short walk of three-quarters of an hour brings you to the tranquil Lac de Gaube from where there is a view of the Pique Longue du Vignemale, the highest point of the Pyrénées (10,820 ft); you can also reach the lake by *téléférique* in ten minutes. Otherwise, you can continue by car on a very rough track up the wild but beautiful valley of Marcadau, until you reach a dead-end in a vast clearing. Here there is ample room to park and find a picnic spot, well away from anyone else, on the banks of the Gave which here is wider and less noisy than further downstream, although it still runs very fast over the boulder-strewn riverbed. We once spent a long, languorous afternoon here, eating a delicious picnic with a crisp white wine chilled in the Gave and watching a dipper perched on a rock in the middle of the stream and every so often plunging into the water after a fish. Thousands of feet above we caught a glimpse of an enormous bird that could have been an eagle, wheeling over the mountain crest.

The valley of Marcadau is in the beautiful Parc National des Pyrénées, created in 1967 to protect the ecology of the Pyrénées and covering an area of nearly 20,000 acres. Lighting fires, camping, dogs and picking flowers are all forbidden in the Parc but there are recognized mountain refuges where back-packers can stay overnight.

East of Lourdes is Bagnères-de-Bigorre, an agreeable resort which, although much smaller than Lourdes (population 9,880 as against 17,619 for Lourdes), may be preferred by those who find the cult of Bernadette excessive. Bagnères can be reached by taking the D937 from Lourdes or the D935 south from Tarbes.

Ten miles east of Bagnères is the Château de Mauvezin, a frontier fortress built on a promontory with superb all-round views. The name is thought to derive from *mauvais voisin* (bad neighbour), which seems to be borne out by a verse found in an old book:

Je suis le vieil castel qu'on nome Malvezin
Du haut de mon haut roc à tous je fais la nicque

Estant à qui m'entoure un fort malvais vesin
A moi qui se frotte se picque.

Roughly translated this means:

> I am the old castle called Malvezin
> From the top of my crag I cock a snook
> A bad neighbour to those around me
> Rub me the wrong way and you'll feel my sting.

It is not known when Mauvezin was originally built but it is mentioned in a document dated 1079 when Centulle I was Count of Bigorre. The present building dates from the thirteenth and fourteenth centuries. It has a square plan with massive buttresses at the corners and middles of three sides; the fourth, east side is dominated by a rectangular keep, one hundred and eighteen feet high, which guards the entrance.

In 1373 Mauvezin, which was at that time held by an English garrison under the command of a Gascon called Raymond de l'Epée, was invested by French troops led by the Duke of Anjou. The siege that followed is described by Froissart:

The castle of Malvoisin held out about six weeks; there were daily skirmishes between the two sides and the place would have held out much longer, for the fortress was so strong it could have withstood a very long siege, if it were not for the fact that the well was outside the walls and the French cut off the supply of water. The weather was very hot and the cisterns inside quite dry, for there had not been a drop of rain for six weeks; but the besiegers were at their ease on the banks of this clear fine river which they used for themselves and their horses.

The garrison of Malvoisin were alarmed by their situation for they could not hold out any longer: they had plenty of wine but not a drop of sweet water. They decided to parley and Raymond de l'Epée requested a safe-conduct to the duke, which having been granted he said 'My lord, if you will treat my companions and me honourably we will surrender the castle.' 'What is it you want?' replied the Duke of Anjou, 'get about your business, each of you to your own countries and don't go to any other castle that is holding out against us, for if you do and I catch you I will hand you over to Jocelin[1] who will shave you without a razor.'

'My lord,' said Raymond, 'if we leave, we must take what belongs to us and what we have gained by force of arms with great risk.'

The duke paused and then said, 'I agree that you take with you whatever you can carry in trunks or on horseback; any prisoners must be surrendered.'

All who were in the castle departed after surrendering it to the Duke of Anjou and took all they could with them. They returned to their own countries or elsewhere in search of adventure: but Raymond de l'Epée turned to the French and served the Duke of Anjou a long time, passed into Italy with him and was killed in a skirmish before the city of Naples.

After the English were driven out of Bigorre, Mauvezin was granted by the French King in 1376 to Gaston Fébus, Count of Foix (1331–91), one of the most powerful figures of the south-west who ruled not only the County of Foix, to the east of the Couserans, but also the Kingdom of Béarn, which lay to the south and west of Bigorre.

After Henri of Navarre and D'Artagnan, Gaston Fébus is the most famous of Gascon heroes. The soubriquet 'Fébus', which is Gascon for 'brilliant' or 'shining', was given to him as a young man because of his magnificent head of golden hair but, such was the force of his personality, it soon came to be applied to the man himself and acquired the additional meaning of illustrious; in fact, by implication he was being compared to Phoebus Apollo, the Sun God, thus anticipating Louis XIV by some three hundred years.

It is easy to see why Gaston Fébus was so popular; he possessed all the qualities admired in the Age of Chivalry: he was a brave and successful warrior, a fine poet and a great hunter who enjoyed the chase so much that he wrote a book about it, which became the standard work on the subject during the late Middle Ages.

An early feat of arms, which made Gaston Fébus's name famous throughout France, occurred in 1358, when he was only twenty-seven. He was on his way home with another famous Gascon leader, the Captal de Buch, from a 'crusade' against the pagans in

1 The French executioner.

9 This sculpture embedded in the wall of Saint-Aventin shows the bull that, directed by an angel, led the faithful to the body of the saint.

10 This curious Celtic sculpture, depicting a twin deity, was incorporated into the walls of Saint-Aventin when it was built.

11 This remarkable capital from Saint-Sever depicts Salome dancing before Herod. On the right-hand side the head of John the Baptist is given to Salone.

OPPOSITE PAGE: 8 The rugged Pyrenean church of Saint-Aventin.

12 The Gallo-roman sarcophagus of Sainte-Quitterie in the crypt of Saint-Pierre, Aire-sur-L'Adour.

13 The front of this house at Jouanhaut is a beautiful example of the fine carpentry to be found in the Landes.

the deep forests of what later became Prussia. It was the time of the Jacquerie, the French peasants' revolt, and Gaston Fébus heard that the rebels were threatening to take prisoner the Dauphin's wife, sister and daughter who had taken refuge in the town of Meaux. At once the two knights rode to the rescue with a small force of 120 men. Despite being heavily outnumbered the Gascons succeeded in reaching the royal party ahead of the rebels and placing them under their protection:

> The Dauphine had taken refuge, along with a number of noble ladies and their children in the market-place at Meaux. This had a natural moat on three sides formed by a loop in the river Marne; the fourth side by which the market was entered was closed by a wall with a gate in it. The rest of Meaux rapidly filled up with Jacquerie from Paris and the surrounding countryside who threatened to storm the market-place.
>
> The noble ladies who were lodged there were terrified to see such crowds advancing on them. At this, the two Gascon lords and their men marched to the gates of the market-place and threw them open. Standing under the banner of the Count of Foix and the pennant of the Captal de Buch they confronted the badly armed Jacquerie. When the rebels saw such a well-equipped company of noblemen sally forth to guard the market-place, those in the vanguard began to fall back; the noblemen followed them striking at them with their swords and lances. Feeling the weight of these blows the terrified Jacquerie retreated so quickly that they fell over one another in their haste. More armed men charged out of the market-place and drove the rebels before them, striking them down like beasts and clearing the town of them, for there was no order or discipline and they slew so many of them that they were tired, flinging them in great heaps into the river and no one would have escaped if they had chosen to pursue them.
>
> When the men-at-arms returned to Meaux they set fire to the town and all the peasants they could find were shut up in it because they had supported the rebels.

Returning home after the massacre of Meaux, Gaston Fébus discovered that in his absence his great rival, Jean I, Count of Armagnac, had been putting forward claims to the County of Bigorre. Despite attempts at mediation by the Pope, war broke out in 1362, culminating in the Battle of Launac. This encounter was on a scale that rivalled any battle of the Hundred Years' War and involved all the great Gascon lords: the Counts of Astarac and of l'Isle Jourdain fought on the side of Gaston Fébus, while against them were ranged the Count of Comminges, the Viscount of Fézensaguet and the Lord of Albret on the side of Jean I. The result was a catastrophic defeat for the Count of Armagnac who was captured and held to ransom, along with many other nobles, including the Lord of Albret.

Gaston Fébus demanded the enormous sum for those days of 300,000 florins for the release of his fallen foe and altogether collected 600,000 florins from his noble captives. This fortune, together with his extensive territories, made Gaston Fébus the most powerful political figure in the whole of south-west France.

That Gaston Fébus was also a fine poet is attested by his famous lyric *The Song of Gaston Fébus*:

> Aqueres mountagnes
> Que ta hautes soun
> M'empechen de bede
> Mas amous oun soun
>
> Se canti quan canti
> Canti pas per you
> Canti per ma miga
> Qui-ey tant loegn de you
>
> Si sabi las bede
> Ou las rencountra
> Passari l'ayguete
> Chens pou d'em nega
>
> Aqueres mountagnes
> Que s'abacheran
> Et mas amouretes
> Que parecheran

Roughly translated this means: These mountains, which are so high, prevent me from seeing my loved ones. If I sing, when I sing I do not sing for myself. I sing for my loved ones who are far away from me. If I thought I would see them or meet them, I would cross the waters without fear of drowning. The mountains will stoop and my loved ones will reappear.

But there was a darker side to Gaston Fébus's nature. During the siege of Lourdes he summoned to his presence its commander, Sir Peter Arnant, a knight of Béarn, and demanded that he surrender the castle. The unfortunate man was in an impossible position for he was the vassal of both Gaston Fébus, who as ruler of Béarn was his immediate overlord, and of the King of England, whose son the Black Prince had actually appointed him to his post. Sir Peter steadfastly refused to submit to the Count of Foix, swearing that his greater loyalty was to Edward III, whereupon, in an ungovernable rage, Gaston Fébus seized a dagger and struck him dead on the spot.

Even worse was Gaston Fébus's treatment of his son, Gaston. At that time (1377), Gaston Fébus's estranged wife was living with her father, the King of Navarre, in Spain and the young Gaston had paid them a visit. On his return, he was denounced by his half-brother Yvain who accused him of having in his possession a pouch containing a white powder given to him by the King of Navarre:

The Count of Foix thought deeply about what he had been told and remained alone until it was time for dinner when he sat down as usual at his table in the hall. His son Gaston always tested the dishes and placed them before him: as he served the first course the Count noticed the strings of the pouch tucked inside his doublet and his blood boiled. 'Gaston come here!' he said. 'I want a word with you.' The young man approached the table, whereupon the Count seized him, undid his doublet and taking his knife cut the strings of the pouch. The boy was thunderstruck: he spoke not a word but turned white with fear and trembled violently, for he knew he had done wrong. The Count opened the pouch and took some of the powder which he sprinkled on a slice of bread and calling one of his dogs gave it to him to eat. No sooner had the dog taken a bite of the bread than his eyes rolled in his head and he fell dead. The Count was furious and with reason: rising from the table he made to strike his son with his knife but was restrained by his knights and squires saying, 'For God's sake, Sire, don't be hasty; find out more before you harm your son.'

The first words the Count spoke were in his native Gascon '*Zo, Gaston traitour*, I have waged war and made enemies of France, England, Spain and Navarre and fought gallantly against them all for your sake and now you want to murder me!' And leaping over the table with a knife in his hand he would have killed Gaston if the knights and squires had not come between them, imploring him with tears, 'Ah my Lord, for God's sake don't kill Gaston. Put him in prison while you make enquiries, perhaps he didn't know what was in the pouch and is innocent.'

'Take him to the tower,' said the Count, 'and see that he is well guarded.'

So Gaston was confined to a room in the keep where he remained for ten days. He scarcely ate or drank any of the food which was brought to him but pushed it to one side. It is said that, after he died, all the meals were found untouched, so it was a marvel that he survived so long. The Count would not allow anyone to remain in the cell to advise or comfort him and he only had the clothes he was wearing when he was arrested. So he became furious and melancholy for he had not expected such harshness and he cursed the hour he was born. On the day he died they brought him food saying 'Gaston, here is meat for you' but he ignored them and said 'Put it down'. The servant, seeing all the food he had previously brought untouched, went to the Count and said 'My Lord, for God's sake watch out for your son, he is starving himself to death and has eaten nothing since he was imprisoned. The Count was enraged and without a word left his chamber and went to the tower. As ill-luck would have it, he had in his hand a small knife with which he had been cleaning his nails.

'Ha, traitor!' cried the Count, 'Why don't you eat?' and he held the point of the knife against Gaston's throat, then he stormed out of the room.

Small as it was the knife cut a vein in Gaston's throat and feeling this he turned his face away and so died.

The Count had scarcely regained his chamber when the servant came in and said, 'My Lord, your son Gaston is dead.'

'Dead?' said the Count.

'As God is my witness, he is indeed, my Lord.'

The Count could not believe it and sent a knight to find out if the news was true. He returned and confirmed that Gaston was, indeed, dead.

The Count was deeply moved and cried, 'Ah Gaston! What a sorry business. It was an evil day when you went to see your mother in Navarre. I shall never be happy again.'

Gaston Fébus's great passion in life was the chase and, according to Froissart, he kept a pack of sixteen hundred hounds. In 1391 he was returning from a bear hunt in the Pyrénées and had stopped for refreshment at an inn near Orthez when he collapsed and died: he was sixty. Gaston Fébus may not appeal to modern readers but in his own times there was no greater Gascon hero.

Above the entrance to the Château de Mauvezin is a marble plaque bearing the sculpted arms of the Counts of Foix: at the top a quartered shield with three vertical bands signifying Foix and Bigorre and two belled cows representing Béarn. Underneath is a beautifully carved helmet surmounted by the cow's head of Béarn while below is a winged dragon. Across the middle is an inscription *Jay Belle Dame*. The significance of these enigmatic words is now lost but it is thought that they may refer to the marriage of Gaston Fébus's son Gaston to Beatrice of Armagnac.

Inside the castle you can make a tour of the ramparts and then enter the tower where there is a gruesome waxworks reconstruction of Gaston Fébus murdering his son. From the top of the tower there is a magnificent panorama: to the south is the Pic du Midi de Bigorre which, although not the highest mountain, dominates the plain by virtue of its isolation from the rest of the chain. It is easily recognized by its T.V. station. Standing here it is not difficult to see why the castle was built on this site, dominating, as it does, the passages from the high valleys of Bigorre to the plain and the vital east-west route from Toulouse to Bayonne.

A favourite excursion from Bagnères is to the Grottes de Medous, only a mile to the south, off the D935, where you can glide in a boat through a series of magnificent underground caverns. A little further south is the charming valley of Lesponne with a number of traditional small stone barns with stepped gables and thatched roofs. The road comes to a dead end at Chiroulet where there is a good small hotel. From here a long, but relatively easy climb of four hours (there and back) brings you to the beautiful Lac Bleu.

The main road (D935) continues south following the valley of the Adour through Campan to Sainte-Marie-de-Campan where there is an attractive mountain church with a typical slate-covered spire. Here the road divides: the right (west) fork leads up the pleasant pastoral valley of Campan to the popular ski resort of La Mongie. *En route*, at Artigues, is a well-known beauty spot with a waterfall, the Cascade du Garet.

Just beyond La Mongie is the *téléférique* which takes you to within seven hundred and fifty feet of the summit of the Pic du Midi de Bigorre (9,400 ft). Here you will be rewarded (weather permitting) by the finest view in the whole Pyrénées. In the right conditions it is possible to see all the way from the Montagne Noire, to the north of Carcassonne in the east, westwards to La Rhune in the Pays-Basque and sometimes it is even possible to glimpse the glow of the lighthouse at Biarritz. Immediately to the south are all the highest peaks of the chain, culminating in the Pic d'Aneto (11,168 ft) over the border in Spain. No wonder Henry Russell said that sunrise here was enough to make the saints nostalgic for the earth.

The Pic du Midi can also be reached by car from the Col du Tourmalet but it is a very difficult climb and anyway the pass is only open in the three summer months. After the Col the road winds down to Barèges and thence to Luz-Saint-Sauveur and the Lavedan (see pages 154–8).

The left-hand fork at Sainte-Marie-de-Campan leads over the Col d'Aspin (4,885 ft) to the Vallée d'Aure, which can be reached more easily by taking the D929 south from Lannemezan. In the early Middle Ages the Vallée d'Aure was a viscounty whose feudal overlord was the King of Aragon. In the fourteenth century the Viscounty of Aure was united with the valleys of Magnoac, Neste and Barousse to form the Four Valleys, a virtually independent enclave in the mountains enjoying many ancient rights and privileges. In 1398 the Four Valleys fell into the hands of the Counts of Armagnac and remained part of their territories until 1475 when they were surrendered to the French crown.

During the rule of the last Count of Armagnac, Jean V, the Vallée d'Aure provided a convenient escape route for the Count whenever, as constantly happened, he had incurred the wrath of the French King. Once across the border and into Spain the Count knew that he could rely on the protection of his father-in-law, the King of Navarre.

At its northern end, between La Barthe-de-Neste and Arreau, the Vallée d'Aure is not particularly attractive, especially at Sarrancolin, where the bleak red cliffs are disfigured by marble quarries. Arreau, on the other hand, is a lively market town, often so packed with traffic that it is difficult either to negotiate it or to find a parking spot. Nevertheless it has some nice old houses, including the sixteenth-century half-timbered Maison Valencia-Labat, opposite the town hall. It is also a good place to buy the strong mountain cheeses, made by traditional methods in the surrounding valleys. The sheep's cheeses are particularly good.

Arreau, which was formerly the capital of the Four Valleys, marks an important crossroads where the east–west mountain routes over the passes of the Col de Peyresourde from Luchon and the Col d'Aspin from the high valleys of the Lavedan meet the main north–south route from the lowlands to the Spanish border.

After Arreau things improve, the valley looks more pastoral and there are some attractive villages. At Bourisp, six miles south of Arreau, the porch of the Gothic church contains a sixteenth-century wood carving of the seven deadly sins with the sins depicted as women in the costumes of the period of Henri III of France (1574–89). At nearby Vieille-Aure is a church with twelfth-century apse and side chapels. The nave and solid west tower are sixteenth-century.

Soon afterwards you reach Saint-Lary-Soulan, one of the most popular Pyrenean resorts and a good place from which to explore the Massif de Néouvielle and the Vallée de Rioumajou. South of Saint-Lary, the road enters a narrow gorge. After two miles you come to the village of Tramezaigues and the remains of a castle that defended the valley against incursions by the Aragonese. Immediately afterwards a left turn brings you to the beginning of the valley of Rioumajou. The unmade road climbs up through magnificent woods, alongside a rapidly flowing stream bordered by grassy banks. As the scenery gets prettier the track deteriorates until it finally peters out in the clearing of Frédançon. From here an easy four-mile walk brings you to the Hospice de Rioumajou in a beautifully grassy amphitheatre.

Three miles south of Tramezaigues, on the D929, is Fabian where a turning to the right leads to the *massif* of Néouvielle. The great attraction of this region is the hundreds of lakes scattered throughout it, most of them only accessible on foot. By car you can follow an eight-mile bone-crushing track along the narrow valley of the Neste de Couplan to the Barage de Cap-de-Long. After three miles you come to a spectacular waterfall, the Cascade de Couplan, that crashes down over three hundred feet from the Lac de l'Oule. After this a series of seemingly endless bends brings you to a chalet hotel, high up overlooking the Lac d'Orédon, whose boulder-strewn slopes are covered with pines. The far end of the lake is closed by the massive dam wall of the Barage de Cap-de-Long.

A narrow track along the south side of the Lac d'Orédon brings you to the foot of the dam after which you must proceed on foot. The view is austere but impressive with the still water of the lake surrounded by sharp mountain crests, dominated by the peak of Néouvielle (10,141 ft). Another track takes you up the east side of Lac d'Orédon to the Lac d'Aumar and Lac d'Aubert, beyond which a car can go no further.

Back at Fabian, the main road continues south to Gela and then follows the course of the Neste de Saux to the tunnel of Bielsa, which takes you across the border into Spain.

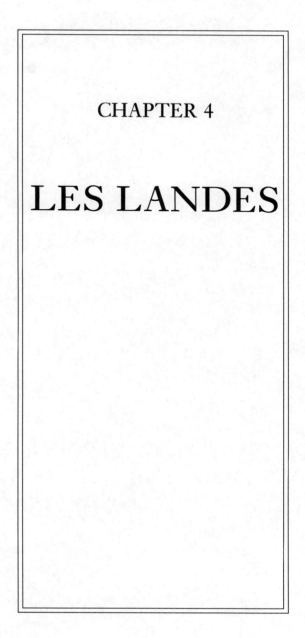

CHAPTER 4

LES LANDES

'... a desolate landscape where a man can find no comforts whatsoever, no wine, no meat, no water. There is only honey, millet and pigs.'

SO WROTE THE twelfth-century author of the *Liber Sancti Jacobi*, a guide written for pilgrims on their way to Santiago de Compostella. And indeed the medieval traveller had every reason to fear the Landes, for in those days it was one of the poorest and most inhospitable parts of France, a desolate region little better than a desert. Few outsiders would brave the fevers and hardships of a journey across the Landes and those who did regarded the inhabitants as little better than savages.

As late as 1860, Henri Maret, a Parisian who made an excursion from Bordeaux into the Landes, could write: 'I was stupid enough to venture into this region on a fine day in February ... the Landes are for the most part immense deserts with occasional stunted shrubs. The monotony of these plains is fatiguing to both the traveller's eyes and feet. From time to time a pine forest stands out against the horizon but without changing the sad, still landscape. You can sometimes journey for twenty leagues without meeting another human being or seeing a house, and should you come upon a shepherd striding on gigantic stilts, driving a milk-white flock before him, he will suddenly disappear as you approach, like a ghost.'

Yet by 1860 a vast programme of reclamation, started at the end of the eighteenth century, was already over seventy years old and within another twenty would radically transform the desert into the vast forest that we see today.

The Landes has the form of an enormous triangle with its base the Atlantic coast, stretching south from the Arcachon basin to the mouth of the river Adour and its point over sixty miles inland in the vicinity of Nérac. The coast consists of a strip of sand dunes about seven miles wide. Some of these dunes are the size of small hills and the most famous of them, the Dune du Pilat, near Arcachon, is three hundred and twenty-eight feet high and the highest in Europe.

Behind the dunes is a serious of lagoons, running north to south, which originally formed because the few small streams flowing through the Landes were blocked by the shifting sands and prevented from reaching the sea. The water spread to become swamps which have now been drained and turned into lakes where there are attractive holiday resorts, offering swimming and boating. Small streams called *courants* flow out of some of the lakes and eventually find a circuitous way to the sea. Some of these meander through beautiful scenery reminiscent of the Everglades of Florida. They are navigable by canoes and punts and, as he drifts with the stream, the voyager will see around him all kinds of interesting flowers and birds.

Until the nineteenth century, however, there was nothing behind the lagoons but a mournful landscape composed of barren heathland and fever-ridden marshes, inhabited for the most part by a few wretched shepherds, like those described by Henri Maret, who journeyed through the fens on stilts, guarding large flocks of sheep. In those days the Landes had more head of sheep than any other part of France: in 1857 there were 300,000 of them. Except for sheep farming, the only source of income came from bee-keeping. The heathland flowers give the honey a delicious flavour and it can still be bought from farms in the Landes to this day.

Apart from the wandering shepherds most of the inhabitants of this sad country lived in small oases of grassland called *airials*. These were to be found in isolated spots where for some reason, usually because the land was slightly higher than the surrounding

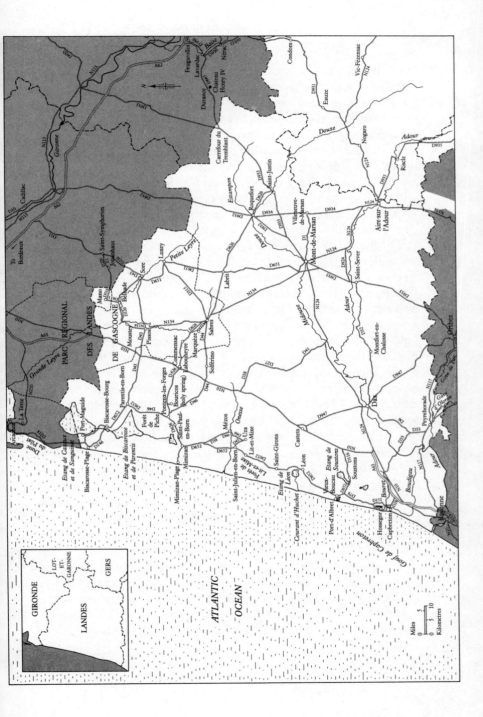

flat country, conditions were a little more favourable. The *airials* consisted of a few half-timbered houses, some pigs and poultry.

Nearby were one or two small fields where millet and rye were grown but this was for subsistence only. *Airials* are still to be found in clearings in the Landais forest but the old houses have been smartened up and there are bright flowers where crops once grew; the subsistence farmers are long since gone, to be replaced by well-off local businessmen or foreigners from northern France. If you would like to see what an *airial* would really have looked like, you will find one at the Ecomusée de la Grande Lande at Sabres, which is part of the Parc Naturel Régional des Landes de Gascogne, described in detail on pages 186–89.

For hundreds of years nothing was done to improve the Landes or to alleviate the miserable existence of the people who lived there. Feeble attempts were made at the beginning of the eighteenth century when the first pines were planted at Mimizan and Parentis-en-Born but it was not until 1788 that Brémontier, a famous French construction engineer, started on the immense task of holding back the dunes, which were advancing inland at a rate of between thirty and eighty feet a year, burying whole villages that lay in their path. Until this was done there was little point in trying to reclaim the interior. Brémontier began by constructing a palisade, well above the highest tide line, against which the sand accumulated. As the sand built up, the height of the palisade was increased until eventually there was an embankment forty feet high, forming a permanent coastal barrier. The next step was to prevent the tops of the dunes being whipped off and blown inland by the gales. This was done by planting a species of coarse grass called *gourbet* whose roots spread very quickly, forming a dense network that held the sand in check. Behind this first line of defence Brémontier planted a mixture of gorse and pine seeds. The gorse and broom grew quickly and helped to protect the slower-growing pine trees. By 1867 the dunes had been fixed and 198,000 acres had been planted with pines.

The problem of how to improve the fertility and drainage of the interior had still to be solved, however, and this task was under-taken by another engineer called Chambrelent at the beginning of the nineteenth century. The bleak conditions in the Landes were due to a thin layer of sandy topsoil covering a layer of impermeable red sandstone called *alios*, or, in the local patois, *garelouche*, lying at a depth of twenty inches, that stopped the growth of plant roots and created marshes in low-lying areas. Chambrelent put forward a scheme which included breaking up the hard rock, draining marshes, introducing fertilizers and planting pine trees. For a long time progress was painfully slow because of lack of money, until Napoleon III took a hand. A law was passed obliging the local communes to drain their land and plant trees. The Emperor himself set an example by buying and planting an enormous tract of land near Sabres, called Solférino after his famous victory. By the end of the century the forest covered a vast area of over 2,000,000 acres.

This dramatic alteration in the physiognomy of the Landes brought about far-reaching changes in the ecology and economy of the region. The hundreds of miles of forest were soon populated by all kinds of birds, including many that the French love to hunt and eat: pheasant, snipe, woodcock, *ortolan* and above all the *palombe*. Great flocks of these wild pigeons fly across south-west France every autumn on their way from Scandinavia and northern Europe to the warmer climates of southern Spain and North Africa. This annual migration arouses the same degree of fervour and excitement in the Landes that the World Series does in the U.S.A. or the F.A. Cup in England. From the beginning of October the arrival of the *palombe* is eagerly awaited, not only in the Landes but in the Pays-Basque and Armagnac as well. Workers take time off from their factories, shopkeepers shut their shops and professional men close their offices, all of them intent on bagging as many *palombes* as they can.

With such a reception committee it is a wonder that any of the birds survive at all but the *palombes* are easily frightened and it is very hard to get near them. To overcome this difficulty, elaborately camouflaged hides are set up, both on the ground and in the trees. Some of these hides are big enough to hold several sportsmen, who may have to stay there all day for several days. Naturally, they take a good supply of food and wine and great camaraderie grows up between members of the group who may well meet each other in the same hides year after year. From the hides, the huntsmen manipulate a complicated system of decoy birds set high in the trees to attract the *palombes* and persuade them to settle long enough for the *chasseurs* to get in a shot. The decoys are controlled by an intricate network of lines leading back to the hide, which when they are pulled make the decoy flap its artificial wings, thus catching the attention of the *palombes*. It is a highly skilled operation requiring great patience. Some hunters use live birds attached by their legs to the perches, as decoys, which are kept hooded until the *palombes* approach.

The *palombe* is considered to be a great delicacy and is quite often found on restaurant menus. It can be roasted but the best-known recipe is a rich casserole dish called *salmis de palombe* which can be bought in tins in the better *charcuteries* – and very good it is too.

The maritime pine soon proved to be a valuable resource: it was tapped for its resin, which was distilled to produce turpentine, while the wood was converted into paper, planks or pit-props. From being the poorest part of France, the Landes became for a while the richest. Unfortunately, this prosperity did not last; the industries on which it was based have all declined since the Second World War and now the French Government is pouring money into the region to help promote tourism, especially on the coast where small resorts, like Port d'Albret, have been transformed into architect-designed leisure complexes with smart flats and villas, pedestrianized shopping precincts and all kinds of sports facilities including, at Port d'Albret, a bull-ring.

It is a shame that so few of the motorists who dash through the Landes on their way to Spain ever stop to explore. Speeding down the N10 you get an impression of an endless vista of trees which is quite misleading. Of course, there are boring stretches but it is not all monotone; there are other trees besides the ubiquitous pine, oaks and acacias, for instance, and there are heather-covered clearings which are sometimes a mass of nectar-seeking butterflies. There are many delightful villages in the interior and, of course, the *airials* with their clusters of half-timbered houses. On the coast there is a wide variety of resorts from gracious Hossegor with its elegant pre-war villas to the brand-new Port d'Albret, while behind the coastal dunes are some beautiful lakes. There is also the Parc Naturel Régional des Landes de Gascogne, covering an area of over 500,000 acres, including two interesting open-air museums.

The Ecomusée de la Grande Lande at Marquèze is situated deep in the heart of the Landais forest at the southern end of the Parc Naturel Régional des Landes de Gascogne. To reach Sabres, starting from Agen, take the D119 towards Bordeaux. After twenty miles turn left at Feugarolles onto the D930 to Lavardac. A slower route to Lavardac, but passing through more attractive scenery, is via Nérac on the D656 and D930.

From Lavardac follow the D665 to Durance, a thirteenth-century fortified bastide, of which only the original gateway and one defensive tower remain. Nearby are the vestiges of the so-called Château Henri IV, where the Vert Galant is supposed to have stayed when hunting. Durance lies on the border of the Pays d'Albret; you enter the Landes about a mile east of the Carrefour du Tremblant where the D665 meets the D933, although the landscape here, while flat, is still open with stands of trees rather than thick forest.

Seventeen miles south of the Carrefour du Tremblant is Saint-Justin where, on a baking hot day, Sybil and I witnessed our first *Course Landaise*, a colourful and exciting spectacle peculiar to the Landes and the extreme west of Armagnac. The *Course Landaise* is often confused with the bull-fight but, although there are some similarities, there are fundamental differences. In this sport the object is not to kill the wild cows, which are used here instead of bulls, but to display the skills of a daring athlete who confronts a dangerous, confused animal with no other weapon than his self-confidence. The wild cows are two years old and specially reared for the *Course Landaise* on local ranches. They are savage and powerful and, unlike the victims of the *Corrida*, are not weakened by having darts planted in their shoulders before they are challenged.

The day we went to Saint-Justin the temperature was in the hundreds. Gasping in the heat we walked down an avenue of brutally pollarded plane trees to a small concrete stadium. Inside, two thousand ardent fans were crammed together on the shady side of the area, out of the searing sun. Because of the heat, the start had been delayed until early evening: there was a long wait and then a fire engine arrived, a hose was unwound and a *sapeur-pompier*, looking very hot in his thick uniform, slowly and meticulously sprayed water over the sand to lay the dust.

The programme began with the arrival of the band, dressed in black trousers, white shirts and black berets, playing 'The Entry of the Gladiators'. Behind the band were girls and boys wearing traditional Landais costume: the girls were dressed in long, flowered skirts and aprons, white blouses covered by pink shawls and white bonnets; the boys wore black trousers, white shirts with red tassels at the throat and black berets. They all paraded round the arena on stilts to great applause. Finally, out strutted the *Cuadrillas*, teams made up of *cordiers* and *sauteurs*, clad all in white with red ties and red or blue cummerbunds, and the splendidly attired *écarteurs*, wearing short embroidered jackets, waistcoats, white ducks and coloured cummerbunds. The *Cuadrillas* marched towards one end of the arena, where the judges sat, high up in the stand, and, standing on tip-toe with their arms above and in front of their heads, their hands open and fingers together, pointed at them – a very graceful greeting.

Now at last the *Course Landaise* could start: the gates were opened and out charged the first wild cow to an excited fanfare from the band. The cow had a leather halter round its horns to which was attached a long rope at the end of which were the *cordiers*. Their job is to control the movements of the cow from a distance, using the rope as a break, and to manoeuvre it into position at one end of the arena, in line with the judges. If the cow shows an inclination to attack the *cordiers*, they take refuge behind one of the wooden barriers erected at intervals round the arena, which are just wide enough for a man to squeeze into but too narrow for the cow to follow. A great deal of the success of the *Course* depends on the skill of the *cordiers* in controlling the movement of the cow. The knack is to turn the animal so that it sees before it the *écarteur*, standing on tiptoe, arms outstretched before him. Behind the *écarteur* crouches another member of the team waving a handkerchief to attract the attention of the beast. When the *écarteur* judges that the moment is ripe, he signals to the *cordiers* who slacken the rope so that the animal is free to charge. The *écarteur* stands his ground as the animal thunders towards him, only turning sideways at the very last moment, arching his body so that the horns pass just inside the small of his back, while the cow's haunches brush his buttocks in passing. If done correctly the effect is both elegant and spectacular. The *écarteur*'s most difficult feat is to make his pass on the inside, that is to say the side of the cow to which the rope is attached. This means that the *cordiers* cannot tauten the rope until the *écarteur* has stepped over it, making it easier for the cow to gore the *écarteur* if something goes wrong. If all goes well, the bewildered cow is restrained by the *cordiers* and persuaded into position for another charge.

Unfortunately, the day we went, the first pass was a disaster. A young *écarteur* in a green jacket misjudged his timing and was knocked over by the cow and gored. Immediately the rest of the team rushed forward to distract the angry beast while *cordiers* tailed onto the end of the rope, trying to impede its progress as the *écarteur* struggled to his feet, sprinted to the side of the arena and jumped over the barrier to safety. Luckily, the cows' horns are always tipped with leather to prevent a serious wound, but even so they can and do draw blood.

The show continued with a great many disasters. One particular cow had a nasty habit of lifting its left-hand horn as it charged and this trick caught nearly all the *écarteurs*. One of them, Ramuncho, a past champion, was knocked over twice and the second time received a nasty wound in the back of his head.

The most successful competitors were the *sauteurs*. Like the *écarteurs* they wait for the cow to charge but, instead of standing their ground, they jump over the animal. Their first jump is a shallow dive with arms outstretched, landing on both feet behind the cow. If the dive is well executed, the *sauteur* will be horizontal just above the cow's back as it passes beneath him. The closer he is to the animal's back the better the jump. To achieve this, the *sauteur* runs to meet the cow as it charges and takes off at the last possible moment. Perfect timing is vital. If the jump is performed well, it looks just like the famous paintings of athletes leaping over the backs of bulls depicted on ancient vases found in Crete: could there be some distant connection? The *sauteur*'s second jump is a forward somersault but his most sensational trick is to tie his legs together with his sash, stuff his feet in a red beret and do a standing jump over the horns of the charging beast.

During the interval, the boys and girls returned and danced on stilts, after which they formed a circle, still on stilts, and lifted a small girl clutching a French flag on a tray above their heads to furious applause. The second half of the show went very much better with some skilful displays, the best of them being greeted by enthusiastic fanfares from the band, which during the first half had remained rather quiet. At the end the *Cuadrillas* lined up before the judges to learn their verdicts. There were awards for the best *Cuadrilla*, the best individual performance by an *écarteur* and a *sauteur* and the best team of *cordiers*. Points were awarded to everyone including the most successful *Ganaderia*, the ranch that reared the best cows, and even the best cow of the show, that is to say the one whose charges were the most determined and the most direct: the cow which lifted its left horn did not rate highly. All these points accumulate over the season in a league table which produces a supreme champion in each of the different classes, including, yes, a champion cow. A very different ending to the bloody climax of the *Corrida*.

The Gascons are mad about sport: where else would you find a chapel dedicated to rugby like Notre-Dame-du-Rugby at Lar-rivière? But then the South-West is a rugby stronghold and Agen supplies no less than five of the current national teams. Another purely local sport is the *Jeu de Quilles*, a form of skittles played with six pins about three feet high on any piece of level ground – including the high road. The pins are set up with three large ones behind and three slightly smaller ones in front. Instead of a ball, you try to knock them down with a half-size pin called a *maillet* from a distance of thirty feet. Teams of three compete with the object of leaving only one *quille* standing. If the first throw is successful the next man in the team has a free go, as does the third if the second man achieves the same result. The maximum score in each round is three points and the first team to reach eleven points is the winner.

From Saint-Justin take the D626 to Roquefort, a *castelnau* that takes its name from an early castle built on a rock, around which in the early Middle Ages the town grew up. Situated at an important crossroads, where the main road from Marmande to Mont-de-Marsan crosses the rivers Estampon and Douze, Roquefort was the ancient capital of the *petit-pays* of Marsan, before the foundation in 1141 of Mont-de-Marsan.

The formidable church has a twelfth-century apse and side chapels but the roof level of the apse was raised when the church was fortified in the fourteenth century; the crenellation, massive buttresses and square tower belong to the same epoch. The nave is fifteenth-century as is the flamboyant entrance at the south-west corner.

Twelve miles west of Roquefort is Labrit, a hamlet so small that you might easily speed through it without noticing; yet this was the site of the first primitive castle of the Albrets.

Although it has been known for a long time that the vestiges of the Château des Albrets were to be found at Labrit (the name is obviously a corruption of Albret), it was not until 1987 that the site was granted the status of Monument Historique and plans were made to excavate it. The local commune has acquired the twenty-five acres covered by the ruins of the château and work has begun to clear the site, which is heavily overgrown. Professor Marquette of Bordeaux University has undertaken a preliminary survey which has revealed the outline of the primitive castle and, despite thick woods and despite an almost impenetrable under-growth that have hidden the ruins for so long, it is possible to see the deep ditches and massive earthworks that mark the line of the original walls.

The plans show that this was a motte and bailey castle, probably originally built of wood, and the huge mound on which the original keep stood can clearly be seen inside the ditch as can the bases of the towers that guarded the entrance. The limits of the bailey are easily made out because it has remained an open field, planted with crops, surrounded by a ring of woods concealing the earthwork foundations of the original walls.

Until the site has been thoroughly excavated, the date of the castle is pure guesswork: the keep could be as early as tenth-century but elsewhere on the site are the remains of stone walls which are much later, probably thirteenth- or fourteenth-century. The castle seems to have been demolished by being blown up but when this happened is not clear. Perhaps by the time this book is published a great deal more will be known about the Château des Albrets at Labrit. We certainly intend to keep a close eye on the progress of the excavations.

Sabres is only ten miles further down the road but already deep in the Landais forest. To visit the Ecomusée de la Grande Lande at Marquèze, park your car under the trees and buy a ticket at the small station: the price includes a visit to the museum.

A little old-fashioned train that once carried resin-tappers and lumberjacks to their work chugs slowly through the forest for ten minutes before stopping in a clearing containing a number of typical Landaise houses and their out-buildings. The Ecomusée de Marquèze was created in 1968 to conserve an example of a Landais *quartier*, that is to say, a small self-supporting community living in an *airial*. Before exploring Marquèze, it is a good idea to visit the information office where you can buy a map of the *quartier* and a guidebook.

Close by is the Maison des Maîtres, built in 1824, a fine example of local domestic architecture. The old Landaise houses have a distinctive style which is very attractive: the roofs are low-pitched and covered with Roman tiles, while the walls are half-timbered, the spaces between the uprights being filled with *torchis* a mixture of straw and plaster made from clay mixed with sand. But what sets these buildings apart from those found in other parts of Gascony is the splendid way that carpentry is used to make the façades more interesting. The fronts of Landaise houses often have a covered vestibule in the centre with the supporting cross-beams and uprights deliberately left exposed. Apart from providing a cool, shady area outside the living quarters proper, this is visually very pleasing because of the contrast of light and shade it creates

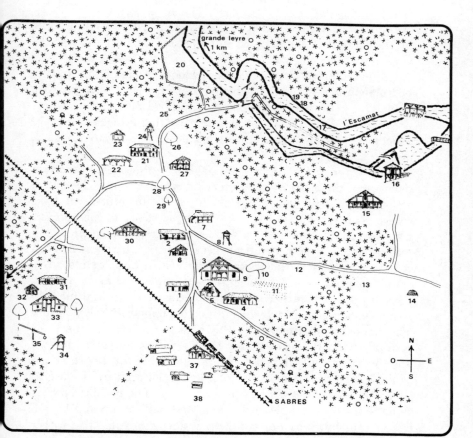

grande leyre
1 km

l'Escamat

N
O — E
S

SABRES

1. Reception
2. Information, shop, toilets
3. *La Maison des Maîtres* The Master's house
4. Servants' quarters
5. Hut used as barn and stable
6. Barn
7. Bread-oven
8. Hen-coop on stilts
9. Garden
10. Pines
11. Cultivated plot
12. Resin-tapping
13. Pine-seedlings
14. Charcoal oven
15. Miller's house
16. Water-mill
17. The Escamet
18. Royal Osmond (a rare fern)
19. Willows
20. Meadow
21. Sharecroppers' house
22. Barn with wagons
23. Pig-styes
24. Thatched hen-coop
25. Bee-hives
27. Barn
28. Large oak tree
29. Chestnut trees
30. Sheep
31. Exhibition Hall
32. Hut
33. Maison *Le Mineur*
34. Hen-coop on stilts
35. Well
36. Picnic area
37. Warden's house
38. Railway

in the façade. In the Maison des Maîtres this effect is emphasized by the pattern of the exposed uprights and tie-beams above the vestibule.

Inside the house is a large central room surrounded by smaller bedrooms and a kitchen. The main room has a large open fire with a spit. One of the bedrooms contains a box bed with curtains whose drapes hang down from a central point so that it looks rather like a medieval tent. It must have been wonderful to retire to this warm nest on a long, cold winter night.

The Maison des Maîtres belonged to the most important member of the *quartier*, the farmer on whom the rest depended, and the size of his house and quality of his furniture reflect his status. Nearby is the much humbler abode of one of the *métayers* who worked the land under a share-cropping arrangement.

Further along the path are a bakery, pig-sty, a barn and chicken coops set high above the ground to protect the birds against foxes and other predators. A bend to the left brings you to *Le Mineur*, a beautiful eighteenth-century house transferred to Marquèze in 1971 from a nearby *airial* when it was threatened with demolition. The standard of carpentry in this house is very high: the front vestibule has a tie-beam at roof level which is supported by two uprights that divide the space below into three equal parts. Each of these segments is made to look like a tall arch by the use of curved brackets below the horizontal beam. The middle 'arch' is emphasized by a double-curved cross-tie halfway up and by the fact that the lower portions of the two side arches are filled with a low fence. It is a highly sophisticated effect created by a master craftsman who possessed the skills of an architect.

A path near the bakery leads past some small fields planted with a mixture of crops, vines and fruits, down to the miller's house and the water-mill, a pretty single-storey half-timbered house built on stilts above a sluice that conducts water from the river Escamat to a small reservoir. After the water-mill there is a charming riverside walk alongside the Escamat. The waters of this small stream have a reddish tinge that comes from a layer of iron-sandstone twenty inches below the surface of the ground. Shading the banks of the Escamat are willows, alders, chestnuts and two kinds of oak, proving conclusively that the maritime pine is not the only tree to be found in the Landes. The holly bush also flourishes here and there is a rare fern, the Royal Osmond.

After a pleasant stroll alongside the meandering stream, you find the path swinging back to the *airial* where, if you still have the energy, you can see an interesting exhibition on the art of bee-keeping; otherwise you can board one of the trains that return at regular intervals to Sabres.

The Escamat is a tributary of the Grande Leyre which rises near Sabres and flows northwards to its confluence with the Petite Leyre near Moustey. The river then continues north-westwards, under its new name, the Eyre, to the basin of Arcachon. The Grande Leyre, Petite Leyre and Eyre together constitute the most important river system of the Landes, which accounts for the larger number of villages and *quartiers* in this region. On the Grande Leyre, near Commensacq, is the Base de Mexico, a water-sports centre where you can learn to canoe and which is the starting point for an excursion by kayak downstream to the mouth of the Eyre.

Commensacq is a tiny village six miles north-west of Sabres on the D626. It has a fifteenth-century church which stands in an attractive green setting backed by fields. An unusual feature is the narthex preceding the west end and the stone pendants which decorate its ceiling.

A cross-country route (D315) leads through thick forest from Sabres to Luxey, fourteen miles away. Here is the second Ecomusée of the Parc Régional, the Atelier de Produits Résineux Jacques et Louis Vidal. In a modest building that looks more like a large barn than a factory you can see how the resin tapped from the pines was distilled into turpentine. The atelier functioned from 1859 to 1954 and, although it only employed three workmen, at least two hundred local resin-tappers depended on it.

Eight miles due west of Sabres on the D44 is Solférino, the model village created in 1863 by Napoleon III. Solférino was part of a vast estate covering six neighbouring communes bought by the Emperor with the idea of setting an example to local land-owners who were ignoring the law, promulgated in 1857, obliging them to drain their land and plant pines.

At the start of the village is a small church in the middle of the road. Behind is a single street lined with identical brick houses which, although obviously a great improvement on the traditional Landaise houses, lack charm. In fact, the village is dead. A small museum has a few souvenirs associated with the Emperor and with Felix Arnaudin, a local historian famous for his photographs of life in the Landes taken at the turn of the century. Many of his photographs are on show at Marquèze.

In the Landes all roads seem to lead to Mont-de-Marsan, which is situated at an important crossroads where routes from Agen, Bordeaux and Tarbes converge and where the dense forest of the Landes gives way to the more open country to the south. It is the departmental capital of the Landes and an important commercial centre but has little to offer the tourist except right in the centre where there are some old half-timbered houses at the junction of the rivers Douze and Midou. Nearby is the fourteenth-century tower built by Gaston Fébus to overawe the rebellious citizens who had risen in revolt against his rule. It now houses the Musée des Beaux-Arts which contains some sculpture by Rodin.

Ten miles east of Mont-de-Marsan is Villeneuve-de-Marsan which, although in the Landes, falls within the area delineated as *appellation bas armagnac* and is an important centre for the production of the brandy. A bastide town, it suffered badly in the Wars of Religion and is now chiefly remarkable for having two excellent restaurants, both with Michelin rosettes, Darroze, owned by a famous Gascon chef, Jean Darroze, and the Europe.

It was at Villeneuve-de-Marsan that Sybil and I watched the succulent Landais dessert, *pastis*, being made. It is an irresistible confection made from the thinnest of flaky pastry with a filling of thinly sliced eating apples. The pastry is rolled very thin, brushed with melted goose fat and folded. This process is repeated over and over again until it is as thin as the finest linen, indeed the traditional name for the pastry is *voile de mariage* or wedding veil.

The landscape south of Mont-de-Marsan is not particularly interesting until you reach the Adour, which is covered in the next chapter. Further north, however, is the country made famous by the great French novelist François Mauriac. The easiest way to reach Mauriac country from Agen is to take the *autoroute* in the direction of Bordeaux and come off at Junction 2, signposted to Cadillac. At the intersection turn left to Saint-Symphorien, fifteen miles to the south.

Saint-Symphorien is the Saint-Clar of Mauriac's most famous novel, *Thérèse Desqueyroux*. A small, one-horse town, even today it feels a long way from civilization; eighty years ago it must have been very remote indeed. Mauriac's own house, a large, rose-coloured brick villa, stands in its own park on the southern outskirts. Two and a half miles away, down a narrow country road (D220E2), is Jouanhaut, the Argelouse of *Thérèse Desqueyroux*, where the eponymous heroine was exiled after her abortive attempt to poison her boring husband. It is a *quartier* in a grassy oasis containing a number of typical Landais houses, including one every bit as good as anything to be found at the Ecomusée de Marquèze: the front has a vestibule with a wooden balcony support on nine arches. Above the balcony is an exposed wooden tie-beam on which is carved an inscription in Gascon saying that the house was built on 29 May, 1781; above the beam is a crown post: all the timber work is beautifully executed. On the road quite near the house is a memorial to two local men 'massacrés par les Boches'.

It was a bright sunny day when we visited Jouanhaut and the little settlement looked so attractive that it took a considerable effort of imagination to visualize how sad and lonely it must have been at the beginning of the century with the sole escape route a rutted cart track leading to Saint-Symphorien and civilization.

> ... It was the silence: the silence of Argelouse! People who don't know this lost land can't imagine the silence: it surrounds the house as if solidified by the thick mass of the forest, where nothing lives except sometimes a hooting owl (in the night it is as though you hear the sound of your own stifled sobs). *Thérèse Desqueyroux*.

Just west of Jouanhaut you cross into the Landes proper and come to Mano, scene of a dramatic forest fire in *Thérèse Desqueyroux*. A left turn onto the D651 soon brings you to Belhade, a pretty village with some nice Landaise houses in amongst the chestnut trees and an interesting Romanesque church, rather larger than one would expect in this out of the way place. It is built for the most part of dressed limestone but patched with the local red sandstone which makes drainage so difficult in the Landes and which is called locally *garelouche*. The west front has a bell-gable with a delightful wooden balcony for the bell-ringers halfway up. Below is a porch with a Roman tiled roof supported on wooden posts which protects an original round-headed arch with four archivolts resting on alternating flat and round piers, the latter having very worn carved capitals. The outermost capital on the right depicts a boat with three figures in it, one of whom is hauling a net. Presumably it depicts the miraculous catch of fish on the Sea of Galilee.

Just outside the village is the Château de Rochefort-Lavie, a small manor house whose presence no doubt explains the size and sophistication of the village church. The château occupies the site of an earlier castle and is still surrounded by the original ditches, while the entrance is flanked by two round medieval towers. Inside is a large courtyard where the outer bailey must have been; on the far side is a typical fifteenth-century manor house flanked at either end by rectangular towers with pointed tiled roofs. On the left a later wing is faced with *garelouche*.

From Belhade the D120 leads to Moustey, near the confluence of the Grande and Petite Leyre. Here there are two medieval churches, both with bell-gables, close to each other on a grass common, planted with lime trees – a charming scene. Another four miles down the N134 brings you to Pissos, a crossroads where you can go east, via Sore to the Ecomusée at Luxey; south to Sabres and the Ecomusée de Marquèze or west on the D43 to Parentis-en-Born and the coast.

The quickest route to the coast from Agen is to take the *autoroute* to Bordeaux, turn off at Junction 15 onto the autoroute 63 and leave this at Junction 22. Now follow the N250 to La Teste-de-Buch, just south of Arcachon. There is no particular reason to stop at La Teste, other than to sample the oysters, but in the Middle Ages there was a castle here, built of the red sandstone called *alios*, which belonged to the Captals de Buch. During the Hundred Years' War the Captals (the word is Gascon and means chief) were staunch allies of the English and the most famous of them, Jean de Grailly (1343–77), was a friend of the Black Prince. He played a crucial role in the defeat of the French at the Battle of Poitiers and was rewarded by being made a Knight of the Garter. The original town of La Teste was overwhelmed by the sands and all that remains of the Captals' castle is the much-restored chapel with its massive square tower.

On the coast, west of La Teste, are some huge dunes, including the biggest of them all, the Dune du Pilat. They were amongst the first to be planted with pines at the end of the eighteenth century, a fact commemorated at La Teste by a marble block raised on a small dune, the 'cippe Brémontier'.

A minor road (D218) runs southwards behind the great dunes to the first of the lagoons, the Etang de Cazaux et de Sanguinet. The lake is large enough for the distant shore to be out of sight (it is seven miles long by six at its widest point) and such a vast stretch of protected water is ideal for sailing: on the west shore is a very smart marina, Port Maguide, with berths for boats up to twenty feet in length.

Two miles west of the Etang de Cazaux et de Sanguinet is the old-fashioned seaside resort of Biscarosse-Plage, but south of the lake is Biscarosse-Bourg, one of the ultra-modern tourist towns built with Government money in the seventies and eighties. I cannot pretend that such places appeal to me but I have to admit that, of its kind, Biscarosse-Bourg is not bad. The colour of the synthetic building material has been carefully chosen to match the local red sandstone and blends well with the green of the surrounding pines. The streets are pedestrianized with attractive floor-scaping and the scale of the architecture is human. All in all, the planners have done a good job.

Immediately south of Biscarosse is the Etang de Biscarosse et de Parentis. Unfortunately, the appearance of the lake is ruined by unsightly oil derricks. Oil was discovered here in 1954 and proved to be the most important find in France. The Esso oil refinery has a museum where the public can go and learn about the techniques of oil research and exploitation. The west side of the Etang de Biscarosse et de Parentis is a military zone and access is forbidden. On the east is the village of Parentis-en-Born.

Ten miles south of Parentis-en-Born, via the Forêt de Piche, is the hamlet of Pontenx-les-Forges, where we once enjoyed an outstanding lunch, but first we went to see the holy spring of Bouricos. You take the D626 eastwards to Labouheyre and after about two miles look for a small turning on the right to Bouricos. Apart from the miraculous fountain in its dell, there is a small chapel dedicated to St John the Baptist and a community of monks living in attractive old Landaise houses. There is a midsummer festival (June 24) held at Bouricos which suggests that originally this was a pagan shrine.

West of Pontenx-les-Forges is Saint-Paul-en-Born, a pretty village in a sylvan setting with an interesting church. In front of the porch is a covered area with a pyramidal roof, covered by fish-scale terracotta tiles supported on six wooden piers. The entrance porch proper is on the west side of the very solid belfry which is covered by a curious, two-stage, slate-covered roof. The lower third has broad, obtuse-angled slopes, above which is a slim candle-snuffer, octagonal spire. Inside there is a wooden roof and a Gothic vaulted choir.

Another five miles bring you to Mimizan, a small resort nestling below a huge dune that destroyed the original village in the Middle Ages. Hard up against the monster dune is a fifteenth-century tower, all that remains of a Benedictine abbey engulfed by the sands. It is built mainly of brick in the Toulouse style but with some in-filling of *alios*, the red Landais sandstone, as well. The top of the tower is marred by a risible cupola with shingled sides. The great dune was one of the first to be planted with *gourbet* at the end of the eighteenth century. A road leads through the dune to Mimizan-Plage, passing a large, smelly paper-making factory *en route*. Just north of Mimizan-Bourg is the small but beautiful Etang d'Aureilhan. Ringed by pine trees the lake makes an ideal spot for picnics.

In the village of Mézos, ten miles south-east of Mimizan, off the D38 is a rugged fourteenth-century church founded by the Knights of Malta. Largely built of *alios*, it has a solid squat west tower with a two-stage slate roof, as at Saint-Paul-en-Born (see previous page). The inside is very plain: there is a four-bay nave, with aisles but no clerestory, surmounted by a quadripartite vault. At the east end is a shallow chancel and side chapels.

Mézos lies deep in the forest and presumably owes its existence in this remote region to the Onesse, one of the few small streams that flow through the Landes. A very minor road (D66) leads south from Mézos to Uza. After the gloom of the pine woods, Uza comes as a delightful surprise: a tiny hamlet at the edge of a pretty lake, bordered by oak trees for a change instead of the inevitable pine, with swans gliding over its calm surface; it is a perfect place for a picnic.

The road (D41) continues to the village of Saint-Julien-en-Born with its Landais houses and old communal wash-house. There you join the D652 which runs south, skirting the forest of Lit-et-Mixe, through the holiday villages of Lit-et-Mixe and Saint-Girons to Léon. Just north of Léon is the Etang de Léon, a very attractive lake, fringed by pines, which has a simple, good hotel at its southern end, the Hôtel du Lac. Apart from the usual attractions, fishing, swimming, sailing and so on, Léon offers a unique excursion down the Courant d'Huchet, the tiny stream that winds its way for eight slow miles to the sea. You glide in a flat-bottomed boat propelled first by oars and then, when the water gets very shallow, by pole under a dim green canopy of alders, willows and giant tamarisks. All kinds of birds and animals may be glimpsed in this secret place but the highlight of the trip is the rare hibiscus which flourishes in this humid micro-climate but is otherwise only to be found in the extreme south of Italy and on the banks of the Nile.

Ten miles south of Léon is Vieux-Boucau and Port-d'Albret. *Vieux-boucau* is Gascon for *vieille embouchure*, for in the fourteenth and fifteenth centuries this was the mouth of the Adour and Port-d'Albret was a prosperous harbour. This favourable situation came to a sudden end in 1579 when Louis de Foix constructed the canal that diverted the course of the Adour back to Bayonne (see page 201). The old mouth of the river at Port-d'Albret silted up and the town went into a long decline that lasted until 1976 when the

Government agency Mission Aquitaine funded a large leisure complex designed to attract the growing holiday trade. Unlike the development at Biscarosse, however, Port-d'Albret looks and feels totally artificial. Nevertheless, the plan has clearly worked and during the season the resort is full.

East of Port-d'Albret is Soustons, a small holiday town in a very agreeable setting on the shores of the Etang de Soustons. There is an excellent restaurant here, the Pavillon Landais, which has a Michelin rosette.

Capbreton, which lies ten miles south of Port-d'Albret, was a flourishing port in the Middle Ages whose fishermen hunted the whale as far north as the waters of Greenland and fished for cod off the coast of Newfoundland. In fact, according to the Capbretonnais, they were the first to discover the mainland coast of America, long before Columbus.

Off the coast of Capbreton is the Gouf de Capbreton, an underwater valley, twenty-one miles wide and between three and five thousand feet deep, which is thought to have been formed in the same era as the Pyrénées. The gulf has the effect of diminishing the height of the Atlantic waves, making it a safe anchorage in bad weather; it also means that Capbreton is one of the few places on this coast where bathing is safe.

Up to 907 AD the mouth of the Adour was at Capbreton after which this capricious river switched northwards to flow into the Atlantic at Port-d'Albret. In 1164 the Adour deserted Port-d'Albret for Bayonne and soon afterwards returned once more to Capbreton. After a terrible storm in the fourteenth century the wandering river switched back to Port-d'Albret but Capbreton was not seriously affected until 1579 when the Adour returned to Bayonne. Even so, unlike Port-d'Albret, there is still a narrow outlet to the sea at Capbreton and an inner harbour big enough to hold a small fishing fleet and a large marina. Capbreton lies on the south side of the inlet; on the north side is Hossegor, an elegant resort with some extremely expensive villas hidden amongst the trees surrounding the Lac d'Hossegor. The lake is a shallow lagoon which is all that is left of the northern arm of the old harbour whose southern outlet into the existing harbour silted up long ago.

Capbreton, as befits a fishing port, is more down to earth than
Hossegor, although here too there are some handsome houses,
lining the banks of the river Boudigau and its tributary the Bourret
which flow into the harbour. The inlet at the mouth of the harbour
is dead straight and very narrow, causing a bottle-neck which in
strong on-shore winds creates gigantic surfing waves that drive
down the entrance, spilling over the quayside and making entry or
exit impossible. The mouth of the harbour has a mole on the north
side, with a small, striped lighthouse on it, and a jetty to the south
which is usually lined with intrepid fishermen. From the end of
the jetty there is a splendid view down the sandy shore to the
mountainous coastline of the Pays-Basque. From Capbreton it is
only fifteeen miles to Bayonne, the ancient port at the mouth of
the Adour where Gascony and the Pays-Basque meet.

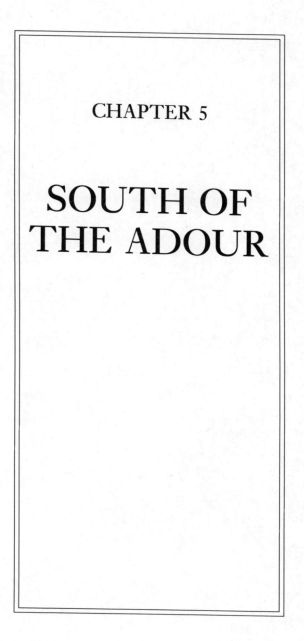

CHAPTER 5

SOUTH OF THE ADOUR

THE GASCONS call the Adour the wandering river because over the centuries it has frequently changed course: in AD 907 it abandoned Capbreton to flow into the Atlantic twenty-four miles further north giving birth to the new harbour of Port d'Albret in the process; in 1164, however, this fickle stream switched south again, first, briefly, to Bayonne and then to its original outlet, Capbreton; in the fourteenth century a terrible storm blocked the mouth of Capbreton and the Adour was forced north once more to Port d'Albret. During this time the port of Bayonne, which during the twelfth and thirteenth centuries had prospered under English rule, was gradually cut off from the sea by sand and suffered a serious recession. Finally, in 1569, Charles IX of France gave orders for a canal to be constructed to save the city. Louis de Foix, the architect of Philip II's Escorial, was recalled from Spain and work began. In 1578, aided by a providential flooding of the river Nive, the Adour was directed into the new cut and Bayonne was saved – at the expense of Port d'Albret.

The Adour rises in the Pyrénées, not far from the Pic du Midi de Bigorre, and flows northwards to Tarbes and then to Riscle where it swings westwards in a great shallow curve before flowing south-west through Dax to meet the sea at Bayonne. South of the river, between Riscle and Dax, is a little-known region which, although administratively and indeed traditionally part of the Landes, is quite unlike the great, flat, sandy pine-covered terrain to the north. Here, in the foothills of the Pyrénées, there are green hills and fertile valleys; to be sure the region is well wooded but there is a much greater variety of trees and here they are only part of the landscape, which is heavily cultivated. Maize is the predominant crop in the valleys, especially the valley of the Adour itself, where the fields stretch monotonously for miles; but the hills are often covered with vines.

Just south of Riscle, beyond the flat, rather boring fields of maize, rise the low hills of Vic-Bilh (*vic-bilh* is Gascon and means 'old village'), one of the many tiny feudal divisions of Gascony whose identity is still jealously conserved by the local inhabitants, even though it has had no independent existence for hundreds of years. What has probably saved Vic-Bilh from complete obscurity is that its south-facing slopes produce two of the most interesting wines of the South-West, Madiran and Pacherenc du Vic-Bilh. There have been vine yards in Vic-Bilh since Roman times but their preservation is due to the Benedictine monks who founded an abbey on the site where the village of Madiran now stands and who planted vines there in the twelfth century. Of the two wines, Madiran is by far the more important. It is a full-bodied red having a minimum alcoholic strength of 11 degrees and a high tannin content that means it ages well in the bottle. The locals recommend keeping it in the cellar for at least five years. The grapes used are the Cabernet Sauvignon and the Tannat, a robust variety that gives the wine its body and longevity while the Cabernet adds finesse. There are about two hundred growers in Vic-Bilh. Most of them send their grapes to the Cave Coopérative de Crouseilles which is responsible for fifty per cent of the area's production of Madiran. There are, however, about twenty *vignerons* who make their own wine, amongst the best examples of which are Château de Peyros, Château d'Aydie and Château Montus.

Pacherenc du Vic-Bilh is a very different wine: it is white and sweet, although in bad years a dry white is produced instead. The latter is perfectly drinkable but the sweet wine is very attractive, lighter than the sweet wines of Bordeaux, like Sauternes or Loupiac, but fresh and clean on the palate with a very distinctive flowery bouquet. Sadly this excellent wine is made in very small quantities by a handful of producers on the same slopes as Madiran.

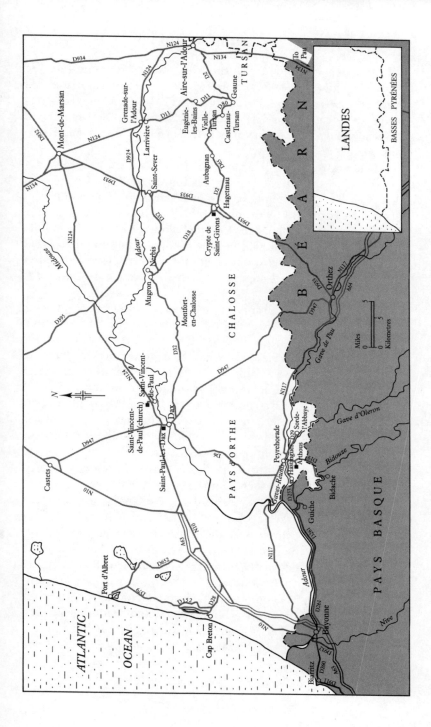

The grapes used are curious: the wine owes its name to the chief grape employed, the Pacherenc, which is a local word meaning *raisin d'échalas* (grape of the vinestake). Besides the Pacherenc grape (also called Ruffiat), Manseng, Semillon, Sauvignon and Courbu, which here is known as Petit Sarrat, are also used to make this wine.

Pacherenc du Vic-Bilh is not to be found outside Vic-Bilh itself, but if you are ever in the vicinity a detour to the Cave Coopérative de Crouseilles, near Lembeye, is well worth while. The countryside is very pleasant with occasional splendid views of the mountains to the south from the ridge that runs along the crest of the hills. At the Coopérative you will be able to sample not only Pacherenc du Vic-Bilh and Madiran but a very pleasant quaffing wine called Vin des Fleurs. The Coopérative also sells Rouge de Béarn and Rose de Béarn.

In the hills to the south-west of Riscle is another wine-growing region, Côtes de Saint-Mont, producing well-made, unpretentious red, white and rosé wines with VDQS status. As at Madiran the vines were originally planted by monks from the nearby priory of Saint-Jean-Baptiste-de-Saint-Mont. The church was built circa 1050 by the local lord, Raymond, as the fulfilment of a vow made after a particularly nasty nightmare. He was given great support by Bernard Tumapaler, the Count of Armagnac, who chose to retire there after his defeat by Guy Geoffroi, the Duke of Aquitaine.

The priory was built on a rocky spur overlooking the river Adour but over the centuries the fabric of the church has suffered greatly from earth movements for the site, though spectacular, was ill-chosen. The building was already in a dilapidated state when Montgoméry's troops attacked and devastated it in 1569. Of the eleventh-century church only the south transept and the chapel leading off it on the east side survive. Seen from the outside the east chapel looks decidedly primitive compared with the square-ended chancel, which, indeed, for the most part is fifteenth-century. The chapel is built of smooth round stones from the river Adour, roughly set in mortar. These stones, known locally as *galets*, are morainic débris left behind when the glaciers melted and are commonly found in old houses and barns in the valley of the

Adour. They are often arranged in horizontal bands, sometimes alternating with brick or stone, and the resulting patterns can be very attractive. At Saint-Mont, however, the stones were used higgledy-piggledy and the result is not at all pleasing. Inside the chapel things are better: the stones are arranged more regularly and at the entrance is an arch supported by piers with well-carved capitals. The one on the right has a very jolly carving with at the top lions' heads emerging from vine-scroll interlacing and below them standing lions and a wild man. That on the left has palm leaves amongst intertwined vine-scrolls. The carved capitals in the south transept are slightly later and less exuberant. The first bay west of the crossing was reconstructed in the fourteenth century but the next three bays on the south side are twelfth-century. The rest of the nave, including the vaults, is fourteenth-century as are the south-east buttress and the inside south wall of the chancel. The north transept, north wall, north-east buttress and most of the east wall of the chancel were rebuilt in the fifteenth century. The three large buttresses on the north side of the nave were added in the seventeenth century. The problem of subsidence continues to this day and a great deal of money has been spent quite recently in reinforcing the foundations on the north side of the church.

Despite its ruinous state, Saint-Jean-Baptiste-de-Saint-Mont still has the power to move the visitor and evoke a sense of its former grandeur.

West of Riscle the valley of the Adour widens and the fields of maize seem to stretch interminably on either side of the river. Ten miles downstream on the D935 is Aire-sur-l'Adour, a busy market town straddling an important river crossing where the road from Bordeaux to Bayonne meets the east–west route from Auch to Bayonne. The Tuesday market at Aire is one of the largest in the region and is famous for its *foie gras d'oie* and *de canard*, on sale from November to February.

Aire-sur-l'Adour was originally the capital of one of the Novem-populani, the Aturenses, conquered by Crassus in AD 56. Little remains of the ancient Atura, as the Romans called it, except for some fragments of sculpture and a mosaic pavement. Perhaps the most interesting find is twenty-nine altars dedicated to the god

Lelhunnus. These remains are housed in the old episcopal palace, now the town hall, which dates from the sixteenth and seventeenth centuries.

Aire-sur-l'Adour was created a Bishopric in the early sixth century but the seat was transferred to Dax in 1933. The former cathedral of Saint-Jean-Baptiste has suffered many alterations over the centuries. Of the original eleventh-century building only the north transept and two chapels leading off it survive. The nave and south transept are fifteenth-century. The choir was completely rebuilt in the eighteenth century while the nave aisles were added in the nineteenth. The lower part of the façade is thirteenth-century but the bell-tower was added in the eighteenth. The fourteenth-century chapter house, now the sacristy, has an elegant central column.

In the suburbs south of the river, just east of the N134, is a much more interesting church, Sainte-Quitterie-du-Mas. Quitterie was a young Visigothic princess who was martyred in 476 because she refused to embrace the Arian version of Christianity, which in the fifth century was the state religion of Gascony. She was put to death on a hill-side just outside the city walls and promptly, as seems to have been a habit of Gascon saints, picked up her head and marched up the hill to the site of the present church. Here, as so often, one is inclined to suspect a Christian legend grafted onto a previously pagan temple.

The earliest part of the church, and the most interesting architecturally, is the east end which is twelfth-century. Here, behind the altar, is a beautiful blind arcade. It has six arches, lavishly ornamented with billet moulding and an interlaced flower motif. The arches are supported on single columns to left and right and twinned columns in between. The finely-carved capitals depict on the right the flight into Egypt and next to it a bird eating grapes; on the left a capital with two figures apparently embracing is thought to represent the Visitation and next to it is a bizarre carving showing wild men (satyrs?) riding on the backs of fabulous beasts.

The rest of the church is frankly a mess: the nave and aisles date from the thirteenth and fourteenth centuries while at the west end is a brick belfry in the Toulouse style which was rebuilt in the seventeenth century. The main entrance below the tower has a thirteenth-century tympanum with sculpture depicting the Last Judgement. It must originally have been rather fine but, alas, it was badly mutilated by the Huguenots during the Wars of Religion.

But the chief reason for visiting Sainte-Quitterie-du-Mas is to see the remarkable Gallo-Roman sarcophagus dedicated to Ste Quitterie, thought to date from the fifth century, which is housed in the crypt. The whole of the front, the lid and the two ends are covered with splendid carvings making the sarcophagus probably the finest survival from this period yet found in France. The front corners of the lid have magnificent portraits of the Gallo-Roman god Mercury, clearly identified by the wings in his hair.

South of Aire-sur-l'Adour lies the first of three *petit-pays*, the Tursan, the Chalosse and the Pays d'Orthe, which in medieval times were semi-independent fiefs. The frontiers of the three *petit-pays* are difficult to define exactly, but they all lie south of the river Adour in an area stretching south-westwards from Aire-sur-l'Adour to Peyrehorade on the Gave de Pau.

Tursan, the most easterly of these former fiefs, is also the smallest, yet it is nevertheless important on two counts: it produces a well-known VDQS wine called Tursan, and at Eugénie-les-Bains is to be found one of the most famous restaurants in France, Michel Guérard's Les Prés et les Sources d'Eugénie. It has three rosettes and its prices reflect its prestige but if you wish to eat impeccably-prepared food in the most elegant surroundings this is the place.

Eugénie-les-Bains can be reached cross-country from Aire but it is more sensible to take the longer route via the main road to Grenade, a fourteenth-century bastide which still retains its arcaded main square. Across the river at Larrivière is the chapel of Notre-Dame-de-Rugby. Amongst other devotional objects to be found here is the sculpture of a child offering a rugby ball to the Madonna.

Six miles down the D11 is Eugénie-les-Bains itself, a tiny spa town which was put on the map by its most illustrious visitor, the Empress Eugénie, wife of Napoleon III. Today, however, her memory is overshadowed by the fame of one of France's greatest chefs.

South of Eugénie-les-Bains is the capital of the Tursan, Geaune, a *bastide* town founded in 1318 by the seneschal Antoine de Pessagna, acting on behalf of the English King, Edward II, and a local lord, Pierre de Castelnau. The name Geaune derives from the seneschal's native city Genoa in Italy.

Much of the original arcaded square of Geaune survives and happily the local commune is doing its best to ensure that new buildings are in keeping with the old ones. The modernized *hôtel de ville*, for example, has windows and a round-headed arch that harmonize with those of its neighbours.

Behind the *hôtel de ville* is the fifteenth-century church of Saint-Jean-Baptiste. The most remarkable feature of the church is its colossal west tower, built on arches, with massive supporting buttresses and capped by a four-sided red-tiled roof. The tower has only two openings in each face, one at the level of the bell-chamber and another just under the roof, and was clearly designed for defence. The side walls of the nave and the choir, especially, also have huge buttresses.

Inside the west porch is an inscription in Gascon carved high up on the north pillar 'L'An MCCCCLII feit aget pilar la bote de glis' which translated means 'In the year 1452 were made this pillar and the vaults of the church'. On the south side of the church, above a doorway, is a carving of the town's coat of arms with three fleurs-de-lys. The interior of the church is impressive but the vaults were destroyed by the Huguenots during the Wars of Religion and only rebuilt in the nineteenth century.

At the other end of the town is the Tour des Augustins, an elegant belfry which is virtually all that remains of a former fifteenth-century Augustinian monastery.

Before leaving Geaune, you may like to visit the Cave Coopérative which produces annually 25,000 hectolitres of which 15,000 are of VDQS quality. The vineyards of Tursan cover some 5,000 acres in the neighbourhood of Geaune and altogether there are about 1,200 *vignerons*, some of them very, very small, but all the wine that is sold commercially is made at Geaune. The vineyards are, for the most part, planted with the Baroque grape which gives a dry, white wine that is light and fruity. Small amounts of red and rosé wines are also made. Tursan is not an important wine today but in the seventeenth century it was better known and was exported through Bayonne to Holland and England.

A minor road, the D80, leads out of the square to Castelnau-Tursan, a hamlet with a disproportionately large church with another massive west tower, and thence, via the D437 and D65, to Vieille-Tursan. Here there is a twelfth-century church whose south-east apsidal chapel has roof corbels with carvings depicting the seven deadly sins. The interior is much restored and only at the east end is there any sense of the original church, especially at the level of the semi-dome of the choir where there is billet moulding.

The village of Vieille-Tursan is built on a ridge and there is a lovely view south over a pleasant, much cultivated valley.

After Vieille-Tursan, the D65 continues west through Aubagnan to a junction with the D2 where you turn right for Hagetmau. Somewhere on this last stretch you cross into the Chalosse, the largest of the three *petit-pays* south of the Adour. It is an attractive, well-wooded, hilly region where at last the boring fields of maize give way to polyculture, and here, as in Armagnac, you will find large flocks of ducks and, less often, geese waddling round or floating idly across the muddy farmyard pools, for the Chalosse is famous for its *foie-gras*.

Just outside Hagetmau on the road to Mugron (D18) is the crypt of Saint-Girons, all that remains of a twelfth-century abbey that was destroyed during the Wars of Religion by the Huguenots. It is heartbreaking to think what has been lost for the crypt contains some of the finest carved capitals to be found in Gascony and the great advantage here is that they are only just above eye-level and can be studied much more easily than in most churches.

There are steps down to the crypt on both the right and the left of the entrance at ground level. Having descended you find yourself in a vaulted chamber which clearly follows the pentagonal plan of the choir that once stood above it. The vaults spring from four free-standing columns in the middle of the chamber and eight more which are attached to the walls.

On the back wall are two attached columns, the one nearest the left-hand entrance having beautifully carved stiff-leaves that look as though they are distantly based on the acanthus leaves of a Corinthian capital. Turning round you will see directly ahead the first two free-standing columns: that on the right also has a 'Corinthian' capital but the one on the left depicts monsters, vaguely reminiscent of lions, devouring their human victims, legs first. On another face of the same capital, a bearded man holds a partially devoured man in each hand by their hair. Does this represent Christ rescuing the damned from the jaws of hell?

The capital of the next free-standing column on the left has another bizarre carving: on each corner a man, wearing a long robe, holds the wing of a fierce-looking bird and appears to dangle a fruit or berry in its powerful beak – or is he fighting the bird for possession of the fruit? Whatever the meaning of this strange scene, it is a fine piece of work with details such as the folds of the man's robe and the bird's plumage skilfully carved.

The last of the free-standing columns has a capital carved with biblical scenes: on one face we see the rich man Dives sitting with two cronies at a table set with several dishes. Below the table lies the wretched Lazarus with dogs licking his wounds; further round the capital Lazarus stands supported on either side by an angel, while below him Dives, tortured with thirst, points to his parched tongue. The same capital has a splendid winged dragon with fierce bared teeth.

An attached shaft on the right-hand wall close to the Lazarus sculpture has a capital showing St Peter being released from prison. The figures are enclosed by arches carved with an inscription quoting from the Acts of the Apostles (Chapter XII, verses 6–9). On the right of the capital an angel is shown cutting St Peter's bonds while on the left, guarding the apostle, are two soldiers dressed in twelfth-century armour with pointed shields.

At the east end of the crypt are two shafts with capitals depicting pairs of fabulous birds with their claws joined in the middle. One of the shafts on the north side has a 'Corinthian' capital while the other, nearest the entrance, has a carving of smiling lions (looking forward to devouring Daniel?) as does the one opposite on the south wall.

Some idea of what the rest of Saint-Girons must have looked like can be gained by visiting the abbey-church of Saint-Sever eight miles to the north on the D933.

The great abbey of Saint-Sever, and the small town that grew up round it, stand at the summit of a high hill overlooking the Adour. It is a splendid vantage point right at the edge of the Chalosse where the high land gives way to the plain and there is a magnificent view from the top, northwards over the dark forest of the Landes.

Severus was a fifth-century evangelist sent by the Pope to convert the Novempopulani. He was martyred by the Vandals and, like Sainte-Quitterie, obligingly picked up his head and showed his followers where he was to be buried. A monastery was established on the site in the seventh or eighth century but this early building was destroyed by the Normans.

The Benedictine monastery that stands today was founded in the late tenth century by Guillaume Sanche, Duke of Gascony, after he had inflicted a heavy defeat on the Normans at the Battle of Taller in 982. The building of the abbey was largely the work of one remarkable man, Gregory of Montaner, a Spaniard who was abbot for forty-four years from 1028 to 1072 and also Bishop of Lescar and Dax. It was during his rule that the Spanish manuscript *Commentary of Beatus on the Apocalypse*[1] was copied and illuminated at Saint-Sever, the finest example surviving from this period.

Over the centuries, the abbey-church and its monastic buildings have suffered greatly. During the Hundred Years' War the town was a possession of the English crown and was attacked and taken three times by French troops, once in 1295 after a siege of three months, again in 1360 and finally in 1435 when the troops of Charles VII sacked the monastic buildings and set fire to them.

In 1372 an earthquake damaged the fabric of the church; but the tale of woe was not yet at an end: in 1569 Huguenot troops, inevitably under the command of Montgoméry, occupied the town

1 Now in the Bibliothèque Nationale, Paris.

for eleven months during which time they pillaged what was left of the monastic buildings and did considerable damage to the church itself.

It was not until the end of the seventeenth century that a major programme of repairs was embarked on, including the addition of an unfortunate classical entrance at the west end. This was replaced by the present neo-Romanesque porch in 1840.

The original Benedictine plan of Saint-Sever is preserved unaltered: there is a five-bay tunnel-vaulted nave flanked on either side by a single groin-vaulted aisle. Beyond the nave is a short transept followed by a two-bay chancel with aisles terminating in an apsed choir. On either side of the chancel are three stepped chapels, also with apsed ends.

The best view of the abbey is from the place Verdun at the north-east end. Here you can get a good idea of what the original church must have looked like, even though all but the first apsidal chapel, the one nearest the apse itself, are heavily restored. The chapel has flat buttresses either side of the central window which extend halfway up the wall and taper at the top where two attached shafts begin. The shafts have carved capitals and there are carved corbels supporting the tiled roof.

Beyond the chapels is the north transept, the end of which is covered by a large bell-tower. The top of the tower was restored, very badly, in the 1930s. At the base of the tower is a porch with an original tympanum, alas badly mutilated, depicting the Last Judgement. Christ in Majesty is surrounded by Cherubim and Seraphim. On the left St Michael strikes down the devil with his lance and on the right an angel embraces a figure prostrate before the vision of glory.

Rather than enter the church at this point, it is best to go to the west end, noting the Gothic flying buttresses of the nave on the way. Inside, the first three piers on the right are fourteenth-century and all the vaults of the aisles, except the last on the right before the transept, have been restored. The false tribune of the nave was added in the nineteenth century.

Despite all this rebuilding, you cannot help admiring the grandeur and spaciousness of the church. This is especially true as you stand in the crossing and look into the complex spatial pattern created by the chancel with its apsed choir and six staggered chapels. On either side, the tunnel-vaulted transepts end elegantly in two-arch arcades surmounted by graceful four-arch galleries. Here, and in the chapels, you will find the best sculpted capitals. Those on the north side are earlier and simpler in design, although skilfully executed. The central column of the arcade, for example, has two rows of plain but crisply carved leaves. The capitals of the gallery above and on the opposite side of the church were probably carved in the twelfth century and are much more richly decorated. One, in the intermediate chapel, shows Daniel standing between two splendid lions' heads with his hands in their mouths. Elsewhere, there are capitals with smiling lions like those at Hagetmau. Similar capitals are to be found at Moirax (page 3) and elsewhere in the Agenais and the style may well have spread south from there to Saint-Sever.

The westernmost bay of the nave also has some interesting capitals in the different style of Toulouse. One shows Salome dancing before Herod, the beheading of John the Baptist and the Saint's head being brought to Salome.

The town of Saint-Sever was originally called Cap de Gascogne. *Cap* means 'chief' in Gascon and the name could well have been given to the town by pilgrims coming from Bordeaux. Certainly no sight could have been more welcome to the weary medieval traveller than that of the Cap de Gascogne rising abruptly over three hundred feet above the flat plain, surmounted by the small town with its Romanesque abbey. Here he knew that for the time being the worst was over. The next stage of his pilgrimage would be through the pleasant, gently rolling landscape of the Chalosse where he would find comfortable inns where he could dine well and prepare himself for the difficult journey across the mountains.

The reputation of the Chalosse continues to this day. Saint-Sever itself, although it only has a population of 4,800, has two excellent restaurants, one of them, the Relais du Pavillon, with a Michelin rosette. This is because the town is an important market centre not only for *foie-gras* but also for the plump, yellow, maize-fed chickens whose flesh is particularly succulent and which are famous throughout France for their quality. In fact, Saint-Sever is the headquarters of the oddly-named Syndicat de Défense du Poulet Jaune des Landes, which exists to make sure that standards are maintained. Incidentally, a subsidiary industry has grown up in Saint-Sever using feathers from the ducks and geese to stuff pillows and duvets.

From Saint-Sever take the D32 to Mugron. The road runs along the top of a ridge with splendid views to north and south. About a mile short of Mugron a turning to the right leads via a charming leafy lane to Nerbis. Here there is a small, rustic-looking church founded in the early eleventh century by Guillaume Sanche, Duke of Gascony, on the site of an earlier Benedictine priory.

Work began on the church before 1050 but only the apse of the choir and the apsidal chapels survive from this period, built of rough undressed sandstone, set unevenly in mortar.

The nave and transepts were completed round about 1100, although the vaults are later: one boss in the choir bears the date 1237 but the vaults of the nave are fifteenth-century. The church was set on fire by French troops in 1435 and, judging by one of the bosses which bears the three lilies of France, the nave vaults were constructed after the English were driven out of Gascony in 1453. The south aisle, with its lierne and tierceron ribs, was built about the same time.

In 1569 the church was again burned and its treasure stolen by Montgoméry's troops. During this attack the fourteenth-century tower over the transept was badly damaged. The original roof was replaced by a curious bell-cote covered with chestnut shingles. The south wall of the aisles and its supporting buttresses were rebuilt in the late sixteenth or early seventeenth century.

The entrance to the choir has a capital on the right rather like the one in the north transept of Saint-Sever, with two rows of plain stiff leaves. Opposite is a bizarre capital with equine monsters with claws rather than hooves gripping terrified, squatting mannikins in their talons.

Like Saint-Sever, Nerbis is beautifully sited and there is an agreeable picnic spot nearby with fine views over the Adour.

The D32 continues along the ridge to Montfort-en-Chalosse, a *bastide* town founded in the fourteenth century and built on a hill that dominates the whole of the area. Of the original town little survives except for a couple of streets and a stretch of the old walls on top of which is built the rue des Ramparts. Unusually, the church is outside the town on a promontory jutting out to the south: it may well be that there is yet another pagan site adopted by the early Christian fathers.

The nave and apse are Romanesque, perhaps eleventh-century, but the squat west tower and the aisles were added in the fifteenth century. The three-bay nave has heavy pointed arches with no gallery or clerestory but a low somewhat oppressive roof. The most interesting part of the church is the back of the choir, behind the altar, where there is a four-arch blank arcade with some remarkable capitals. Unfortunately, they are painted in hideous colours, greens and browns predominating. However, one has to remember that all Romanesque churches were originally decorated in this way, though whether in quite such disgusting colours is doubtful.

The first capital on the right has a figure in the middle of two others who have hold of his hair; he, in turn, is holding each of them by one of their legs. The long hair suggests that the central figure may be Samson. The next capital on the left has a crowned figure with arms outstretched and his hands in the mouths of two monsters. This is similar to a capital at Saint-Sever and may represent Daniel in the lions' den. The third capital has a strange head with staring eyes and ribbons coming from its mouth that are intertwined with corn stooks – a very pagan motif. The fourth capital has a bird, between bunches of grapes. It has its head bent and its beak apparently pecking at something between its feet. The last capital shows a figure on the right and a musician holding a viol on his left. Scholars suggest that the scene represents a troop of acrobats and that the middle figure is supporting a ball with his feet. It is not clear when these capitals were carved: all of them, except the pagan-looking head, have counterparts at Saint-Sever and at another important church at Saint-Paul-lès-Dax and it may be that the ones at Montfort are later copies.

There is a good, simple restaurant at Montfort, Le Relais de Chalosse.

After Montfort-en-Chalosse the D32 descends to the plain. An easy drive of ten miles brings you to Dax, a health resort whose healing water and mud baths have been famous since Roman times. Originally Dax was called Aquae Tarbellicae when the town was capital of the Tarbelli, one of the Novempopulani. The name was changed to Aquae Augustae after the emperor's wife Octavia and his daughter Julia visited the town between 27–25 BC to take the waters. It is possible that Augustus himself may have accompanied them. Subsequently, the name contracted to Acqs and then Dacqs.

Dax was created a bishopric in 360, making it one of the earliest in Gascony, but this was suppressed after the Revolution. During the tenth and eleventh centuries there was a small independent Viscounty of Dax which, after the marriage of Eleanor of Aquitaine and Henry Plantagenet, passed to the English crown. Dax remained under English control until 1451.

Dax is an agreeable town with pleasant riverside walks and smart tea-shops. It also has a casino. Its most notable sight is in the place Borda where a hot spring, the Fontaine de la Nèhe, flows into a large pool surrounded by an elegant Tuscan arcade. The cathedral, which was rebuilt in the seventeenth century, preserves a beautiful Gothic doorway, the portail des Apôtres, in the north arm of the transept.

Across the river is a much more interesting church, Saint-Paul-lès-Dax. To find it take the main road north to Castets and turn left immediately after the railway crossing.

The church stands on the edge of a promontory which in Roman times was the starting point for an aqueduct which carried cold water to Aquae Tarbellicae. Originally, a Gallo-Roman temple stood on this site but this was replaced in the eleventh century by a magnificent Benedictine church of which, alas, only the apse survives. A Latin inscription behind the altar records the consecration of the church: 'This altar was consecrated on the evening of the Ides of June in honour of Saint Martin and all the Saints by Raymond, Archbishop of Auch.' This establishes a starting date of 1045.

The church was badly damaged in the Wars of Religion and the nave was rebuilt in the seventeenth century; the tower is nine-teenth-century.

It is heartbreaking that so little of the original Benedictine church is left for, to judge by the apse, it must have been very beautiful. Certainly, the decorative scheme and sculpture of the exterior are the finest in Gascony. The wall surface is divided vertically into three equal parts by shallow buttresses and hori-zontally by a band of billet moulding below the windows. The lower half of each section has blind arcading consisting of three arches springing from four columns with elaborately carved capitals. The upper half has a series of marble panels, carved in low relief, depicting scenes from the Bible. They are inserted either side of the windows and on the buttresses. Each section has a round-headed window in the upper half with a round-headed arch, decorated with zig-zag moulding, springing from recessed columns with leaf capitals.

Working from left to right (i.e. from north to south) the capitals of the arcading depict: 2. A siren-bird flanked by lions with drooling tongues; 3. Two birds, joined at their breasts and necks, with heads turned backwards to peck at grapes; 5. Eagles; 8. A weird capital with a central figure flanked by two more who are gripping him (her?) by the hair, who, in turn, holds them by one of their legs. The long-haired figure could represent Samson fighting the Philistines or it may just be a scene showing acrobats; 9. This last interpretation seems borne out by the next capital which shows a figure standing on his head and balancing a ball on his feet with a musician playing a viol at his side. Capitals of the same design as this and the previous one are also to be found at Montfort-en-Chalosse; 10. Two lions; 11. Birds with their beaks between their legs, framed by grapes; 13. A large lion's head devouring its victims with bearded heads on either side; 14. Two big cats with enormous paws; 15. A figure with outstretched arms with his hands in the mouths of two lions. Is this a lion-tamer or does it depict Daniel in the lions' den? This capital is also to be found at Montfort-en-Chalosse and at Saint-Sever; 17. Birds with long claws, pecking their breasts: perhaps a representation of the pelican that pierces its breast to feed its young, a medieval fable which symbolizes the sacrifice of our Saviour; 18. A recent restoration (as in 4); 20. Another bizarre capital with a figure held from behind by his hair; 21. Strange, elongated horses with their heads turned backwards, chewing their tails.

The theme of the low-relief panels that run round the upper half of the apse is the Salvation but the scenes do not appear in any particular order. From right to left they are: 1. An architectural scene depicting a church, perhaps representing Jerusalem the Blessed. A figure in a niche in the top half of the church may represent Raymond, Archbishop of Auch, the church's founder but the meaning is not clear; 2. A monster; 3. A woman holding a viol; 4. Samson on the back of a lion whose jaws he is forcing open; 5. The Crucifixion; 6. The arrest of Jesus: Christ and Judas are the fourth and fifth figures from the right; St Peter, holding a sword, is second from the left; 7. The Last Supper; 8. Two lions with large paws; 9. Three apostles (on the buttress); 10. The discovery of the empty tomb; 11. A lively carving of weird monsters perhaps representing some of the beasts summoned by the fifth and sixth trumpets of the Apocalypse. The last two reliefs seem to have been carved by a different, more assured hand.

Five miles north-east of Dax, just off the N124 to Mont-de-Marsan, is Saint-Vincent-de-Paul, the birthplace of the saint (1581–1660) who created the orders of Lazarists and Filles de la Charité.

South of Dax the land is flat and sandy and covered with pine-forests, interspersed with vineyards. However, a short journey of fifteen miles brings you to Peyrehorade, capital of the Pays d'Orthe, a small town commanding an important river crossing of the Gaves-Réunis, a short stretch where two mountain rivers, the Gave d'Oloron and the Gave de Pau, join forces before flowing into the Adour.

The Pays d'Orthe was a small semi-independent medieval Viscounty and Peyrehorade is still dominated to the north by the ruins of the Viscounts' castle, which was destroyed by Montgoméry in 1569. Down by the river is the sixteenth-century Château de Montréal, a massive square fortress with round towers at each corner and a fine wrought-iron grille in the entrance gateway.

Just across the river, in a typically beautiful setting below a wooded field, are the ruins of Arthous, a Premonstratensian abbey founded in 1160. It was an important stage on the route to Santiago de Compostella and, during the Middle Ages, grew rich and powerful, but like so many other churches it suffered dreadful damage at the hands of Montgoméry's troops in 1569.

Despite scrupulous restoration, the abbey is a sad sight. The best part is the east end: the apse is articulated by twin columns either side of the central window and flat pilaster-like buttresses to the west of the side-windows. At roof level is an arched corbel table with sculpted corbel ends. Amongst the scenes depicted are Original Sin, the Expulsion from Eden, the Holy Family's flight into Egypt and the Three Wise Men. The south apsidal chapel has corbels with Adam and Eve standing side by side; a man drinking from a barrel; a creature that looks like a bear; a musician playing a viol, a wolf preying on a lamb and a dog and duck.

The interior of the church is very ruined and rather depressing, although the walls survive up to roof level. The most interesting thing here is the remains of a beautiful tympanum that once was situated above the north doorway depicting the Adoration of the Magi.

Attached to the abbey is a small museum, mostly devoted to prehistory, for this area has been inhabited since Palaeolithic times, over forty thousand years ago. Amongst the exhibits are the remains of a boat, hollowed out of a log, salvaged from the river near Sorde-l'Abbaye, two miles east of Peyrehorade. This primitive craft corresponds closely to a description in a guidebook written sometime in the twelfth entury for pilgrims on their way to Santiago. At that time Sorde was the only place where it was possible to cross the Gave d'Oloron, for there were no bridges then. The anonymous author describes first how, after the dreadful crossing of the Landes, the pilgrim came to the Chalosse:

> Once having crossed the Landes, you come to Gascony, rich in white bread and excellent red wine. It is well-wooded with meadows and rivers and pure springs. The Gascons are witty, talkative, jokers, dissolute, drunkards, gluttons, ragged and penniless. But they are skilled in warfare and very hospitable to the poor. Instead of eating at

table, they are accustomed to sit round the fire sharing the same cup. They eat and drink a great deal and are badly dressed. Servants, masters and mistresses all sleep together, without embarrassment, on the same thin foul mattress. Quitting this country by the pilgrim road of Saint-Jacques you come to two rivers near the village of Saint-Jean-de-Sorde, one on the right and one of the left. One is called 'gave' and the other 'river'. It is impossible to cross without a boat. A curse on those boatmen ... the boat is small, made entirely of the trunk of a single tree; they frequently take on board so many pilgrims, after making them pay first, that the boat capsizes, the pilgrims drown and the boatmen rejoice evily after seizing and stripping the corpses.

Presumably 'river' (*flumen* in the original Latin) refers to the Gave de Pau although it could just mean the Gaves-Réunis, a much broader stream than the Gave de Pau or Gave d'Oloron. The reference to Saint-Jean-de-Sorde clearly identifies the 'gave' (*gaver* in Latin) as the Gave d'Oloron.

Sorde-l'Abbaye, as Saint-Jean-de-Sorde is now called, stands on the north bank of the Gave d'Oloron, two and a half miles east of Peyrehorade. This small, sleepy town, which at first sight looks rather dull, occupies one of the most remarkable sites in Gascony which has been continuously inhabited from Palaeolithic times to the present day. A great deal of archaeological evidence from different periods has survived, so that Sorde is a kind of time capsule where the past comes vividly to life.

The prehistoric site lies just south of Sorde at the foot of the cliff-wall of Pastou where a collection of stone tools dating from the upper Palaeolithic period has been found, including needles, spears, scrapers and knives. These can be seen in the museum at Arthous.

A prehistoric track ran just to the east of Sorde from Dax, southwards to Astorga in north-west Spain. This route was subsequently adopted by the Romans and traces of the road they built still survive, although now it is so thickly overgrown that it is very difficult to find. In the Middle Ages the road was called the Pas de Charlemagne because the emperor was supposed to have passed this way *en route* to Spain to fight the Moors. Colloquially, the road was known as the *Chemin de la Chaudière*. A *chaudière* is a pot in which water is boiled and the reference is to the hot springs of Dax.

According to Book IV of the *Liber Sancti Jacobi*, Charlemagne stopped at Sorde on his return from Spain and built a church here with gold captured from the Moors. Book IV is believed to have been written by Turpin, the famous fighting Bishop, who was a friend and companion in arms of Charlemagne, and legend has it that he is buried at Sorde.

The Benedictine monastery of Saint-Jean-de-Sorde was founded in the tenth century. The monks chose an admirable site on the north bank of the Gave d'Oloron where the rich alluvial soil was ideal for growing crops and vegetables, while the river could be relied on for an abundant supply of salmon. Alas, this is no longer true: pollution has reduced their numbers sharply in recent years.

Like Arthous, Saint-Jean-de-Sorde was a stage on the pilgrim route to Compostella and for three hundred years the abbey's wealth and fame increased. All this came to an abrupt end in 1532 when the monastery was sacked by Spanish troops during the Franco-Spanish War. Barely had the monks had time to get over this shock when Saint-Jean was attacked again, this time by Montgoméry's troops, and set on fire. During the seventeenth and eighteenth centuries there was a slow recovery but the *coup de grâce* was administered in the French Revolution when the monastery was dissolved. The abbey, however, became the local church and was restored, very badly, between 1868 and 1871.

The earliest surviving part of the church is the east end, which is twelfth-century. The semi-circular apse is much larger than the apsidal chapels and has a diameter of twenty-six feet. The roof level was raised at a later date but this work was very inexpertly carried out so that the join is obvious. In fact, the whole apse has a rather battered look, although when you look closely you can see details like the billet moulding between the windows and the remains of attached columns which show that it must once have looked very imposing. Of the two apsidal chapels, that on the south seems to be earlier.

The transept is also twelfth-century, although the Gothic

windows and the blank arcade inside were added later. The north transept is flanked to the west by a belfry whose base some scholars believe to be the remains of an eleventh-century defensive tower; on the east side is a huge diagonal buttress.

The nave and the aisles date from the late thirteenth or early fourteenth centuries but were heavily restored in the seventeenth and nineteenth centuries. At the west end the entrance porch has a badly mutilated tympanum depicting Christ in Majesty surrounded by the signs of the evangelists. The voussoirs of the arch above have carvings of the wise and foolish virgins, ten sitting figures that may be elders or prophets and signs of the zodiac and labours of the months.

Inside, it soon becomes apparent that the south wall is badly out of alignment. This can be seen most clearly by comparing the north and south aisle vaults of the westernmost bay of the nave.

There are some interesting capitals at the entrance to the apsidal chapel. Those in the south chapel depict two scenes from the childhood of Christ: on the right Mary sits with Christ on her knee, flanked on either side by an angel standing on a cloud and pointing at the holy pair. On the left Mary, with Joseph beside her, presents Jesus to Simeon who kneels before her. Behind Simeon is a small building, perhaps his home. In the sky above are angels and the two doves that were sacrificed in the temple.

In the north chapel, a capital shows on one face Christ's arrest and, on the other, Daniel, representing the triumph of Christ, sitting holding a book with his hand raised in blessing, surrounded by lions. The worn Latin lettering describes the scenes: 'JUDAS ISCARIOT/DEI TRADICCIO' and 'DNI H ... TRADIDIT' and 'HISTORIA DANIEL PROPH ...'

Behind the altar is a remarkable mosaic. At one time it was thought that it belonged to the Roman villa that once stood here but scholars now believe that it is medieval. Note in particular the dog chasing a hare.

South of the church are the ruins of the monastic buildings, dating from the seventeenth century. There is not a great deal to see but it is well worth a visit, to walk along the subterranean groin-vaulted corridor whose windows offer beautiful views of the Gave d'Oloron.

At the south-east corner of the church is the Abbot's House, a fifteenth-century building with a corner tower and mullion and transom windows. Its modest exterior hides some fascinating archaeological discoveries: the manor house was built on the site of a fourth-century Gallo-Roman bath house and excavations undertaken in 1958 revealed not only some very fine mosaic pavements but, in the middle of them, a grave containing several skeletons. These have been identified as belonging to Barbarians, probably the ones who destroyed the baths, for it was apparently a Barbarian practice to bury their dead amid the ruins of buildings they had destroyed. Here, for once, is rare evidence that the Barbarian tribes who overran the Roman Empire really did exist. Upstairs is an exhibition devoted to life in the monastery, including an ingenious construction, rather like a water-wheel, with paddles instead of spokes which flipped the fish into a net as it turned. No wonder some of the monks complained of having too much salmon in their diet. The upper windows of the Abbot's House offer splendid views of the river and the gentle country beyond.

Five miles south of Arthous, at Bidache on the D19, are the magnificent ruins of the château of the Dukes of Gramont. The first mention of a castle at Bidache is in 1250 when the stronghold of a local robber baron was destroyed by Simon de Montfort on the instructions of Henry III of England. The Gramont family seems to have settled here in the fourteenth century but the castle they built was almost totally destroyed in 1523 by invading Spanish troops. Work soon began on a new building in the latest Italian style but this, in turn, was modified in the seventeenth and eighteenth centuries. The château was finally abandoned after being set on fire during the French Revolution.

The Count of Gramont was a companion in arms of Henri of Navarre, and the Vert Galant met one of his favourite mistresses, 'la belle Corisande', Diane of Andoins, Countess of Gramont, at the château. But the most famous of the Gramonts was Antoine III (1604–78) who became a Marshal of France and was created a Duke in 1648. He was a successful diplomat and received Mazarin at the château in 1658 during peace negotiations with Spain.

The ruins stand on a gentle, grassy slope just north of Bidache, close to the river Bidouze. The monumental, eighteenth-century entrance, with its heavy rustication and triangular pediment, is flanked on either side by two massive towers belonging to the original medieval barbican. To the right are the remains of the seventeenth-century wing built by Antoine III: its windows have triangular and semi-circular pediments while above them pedimented gables project skywards where the roof should be.

Once through the gateway you are in a courtyard and facing you is the earlier Renaissance wing. A seventeenth-century Baroque gateway on the right leads to what remains of a large second courtyard, a short stretch of a west wing and all that survives of the massive medieval keep.

The château of Bidache stands right on the southern border of Gascony and Bas-Navarre, now part of the Pays-Basque, and the strategic importance of the site is reflected in the size and extent of these impressive ruins.

Back on the south bank of the Gaves-Réunis, about two miles west of Peyrehorade, is Hastingues, a *bastide* town built on a hill overlooking the river. It was founded in 1305 by Sir John Hastings, the seneschal of Edward I of England, and remained in English hands until 1451. The town was subsequently burned and pillaged by Spanish troops in 1523 but, even so, it retains much of its original character. A stretch of the old walls still survives on the south side of the town together with a stone gateway. Inside is the usual grid pattern of streets with fine views down some of them to the river below. The church in the square has a fourteenth-century tower but the rest is nineteenth-century; opposite is a handsome sixteenth-century house with mullion and transom windows. The narrow main street leading down from the original southern gateway looks very medieval, although many of the houses are actually built in the style of the Pays-Basque. On the east side is the façade of a medieval house whose doorway has a Gothic ogee arch surmounted by an angel holding a shield with armorial bearings. The arch is supported left and right by grotesques.

From Hastingues, the D253 leads to the nearby ruins of the

château of Guiche, built on a promontory dominating the left bank of the Bidouze. The first château dates back to the eleventh century but by the thirteenth century there was an important fishery here which was a hazard to navigation. This gave rise to a bitter feud between the fishermen of Guiche and the boatmen who regularly used the river, culminating in 1257 when the boatmen set fire to the château. In the fourteenth century the château came into the possession of the Albrets, Viscounts of Tartas, and a furious rivalry grew up between them and the Counts of Gramont. In 1449 Guiche was captured by Gaston IV of Foix-Béarn and although the Albrets recovered the château, they were forced to surrender it to the Counts of Gramont in 1485. The *coup de grâce* was administered to the château of Guiche by invading Spanish troops in 1523; what little remains is thickly covered by vegetation.

From Peyrehorade it is just over twenty miles along the N117 to Bayonne. A slower but more enjoyable route follows the south bank of the Gaves-Réunis and the Adour, the first part, west of Hastingues, running along the top of a narrow embankment. But the usual approach is from the north, via the N10. You descend a long hill, pass through a rather scruffy northern suburb and, suddenly, you are crossing the wide Adour and, immediately afterwards, its attractive tributary, the Nive.

Bayonne is a delightful place: a quiet cathedral city whose picturesque medieval streets and pleasant riverside boulevards belie its turbulent past. It occupies a strategic position, astride the rivers Nive and Adour, close to the western end of the Pyrénées, which has made it a vital frontier fortress since Roman times. At the end of the third century AD, Lapurdum, as it was then called, was the headquarters of a Roman cohort stationed there to guard the Novempopulani and there are still traces of the fourth-century defensive wall that they built. During the ninth century, the city became a base for Norman pirates who made raids inland as far as Saint-Sever.

By the twelfth century, the name had changed to Baïona, derived from the Basque word *ibai-one*, beautiful river, but the diocese of Bayonne retained the old name of the westernmost region of the Pays-Basque. Bayonne is, in fact, as much a Basque town as a

Gascon one and *euskara*, their strange language, can often be heard in its cafés and bars.

For nearly three hundred years, from 1152 to 1451, Bayonne was part of English Gascony. Under the benign rule of the English kings, the port of Bayonne prospered and a thriving trade, especially in wine, developed with English ports such as Bristol and London. So much so that, when Dunois, at the head of a French army, besieged the city, the Bayonnais resisted fiercely. The story goes that on 20 August, 1451, the defenders saw in the sky white clouds in the shape of a cross surmounted by a crown which changed into a fleur-de-lys. The Bayonnais took this as a sign that God was on the side of the French and surrendered. One cannot help thinking that the canny Gascons saw not so much a sign in the sky as the writing on the wall and used the celestial manifestation as a face-saver.

The change to French rule did the port of Bayonne little good. The trade link with England was lost and, instead of the special privileges granted by the English monarchs, a heavy indemnity was imposed by the new masters. To make things worse, all through the fifteenth century the mouth of the Adour was silting up and finally, after a terrible storm, it was completely blocked and the river turned northwards to find a fresh outlet at Port-d'Albret. In 1569 Charles IX of France decreed that a way should be found to open up the port again. A canal was dug across the dunes and, aided by a providential flooding of the river Nive in 1578, the Adour was turned into its new channel.

The sixteenth and seventeenth centuries saw a revival of the fortunes of Bayonne. Realizing the strategic importance of the city, François I had new fortifications built and was rewarded by the Bayonnais' heroic resistance when they were besieged by Spanish troops in 1523, justifying the proud boast on their coat of arms, *jam polluta* (never violated). By 1680 these fortifications were no longer considered adequate for modern conditions and the great engineer Vauban was despatched to bring them up to date. Most of his defensive system of ramparts and ditches survives to this day on the south side of the city.

In the seventeenth century Bayonne became a base for corsairs, a kind of legalized piracy in which ships were licensed to attack the merchant ships of other nations with which France was at war and their owners and crews allowed to keep a proportion of the profits of the cargo, the rest going to the crown. The local bourgeoisie grew rich by building and commissioning their own ships to take part in this lucrative business and the whole community benefited from their foresight.

Bayonne's boom period was during the eighteenth century. Huge profits accrued from numerous prizes captured during the Seven Years' War between England and France; the fishing fleet sailed as far afield as Newfoundland; ship-building flourished and an iron-foundry was built which created the famous *baïonette*, used by all French armies after 1703. In 1748 Bayonne was made a free port and its traffic tripled.

This period of prosperity came to an end with the French Revolution. During the Napoleonic Wars the port was blockaded by the English fleet and never fully recovered afterwards. Today its chief exports are maize and sulphur, a by-product of the natural gas exploited at Lacq in the Pyrénées.

Immediately after crossing the Nive by the Pont Mayou, you come to the Place de la Liberté, the lively centre of Bayonne. Here, in the elegant, arcaded eighteenth-century *hôtel-de-ville* is a café where you can drink your first cup of chocolate. Bayonne has been famous for this beverage ever since the sixteenth century when the art of making it was brought from Spain by Jews fleeing the persecution of the Inquisition.

Behind the *hôtel-de-ville* are the narrow streets of Grand Bayonne, that part of the old city, west of the Nive, where the cathedral and the Château-Vieux are to be found. The rues Albert I, Thiers and Victor Hugo all lead towards the cathedral but the arcaded Rue du Pont Neuf is the most agreeable. Here you will find the best chocolate shops, *patisseries* and *salons de thé* where you can relax after the rigours of sight-seeing.

Here, too, you can buy the famous Bayonne ham, which is not actually produced here but comes downriver from the mountains of Béarn. The individual flavour of the ham is due to the method of curing and the mixture of salt and herbs that is used.

The rue du Pont Neuf is followed by the rue de la Monnaie, which leads to the place Louis Pasteur and the cathedral. The square is a pleasant secluded spot, planted with magnolia trees and bounded to the north by interesting small shops and to the south by the north porch of the cathedral. A little way to the left is a fountain on the site of a former pillory built with stones from the château of Hastingues, which was stormed by the Bayonnais themselves in 1377.

The Cathedral of Sainte-Marie is unique in being the sole example in Gascony of the high Gothic style of Champagne and the Ile-de-France. The original church, which stood on the site of a Roman temple, was destroyed by fire in 1213 and work on the new cathedral began soon afterwards.

At that time Gascony, including of course Bayonne, was under English rule. It was a period of intense rivalry between the English King, Henry III, and Louis IX of France. The English King was deeply impressed by the new Gothic cathedrals of northern France, such as Chartres and Rheims, and was determined not to be outdone. So, under his influence, Bayonne was designed in the very latest style. This can be seen most clearly at the east end where the two-light windows are crowned by roundels with sexfoil bar tracery, an innovation first found at Rheims in 1211.

The nave was built in the fourteenth century and has the three-storey elevation of the high Gothic period but the tracery in some of the clerestory windows is in the later flamboyant style. Work on the church continued until 1544 when the money ran out. The west front remained unfinished until 1847 when work was resumed on the initiative of a wealthy Bayonnais called Lormand. The west towers and spires belong to the same period. They are built of a lighter coloured stone than the rest of the building but even so they blend very happily with the earlier parts of the cathedral and their elegant spires are a landmark all over the city.

The north porch was badly damaged during the French Revolution but on the left there is an amusing sculpture (clearly not original) of a mason sculpting a capital. On the left-hand door there is a thirteenth-century bronze sanctuary knocker. Inside, to the left, is the choir and ambulatory where the high Gothic influence can be seen not only in the windows but also in the cylindrical piers with their attached shafts and the combined vaulting of the chapels and the ambulatory whose ribs share common keystones, as at Soissons.

The fourteenth-century nave with its harmonious proportions, its simple three-stage elevation and quadripartite vaults, is very impressive. The keystone of the first vault west of the nave bears the arms of England, three lions against a red background. Other keystones display the fleurs-de-lys of France.

The glass in the clerestory is unfortunately all restored but there is a Renaissance window in the second chapel to the right of the north entrance. It shows the woman of Canaan kneeling before Christ, who is surrounded by his apostles, imploring him to heal her child. In the background is a rocky landscape and a city, presumably Jerusalem the Blessed. On the left a bat-winged devil is in flight after the curing of the woman's child. At the top of the window is the salamander, the emblem of François I, and the date 1531. Below are the donors François de Laduch and his wife Laurencine de Lagarde and their motto *Nunc et semper* (now and for ever). Continuing along the north aisle the last but one chapel to the west contains a tablet commemorating the Miracle of Bayonne which gave the French victory over the English in 1451. The last chapel has a fifteenth-century fresco of the Crucifixion.

A doorway at the opposite side of the nave leads to the beautiful fourteenth-century cloister, from the south side of which there is a splendid view of the complicated tracery of the clerestory windows. The vaulted passages have openings subdivided into two arches which are further subdivided into two smaller arches, surmounted by three roundels with sexfoil bar-tracery. In the south-east corner of the cloister is a Gascon inscription which reads: 'In the year 1515 this pillar was begun, noble Auger de Lahet being mason and lay-treasurer of this church, to hold up this tower, begun by the Lord his father, also lay-treasurer when alive. Thanks be to God.'

Part of the cloister on the north side is now sealed off to form the sacristy. Unfortunately, inside is the thirteenth-century entrance to the church with its original sculpture which is now impossible to see without special permission. This is a great pity for the quality of the sculpture is very fine. There are two sculpted tympana: the one of the right depicts the Last Judgement with Christ showing his wounds, surrounded by angels and instruments of the Passion; in the corners are the signs of the evangelists; below are scenes of the Day of Judgement in which the chosen ascend to heaven while the damned are dragged down to hell, among them a king, recognizable by his crown, and a bishop who is already being boiled in a cauldron by an exultant devil.

The left tympanum shows the Virgin Mary and the Christ-child surrounded by angels with musical instruments; below are standing figures of (from left to right) St Paul with a sword, St Peter, St James with his pilgrim's staff, St Matthew, St Andrew with his cross, and an unidentified figure.

Back inside the church, the vault of the choir ambulatory, just outside the sacristy, has an interesting keystone depicting a ship. The five chapels at the east end of the cathedral have paintings by Steinheil, a nineteenth-century artist.

The fifteenth-century porch lost all its sculpture during the Revolution but above it is a rose window, surmounted by the arms of France, born aloft by angels, an unequivocal declaration that God is on the side of the French.

If you turn right after leaving this splendid symbol of spiritual authority, you will quickly come to the powerful representative of the secular arm: the Château-Vieux. This massive square fortress, flanked at the corners by round towers, was built by Bertrand, Count of Bayonne and has part of the original Roman ramparts as its base. Among the famous men who stayed at the château were Don Alonso le Batailleur, King of Navarre in 1130, the Black Prince and his great French opponent Du Guesclin who was captured at the Battle of Auray and held captive in the fortress until a ransom was paid. Don Pedro the Cruel, King of Castile, stayed there in 1367 followed by several French kings: Louix XI in 1463, François I (1526), Charles IX (1565) and Louis XIV in 1660, on his way to meet his future wife and queen, Maria Theresa of Spain. The last famous visitor, albeit an involuntary one, was the Spaniard General Palafox, Duke of Saragossa, celebrated for his heroic defence of Saragossa against Napoleon's troops in 1809, who was subsequently defeated in battle and imprisoned in the Château-Vieux.

From the Château-Vieux, it is but a short step to the splendid ramparts built by Vauban as part of his herculean twenty-year programme designed to strengthen France's frontiers with a ring of modern forts. The ramparts of Bayonne stretch practically intact right round the southern side of the city, affording a pleasant promenade with views south over municipal parks to the nearby mountains.

Halfway round, the line of the ramparts is interrupted by the river Nive which divides Grand Bayonne to the west from Petit Bayonne on the east. In Petit Bayonne there are two excellent museums: the Musée Bonnet, which houses a fine collection of paintings, and the Musée Basque, devoted to the history and culture of the Basque people.

Although historically Bayonne belongs to Gascony, it is also the traditional capital of the Pays-Basque, that mountainous territory to the south of the city inhabited by a mysterious people, speaking a strange tongue, completely unrelated to the Indo-European languages, whose origins are unknown. The word 'basque' derives from the Latin *vascones* which in the mountains became *bascos* and ultimately 'basque', while in the plains the Latin pronunciation 'wascons', because the French language abhors a 'w', changed into 'Gascons'. Thus Gascon and Basque are the same word. Despite this, it seems unlikely that the Basques are the direct ancestors of the Gascons but they certainly share the same roots as the Vascones who, in the sixth century, descended from the mountains, conquered the Novempopulani and by assimilation with their Gallo-Roman subjects formed the indigenous base of the Gascon people.

ENVOI

On the surface little has changed in Gascony in the five years it has taken to write this book. There is some new building between Agen and Auch, and in the Ténarèze, near Condom, some vineyards have been grubbed up and replaced by cereals; but, as you go futher south, into the heart of Armagnac, the landscape still looks invitingly empty and serene.

Yet there have been some interesting developments. In recent years the French have become increasingly aware of their heritage and there has been great stress on local and regional identities. South and west of the Garonne the word 'Gascogne' is being used more and more to describe local products like Côtes de Gascogne, the wine from the region south-east of Eauze. Armagnac, which in the past has had to play second fiddle to its rival brandy, Cognac, is now considered the more fashionable drink. In its promotional literature Armagnac is now always described as originating in Gascony. In holiday brochures more and more Gascon holiday homes are being advertised for the first time. So, the profile of Gascony is much higher than it once was and tourists are beginning to look beyond the Dordogne and the Lot to this unspoiled region further south.

How will the Gascons cope with this increasing tide of visitors? In the Pyrénées they have long been used to looking after tourists and the facilities already exist. Further north, especially in the heart of Gascony, a great deal needs to be done to prepare the locals to meet the demands of this new industry. The authorities are well aware of the problem and surveys of hotel accommodation and other facilities are already in hand. But the Gascons are naturally hospitable people and the traveller who sets out to explore this beautiful and historic region is assured of a genuinely warm welcome.

USEFUL INFORMATION

Tourism in France

Tourism is highly organized in France. The headquarters is: Office de Tourisme, 127 Avenue des Champs-Elysées, 75008 Paris. In Britain the address is: French Government Tourist Office, 178 Piccadilly, London WIV oAL. In the U.S.A. it is 610 Fifth Avenue, New York, 10020.

Each region has its own headquarters. Gascony is covered by:

Lot-et Garonne Comité Départemental du Tourisme et des Loisirs, Centre Culturel Ledru-Rollin, rue Ledru-Rollin, 47000 Agen.

Gers Comité Départemental du Tourisme et des Loisirs, 9 rue Espagne, BP 69, 32002 Auch.

Landes Comité Départemental du Tourisme des Landes, 9 allées Brouchet, 40000 Mont-de-Marsan.

Midi-Pyrénées Comité Départemental du Tourisme, 12 rue Salambo, 31000 Toulouse.

In addition every town of any size has a tourist office in the local information bureau, the Syndicat d'Initiative.

Railways

French Railways, 179 Piccadilly, London WIV oAL.

Touring by Car

Touring Club de France, 65 avenue de la Grande-Armée, 75016 Paris. For touring the best maps are the Michelin yellow series 1/200,000 (1cm = 2 kilometres) published by Pneu Michelin, 46 avenue de Breteuil, 75341 Paris. Gascony is covered by maps 78, 79, 82, 85, 86.

Walking and Backpacking

Comité National des Sentiers de Grande Randonnée (C.N.S.G.R.) is the organization responsible for the administration of the routes for walkers and backpackers in the Pyrénées, Alps and elsewhere. The routes are clearly marked with painted signs, even on the highest slopes and there are refuges and hostels, some of them with wardens in the summer months. Details can be obtained from C.N.S.G.R., 96 rue de Clignancourt, 75018 Paris, or from regional offices:

Landes Cité Galliane, 40000, Mont de Marsan.

Lot-et-Garonne Association Départmentale du Tourisme Pédestre, Centre Culturel Ledru-Rollin, rue Ledru-Rollin, 47000 Agen.

Midi-Pyrénées Grandes Randonnées Pyrénéennes, 4 rue de Villefranche, 09200 Saint-Girons.

Pyrénées-Atlantiques, 83 avenue des Lauriers, 64000 Pau.

The Institut Geógraphique National (I.G.N.), 107 rue de la Boétie, 75008 Paris, publishes the excellent route maps *Cartes de Randonnées* with scale of 1/50,000 (1cm = 5km) which are ideal for walkers. The numbers for Gascony are 3. Béarn-Parc National des Pyrénées 4. Bigorre-Parc National des Pyrénées 5. Luchon-Aure-Louron 6. Couserans-Vicdessos.

The following organizations also supply useful information:

Chalets Internationaux de Haute-Montagne (C.I.H.M.), 15 rue Gay-Lussac, 75005 Paris.

Club Alpine Français (C.A.F.), 7 rue de la Boétie, 75008 Paris.

Touring Club de France, 65 avenue de la Grande-Armée, 75016 Paris.

Union Nationale des Centres de Plein-Air (U.C.P.A.), 62 rue de la Glacière, 75013 Paris.

Regional Parks

Landes Parc des Landes de Gascogne, place de l'Eglise, 33830 Belin-Béliet.

Midi-Pyrénées Parc National des Pyrénées Occidentales, BP 300, 65013 Tarbes.

Watersports

A useful guide to aquatic sports, *Tourisme Fluvial en France*, is published by the Ministère des Transports, Sous direction des voies navigables, 244 boulevard Saint-Germain, 75007 Paris.

Fishing
Conseil Supérieur de la Pêche, 10 rue Péclet, 75015 Paris.

Boating and Sailing
Syndicat National des Loueurs de Bateaux de Plaisance, Yacht-House de la F.I.N., Port de la Bourdonnais, 75007 Paris.
Fédération Française de Yachting à Voile, 55 avenue Kléber, 75116 Paris.

Canoeing
Fédération Française de Canoë-Kayak, 87 quai de la Marne, 94340 Joinville.

Surfing
Fédération Française de Surf-riding et de Skate-Board, Cité Administrative, avenue Edouard VII, 64200 Biarritz.

Horse-riding
Association Nationale pour le Tourisme Equestre et l'Equitation de Loisirs (A.N.T.E.), 12 rue du Parc Royal, 75003 Paris.

Pilgrimage
Sentier de Saint-Jacques-de-Compostelle, Quercy-Gascogne, GR65.
This guidebook to the part of the pilgrimage route to Santiago de Compostella that crosses Gascony is published by the Comité National des Sentiers de Grande Randonnée, 8 avenue Marceau, 75008 Paris.

Hotels and Restaurants
Ownership and standards of hotels and restaurants are constantly changing and it would be a full-time job to keep abreast of them, so, apart from those mentioned in the text, no special recommendations are made here. Instead you are advised to consult the following guides:

Red Michelin Guide to Hotels and Restaurants. This is the most comprehensive and best guide and is published annually by Pneu Michelin, avenue de Breteuil, 75341 Paris. It is widely available in Britain.
Logis et Auberges de France. A guide to modestly priced but good value

hotels published by Fédération Nationale des Logis et Auberges de France, 25 rue Jean-Meroz, 75008 Paris. *Logis et Auberges de France* is available free from the French Government Tourist Office, 178 Piccadilly, London W1V 9DB (send 80p for postage).

Gites de France. This popular handbook offers a wide range of self-catering accommodation in the French countryside, often in very beautiful sites. It is available for a fee of £3.00 from Gites de France Ltd, 178 Piccadilly, London W1V 9DB, who also provide a booking service. Gites de France also publish the *Chambres d'Hôtes Brochure*, which offers short stays in French country homes, and *Loisirs Accueil*, which features rambling and cycling holidays throughout France.

French Farm and Village Holiday Guide. This British edition of *Gites de France* contains 1,200 addresses and is published by FHG Publications Ltd, Paisley, Strathclyde, Scotland.

Le Guide Gascon An enthusiastic local guide by Maurice Vidal published by Art Village, 32380 Saint-Clar, Gers.

French Leave 3 by Richard Binns contains an excellent survey of restaurants in South-West France. Published by Chiltern House Publishers Ltd, Chiltern House, Amersham Road, Amersham, Bucks HP6 5PE.

Camping and Caravanning

The best guide is *Camping and Caravanning in France* published annually by Pneu Michelin, 46 avenue de Breteuil, 75341 Paris.

The Maison des Gîtes de France also publishes *Campings à la Ferme et Gîtes d'Etape*, Maison des Gîtes de France, 35 rue Godot-de-Mauroy, 75009 Paris.

Wines and Spirits

Armagnac

The governing body is GIVISO (Groupement d'Interêt Economique des Vignerons du Sud-Ouest), 50 boulevard Carnot, 47000 Agen. (58) 66 75 99.

Producers

Boignères, Domaine de, Le Frèche, 40190 Villeneuve-de-Marsan, (58) 45 24 05, Léon Lafitte.

La Boubée, 52250 Montréal-du-Gers, (62) 28 41 85, Jean Ladevèze.

Au Bourdieu Lauraët, 32610 Mouchan, (62) 28 41 37, Joel Fourteau

Busca-Maniban, Château du, 32310 Masencôme, (62) 29 12 02, Mme. Jaqueline Palthey de Roll.

Cassagnoles, Domaine des, 32330 Gondrin, (62) 29 12 75, J. Cardeillac and G. Baumann.

Cassaigne, Château de, 32100 Condom, (62) 28 04 02, Henri Faget.
The château was built in 1247 by the Abbot of Condom and remained the abbot's country retreat until the sixteenth century when it was secularized, rebuilt and transformed. The still-house dates from the eighteenth century.

Castarède, Pont-de-Bordes, 47230 Lavardac, (53) 65 50 06, Florence Castarède.
The oldest firm in Armagnac, founded in 1852, Castarède do not distill their own armagnac: they buy in, store in wooden casks and market many fine individual vintages.

Caussade, Marquis de, BP 38, route de Cazaubon, 32800 Eauze, (62) 09 94 22, Michel Coste.

Cyrano, Cadets de Gascogne, 40000 Mont-de-Marsan, (58) 75 26 10, M. Bats. A firm specializing in old armagnacs.

La Croix de Salles, BP 9, 32110, Nogaro, (62) 09 03 01, H. Dartigalongue et Fils.

Dupeyron, 1 rue Daunou, 32100, Condom, (62) 28 08 08, Ryst Dupeyron.

Gayrosse, Domaine de, 40240 Labastide d'Armagnac, (58) 44 81 08, Dr. Charles Garraud, the inventor of Floc de Gascogne.

Gélas, BP 3, 32190 Vic-Fézensac, (62) 06 30 11, Pierre Gélas.

Goudoulin, Domain de Bigor, Courrensan, 32330 Gondrin, (62) 06 35 02, Veuve Goudoulin.

Janneau, 50 avenue d'Aquitaine, 32100 Condom, (62) 28 24 77. The largest and most up-to-date firm in Armagnac.

Larressingle, Etablissements Papelorey SA, rue des Carmes, 32100 Condom, (62) 28 15 33.

Laubade, Château de, GFA de Laubade, Sorbets, 32110 Nogaro, (62) 09 06 02, M. Jean-Jacques Lesgourgues.

Malliac, Château de, 32250 Montréal-du-Gers, (62) 28 44 87, M. Berthelon.
A fine château dating from the Middle Ages which produces some excellent armagnacs, especially their Grand Bas Folle Blanche '47.

Miquer, Domain de, Hontanx, 40190 Villeneuve-de-Marsan, M. Lasserre.

Montesquieu, Marquis de, route de Cazaubon, 32800 Eauze, (62) 09 82 13. The firm was founded by Pierre de Montesquieu, a descendant of D'Artagnan. It is now owned by Ricard. It has some fine old vintages going back to 1942.

Ognoas, Domaine d', 40190 Villeneuve-de-Marsan, (58) 45 22 11, Arthez d'Armagnac. Armagnac made in a still that is one hundred and eighty years old.

Plachat, Panjas, 32110 Nogaro, (62) 09 07 02, Pierre Cournet.

Pomes-Peberère, Château de, 32100 Condom, (62) 28 11 53. Louis Faget.

Roy des Armagnac, Le, Domaine Balenton, Cazeneuve, 32800, Eauze, (62) 09 90 01, M. Gimet.

Ravignan, Domaine de, Perquié, 40190 Villeneuve-de-Marsan, (58) 45 22 04, Baron de Ravignan.

Tariquet, Château du, 32800 Eauze (62) 09 87 82, Pierre Grassa et Fils. You will receive a warm welcome from our friends if you visit this excellent château. Try their fifteen-year-old *hors d'âge* armagnac.

Samalens, 32110 Laujuzan, (62) 09 14 88, Jean and George Samalens. Samalens has one of the largest stocks of old armagnacs.

Sempé, 32290 Aignan (62) 09 24 24, Henri-Abel Sempé.

Pousse Rapière

Monluc, Château de, 32310 Saint-Puy, Valence-sur-Baïse, (62) 28 55 02. Well worth a visit to Blaise de Monluc's birthplace to see the medieval stone *pressoir* and vast cellars.

Wine

Côtes de Buzet

Les Vignerons Réunis des Côtes de Buzet, Buzet-sur-Baïse, 47160 Damazan, (53) 84 74 30.

Côtes de Gascogne

Cassagnoles, Domaine des, 32330 Gondrin, (62) 29 12 75, J. Cardeillac and G. Baumann.

San de Guilhem, Ramouzens, 32800 Eauze, (62) 06 57 02.

Tariquet (Domaine du), Château de Tariquet. 32800 Eauze, (62) 09 87 82. Pierre Grassa et Fils. Château du Tariquet also make Domaine du Tariquet Cuvée Bois, which is aged in cask for six months.

Madiran

Aydie, Château d', 64330 Aydie, (59) 04 01 17, MM. Laplace.

Barréjat, Domaine de, Maumusson, 32400 Riscle.

Montus, Château, Maumusson-Laguian, 32400 Riscle, (62) 69 74 67, Alain Brumont.

Peyros, Château, Corbères, 64350 Lembeye, (59) 33 70 51 M. Denis de Robillard.

Côtes de Saint-Mont

Union des Producteurs Plaimont, Saint-Mont, 32400 Riscle, (62) 69 78

87. This cooperative also sells Côtes de Gascogne, Pacherenc du Vic-Bilh and Madiran.

Tursan

Les Vignerons du Tursan, 40320 Geaune, (58) 44 51 25.

Pacherenc du Vic-Bilh

Aydie, Château d', 64330 Aydie, (59) 04 01 17, MM. Laplace.

Crampilh, Domaine du, Aurion-Idernes, 64350 Lembeye, Lucien Oulie.

Barrejat, Domaine de, Maumusson, 32400 Riscle, M. Capmartin.

Union des Producteurs Plaimont, Saint-Mont, 32400 Riscle, (62) 69 78 87.

Les Vignerons Réunis du Vic-Bilh-Madiran, Crouseilles, 64350 Lembeye, (59) 33 70 93.

Gastronomy

Art Village, Promotion Guide Gascon, 32380 Saint-Clar, (62) 66 48 22. *Foie gras, magret de canard, magret de canard séché, confit de canard cassoulet.*

Barthouil, 40 Peyrehorade, Landes, (58) 73 00 78. *Saumon fumé, jambon de Bayonne, foie gras.*

Caban, J'le Barail' Brax, 47310 Laplume, (58) 66 95 43. *Prunes d'agen, fruits en Armagnac.*

Casteran, Christain, 'Ramoun', 65170 Saint-Lary-Soulan, (62) 39 43 40. Excellent mountain cheese, especially *brebis* (sheep's cheese) and local wines.

Comtesse du Barry, 32200 Gimont, (62) 67 70 10. An excellent range of tinned local and regional specialities, including *foies gras de canard* and *d'oie, cassoulet, salmis de palombe*, etc.

Conserveries Lafitte, 49 rue des Carmes, 40 Dax, (58) 74 19 39. *Foie gras, pâtés, confit de canard.*

Dubernet, M. 40500 Saint-Sever, (58) 76 01 20. *Jambon de Bayonne, graisse d'oie, saucisses, confits.*

Espiet, Roger, 32800 Eauze, (62) 09 80 26. *Conserves regionales, jambon de Bayonne.*

Plante, R., place Sterling, 40 Soustons, Landes, *Confits, foie gras, pâtés, conserves de gibier, jambon de Bayonne.*

Gracia, Richard et Marie-Claude, La Belle Gasconne, Poudenas, 47170 Mezin, (53) 65 71 58. The finest *foie gras.*

BIBLIOGRAPHY

General Background
BUGE, Jean-Marc, *Habiter en Lomagne, Hier et Aujourd'hui*, Editions CTR, Lectoure, 1986.
CASTEX, Jean, COURTES, Jean and LASPALLES, Louis, *Gascogne d'Autrefois*, Editions Horvath, Roanne, 1981.
DUPUY, André, *Petite Encyclopédie Occitane*, Saber, Montpellier, 1972.
Petit Larousse en Couleurs, Libraire Larousse, Paris, 1972.
PESQUIDOUX, Joseph de, *Chez Nous en Gascogne*, Plon, 1921.
YOUNG, Arthur, *Travels in France during the years 1787, 1788, 1789*, two volumes, Bury St Edmunds, 1794.

Guides
Michelin Guides Verts: *Pyrénées-Aquitaine, Côte de l'Atlantique*, published by Pneu Michelin, Service de Tourisme, 46 avenue de Breteuil, Paris.
AMBRIÈRE, Francis, *Poitou-Guyenne*, Guide Bleu, Libraire Hachette, Paris, 1958.
AMBRIÈRE, Francis, *Pyrénées-Gascogne*, Guide Bleu, Libraire Hachette, Paris, 1972.
BAEDEKER, Karl, *Southern France*, Karl Baedeker, Publisher, Leipzig, Dulau and Co., London, 1907.
BRUNET, Roger, *Le Midi Toulousain*, Libraire Larousse, Paris, 1974.
BRUNET, Roger, *Les Pyrénées*, Libraire Larousse, Paris, 1974.
FAUCHER, Daniel, d'ESTALENX, J.-F., de GORSSE, Pierre, CUZACQ, René, *Visages de Gascogne, Béarn, Comté de Foix*, Horizons de France, 1968.
FÉNELON, Paul, SECRET, Jean, CROZET, René, GOT, Armand,

Visages de Guyenne, Horizons de France, Paris, 1966.

LERAT, Serge, *l'Aquitaine*, Libraire Larousse, Paris, 1974.

MYHILL, Henry, *North of the Pyrénées*, Faber and Faber, London, 1973.

Regional Guides

Les Gers: Gascogne-Armagnac, a beautifully illustrated essay published by le Comité Départemental du Tourisme et des Loisirs du Gers, Auch, 1981.

Guide de Haute Garonne, Collection-connaissance du Pays d'Oc, Editions de la Source, Montpellier (no date).

BOTTACIN, Abbé, *Le Pays d'Albret et ses Origines*, Nérac, 1972.

DELPAL, Jacques-Louis, *Pays Basque-Béarn*, Livre de Poche, Paris, 1977.

DELPAL, Jacques-Louis, *Pays Basque-Béarn*, Livre de Poche, Paris, 1977.

DELPONT. Jacques-Louis, *Le Pays d'Albret*, Editions Saber, Saint Christol, 1987.

DUFOR, Henri, *A la Découverte du Pays Gersois et de l'Armagnac*, Privat, Toulouse, 1980.

FAGET, Roger, *Les Landes*, Guide Touristique, Dax, 1976.

HENRY, Simone, *Comminges et Couserans*, Collection Pays du Sud-ouest, Privat, Toulouse, 1985.

PÉRÉ, André, *Armagnac coeur de la Gascogne*, Bibliothèque de Travail, Cannes, 1967.

SENDRAIL, Geneviève and DURAND, Philippe, *Guide du Haut Salat*, Saint-Girons, 1981.

TORRE, Michel de la, *Guide de l'art et de la nature, Gers*, Berger-Levrault-Banque National de Paris, Paris, 1981.

TORRE, Michel de la, *Guide de l'art et de la nature, Landes*, Nathan-Banque National de Paris, Paris, 1985.

TORRE, Michel de la, *Guide de l'art et de la nature, Lot-et-Garonne*, Levrault-Banque National de Paris, Paris, 1979.

Guidebooks: Local

CAILLAU, Georges, *Nérac, Histoire resumée de la capital de l'Albret*, Laplume, 1977.

Condom-en-Armagnac, Annuaire-Guide, Condom (no date).

Ecomusée de la Grande Lande, Guide du Visiteur, Bordeaux, 1983.

LAURENTIE, Dr and BRACH, Abbé, *Saint-Clar de Lomagne*, Edi-Service, Auch, 1981.

Mauvezin, regards sur le canton de, Edi-Service, Auch, 1981.
Le Savès Gersois, Cantons de l'Isle Jourdain, Lombez, Samatan, Edi-Service, Auch, 1978.

Guidebooks: Monuments and Sites
Midi-Pyrénées, Monuments Historiques no. 115, Juillet-Août, 1981.
Ouvert au Public, châteaux, abbayes et jardins historiques de France, Editions de la caisse nationale des monuments historiques et du sites, Paris, 1983.
BURIAS, Jean, *Sites du Lot-et-Garonne*, Nouvelles Editions Latines, Paris (no date).
Monuments and Sites
BABONNEAU, Lucien, *l'Eglise Fortifiée de Simorre*, Coueilles (no date).
BRIAT, René, *Le Château de Gramont*, Monuments Historiques no. 107, Paris (no date).
DONZE, Henri, *Saint-Savin en Lavedan*, Lourdes, 1982.
DUBARRY, Séverin, *Le Château-fort de Mauvezin*, Tarbes, 1962.
DURLIAT, Marcel, *Laressingle*, Privat, Toulouse, 1973.
Flaren, Auch (no date).
FOUET, Georges, *La Ville de Montmaurin*, Société des Etudes du Comminges, Saint-Gaudens, 1969.
JACQ, Christian and BRUNIER, François, *Saint-Just-de-Valcabrère*, Éditions des Trois Mondes, Paris, 1975.
LAFFARGUE, André, *En Visite chez Monluc*, Marsolan, 1980.
LARRIEU-DULER, Mary, *Le Musée de Lectoure*, Nouvelles Editions Latines, Paris (no date).
PÉMAN, Abbé-Louis, *l'Abbaye de Saint-Sever-de-Rustan*, Editions Pyrénénnes, Bagnères-de-Bigorre, 1982.
Seviac, Association pour la Sauvegarde des Monuments et Sites de l'Armagnac, Tour da Lamothe, Bretagne d'Armagnac (no date).
Biography
BARBER, Richard (editor and translator), *The Life and Campaigns of the Black Prince from contemporary letters, diaries and chronicles, including Chandos Herald's Life of the Black Prince*, Folio Society, London 1979.
EMERSON, Barbara, *The Black Prince*, Weidenfeld and Nicolson, London 1976.
EVANS, A. W., *Blaise de Monluc*, Herbert and Daniel, London (c. 1909).
SAMARAN, Charles, *D'Artagnan, Captaine des Mousquetaires du Roi*, Auch, 1967.

SAMARAN, Charles, *Louis XI, Jean d'Armagnac et le Drame de Lectoure*, Revue Historique XXXIII, Paris, 1885.
SPEAIGHT, Robert, *François Mauriac, a Study of the Writer and the Man*, Chatto and Windus, London 1976.
WILLIAMSON, Hugh Ross, *Catherine de' Medici*, Michael Joseph, London, 1973.

Architecture: General

BLUNT, Anthony, *Art and Architecture in France 1500–1700*, Penguin Books, London, 1953.
Congres Archéologique de France 128ᵉ Session 1970, Gascogne, Société Française d'Archéologie, Paris, 1970.
EVANS, Joan, *Art in Mediaeval France 987–1598*, Oxford University Press, London, 1948.
MARKHAM, Violet R., *Romanesque France*, John Murray, London, 1929.
MARTIN, Henry, *l'Art Roman*, Flammarion, Paris, 1946.

Church Architecture: Regional Guides

BROSSE, Jacques (editor), *Guyenne*, Dictionnaire des Eglises de France, Robert Laffont, Tours, 1967.
BURIAS, Jean, *Eglises du Lot-et-Garonne*, Nouvelles Editions Latines, Paris (no date).
BURIAS, Jean, *Abbayes, Prieurés, Commanderies en Lot-et-Garonne*, Art et Tourisme, Paris (no date).
CABANOT, Abbé Jean, *Gascogne Romane*, Zodiaque, Pierre-qui-Vire, 1978.
CAZAUX, Paul Raôul, *Historie et Description de quelques églises de l'Astarac*, Miélan, 1982.
DUBOURG-NOVES, Pierre, *Guyenne Romane*, Zodiaque, Pierre-qui-Vire, 1979.
DURLIAT, Marcel and ALLÉGRE, Victor, Pyrénées Romanes, Zodiaque, Pierre-qui-Vire, 1978.
MESPLÉ, Paul, *Églises du Gers*, Art et Tourisme, Paris (no date).

Secular Architecture

BERESFORD, Maurice, *New Towns of the Middle Ages: Town Plantation in England, Wales and Gascony*, Lutterworth Press, London, 1967.
BUGE, Jean-Marc, *Habiter en Lomagne, Hier et Aujourd' hui*, Editions CTR, Lectoure, 1986.

BURIAS, Jean, *Le Guide des Châteaux de France*, Lot-et-Garonne, Hermé, Paris, 1981.

CAYLA, Dr A., *Maisons de Guyenne et de Gascogne*, Editions Serge-Reprint Eddibor, 1980.

COUSTEAUX, Fernand, *Le Guide des Châteaux de France, Gers*, Hermé, Paris, 1981.

GARDELLES, Jacques, *Le Châteaux du Moyen Age dans la France du Sud-ouest, La Gascogne Anglaise de 1216–1327*, Bibliothèque de la Société Française d'Archéologie, Droz, Geneva, 1972.

POLGE, Henri, *Châteaux du Gers, Art et Tourisme*, Paris (no date).

SPENS, Willy de, *Le Guide des Châteaux de France, Gers*, Hermé, Paris, 1986.

History

BORDES, Maurice, *Histoire de la Gascogne des Origines à nos Jours*, Editions Horvath, Roanne, 1982.

CASTEX, Jean, COURTES, Jean and LASPALLES, Louis, *Gascogne d'Autrefois*, Editions Horvath, Roanne, 1981.

COURTEAULT, Paul, *Histoire de Gascogne et de Béarn*, Boivin, Paris, 1938.

FROISSART, Sir John, *Chronicles of England, France and Spain*, translated by Thomas Johnes, Esq., two volumes, William Smith, London 1839.

GROSCLAUDE, Michel, *La Gascogne, Témoignages sur deux mille ans d'Histoire*, Sources de l'Histoire Occitane, Béarn, 1986.

HIGOUNET, Charles, *Le Comté de Comminges de ses Origines à son Annexion à la Couronne*, two volumes, Privat, Toulouse, and Marcel Didier, Paris, 1949.

LABARGE, Margaret Wade, *Gascony, England's First Colony, 1204–1453*, Hamish Hamilton, London, 1980.

MANCIET, Bernard, *Le Guide des Chateaux de France, Pyrénées-Atlantiques*, Hermé, Paris 1986.

MARRIOTT, Sir J. A. R., *A Short History of France*, Methuen and Co., London, 1942.

OMAN, Charles, M.A., F.S.A., *The Dark Ages*, Rivingtons, London, 1905.

SAMARAN, Charles, *La Maison d'Armagnac au XVe Siècle*, Libraire Alphonse Picard et Fils, Paris, 1908.

SUMPTION, Jonathan, *The Albigensian Crusade*, Faber and Faber, London, 1978.

THOMPSON, James Westfall, *The Wars of Religion in France, 1559–1576*, University of Chicago Press, Chicago, 1909.

WEBER, Eugen, *Peasants into Frenchmen, The Modernization of Rural France, 1870–1914*, Chatto and Windus, London, 1977.

Pilgrimage in Gascony

Sentier de Saint-Jacques-de-Compostelle, Quercy-Gascogne GR 65, Topoguide du Sentier de Grande Randonnée, Paris, 1979.

SUMPTION, Jonathan, *Pilgrimage, an Image of Mediaeval Religion*, Faber and Faber, London, 1975.

TATE, Brian and Marcus, *The Pilgrim Route to Santiago*, Phaidon Press, Oxford, 1987.

TREUILLE, Henri, *Memoire sur les chemins et 'routes de Compostelle' dans les Landes*, in *Bulletin de la Société de Borda*, Dax, 1978.

Gastronomy

BINNS, Richard, *French Leave 3*. Chilton House, Amersham, Bucks, 1988. A useful restaurant guide.

BUSSELLE, Michael, *The Wine Lover's Guide to France*, Pavilion-Michael Joseph, London, 1986.

FAITH, Nicholas, *Pocket Guide to Cognac and other Brandies*, Mitchell Beazley, London, 1987. An excellent introduction to Armagnac brandy.

SAMALENS, Jean and Georges, *Armagnac*, Christie's Wine Publications, London, 1980.

TINGEY, Frederick, *Wine Roads of France*, Charles Letts and Co., London, 1977.

VIDAL, Maurice, *Le Guide Gascon*, CRI Art Villlage, Auch, 1987. A comprehensive local guide to restaurants and vineyards in the Armagnac region.

INDEX